Secrets In Scarlet

The Rookery Rogues
Book 2

Erica Monroe

Quillfire Publishing

SECRETS IN SCARLET

Quillfire Publishing

ISBN: 978-0990022954

For information, address Erica Monroe at ericamonroe.com.

✾ Formatted with Vellum

Dedication

To my father, who taught me never to apologize for the things I love.

Prologue

S pitalfields, London
    April 1832

The last time Sergeant Thaddeus Knight had encountered so much blood, he'd been seventeen. That death had shaken him to his core, setting him on a path to join the Metropolitan Police.

But in his three years with the Met, he'd been lulled into a false sense of security by arrests of pickpockets and mendicants. He wasn't prepared for this violence.

He found the bruised, bleeding girl outside of a factory on White Lion Street. His body went cold, starting in his spine and settling deep into his tailbone. For a second, he was transfixed, staring at the crimson that stained her tattered wool gown and clotted in her russet curls. Her hands were scraped, the knuckles chafed.

Was she still alive? The cut on her forehead had streamed so profusely, he couldn't imagine she maintained consciousness.

He yanked off his gloves and stuffed them in his pocket.

Kneeling down beside her, Thaddeus placed two fingers to her neck to check for a pulse. Her eyes fluttered open. Catching sight of his blue uniform, she attempted to move away from him. But she was too weak.

"Peeler," she croaked. Her bottom lip was split. "Don't 'urt me."

"I've no intention of the sort." Sitting on his haunches, Thaddeus's tall frame towered over the girl's huddled body. He rested his elbows on his knees, trying to keep his expression bland. Unassuming. All he wanted to do was turn his head to the side and vomit, for the saccharine stench of blood drenched her entirely.

Don't give any indication that you believe she cannot survive.

The girl whimpered. If he didn't get her help soon, she'd die.

Thaddeus reached for her, expecting that he'd have to carry her slung over his back. He didn't trust that she'd be able to stand on her own.

From this new angle, he saw a gaping wound in her back, right underneath her shoulder blade. Her dress was split, the tears confirming his initial theory that she'd been stabbed. The knife had been dragged down a few more centimeters and twisted, for the bottom of the wound was far larger.

Christ.

Her head lolled back against the factory wall.

"Stay with me now," he urged. "I'll get you to safety."

Still stooped, he gathered her up in his arms, careful not to hit the wound on her back. Her legs dangled in the air, and one shoe fell from her foot. Cascading to the ground, the tiny slipper barely made a sound as it hit the dirt. She couldn't have been more than fourteen. A sense of helplessness surged through him. She was too damn young for this.

Too damn young to die.

Not again, please, not again. He'd already been through this with another girl around her age. That girl had been found seven years ago in a different alley, south of Spitalfields and into Whitechapel.

Thaddeus hadn't been able to save Elizabeth Stewart, but damn it, he'd save this girl.

He jogged toward the hack stand. Every step he took jarred her body a little, sending a spasm of pain across her round cheeks. She had the face of a child, her lithe frame on the edge of blossoming. She was tall for her age, thin and willowy. Yet her hands bore the blisters of an older woman.

He tightened his grip around her body, shouldering her weight. Moving carefully down the street, he dodged jagged bottles and piles of rubbish that lined the alleyway. A soiled broadsheet floated past on a spring breeze.

They were getting closer to the hack stand. From there, he'd get the driver to take them to the London Hospital in Whitechapel. He knew a nurse there who wouldn't blink at her lack of funds.

Hell, he'd pay for her treatment himself, if needed.

"A little farther," he told her when she shivered. "We're almost there. The hospital will take care of you."

Her eyes had closed again.

"Come on, come on," he pleaded, running his thumb across her cheek. "Don't die on me, lass!"

He ran the last few steps to the hack stand. No carriages were waiting. A curse fell from his lips as he held her close to him. His arms were leaden after the trip, but he would not drop her.

She drew in a shaky breath, her bleary eyes focusing on him. Underneath the lamplight of the hack stand, her face was ashen. She would not be long for this world.

If he could not get her help in the time, the best thing he could do was find out who had done this to her and bring them to justice.

"Who hurt you, lass?" he asked.

"Can't tell ye," she murmured.

"Whoever hurt you, I'll find them. You don't have to be scared of repercussions. I'm going to protect you."

With what strength she had left, she lifted her head to look him directly in the eye. "Ye can't keep me safe. They got people the likes of ye Bobbies can't imagine." Nervously, her fingers kept sketching the same *L* across her skirt.

He kept half of his attention on her, half on the street, searching the horizon for a hack. "Did the name of the person who hurt you start with an *L*?"

She didn't reply, but neither did her fingers cease.

"The police can do a lot more than you think, miss," he told her. "If you believe in nothing else, believe in the power of the Met. I'll catch whoever did this to you. I swear it on my life."

The clomp of hooves upon cobblestone echoed, and a hack appeared farther down the street. Thaddeus came forward so that they were directly underneath the lamplight. The driver pulled the hack up in front of them, jumping down from his seat.

The coachman looked at him askew, his eyes drifting from Thaddeus's black regulation top hat to the solid black boots on his feet. He did not move to open the door. "What ye got 'ere?"

Thaddeus readjusted the girl in his arms, fumbling in his pocket for the fare. "She's been attacked. We must get her to the hospital." He handed the fare over to the driver.

The coachman regarded the fare, then the girl. "I don't be wantin' any trouble."

"You'll get trouble if you don't open the damn door now," Thaddeus barked.

"Don't get yer breeches in a twist, lad," the coachman grumbled, but he opened the door.

Thaddeus scooted her limp form into the carriage before him. As he was about to climb in after her, his hand brushed against her ankle. Her skin was cold to the touch, colder than it had been moments before. Her chest did not rise and fall any longer.

Raising his thumb to her neck, he felt no pulse.

The girl was dead.

Chapter One

"You're meant for great things, my boy." Leaning back in his claw-footed chair, Inspector Jonah Whiting smoked a cheroot and regarded Thaddeus with barely veiled impatience. "That business with the resurrectionists ring was the luckiest break you're liable to get in this business."

Three months prior, Thaddeus had apprehended Jasper Finn in a workhouse cemetery in East Smithfield. While the arrest had led to the captures of most of Finn's grave robbing ring, the real bounty had been in tying Finn to several other unsolved murders in London.

Whiting wouldn't let Thaddeus forget this grand success for the rest of his whole damn life.

The inspector smiled one of those simpering smirks meant to ingratiate Thaddeus to him. "Superintendent Bicknell has taken notice. If you play your cards right, you too could have one of these offices. Inspector Doughty is set to retire in a month."

"Aye, it'd be an honor to be considered, sir." Nervousness quivered in his stomach at the thought of taking Doughty's place. To be an inspector at twenty-four years of age was unheard of in the Met, but Thaddeus had worked harder than anyone else on their route. Certainly, harder than the other contender for the job, Michael Strickland.

As an inspector, Thaddeus would be able to make a real difference in the Spitalfields rookery. But he wasn't sure he was willing to give up investigating cases like Anna Moseley's for a chance at a loftier position. The trail of Miss Stewart's murder was long cold, but he could find out who had killed Miss Moseley. Her family deserved answers.

"If you'd stop insisting upon investigating cases like this one..." Whiting scooped up the folder, dropping it unceremoniously back down. The papers scattered every which way, lost in the sea of Whiting's untidy desk.

Thaddeus grimaced, and then promptly tried to hide that grimace with a not-so-well-placed cough. Whiting's brassy glance fixed upon him.

"Sir, if you'd take a moment and look through the papers..." Thaddeus resisted the urge to grab the file and start rearranging it. It had taken him three hours to put together that file for Whiting, and now it would take him three more hours to put it back into proper order.

Whiting snorted, resembling more of a pig than a commanding officer. He had an up-turned long nose, short ears, and copper eyes the color of clock gears. At fifty years of age, he'd been a member of the old Watch until the Met was formed. Whiting never hesitated to inform his officers—mostly, Thaddeus—of what working with the Met meant.

"It's a simple case of rookery violence, Knight," Whiting said. "We're Peel's men, and Peel's men don't spend their time on these foolish enterprises. We *prevent* crimes from happening in the first place."

Their work was noble. Triumphant, even. They were a solution before there was ever a problem. Of course, certain leniency could be granted. Arrests had to be made, and thus cases had to be looked into when the culprit wasn't found on the scene. The Bow Street Runners wanted little to do with the East End.

"Investigating the deaths of every low-down bunter who crosses your path will get you nowhere," Whiting lectured. "You've got a quick mind, Knight, and the boys in Westminster like you."

Thaddeus shifted in his chair. "Sir, the logic is sound here. If you'd just give me some time, I think I'll find out that the Larkers are involved in far more."

If Whiting didn't assign Thaddeus leave to investigate the Moseley death, he'd have no other recourse. Whiting was his superior by assignment. If Thaddeus went over Whiting's head, he could say goodbye to the inspector job. And Whiting would make damn sure he didn't have a job to come back to, prior brilliant arrest of Jasper Finn or not.

Whiting's cheroot dangled from his fingers, above the file. "Apparently, you helped out some countess?"

"Sir, if you'd be a bit more careful with that file..." Thaddeus began, biting back a groan as Whiting blinked at him.

Whiting set down the loosely rolled cheroot. It spilled upon impact, the uncut ends leaving foul traces all over the parchment. There'd be no hope of rereading the paperwork.

Why, oh, why did people treat his efforts at organization with such blatant disregard? Thaddeus would never understand this. Order brought the needed clarity to discover solutions in the most disjointed of fragments. What was so wrong with a little clarity?

"Tell me about this countess," Whiting demanded, ignoring Thaddeus's pained stare at the cheroot.

"I found the countess's jewels for her," Thaddeus explained.

"My brother brought the case to my attention. The countess was one of his clients at Barclay's."

That had been a slow week. Any more cases like that one and his brains might dribble out of his ears from boredom.

"That is the type of outside work you take, my boy," Whiting praised. "You ought to be doing your route, not sitting across from your superior whining about why you can't investigate a random whore's murder."

Thaddeus was most assuredly *not* whining. "If you had seen her—"

"I would be saying the exact same thing."

"She died in my arms." Thaddeus couldn't shake the memory of her once-warm flesh against his blue coat. "She couldn't have been more than fourteen. A young girl."

"Terrible incident," Whiting hedged. "But it's Spitalfields, and it's to be expected. Those weavers are a sordid sort, turning to brew and promiscuity to while away the hours between shifts at the factory. She was probably beaten by some bullyback."

"This was more than some brothel scuttle," Thaddeus insisted.

Murder was foul in all forms, no matter who had been murdered. Wasn't it their job to stop it? They were supposed to protect these people.

Whiting wouldn't understand. He was not a sentimental man. But Whiting might grasp hard facts, so Thaddeus led with that.

"Miss Moseley said we couldn't protect her. That 'they' have people working for them we don't know about. I think it's the Larkers, sir. They own the factory where she was found. When she died, her fingers were sketching the letter *L*."

"It's not enough to go on," Whiting said. "Besides, the Larkers have never caused trouble before. Boz Larker is a respected man of business. If you falsely accuse him, you'll have a lot of explaining to do."

"I can get more information," Thaddeus insisted. "I've compiled a list of everyone the Larkers have associations with."

In the file that Whiting's cheroot had destroyed. Damnation.

"Considering most textile factories are moving to Manchester or Lancashire, dismissals should have happened in spades. It's not a union factory. Nothing is stopping them from dismissing workers," Thaddeus said. "Still, they retain a full staff of thirty weavers, mostly using Jacquard looms."

"The French looms, as if it wasn't enough that the Frog tried to invade our country." Whiting sniffed. "How quickly people forget these things when money is to be involved."

How quickly we forget the idea of justice when money is to be involved, Thaddeus should have said. Instead, Thaddeus stared blankly at Whiting, who held in his stupid, bloated hands the fate of far too many poor men and women in this district.

Whiting was a cancer, eating away at a system that had been meant to instill faith. Every day, Thaddeus saw people shivering in the doorways of their rundown tenement houses, barefoot and desperate in the streets, drunk off the penny drams sold in the gin palaces.

Those people had no one else to fight for them, and Thaddeus would rather be damned than give up on them. If that made him foolish and egotistical, so be it.

"That money's coming from somewhere," Thaddeus insisted.

Whiting let out a much-harassed sigh. "The Larkers have money, Knight. Maybe he's funding the factory from his pocket."

"You know as well as I do that people don't run factories because they care for the workers. If there's no profit, why is the factory still in business?" Thaddeus asked. "I want this case. I'll work it in addition to my regular shifts. I'll take those meetings you wanted me to with Superintendent Bicknell. I'll tell him it was *your* planning that set me up to get Trigger Jem."

A calculating gleam shined in Whiting's eyes. "If you're willing to speak to Bicknell, then I think we can get the younger Strickland to look into your route."

Thaddeus winced. Michael Strickland was not only his competition for the inspector spot, but he was a rash imbecile. Strickland's lone good trait was that he was less of an arse than his father—Claudius Strickland had arrested Daniel O'Reilly three years ago for a murder Jasper Finn had committed.

Finn couldn't hurt anyone again. He'd hung in a widely attended execution that hearkened back to the days of Tyburn.

Yet there were still villains out there. If Strickland was what he had to endure to find Miss Moseley's murderers, then Thaddeus would deal with Strickland.

He nodded.

"Very good," Whiting agreed. "Two weeks."

"That's not enough time." Thaddeus pointed to the beleaguered file on Whiting's desk. "I believe there's more at stake here than the girl's death. I outlined some of my conclusions—"

"Fourteen days," Whiting stated firmly. "Fourteen days and then you're done. No more of this nonsense. You'll do as I tell you, Knight, or so help me God, I'll have you removed, genius or not."

Fourteen days. A day for every year of the girl's too-short life.

* * *

The Larker Textile Factory was not anything special. It was like everything else in Spitalfields, once beautiful but now moldering. The majority of the factory workers had seen their fortunes dwindle, as new machinery and the repeal of the weaving acts outlawing foreign imports made the handloom weavers irrelevant.

Poppaea "Poppy" O'Reilly was neither Protestant nor French; nevertheless, she felt a kinship with the Huguenot weavers. Like them, she had come to London expecting to find sanctuary. An escape from her wicked past.

This April evening, a bell tolled portentously throughout the factory. Poppy glanced over toward the clock hanging on the wall. It was a quarter past five—there was no way the closing bell should have been ringing. The Larkers cared little for the diatribes of reformers. If they could force their workers to stay after the designated twelve-hour shift, they would.

"Come along before they change their minds!" Abigail Vautille cried, skidding by. Her light-blue dress was creased from where she'd been sitting at a loom all day, dust lining the hem, but no amount of dirt and grime could take away from Abigail's beauty.

At nineteen, Abigail was the same age as Poppy. With almond-shaped blue eyes and a small nose, Abigail was everything that was fresh-faced and innocent.

Poppy was used and tarnished.

Abigail's younger sister, Bess, trailed behind her. Bess offered her hand to Poppy shyly, a dingy ginger curl falling across her eye. Beige, ocher, and blue threads tangled with her unruly hair. Children as young as six quilled silk until their small hands were blistered and bleeding.

Leading Bess by the hand, Poppy kept walking through the factory. Abigail followed behind them.

"Why do you think they're letting us go so early?" Abigail asked, careful to keep her voice low lest the Larkers overhear her.

Boz Larker's office door was closed. It'd been closed since four that afternoon, though little sound carried from the office when the looms were in motion. Larker closed the door when he didn't want the workers to know who was visiting him.

Poppy nibbled on her bottom lip. "I don't know."

Bess peeked up at her. One look at Bess was enough to convince Poppy that she was doing the right thing. She might not be able to save Bess from a hard life, but devil take it, she'd sell her body before she allowed her own daughter to work in one of these factories.

Every shift brought money home to support Moira.

"Let's not question their generosity, shall we?" Poppy quickened her pace, and Bess trotted after her.

Abigail nodded, lifting her skirts up so that she'd not trip on them as she walked. Though Poppy was shorter than her, Abigail's strides were never regular. As a child, Abigail had worked as a piecer, sliding underneath the machinery and resting on her right side to mend the broken threads. Her right knee bent inward, giving her an awkward, almost waddling walk, but if she was careful, she could move at an almost parallel speed to Poppy.

They fell into step with the rest of the workers. What had once been an orderly line at the first toll of the bell had quickly descended into a mob. No one wanted to be present should the Larkers change their minds about the early exodus. Poppy kept one hand on her lantern and the other on Bess, shielding her as people pushed to and fro in their attempts to fit through the slim doorway. Abigail stumbled as a man slammed into her but caught herself on an iron stand used to hold gingham bags, scrapers, and netting.

Finally, it was their turn to leave.

Cool, crisp air washed over Poppy's face as they stepped outside. She let out a deep breath, readjusting to the new smells of the outdoors. The factory was all iron and rust, silk and fibers, but here in the open, the scents varied. Down the street, someone was baking bread, while the odor of juniper laid finely over everything from the several open dram palaces.

She could locate gin within a five-meter radius, thanks to her brother, Daniel.

The first traces of nightfall had descended over Spitalfields. Poppy stopped for a moment to allow Abigail to catch her breath and lit the lantern with a lucifer match. She leaned back against the wall. As soon as the crumbling brick side met with the thin cotton of her dress, she sprang forward as if stung.

Not more than a week ago, Anna Moseley had been found against this wall, beaten and stabbed. Some fool Peeler had lifted her up from the spot, probably worsening her injuries.

The Met didn't give a whit about Anna's death. They hadn't cared when they arrested Daniel for a murder he didn't commit. He'd been in the wrong place at the wrong time, a victim of circumstances. The bloody Peelers didn't care about the victims.

But Poppy cared, damn it, and Anna had been a good person. A sweet girl with her whole life ahead of her.

"I miss her too," Abigail remarked.

Poppy sighed. "It isn't fair."

Bess blinked. She looked from Poppy to her sister and back again, her brows furrowing with consternation.

Pulling Bess to her, Abigail covered the girl's ears with her hands. "There's no sign that the Larkers had anything to do with Anna's murder," she whispered.

"And no sign that they didn't," Poppy murmured.

"You could go somewhere else," Abigail suggested, unclasping Bess's ears. "The way you fix up the clothes you find in the rag and bone shops... I'd be lucky to ever be half as good, and I've been at this my whole life. You could easily make twice as much in the pretty shops on Bond Street."

"No." Poppy shook her head. She didn't tell Abigail she'd worked as a dressmaker's assistant until she'd been dismissed from that post. She didn't tell Abigail anything that remotely resembled the truth because she knew better.

Some lies had to be upheld.

"Besides, what would you do without me?" Poppy forced a grin. Abigail meant well.

"Oh, I'd moan and groan, but I'd muddle through." Abigail smiled back.

They continued walking. The street was empty. It was too early for the gin crowd. The rest of Spitalfields was either at work in another one of the factories, sitting down to supper with their family, or sleeping off last night's bout.

"What are you going to do with the extra blunt you earned from weaving the most silk in a week?" Abigail asked.

"I haven't thought about it." Another lie, for Poppy knew exactly what she'd do with the bonus: it would go in the fund for Moira to attend a finishing school someday.

"You must have a plan," Abigail teased. "I'd buy more books, of course. I finished *The Italian* last night. Thank you for loaning it to me."

"You're welcome." Poppy smoothed her skirt with aching fingers, tingling from too many hours spent at the loom. "I suppose Moira would like some fruit."

"*Fruit?*" Abigail repeated, her button nose wrinkling. "Ack. You're so practical. I long for adventure, something scandalous."

Poppy had been scandalous once, and she'd paid the price.

"Eventually, of course, I'd like to marry," Abigail continued. "It seems lovely to be married."

"It was lovely," Poppy lied.

Wincing, Abigail reached for Poppy's hand, covering it with her own. "I'm sorry, love. How insensitive of me. Rambling on about my problems when the loss of your Robert is still fresh with you."

Abigail's soft blue eyes shone with sympathy for the supposed demise of a man she thought had meant the world to Poppy. If Abigail knew that the picture of her supposed husband Poppy carried with her had been purchased at a pawn shop, would she still feel such pains of sadness for her friend? Unlikely. So, the fictional Lieutenant Robert Corrigan of His Majesty's Royal Navy must remain Moira's purported father.

Abigail stopped in front of a public house on Wheeler Street. In a few hours, this area would be alive with music, scoundrels, and the fancy crowd back from the most recent mill. She held the door open for Bess. The little girl darted inside, waiting by the bar for Abigail to enter.

Abigail turned back to Poppy. "Join us? After I drop off Bess back home, I'm going to the Ten Bells. I heard there's a band tonight."

"Afraid not." Poppy shook her head. "Must be getting back to Moira." The last rays from the sun were disappearing quickly. She'd have an hour or two after Moira ate dinner before the babe needed to sleep.

"See you tomorrow," Abigail called.

Poppy moved away from the public house, eager to get home. Daniel and his wife, Kate, had agreed to watch Moira. Poppy's companion, Edna Daubenmire, was out running errands.

The lamps faded at this point, giving way to the barely lit crevices of back alleys and battered-window tenement houses. Staying close to the public houses would give her enough light to see by on her way home, provided she didn't dally any longer. She had memorized which roads she should avoid at what times, taking a different way out in the morning than she did when returning in the evening. Poppy carried a knife and a pair of scissors in her apron pocket, just in case.

She set off, her pace swift and determined.

Footsteps echoed behind her.

She spun around to confront the person, the lantern high in her grasp. In the shadows, the tall, lanky build of the man was visible, a square hat atop his head.

"Wot ye want?" she snapped, dropping her voice into the cutting dialect of the East End like Kate had taught her.

The man came closer, the lamp's glow hitting him. Clothed in a blue uniform, a regulation truncheon at his side, that damn hat—he was a Peeler if she ever saw one.

Bollocks and the balls that came with them.

Poppy had three core beliefs: protect family, be loyal, and avoid officers of the law at all costs.

"Scurry on now, guv, I don't be wantin' your type," she commanded, gesturing toward the other end of the street. "Ain't nothin' 'ere for ye to see."

The man's eyes narrowed, and all too quickly Poppy realized she'd overplayed her hand. He'd think her a whore, angling for paying bedfellows.

She shook her head quickly, a stray red curl slipping free from underneath her cap at the franticness of the motion. "Oy, I got a family to tend to, and I ain't done nothin' wrong."

"Steady, Miss," he cautioned, one brow quirking with amusement.

He thought her amusing. The wretched man, accosting her on the street.

She steeled herself, gripping the lantern tightly. "*Mrs.*"

He nodded stiffly. "My apologies."

She sniffed. Let him believe she had a man at home to protect her if it meant he'd leave her alone faster. While she'd delivered a stirring performance of guttersnipe worthy of

Covent Garden, there was a flash in the officer's eyes that left her distinctly unsettled.

As if he knew something about her that he shouldn't.

"You came from the factory," he stated. His voice was a smooth baritone, striking at something within her that shouldn't have resonated.

"So, wot if I did?" She didn't have to feign the agitation in her voice. Her free hand fell to her hip. "Is that a crime now, guv? I'm an 'onest one."

She had been honest, once.

"I doubt that," the man replied. "But I'm unconcerned about your true vocation. I care more about the girl who was murdered at the Larker factory last week."

Anna. Poppy swallowed down her discomfort. An investigation into Anna's death was highly unlikely. No piggish Peeler cared for a simple fourteen-year-old girl who couldn't read or write. He must have another reason for stopping her, and it couldn't be a good one.

Poppy's stomach tightened. He'd want to know more about her. Atlas had given her a false history strong enough to hold up to casual observance, but under careful examination...

She couldn't risk this Peeler finding out and revealing Moira's true parentage.

"I don't know anythin' about that, and even if I did, I wouldn't be tellin' ye," Poppy declared. "Go on yer merry way, ye bleedin' blighter. My babe calls."

Chapter Two

T haddeus had stood outside the factory as it closed. The workers streamed out in clumps, men conversing with women in boisterous tones. Children skipped down the path, singing at the tops of their lungs. He scanned the crowd, cataloging each worker in his mind as someone he might speak to later.

Then he saw her.

A woman with fiery red hair, creamy pale skin, and green eyes that shimmered as she laughed. She'd stopped at a public house on the corner of Wheeler and White Lion Street.

He didn't know why, out of all the people, he was drawn to this particular woman, but he felt it in his gut, and he'd learned to trust his instincts. While he believed that the wisest decisions came from thorough introspection, in patrolling, there wasn't often the time for such deep thought. When it came to solving crimes, he was confident of his own prowess.

Women were another matter entirely.

Women were baffling, especially when they lobbed barbs at him in stilted Cockney that reminded him of a cross between an off-tune fiddle and a street hawker. From the way she spoke, he'd initially guessed she was a prostitute, born and bred in the heart of the rookeries. They were somewhat close to the market on Crispin Street, a popular hunting ground for lightskirts.

But he doubted a prostitute would insist on being referred to as a married woman.

"You say you didn't know the girl who died, but your posture stiffened when I mentioned the murder," he observed. "'Blighter' though I may be, I'm not a liar, madam. I've no concern over what you do for your blunt, but I do care about Anna Moseley."

She flinched at his words. He found that peculiar, for he hadn't said anything that should have invoked fear.

As quickly as she had pulled back from him, she recovered, fixing him with a lethal glare. "Are ye calling me a liar?"

"Your accent is slipping. Judging from your prior speech rhythms, you should have asked me if I was callin' you a liar." With a wave of his hand, he rocked back on his feet. "Oh, don't misunderstand me, I quite like the improvements. Too often in these parts, one finds our sovereign language brutally maligned."

"I don't know wot ye yammer on 'bout." She'd slipped back into a grating speech. "Yer a bit of a bounder, aren't ye? Thinkin' ye know everythin'?"

He nodded. "It is not the first time that claim has been made."

In this case, however, he knew he was correct: whoever she was, she wasn't originally from Spitalfields. Her words were too crisp. Real speech had slips and stops, a casual flow.

"Then ye best take 'eed," she cautioned solemnly.

Under the weight of her stare, he attempted to transform his chortle into another misplaced cough and failed miserably. She stood across from him, chin raised, brandishing her lantern as though it was a more effective weapon than his own truncheon. Her chin was not overly sharp, softened by sweet features better suited to laughter than this blatant distrust.

"Walk with me, Mrs..." He let the summons trail off, hoping she'd supply her name.

She didn't. Nor did she follow him.

"I don't have improper motives, madam." He tapped the truncheon against his leg idly, surveying her pale oval face. "I value my position. My supervisor would take me to task if I accosted you. I'd be without work. I need to work. You understand that, of course, for you work at the Larker factory."

She studied him cagily.

If every employee of the Larkers was this forthcoming with information, once the two weeks were up, he'd be back to Whiting empty-handed.

But damnation, he was getting closer. Certainty thrummed through his body. This woman was hiding something, and he'd bet a bottle of good whisky that it had something to do with the Larkers.

"Let me escort you to your destination." He doffed his hat, sketching a bow. Was that a flicker of amusement in her eyes, hurriedly squelched? He couldn't be sure.

She didn't take his proffered arm. He turned to look behind them. Standing in the doorway of the public house were three men. None wore coats, taking advantage of the brief reprieve in the rain. With checkered neckcloths and their hats pulled low across their brows, they were almost identical in appearance. Swarthy, dark-haired, and unkempt.

He raised the truncheon higher in preparation. No one else would be hurt on his watch.

However unpleasant this woman might be.

She followed his gaze, a deep frown setting upon her pouty lips.

"You know them." He'd found that leading statements

received better reactions than open-ended questions. "Do they work for the Larkers? I can protect you, madam."

"I highly doubt that," she spat. "If the men find fault with me, it'll be because I was seen talking to *you*."

Giddiness besieged him, that familiar delight at knowing he'd been right. "I knew you weren't from Spitalfields. Madam, you have my interest. What's a lady from—what is it? There's a bit of eastern in your voice, methinks—Sussex doing in these parts?"

"Surrey," she grumbled. "And that's none of your concern."

He glanced back at the men. They had not budged from the doorway, observing the pair with rapt interest. "Madame Surrey then, allow me to walk with you. Standing here, I'm afraid we're attracting extra attention."

It was now a matter of principle. He'd requested her assistance politely, and he was a Metropolitan Police Sergeant. That ought to mean something.

"Unless you'd prefer that I continue to question you in the street, across from the factory, where everyone can see," he said pointedly.

"Men," she huffed. "Can't leave well enough alone." But with one last look toward the leering group, she stalked off down the road.

He trailed after her, quickly overtaking her. "Surely, your husband would want to know you're protected."

"He wants for nothing," she said. "He's dead. From the Portuguese war."

"Oh." Thaddeus grimaced. "I'm terribly sorry for your loss. If I'd known—"

She held her hand up to stop him from continuing. "It's fine. Thank you for saying so."

Her face softened, and he wondered if this was what she

looked like when with the child she'd mentioned. Gentle. Unperturbed.

They walked down Wheeler Street. Instead of turning left toward the market on Crispin Street, she crossed onto Lamb Street, where he'd never once seen a ewe. Their footfalls were muffled by the sounds of a reawakening London, ready for nocturnal ruckuses. Her lantern burned, wreathing the derelict surroundings in an ethereal glow. Somehow, next to her in that light, this place didn't seem so forlorn.

Ducking underneath a doorway, she set her lantern down on the ground and faced him. "Since you won't leave, you might as well know that I can't help you with Anna's murder. I knew her as you might know your fellow officers from different districts."

He nodded. "What was her function in the factory? I find it odd that your factory is not located next to a water source. One would think that the Larkers would want to harness the new methods of power."

"I don't see how that will help you."

"If the factory has nothing to do with Miss Moseley's death, what's the harm in telling me?"

She let out an exasperated sigh. "We weave raw silk into fabric that will be used to produce clothing, ribbons and trims, linens, and so forth. We have Jacquard looms—that is, dobby looms fitted with a Jacquard head—but we also still have a few figured looms to work on the Ducapes."

Pride shined in her eyes at every sentence. Weaving, he knew now, was the way to get her to talk.

"It sounds like you do grand work," he responded.

"The work we do is the same as weavers have been doing in the top floors of their dingy cottages for years," she said. "Some workers punch out the cards for the looms; others prepare the warp and weft. Still others pattern and thread the looms, and of course, there is the actual weaving itself."

He stayed silent, wanting her to talk, for her natural voice was sweet and powerful. It was music to his ears, more calming than the Anglican hymns his mother pressed on him.

"But doing it this way, in a factory, makes sense." She wasn't as guarded now. "I almost think the cloth turns out better then, that our combined minds make it so."

"You develop a kinship with your fellow workers." He felt similar for the sergeants and foot patrollers that served with him. "What role did Anna play in all of this?"

He'd returned too quickly to his original topic. She appraised him, as if weighing his motives for enquiring.

"You should do better research, Sergeant, or you'd already know that answer."

"Enlighten me." He did know it, in fact, but he wanted to hear it from her.

"I have better things to do." Picking up her lantern again, she pushed past him.

He hustled after her, catching her arm so she couldn't retreat further. She glowered at his hand, thoroughly disgusted. He quickly let go of her, jumping back.

"For all that you claim you can't help, I think you did care for Miss Moseley. If anything happened to the other sergeants I work with, I'd want to do something."

She frowned. "You're insufferable. The other sergeants probably *want* to disappear around you."

"Perhaps," he agreed. They did run when they saw him— unless they wanted his help.

"You'd find this out anyhow, so if it will get you to leave me be..." She started down the path, not bothering to check and see if he was behind her. "Mr. Larker prefers to have three assistants upstairs in the assembly room. He hires young men strong enough to lift the inventory, and one woman who is small enough to maneuver easily in amongst the piles. The inventory is kept upstairs in locked rooms."

Thaddeus stiffened, remembering how easily he'd been able to lift Miss Moseley up from the ground. A stack of thick woolen blankets would weigh more than she had.

"Is that standard procedure?" he asked.

Madame Surrey tilted her head toward him, paying him the first real sign of attention since he'd met her. Distractedly, she patted at her flaming red hair, checking that her bun was still in place underneath her straw hat.

For a second, he forgot about the coming nightfall. He forgot about remaining vigilant, about Whiting, about his career—he forgot everything in his eagerness to hear her response.

Such was the appeal of a new case.

It couldn't have anything to do with the adorable smattering of freckles across her button nose or the way her gingham dress encased her svelte frame.

"I can't speak to other factories." Her voice was melodic, her accent tinged with a hint of Irish. "But I believe Anna was to be moved back downstairs sometime soon."

"Had Miss Moseley failed the Larkers in some way?"

"No." She shook her head. Too quickly.

She was afraid of something. Perhaps the Larkers finding out she'd tattled to him, and that she'd become another victim like Anna? Or was it something darker that had nothing to do with the factory?

He kept his expression impassive. "What was the general opinion of Miss Moseley?"

"Everyone liked her." She pursed her lips. Whatever had unnerved her had taken hold. "Officer, I don't know anything more. I work all day at my loom on the first floor. The one time I get up is when I go home for lunch. Most days, I only saw Anna at closing."

His one lead was slipping away from him. He had remained on the street, out of the arch of the doorway. Now, he edged up on her. She'd turned her back to him to survey the scrawls splashed upon the disintegrating brick and stucco of the tenement house.

"And you never had any conversations with Miss Moseley? Please, madam, it's important. Before she died, I promised Miss Moseley I'd find her killer."

He towered over her petite frame. Close contact didn't appeal to him usually. So why was he compelled to take this woman into his arms? To draw her body against his?

Madame Surrey spun around, almost colliding with him. He caught her, steadying her with one arm wrapped around the small of her back. She was everything fragile and delicate, her subtle curves molding to his touch. What was this strange sensation that took hold of him? His hands had become warm where he touched her.

He stole a quick look at her arms to confirm that she was not aflame. No, her dress bore no singe marks. He smelled no smoke. Nothing but honey and vanilla.

"I—" His tongue was leaden in his mouth.

Her palms stretched out against his chest, yet she didn't push against him to break free. That was surprising. Was she lost in this connection too?

No. He was becoming melodramatic. It was nothing more than a trick of physicality. He shook his head, reminding himself to focus.

Reluctantly, he released his grip on her. She didn't move away from him. Her eyes bored into him, like emerald oceans at high tide. Her breath caught, held for a taut moment.

The world stopped before him.

She blinked, sliding from his arms. Though she had taken but a step back, the distance crashed upon him as though she'd run screaming down the street.

That didn't make a damned bit of sense.

"You don't have to tell me how *important* Anna's death is," she hissed through clenched teeth. "Six days out of the week, I'm at that factory. I'm watching men and women struggle to make enough to feed themselves and their families."

His breath came out in uneven pants. It took him a second to realize she'd returned to his earlier question. "I didn't mean—"

"Don't you think I'd like to tell you exactly who murdered little Anna? But I. Don't. Know." Each word was punctuated with a jab of her index finger into his chest.

He retreated. "I'm doing my job, Madame Surrey."

"Damn your job," she jeered.

At least she'd stopped poking him.

She turned away, picked up her lantern, and headed down Cat and Wheel Alley. At the sound of his advancing footsteps, she stopped in her tracks and swung back around to face him.

"And damn *you*," she avowed, with more venom than he'd thought a small woman could be capable of possessing.

"I've done nothing wrong." He couldn't match her vitriol. Their earlier moment had shaken him. Had he imagined the unsteadiness to her breathing? How her eyes had darkened with something akin to desire?

"You're all alike." She balled up her fist, the lantern shaking wildly in her other hand. "Every last lot of you. You claim you care, and then you leave."

He tilted his head to the side, surveying her quizzically. "You've had other run-ins with the Met?"

"No."

Well, that made no sense. "Then who am I like?"

"*Men.*" She flung the word out as if she'd announced he was a traitor to the Crown.

"I'm not sure I understand." He'd always believed it was wise to admit one's lack of knowledge, but the derisive stare she sent him made him doubt that fact.

She didn't clarify. She was moving again, every step quick, deliberate. He liked the urgency of her. So few people had real purpose nowadays. He suspected that once she made a plan, she'd stick to it.

Mulling her words, he continued after her. Her husband was deceased—but there had been something harder in her condemnation of all of mankind, something that hinted at a personal hurt. Had her husband been a rake?

They'd come to the Ten Bells public house on Red Lion Street. On the same corner was Christ Church, a shop devoted to van and cart works, and a school. He'd always found that an interesting combination: ale, God, transport, and children. Given the prevalence of child thieves, he supposed it had a certain logic.

He expected that she'd try to claim that all along she'd meant to go to the Ten Bells. The tramway was on Church Street, so she might choose that too.

But she strode past the bustling public house with little interest and onto Chick Lane. Closely, he shadowed her, holding the truncheon tight. Chick Lane was a popular place for thieves, yet this woman exhibited no fear for her safety.

She stopped in front of a row of cottages on Finch Street. "Well, this is it," she said, waving nonchalantly at the houses. "You may go now, Sergeant."

In the falling dusk, this portion of Finch Street appeared unoccupied. He doubted these houses had been lived in for years. Once whitewashed, the paint now flecked off in spots, like bits of fresh snowfall.

He gestured to the gate. "I'd like to see you inside."

Was it his imagination, or did she shift nervously? Her nose scrunched up, which might indicate frustration. "Fine," she said through gritted teeth. "Though I don't see why that is necessary."

She peered at the clasp on the gate, her fingers touching it lightly, as though checking for a lock. When the clasp slid back easily, her frame shuddered with relief.

There was absolutely no way in hell that she lived here.

"Where do you truly live?" He tried to sound patient when he felt nothing of the sort. Above all else, he abhorred liars. His profession surrounded him with falsehoods; he couldn't bear them in his personal encounters. And something about this woman made him classify this meeting as distinctly personal.

Farther down Finch Street, there was another grouping of cottages. Lights burned in those windows, and smoke puffed from the chimneys. From that direction, a man and a woman approached, a baby held in the woman's arms.

"Poppy!" The woman's voice echoed from the street. In response, the babe in her arms cried out.

A myriad of emotions flashed across his pretty companion's face: dismay at the call, concern at the cry of the baby, and, finally, fear.

He stepped close to Madame Surrey instinctively, the gate almost smacking into him as she opened it wide and stepped out. He squinted as the willowy brunette woman approached, accompanied by a man with hair as red as Madame Surrey's. He knew them both.

Kate Morgan had led him to a vile ring of resurrection men and the arrest of Jasper Finn.

"Miss Morgan," he smiled, waving at her.

"Sergeant Knight." She did not greet him with equal jubilation, but rather caution.

He understood that, for when he'd last encountered her, he had threatened to turn her into his superiors at H-Division if she continued to fence stolen goods. Madame Surrey looked from him to the newcomers and back again, confusion flickering in her eyes.

Daniel O'Reilly placed a protective arm around Kate, drawing her close. "She's Mrs. O'Reilly now."

"My felicitations." Thaddeus nodded, slightly bemused by her husband's reaction.

Another woman lingered farther down the road, her profile half-shadowed by the light of a lantern in a neighboring cottage on Finch Street. She watched their gathering with interest but did not approach. Shorter than Kate and almost as thin, her posture was stiff. Frigid. The kind of woman who probably strapped a knife on her ankle, in addition to the pocket pistol she carried with her.

There was something peculiar about this family.

Daniel's voice drew Thaddeus's attention back. "So, you've met my sister?"

Madame Surrey nodded, a quick signal to her brother to cease speaking, but Thaddeus jumped in. He didn't want to miss the opportunity to know her name. "I wanted to make sure she arrived home safely when I saw her walking alone, but no, we have not been introduced," he said.

"Poppy Corrigan, may I present Sergeant Knight," Daniel said.

Poppy Corrigan. The name was somehow fitting to her. A strange name for a strange woman.

She didn't curtsy, as women were wont to do, or even acknowledge him. Instead, she lifted the child from Kate's arms. She held the girl so naturally, cooing to her and rocking back and forth. The babe gurgled approval, a wide smile on her lips.

He knew immediately that the babe was hers, even without the matching red hair.

His heart went out to Mrs. Corrigan and the babe. No child deserved to grow up without a father.

He bid them adieu, unable to think of a reason why he should further intrude. As he strode away down the street, he looked back once at the O'Reilly clan. Clustered together, smiling at the babe in Mrs. Corrigan's arms, they were everything that Thaddeus's family was not. He couldn't remember the last time he'd attended a gathering where his father hadn't pulled him aside to discuss a "proper" occupation for him.

But if he wanted to make a difference, sacrifices had to be made.

Chapter Three

That night, Poppy sat at the circular wooden table in the middle of her kitchen with her family. Once Knight had left, everyone had gone back to her cottage on Finch Street for dinner. The savory aroma of beef stew and vegetables saturated the room. The stew was as delicious as it smelled, and Poppy ate with relish.

Poppy snuck a glance across the table at Kate and Daniel. They were immersed in conversation about Daniel's new job with the East India Trading Company. Daniel held Moira on his lap, maneuvering around her each time he took a bite of soup. She babbled out garbled words and random sounds, as her tiny fingers wrapped around his thumb.

For the first few months of Moira's life, when they'd still lived in Surrey, she'd cried daily. Here in London, she had blossomed into a cheerful girl, delighted by all. Some of that was her age—Moira was now fifteen months—but the rest, Poppy believed, was the added influence of family and friends.

The very family and friends she might have put in danger tonight by a bloody Peeler following her home.

Daniel was so much happier now than he'd been in Surrey.

He'd started a new life with Kate, and he'd remained sober. If something happened to take that bliss away from him...she couldn't bear it.

And then there was Jane Putnam, Kate's best friend. She sat to Poppy's right. Jane worked as a barmaid for the Three Boars, and she was the best damn cook Poppy had ever known, able to make even the toughest cuts of meat appetizing. An attractive raven-haired woman with a no-nonsense attitude, Poppy had quickly come to appreciate Jane's undying loyalty to her friends.

Though Jane was honest, she'd grown up with the Chapman Street thieving gang members. Her ties to them would make her a valuable capture for the Met.

When there was a lull in the conversation, Kate turned to Poppy. "Are you all right, Poppy? You haven't said anything since dinner was served."

Poppy set her spoon down, pursing her lips. "I don't understand what happened outside."

"You and me both," Jane agreed. "If Peelers are involved, this is bad for all of us. I don't know about you, but I sure don't intend to join Penn in Newgate."

Poppy sent Jane a sympathetic smile. Jane's brother had been sent to Newgate Prison for housebreaking. While Chapman Street was able to keep him from execution, he remained in the miserable gaol until the gang could figure out a plan to break him free.

"Why's a Trap following you around, Poppy?" Jane asked.

"Apparently, he knows Kate." Poppy turned in her chair, angling her body toward Kate. "I've never known you to like the Peelers, but your reception was almost pleasant."

Daniel grinned. "You should see what she does to people she doesn't like."

"That was one time. I held you at gunpoint *one* time," Kate protested. "I swear, I'm never going to live that down."

Daniel leaned down to give Moira a kiss on her cheek. "Your aunt wasn't so fond of me then."

"Daniel, *no one* was fond of you then," Jane said drolly. "You're lucky you've shaped up, or I'd have fully supported Kate's desire to shoot you."

"Balderdash, I won you over from the moment you saw me," Daniel claimed, grinning at Jane. Ignoring Jane's snort, Daniel gave Moira another bounce that sent her shrieking with giggles.

There was nothing softer, more innocent, than a laughing child. Poppy gulped for air, her throat suddenly tight. What if Knight looked deeper into why she'd left Surrey? Daniel's best friend, Atlas Greer, had crafted her story. Atlas was the cleverest thief in London, and he could make out patterns where others only saw disjointed clutter. Short of putting a record for Robert Corrigan's faux death in the parish register for Dorking, they'd considered all possibilities.

It was a slim possibility that Knight would look that deep, yes, but the idea of a Peeler knowing anything about her put her on edge.

Poppy stood, gathering up her daughter from Daniel. Moira nuzzled close to her as Poppy sat back down. She was still talking, her soliloquy background noise to the adults' conversation.

"How do you know Sergeant Knight?" Poppy pressed.

"He saved my life," Daniel said.

Poppy blinked, once, twice. "Pardon?" There was no way she'd heard him right.

"Sergeant Knight is the officer who helped me find Daniel," Kate explained, sitting down across from her.

Shit.

There was only one Peeler in all of bloody London that Poppy owed a debt of gratitude to: the man who had saved Daniel. When Jasper Finn took Daniel captive, Kate had stopped a patrolling policeman and begged for assistance.

They'd arrived at the workhouse cemetery just in time—any longer, and Daniel would have died. Knight had fought off Finn's associates, giving Atlas Greer time to free Daniel.

Poppy's throat tightened. "Now he knows the street I live on. In addition to knowing about your fencing."

"If Knight was going to turn me in, he would have done it months ago, right?" Kate said, looking at Daniel for reassurance. "I haven't fenced anything since we got married. He'd have nothing current to use against me."

Daniel squeezed Kate's hand. "Did Knight mention anything about us when he walked you home, Pop?"

Poppy thought for a moment. "No. In fact, I don't think he knew who I was until he saw you two."

"*I* hid in the doorway," Jane reminded them.

Kate rolled her eyes at Jane, who smirked in return.

Poppy cleaned off her spoon on a napkin and handed it down to Moira to play with. "Knight asked about the girl I worked with that was murdered a few days ago. He said he's investigating her death, and he wanted to know what I knew about the Larkers."

Jane leaned forward. "Why does Larker sound familiar? I swear I've heard that name before, and not just because of the factory. I work tomorrow, so I'll ask the boys what they know."

Kate stepped toward the table, resting her hands on the upper rim of a chair. "Do you know anything about that girl's murder?"

"No, of course not." Poppy shrugged. "I wish I had information for him, but I don't."

"Good." Jane stood, going to place her dish in the sink. "The less the Peelers know, the better. Bunch of louts, the lot of them."

"I can't resent Knight for being a Peeler when it's his official capacity that sent Finn to trial," Kate said.

Daniel nodded. "I'd still be a fugitive if it wasn't for Knight. He'd followed my case from the start before he joined the Met."

Kate squeezed Daniel's hand. "Knight made sure that the charges against Daniel were dropped completely. The Superintendent wanted to try Daniel as part of Finn's plot, but Knight convinced them that Daniel hadn't been aware of what was going on at my father's company."

"I don't trust him," Jane stated grudgingly. "How do you know he's not working an angle? He could be gathering enough information on your family before he presents a case to his supervisors."

"I can't know that for sure," Kate admitted. "So, you're right, it's best to be careful."

As Poppy got up from the table to clean the dishes, the stew in her stomach churned. She kept a close eye on Moira, who had meandered over to her toy box. The babe picked up her favorite tin plate toy and a cornhusk doll.

With every passing day, Moira grew up a bit more. Poppy longed for those early days when Moira had just learned to crawl, viewing the world with wide-eyed glee. A few years from now, she'd know that the world wasn't so wonderful after all. She'd experience hurt and prejudice.

God, how Poppy wanted to stop time so that Moira never knew that pain.

In the dead of night, Poppy woke up in a cold sweat from dreaming that the townspeople of Dorking had risen up against her again. "You and your bastard daughter are a scourge on this town and the good people in it," they'd said.

But this was London, a sprawling metropolis of over a million people. She could remain anonymous here in this little corner of Spitalfields.

Daniel came up behind Poppy, placing his arm around her

shoulders. "She'll be fine, Pop," he assured her. "Moira's a smart girl."

"It's not just Moira I worry about," Poppy reminded him gently, tilting her head to peer up at him. "I was there when you came home, Danny. I know what the police did to you, the life they stole from you. It almost ate you alive."

Daniel squeezed Poppy's shoulder. "And you brought me back. You were there for me as I should've been for you."

If Daniel had been sober, if he'd paid more attention to her whereabouts, maybe she wouldn't have fallen so easily for Edward Claremont's lies.

But if all that hadn't happened, she wouldn't have her daughter.

"I can't let you blame yourself for my failings." Her gaze never wavered from Daniel's face. They'd had this conversation many times, but still, she felt the necessity of absolving him from responsibility. "I believed Edward. I fell for him. I did those things, not you. Who's to say I wouldn't have chosen the same course if you'd been around?"

"That son of a bitch should've been the one everyone judged, not you. He's lucky he left town shortly after, or I would've strangled him with my bare hands. If I saw him now—"

She sighed. "It wouldn't solve anything."

Daniel frowned. "Doesn't make me hate the bounder any less."

"You can hate him," Poppy agreed. "Lord knows I certainly do."

Poppy leaned back against her brother. Family was everything. When it came down to it, that was the most important notion—family to support you, family to strengthen you. Moira would grow up with family who believed in her.

Daniel was her family, and so were Kate, Jane, and Atlas now by extension.

And Daniel was alive thanks in part to Sergeant Knight.

Poppy pursed her lips. She'd been outright rude to Knight. She'd made a snap judgment about him based solely on his blue uniform, as people in Dorking had done when they'd found out she was carrying a child out of wedlock.

"I've been terribly hypocritical," she murmured.

"Hmm?" Daniel inquired.

"Nothing," Poppy assured him.

She couldn't shake the realization that she'd committed an injustice in her behavior to Sergeant Knight. Though she could no longer call herself honorable, she had her pride. The mistakes she'd made in the past could be justified by youth and inexperience.

This time, she had no excuse.

The second week of April had not been pleasant for Thaddeus. The Romans had declared that the Ides of March were perilous when they should have been focusing on April. But the Romans were known to be wrong about some things, like believing animal entrails could be used to predict the future.

Thaddeus sighed, casting a glance around his cluttered library. He could have chosen to live with the rest of the single officers at the section house on Leman Street, but this space called to him. Encircled by his books, he felt more at home here than he'd ever felt in his family's townhouse.

He flipped open the book he'd left on the end table. He hadn't been able to focus on anything since he'd come home from Finch Street. Leaning his head back against his chair, Thaddeus closed his eyes—expecting that without the distraction of light, he'd be able to piece together these fragments of the case that bothered him so.

But he didn't think of burly Boz Larker. No, the vision that appeared before him was lovelier, a petite redhead with a trim waist and pert breasts straining at the confines of her gingham gown. And the small of her back, nestled against his hand as they'd stood in the alley tonight.

He swallowed, shifting in his chair. For a second, he was tempted to root through his desk until he found a certain pamphlet he read in more amorous moments.

But no. He had a job to do, damn it, and it certainly didn't involve lusting after a woman who wanted nothing to do with him. Regardless of how intriguing she was.

He opened his eyes and focused on the book he'd been studying, Cesare Beccaria's *Dei Delitti e Delle Pene*, "On Crimes and Punishments." It had helped little with his current case, yet Thaddeus found the Italian soothing. It was familiar, and he craved the familiar.

Three days since his meeting with Whiting, he'd found himself in distinctly unfamiliar territory. The majority of arrests he made for the H-Division were for petty thievery and disorderly conduct. Though old case files were stacked on almost every discernible surface in this library, he had worked through those in his leisure, without the added pressure of a deadline. There had also been a distance to those cases: he had not seen any of those victims take their last breaths.

When he'd found Elizabeth Stewart in that alley seven years ago, he hadn't had the skills to solve her murder. But he'd kept checking back with the old magistrate to see how the case progressed. After the discovery that Miss Stewart was a prostitute in one of the most ill-reputed brothels in Whitechapel, the investigation had ceased. The assumption was made that a customer had become irate when Miss Stewart wouldn't provide services at a reduced rate.

But this time with Anna Moseley's murder, Thaddeus was wiser. He knew what he was doing, or so he kept telling himself. If he was going to become an inspector, he needed to become more comfortable with working on a timetable.

His brother, Joseph, was supposed to stop by his flat that night on his way home from work with information on the Larkers' finances. That would at least give him something to pursue.

Thaddeus knew Boz Larker was a factory owner with a reputation no more tarnished than usual. Since meeting with Whiting, Thaddeus had interviewed several dismissed employees, but none had any idea of underhanded dealings. One was dismissed because he'd arrived drunk, another had tried to unionize the workers, and the third had been found smuggling out yards of finished brocade.

Each said they hadn't seen what was kept in the locked room upstairs, so that would be Thaddeus's first order of business when he went to the factory.

Thaddeus closed the book in his lap with a resounding thud. Larker didn't seem to have ties to the Chapman Street gang, so if he was dealing in stolen goods, he'd have to be using a different receiver. Thaddeus had his own contact, a retired fence by the name of Dagobert Gottlieb, looking into criminal connections within Spitalfields for the Larkers.

Fences. Thaddeus tapped his finger to his chin, squinting at the orange flames that danced merrily behind the fire screen. Was Mrs. Corrigan using her sister-in-law's fencing connections to move goods for the Larkers? It was a long shot, but at least it was something.

He frowned. None of this added up. He needed evidence. Something better than a witness statement. Those could be bought. He'd learned that from the O'Reilly case.

Thaddeus reached over the arm of his chair for the half-full glass of whisky on the table. He sipped it slowly, letting the amber liquid splash down his throat. Joseph had bought it, and he had decent taste in liquor. That was all Joseph had good taste in—he'd become a banker and married a woman who resembled a rotting fish.

The knock on his front door resonated throughout the room. Thaddeus knew it was his brother before going to the door. Joseph always announced his presence in the most infuriatingly autocratic manner possible, as if he were the Trojan horse himself set upon the shores.

"Let me in," Joseph hollered. "Put down your confounded book and let me in!"

Thaddeus sighed, pushing himself up and out of the chair. He did not bother to put his boots back on, for damn it all, Joseph didn't warrant boots. Or a jacket.

Flinging open the door, Thaddeus skipped the preliminary greeting. "Did you bring the information?"

Joseph pushed past Thaddeus into the house. He was a larger man than Thaddeus or their middle brother, Nathan, but he was not as tall. Joseph had the frame of a pugilist, thick in the shoulders and square jawed. His face was elongated, his nose straight and bulbous.

"I hope you're happy," Joseph reproached him. "I had to miss dinner at the club. Why couldn't this have waited until Sunday?"

On the second Sunday of every month, Thaddeus joined his family for breakfast, motivated by the desire to get his mother off of his back and not a real need to see his family. Visiting with them meant listening to their diatribes on his profession. At least Nathan was relatively silent, but Nathan lived in Derbyshire and only visited London during the holidays.

Joseph's dark eyes settled on the contents of the room with

displeasure. Thaddeus had added another collection of books on criminal deduction, and a cleaned human skull sat atop the ramshackle ladder, but other than that little had changed in the room since Joseph had last visited.

"Don't know why you choose to live in such sparse conditions," Joseph remarked. "Nathan's house isn't so sparse, and he's a bloody rector."

Thaddeus shrugged. "I live alone. What do I need with more space?"

"You ought to think of the future," Joseph cautioned with the bravado of one who'd been married for six years and thus knew everything about the world. "What shall you do when you find a wife?"

Thaddeus crossed his arms over his chest, fixing Joseph with what he hoped was his best intimidating expression but probably came off as mildly peevish. "I have no imminent plans to marry."

He hadn't met anyone who intrigued him for more than one night. No one but Poppy Corrigan.

And that was merely work.

"You're not getting any younger." Joseph searched the room for the whisky he'd brought, snatching the bottle up from the table by the fire. He made his way to the sidebar, sloshing a generous portion into a shot glass.

Bloody hell. With that much whisky, Joseph intended to stay for longer than the ten minutes Thaddeus had allocated. He'd be completely off schedule.

Intrinsically, he knew that Joseph and the rest of his family meant well. He'd spent most of his childhood observing them with the detachment of one who has failed to find a true equal in modern society.

"I am twenty-four years old," Thaddeus reminded him.

"Plenty of time to be had should I decide to take a wife. I highly doubt I've got one foot in the grave."

"Again, you go with the graves." Joseph grunted in disgust. "Take my advice, Thad, don't talk about work with Father again. He raged for days about you helping to put those resurrectionists in gaol. Claimed the law cares more about how a corpse is obtained than scientific discovery. It was dreadfully uncomfortable for me."

How do you think it was for me?

Thaddeus suppressed the urge to roll his eyes. There was no time for Joseph's tirades, not if he planned to finish making notes on the rest of Larker's known associates tonight. "Did you get the information on the account I asked you to look into?"

Joseph pulled out a bundled package from a pocket in his jacket. He passed it to Thaddeus.

Eagerly, Thaddeus unwound the twine connecting the package and spread the paper out across the liquor cabinet. He hadn't expected to receive so thorough of a report from Joseph—it had been a slim chance that the Larkers held an account at Barclay's.

Joseph had labeled each sheet with what the charts represented. As Thaddeus had predicted, the Larker factory wasn't making enough money to justify the purchase of so many new Jacquard looms, nor could they afford to pay for a staff of thirty who worked early morning to late evening.

"What's this about, brother? Why do you care about a struggling textile factory? Not exactly interesting work, I'll tell you."

"It's a case I'm on," Thaddeus said.

Joseph winced. "I was hoping you wouldn't say that. The last case you had me look into nearly brought my bosses down upon me. If I wasn't such a well-liked chap—"

"But you are." Thaddeus placated him. He highly doubted Joseph was in any real danger of being dismissed at Barclay's.

Most of the clients seemed to find Joseph's smarmy mannerisms to be charming, and his wife's family had important social connections that the bank needed.

Thaddeus flipped another page in the packet. "In your experience, what are some of the reasons for a business to spend exorbitantly more than they make?"

Joseph deliberated for a moment, sipping at his whisky. "When starting a business, there are certain expenditures one must make. The first year isn't profitable, or at least not to the extent expected later. That sheet in the back talks about how the factory ran before the Larkers taking over. You'll see that a lot of upgrades were made once Boz Larker bought the place."

Thaddeus shuffled through the papers to find the sheet indicated. "Would you consider these costs to be normal for a factory?"

"How the devil should I know?" Joseph shrugged. "Case or not, the Larkers are dreadfully dull. Overspending is a way of life, Thad. Why, I've seen some of those young bucks withdraw seven thousand pounds from their account to pay gambling debts."

Thaddeus pursed his lips, combing over the report again. "It concerns me."

Joseph leaned back against the liquor cabinet, crossing his left leg over his right and tucking his thumbs in the folds of his waistcoat. His wide forehead creased with premature wrinkles. There was a sharpness to his features that had not been there when they were boys.

Then, Joseph had been a brother in more than the literal sense of the world.

"Do you remember when you found me hiding underneath my bed at Eton?" Thaddeus asked.

Joseph looked up from pouring more whisky into his glass, his brows furrowed. "Yes," he drawled. "But I don't remember what possessed you to take up residence underneath your cot. It must have stunk dreadfully. Lord knows the maids didn't clean properly. Can never get proper servants."

Thaddeus ran a hand through his hair, tugging at the short ends. How could that moment not have meant something to Joseph, when it had defined Thaddeus's youth?

"There were bullies." Thaddeus hated how weak his voice sounded as if he was again a child longing for Joseph and Nathan to notice him. "I was scared to take meals in the common room. When you found out, you hunted them down in the courtyard."

"And I punched the bounder in the nose," Joseph declared, raising his whisky triumphantly.

"It was the only time in my life I've ever been glad to see someone bleed." Thaddeus forced a smile onto his lips because that was what Joseph would expect, but he was no longer keen on the memory.

"I told you if you take out the leader, you'll stop the rest." Carrying the whisky bottle with him, Joseph sat down in the chair by the fire. "And you listened to me, which I found quite the shocker. I saw you the next week, fighting that bleeder when he picked on that scrawny lad from Norfolk."

"They stole his assignment like they'd done to me. I couldn't let it continue." He'd been so angry; he'd struck out with a ferocious uppercut. The brute's nose had broken from the contact, but the boy from Norfolk had never been a target again.

"For a lanky pain in the arse, you packed quite a punch." Joseph's grin stretched wider, becoming that genuine smile Thaddeus remembered from their youth. The one that said he'd finally earned his brother's admiration after so many efforts to impress him.

"Thanks," Thaddeus said as if that compliment hadn't struck him.

Joseph patted his shoulder as one might pat the top of a dog's head. "You'll thank me more later. I've found a job for you. It'll be all fantastic from here."

Stifling a groan, Thaddeus reached for the bottle of whisky and refilled his own glass. "I have a job."

"No, a real job."

"I have a *real* job."

"One with security. One Father will be proud of."

Thaddeus was curious, though he loathed himself for still wanting his father's approval. Damn Joseph for striking at his weakness.

"The job is at the bank," Joseph continued. "They've got an opening for a representative. Someone who meets with the rich old spats, assures them their money is safe. Eight years since Fauntleroy embezzled funds, and they're still buggered over it. As if that would happen at our bank."

Thaddeus wasn't amused. "You'd like me to give up policing so that I might sit with the elderly?"

"It'd be an easy job," Joseph said. "You'd be a fool not to take it. Plus, women love a banking man. How'd you think I snared Catherine?"

Thaddeus didn't think Joseph would appreciate hearing his real thoughts on Catherine. He took a seat upon the settee, for as eldest brother, Joseph had claimed Thaddeus's usual spot. Just as Joseph claimed that he knew what was best for Thaddeus. And a little, niggling part of Thaddeus couldn't help but wonder if his brother was right.

Wouldn't it be easier? To no longer roam the cold streets of Spitalfields, armed with a truncheon while the scoundrels of the world had flintlocks and knives? Whose life was he really changing?

Thaddeus's gaze roamed the library. Encased in shelves that spanned from floor to ceiling, he had amassed one of England's premier collections on crime deduction and criminal motivation. If he were not a police officer, what would he be? How would he function? He'd never met anyone who had cared about *all* of him, outside of what he could do for them. In school, he'd been the boy to befriend if one wanted to ace an exam. At work, he was the man people came to if they wanted a difficult case solved.

Thaddeus lowered his head to look Joseph directly in the eye. "I'm part of the Met, and that's not going to change. I do what I do because I believe it's the right thing. These people deserve protection, as you or I do, and I'm not going to give that up."

"Have it your way." Joseph attempted to be flippant, but the slightest bit of sadness had flashed across his weathered face.

Thaddeus nodded stiffly, raising his glass in salute. "I intend to."

Chapter Four

The next morning, Poppy sat once more at her kitchen table. She dipped the last hunk of bread into her bowl of leftover stew and chomped down with renewed gusto. There. The stew made the old bread passable, and it'd do to keep her sated as she worked at the factory today. Moira played on the floor next to the table, amusing herself with a collection of thimbles.

This was her life, an endless cycle of late nights and early mornings. Falling asleep to the noise of the streets outside her window, for it was never silent in London. She was never alone. At work, there were twenty-five other weavers on the same floor. At home, she shared a room with Moira. The cottage had two rooms in total besides the central living area that doubled as a kitchen. Edna had the other room.

"You never stop, Pop," Daniel had said. "You need to rest. You'll run yourself ragged."

But if she stopped—if she broke from this hectic pace for more than a moment—she'd think, and above all, Poppy wanted to avoid lengthy introspection. Thoughts led to self-doubt. Self-doubt led to failure, and failure wasn't an option.

Every day spent in the Larker factory was for the single goal of putting Moira into a finishing school when she was older. Giving her daughter the chance to be something more than she had been. At nineteen years old, Poppy was already ruined. But for Moira, a new life was before her, unwritten.

Poppy nibbled on her bottom lip, staring out the window. Jimmy, the elderly gentleman from one cottage down, was outside sweeping up the rubbish dumped into the street with the last storm. Several of her other neighbors were out enjoying the sunshine.

Once, this little section of Spitalfields would have sent her into a panic. She'd been sheltered growing up on Uncle Liam and Aunt Molly's farm in Dorking. While they had not been wealthy by any means, Poppy had never wanted for anything. She'd been content to accept Aunt Molly's help in getting an apprenticeship with a mantua maker in town.

Until her seventeenth birthday, she'd never known more. She didn't remember her parents clearly. They'd died when she was young. They were a thread, snipped before it could develop into something truly influencing.

And until her seventeenth birthday, she'd followed society's strictures. She'd known her place. As an Irish Catholic woman with no dowry, she couldn't hope for anything more than an inconspicuous life in Surrey. She possessed no great beauty to trap men, and she spent too much time with her nose in a book.

But Edward Claremont changed all of that. He'd reminded her of the heroes in Ann Radcliffe's novels. He'd made her want, for the first time in her life, to be something more. In that week he'd courted her, she'd believed him when he said she was beautiful. She'd believed that was how love should be: overwhelming and intoxicating. It didn't matter that Edward cared little for literature or any of her other interests. He was gloriously handsome and rich. For some reason, he wanted *her*.

So, she'd allowed him to take her maidenhood. She had not protested. No, she'd gone willingly into her destruction, thinking that she'd achieve a happy ending fit for a story tale.

And instead, she'd learned that those with lofty expectations have the furthest to fall.

"Mama, Mama," Moira cried, tearing Poppy from her thoughts. Moira held out the largest of the thimbles, which encompassed her entire palm.

"It's very pretty, Moira," Poppy agreed.

Moira nodded. "Bobs."

"Are you building a castle?" Poppy asked as Moira stacked each of the thimbles like turrets on an empty wooden box.

"Mine," Moira declared, following up this assertion with several mashed words that Poppy couldn't quite identify. But she sounded excited, so Poppy nodded along with her.

"They have castles all over Ireland, you know. Ireland's where our family comes from. Someday when you're older, we'll go there."

She didn't know why she'd said that. It was another lie to add to a multiplying list of untruths. They wouldn't go back to Ireland—not when Poppy would have to look her relatives in the face and lie about Moira's origins.

A bastard shall not enter into the Congregation of the Lord: even to his tenth generation shall he not enter. So said the Bible, and so said the Magdalene Hospital representatives when they'd come to Uncle Liam's farm. They'd claimed they wanted to help her find her way back to the Lord. That they'd learned of her plight from the concerned citizens of Dorking.

Better to trap her in the asylum, quartered with the hopeless, the mentally deficient, the tainted, and the prostitutes. Clothe her in an inoffensive little cap and apron, and a dark-colored dress designed to hide her womanly curves. All because she was a creature of sin. Moira was thus the devil's helper, born in shame and malevolence.

There was nothing left for Poppy in Ireland or Surrey. London was the last place she could go where family would accept her.

Tiring of the thimble collection, Moira reached out with both hands for Poppy to pick her up. Poppy complied, scooping Moira up from the floor and settling the babe on her lap. She laid her head down on top of Moira's.

Edna Daubenmire emerged from her room, straw bonnet in her hand. At sixty-five, Edna was as spry as a woman half her age. With squat arms and a spindly frame, she stood two heads shorter than Poppy, making her the smallest woman Poppy had ever encountered.

Edna set her hat down on the counter. "How are you feeling this morning?"

"Acceptable," Poppy said, not wanting to worry her friend.

Edna pushed her wire-rimmed glasses up on her bulbous nose. "I don't believe you."

"The sun is shining, and I've got a day off tomorrow. Why shouldn't I feel content?" Off the top of her head, Poppy could think of seventeen different reasons why.

Peering at Poppy dubiously, Edna scooped stew into a bowl. Coming to the table, she took a seat across from Poppy. Moira cooed, delighted to see her companion.

"When I came home last night, you'd already gone to bed," Edna observed. "That's unusual for you. I expected Kate and Daniel to stay longer too."

Poppy shrugged. She'd told them she was fatigued after a long day at the factory when she'd wanted solitude to think over the night's events. Another lie to add to her long list, and no clearness gained from it.

"Jane came by, too, and she had to work early," Poppy said.

"Jane," Moira repeated, waving her hand jubilantly.

Edna let out a low laugh. "I've never seen anything quite as awkward as Jane Putnam speaking with a child. Last time she was over, I heard her explaining to Moira about the seven different types of housebreakers."

Moira shifted in her lap. Poppy grasped the girl's hands, allowing her to stand up on her knees. Moira bobbed, squealing boisterously.

"While I do wish she'd choose a different subject matter, I think it's kind that she cares," Poppy said.

"Miss Jane has a good heart," Edna concurred. "But enough about that, my dear. You haven't answered my question truthfully."

Poppy sighed. She couldn't lie to Edna. They'd been through too much together, and never had Edna faltered in her devotion to Poppy. "I met someone last night."

"How delightful!" Edna exclaimed.

"No, no, it is nothing like that." Poppy hurried to correct her. It wasn't supposed to be like that, at least. There'd been that one moment when their eyes had met. Her palm had pressed against the side of his strapping chest.

"You know my feelings on that subject. I'm not going to court anyone. Moira deserves a steady home."

"Men are not all like that rapscallion Claremont," Edna said, as she had many times before. "My Ernest was honorable until the day he died. The right man will love Moira, and he'll love you all the more for everything you've been through."

Poppy knew that was the worst of lies. Men cheated, and men lied. Even Daniel had left Kate for years. A woman's sole chance at happiness was independence through a good education and a good position. She'd make sure Moira had that chance.

"I'm glad you found happiness with Mr. Daubenmire,"

Poppy said. "But I doubt that such a man exists for me, and I'm in no haste to find him."

And if she embarked on such a relationship again, it would certainly not be with the man who knew all her family secrets.

No. Not all. Knight knew *most* of their secrets.

"If he is not a suitor, who is this man?" Edna asked.

Poppy bounced Moira again, holding onto her hands. "He's a sergeant with the Metropolitan Police. He followed me from the factory and kept asking questions about that girl who died last week."

"Dreadful." Edna frowned. "But why did he choose you?"

"I suppose I was the easiest to get to when the factory let out. Most of the workers dispersed in groups." She remained uncertain.

"I'm sorry you had to go through that." Edna ate a spoonful of stew before continuing. "I know how you dislike the Met after what happened to your brother."

Poppy frowned. "That's where it starts to get odd. Thaddeus Knight is the man who saved Daniel." Saying it out loud made it no less peculiar.

Edna's eyebrows shot up. "Well, I suppose of all the Met for you to meet, he'd be the least likely to earn your disapproval."

Poppy forced a small smile and nodded.

"Oh, dear," Edna remarked. "It didn't go well, did it?"

"I was a tad rude." Poppy covered Moira's ears with her hands and lowered her voice. "I may have told him he was a blighter and a bounder."

"Poppy!" Edna chided. "He saved Daniel! That's no way to behave. Your aunt taught you better than that."

Aunt Molly had been friends with Edna before she passed. No matter how old Poppy got, she'd always be a young girl in Edna's eyes. How Poppy longed to have Aunt Molly back beside her to give her advice. She, unlike Uncle Liam, would have understood her predicament. Aunt Molly had never been the type to judge.

Poppy removed her hands from Moira's ears. "I know. In my defense, I didn't know that's who he was."

"Still, manners," Edna scolded.

"I thought if I was belligerent, he'd consider me too much trouble to ask further questions. And I was doing fine with the accent Kate taught me until I got distracted and slipped up. Sergeant Knight is different from the rest... My mistake intrigued him. He wouldn't stop asking me questions, as if I knew who killed Anna."

"Which you don't, correct?" Edna inquired.

"Of course not. Why does everyone seem to think I do?" Poppy grimaced. "I'm not going to cast stones when it's all rumors. The Larkers are wretched people, to be sure, but I can earn a decent amount with them."

Edna harrumphed. "Provided you work long hours until your back is sore, and your eyes are blearing from staring at the weaving."

"If that's what it takes to give Moira a chance at a new life, that's what I'll do," Poppy vowed.

"I'm not disapproving, Poppy, merely wishing there was another way." Edna patted Poppy's hand. "It's not fair that you must spend all day away from this beautiful girl."

Poppy stood, pushing her chair back from the table. She carried Moira over to the blanket serving as Moira's play area. An empty apple box crate housed Moira's toys, and Daniel had crafted some blocks for her. Sitting Moira down, Poppy knelt by her.

Moira grabbed onto the edge of the coffee table, using it to pull herself up. She waddled over to her toy box, drawing out a stuffed bear. Jamming the bear's ear into her mouth, she sucked on the cloth, grinning all the while.

"Mama!" She waggled her fingers at Poppy.

"Yes, dear," Poppy replied.

Edna sat down in the rocker next to the fireplace. "Tell me what is truly bothering you."

Poppy ran a hand across her skirt. "London was supposed to be a fresh start. A chance for Moira to grow up without my mistake over her."

Edna tilted her head toward Moira. "She's doing well here because of you."

"I cannot help but sometimes wonder if it's all for naught." Poppy ran a hand along the hem of the blanket, where flecks of red paint lined the edge. Red paint that had once spelled out "whore" across Madame Genet's shop window. She'd used the blanket to wipe up the paint, but the stains had persisted through multiple washes.

The same people she'd grown up with in Dorking had turned against her as soon as they found out she was having a bastard child.

"I wish you hadn't kept that," Edna commented. "After the mess was cleaned, you should have allowed me to burn it."

Poppy folded the blanket over to hide the red mark. "It is perfectly good linen. We cannot afford to dispose of something simply because it is slightly soiled."

"You're not a whore," Edna stated. "Child, I agreed to go along with your widow scheme because I thought it'd be best for you to get a chance to move on. Don't allow your past to anchor you. If you do, you'll never be free, and there are so many opportunities for you here in London."

"I like it here," Poppy replied. "The people are lively. I like that I can go down the street and see Irishmen mingling with the Jews and the Huguenots."

"I imagine that's comforting," Edna agreed. "To have people of your home land with you."

"Ireland isn't home," Poppy said, with more vehemence than she'd realized she felt. "In Ireland, they'd throw me into a Magdalene asylum, worse than the ones here. At least in the factories, they *pay* me."

Edna reached for her hand, giving it a tight squeeze. "You avoided that life, lass. No good to come from thinking of it now."

Edna had been there the night the nuns visited Uncle Liam's farm. "You're not a sinner," Edna had said. "You're Molly's beautiful niece, and I believe in you."

Edna swiveled in her chair, inspecting the outside. "These rookeries are an odd place. All the same, I think this is the right place for you."

"But this isn't a place for Moira when she gets older." Poppy waved at Moira as she explored the room. "There's no proper schooling. Even if she's lucky enough to get into a school for the lower class, it'll never set her up for anything more than a life of manufacturing work. I want more for her. She could be a house-maid. Or a governess. A teacher. Anything but like me."

"What's so bad about being like you, lass?" Edna smiled. "You're a sweet girl. You're loyal to your family, and you'll fight for them. I didn't agree to come to London because I like the city, Poppy. I came here because I believe in what you can accomplish."

"Thank you," Poppy murmured.

"It is the truth," Edna said. "London can be whatever you want it to be."

"What if I've spent so much time preparing this new identity that I've forgotten how to be me?" Poppy asked. "All I could think about when I met Sergeant Knight was how the Peelers have hurt my family. And you know, if he hadn't been the man who saved Daniel, I don't think I'd care how badly I acted. How can I raise Moira to be accepting of other people when I act like that?"

"Then go apologize," Edna suggested. "Make amends for how you acted. We all make mistakes, dear girl. It is how we recover from them that defines us."

"Jane pointed out that any contact with the Met could mean trouble," Poppy said. "That's the last thing I want, for the Larkers to think I'm helping a Peeler take down their factory."

"You don't necessarily have to help him," Edna wheedled in a singsong voice. "You can go talk to him."

Poppy tucked a loose red curl behind her ear, ignoring Edna's grin. "I'm telling you, Edna, there is nothing more to this."

However handsome Sergeant Knight might be, he was dangerous. She didn't want a man whose job involved infuriating her neighbors and friends. No matter how her heart had sped up when she'd been so close to him.

If she were going to give Moira autonomy, it wouldn't be as the daughter of a Met officer. In rookery standards, Poppy highly suspected that was several steps below bastard.

Edna was undaunted. "If you're worried about him suspecting things are amiss, wouldn't the proper thing to do be to apologize to him? It's less suspicious that way. You recognize you made a mistake, and you want to thank him for what he did for Daniel. You'll appear as if you have nothing to hide. Plus, you'll get to appease your guilty conscience."

"I suppose that could work," Poppy mused.

All she had to teach her daughter right from wrong was her own example. As for the threat Knight presented, Edna had a good point. Poppy owed Knight her thanks for saving Daniel. It would be normal to visit him, expected.

It was about doing what was right, *not* about how his athletic body had set her heart afire.

Poppy nodded swiftly. "I'll write to Atlas and ask if he can find out where Knight lives."

"That sounds like a good plan," Edna agreed. "Now off with you, before you're late for your shift."

* * *

To the average onlooker, the police station in Spitalfields was not an impressive building. Located at the corner of St. Matthew's Churchyard and Wood Street, it reeked of standard protocol. It had once been the old watch house for the Charleys, appropriated two years prior by the H-Division.

But to Thaddeus, the station house on Wood Street contained everything he'd spent his adult life working toward. Fifteen other sergeants worked in the H-Division, a portion reporting to Whiting and the rest to the other two inspectors. With the exception of Michael Strickland, Thaddeus felt a kinship to these sergeants. Unlike his family, these men understood why he toiled here. They didn't care that they made a measly twenty-two shillings per annum. They expected to walk twenty miles every day around their district. And they knew damn well that the wear and tear upon their bodies from this job would end them in their prime if a bullet from a criminal's pistol didn't kill them first.

They were in it for justice, for the country, and for the people they served.

They were the ones who'd stayed.

As Thaddeus walked through the double doors, he passed the central lobby, waving at the secretary. The section house smelled of lemons, strong tea, and sweat. A combination that should have been outright grotesque, but instead comforted him.

This was home.

He had plenty to do on the Larker case. That encounter with Poppy Corrigan had set his mind to work. He'd reached out to a foot patroller he knew in the A-Division of Westminster to see if Boz Larker was a known fixture in the rookery of St. Giles. It was unlikely, for St. Giles was a carriage ride away on the west side of London. His contact's missive had landed on his desk that morning.

Thaddeus unfurled the parchment. "No one has heard of him," the message said. Thaddeus flipped over the paper to see if maybe the foot patroller had written something on the back. It was blank.

He sighed, setting the parchment on the stack at the right side of his desk for ideas that hadn't panned out. The pile was twice the size of that on the left side, for ideas that had produced solid leads.

Thaddeus pulled at his neckcloth to loosen it. He sucked down the last of his tea, icy cold, and frowned at the clay mug. Just once, he'd like to drink a full cup of tea when it was piping hot. But that was as unlikely as Strickland solving a case with his wits, not his fists.

The clock on the wall tolled three in the afternoon.

He leaned back in his chair, feet perched on his awkwardly shaped desk. No more than a single board of sanded—but not stained—wood, nailed onto two logs that made up the legs. Designed with a far shorter person in mind, the opening where he should have been able to pull up his chair was at the exact height of his shins. In consequence, Thaddeus sat with his long legs spread out on either side of the desk, hunched over to access his papers.

Strickland strode down the hall toward him. "You'd think that they could buy the best sergeant a new desk."

Thaddeus was not a violent man by nature, but damnation, every time he saw Strickland, he wanted to punch the man in his nose.

Strickland crept closer with an aquiline grace better befitting a dancer at the coster halls than the well-built Corinthian he was. Thaddeus knew for a fact that the bounder spent most of his nights off either at the Red Fist, where the fancy crowd gathered, or at the pugilist gymnasium in Shadwell.

"I don't need a new desk," Thaddeus said, with the particular degree of hauteur he reserved for people he knew to be significantly below his intelligence.

Strickland snickered. "Aye, that's a good chap, Thaddy. You'll make do. You always do."

"Don't call me that," Thaddeus replied, though he knew it would do little good. No one but his mother—and Strickland—had called him Thaddy since he was a child.

"Why not, Thaddy?" Strickland stood behind him, peering over his shoulder at his parchment.

Thaddeus heaved a great sigh. He turned the foolscap over so that Strickland couldn't read it. Returning his quill to the inkwell, he pushed his chair out from the desk and faced the other officer. "Why are you here? Don't you have a route to patrol? *My* route, in fact."

Strickland's sneer faltered, but he recovered hastily. "Whiting called me in for a meeting. Said the route could wait."

Thaddeus's eyes narrowed. "Excuse me?"

"You'll have to take it up with Whiting. I'm merely a humble servant following orders." Strickland leaned back against Thaddeus's desk, his hands folded behind his back. "I don't know how you do that route every night, Thaddy. It's all balls and bores down Cat and Wheel Street. You'd think there'd at least be a brothel to toss it up a bit."

"I *asked* for that route," Thaddeus retorted. "Did Whiting tell you what this meeting was about?"

"He didn't, but even a fool could figure it out. Inspector Doughty is taking leave soon. He's got tots crawling out of his ears, that one. Needs to watch them during the day, or they'll burn his home to the ground." Grimacing, Strickland ran a hand through his wavy brown hair. "Can't imagine a worse fate."

Unbidden, Poppy Corrigan appeared in his mind's eye, with her laughing babe in her arms. He wondered what it'd be like to come home to a woman like her, strong and independent. To have a family of his own, a daughter to raise and protect.

"Must be wretched," Thaddeus remarked dryly.

"They need somebody to replace him soon. 'Course it'll be me." Strickland cuffed Thaddeus on the shoulder so hard that Thaddeus fell forward, almost hitting the desk. "I'll expect a pint from you when I get the job."

Thaddeus was saved from a choice remark by the appearance of Whiting. The inspector motioned for Strickland to enter his office.

Watching Strickland leave out of the corner of his eye, he sifted through the piles of parchment for the sketch he'd had drawn up of Anna Moseley. If Strickland was selected for the inspector job, he wouldn't do anything to help the rookeries. His main concern was fame and fortune from solving cases for the aristocracy. Strickland craved his name in the broadsheets. More and more people would fall through the cracks in the law, with no one there to support them.

Thaddeus *had* to get that post.

With the sketch in his hand, Thaddeus went after Strickland to join the meeting in Whiting's office. If anyone was going to be promoted, it was going to be him, not Strickland.

No matter how much he'd rather be out investigating, he'd play these petty bureaucratic games if it saved more Elizabeth Stewarts and Anna Moseleys.

He'd failed them once, but he would not fail again.

Chapter Five

Thaddeus Knight lived in a two-story townhouse, set on the edge of Spitalfields, a stone's throw away from the crime and vice of the rookery. Poppy had heard that Peelers didn't make much in the means of salary, but Atlas claimed that Knight was from a family of decent means. She'd expected him to be in Cheapside, an area befitting his class.

It was hellishly early, but the only time she could see him. Two days had passed since she'd met him outside the factory. Whatever leniency the Larkers had been exhibiting that day had surely passed, for she'd worked sixteen hours yesterday.

She readjusted her bonnet so that it better shaded her eyes from the rising sun. A short visit, not longer than fifteen minutes at most. Not worth the time it had taken for her to walk here, if not for the fact that she'd be absolved of the guilt. Atlas had claimed Thaddeus Knight worked morning to evening, getting off work as the sun dipped down. Most likely, he wouldn't be home, and that was a much preferable alternative. She'd simply drop the note she'd written and the box with the scarf on his stoop and run.

She knocked on the door.

A moment later, the door opened. Knight dipped his head, surprise flitting across his face but quickly suppressed. God, if he didn't look spectacular in the sunlight, the intense morning rays lightening up his tousled dark hair. Without his police uniform, he seemed freer. He wore gray breeches that high-lighted his well-developed legs, and a white cambric shirt that was not fine in quality but somehow made him appear rustic and utterly masculine.

She gulped, desperately averting her eyes from his arms, clad in shirtsleeves. The last time she'd seen a man like this...

She'd taken him to bed.

And afterwards, she'd learned that every whispered word, every caress, every kiss had been part of a larger scheme to ruin her. A bet made with his friends to pass the time while trapped in a dull town.

Poppy looked up, but that was a mistake, for Knight hadn't bothered to put on a neckcloth. How could the bare line of his neck look so tempting? She swallowed again.

"Mrs. Corrigan," he said mildly, as though it were quite a usual occurrence for a random woman to show up outside his door at dawn.

"I wanted—" No, that wasn't right. She didn't want anything from him. "Might I come inside?"

"Certainly." He nodded, stepping back from the door so that she might enter.

The door closed behind her with a resounding click. "This is for you," she announced, thrusting the box with the scarf in it.

He took the box and opened it, lifting out the scarf. "It is quite wonderful." He ran his fingers over the smooth silk. "But I'm not entirely certain why?"

"I came to apologize," she said.

Knight blinked. "Apologize for what?"

"For how I treated you," Poppy clarified. "My brother told

me what you did for him. You saved his life, and I acted as though you were the most dastardly of villains. I should have been thanking you."

Knight was unruffled. "While I appreciate your apology, your reaction was expected, given the circumstances."

"What circumstances?" she squeaked, her stomach roiling.

"I'm a Peeler," he stated. "In Spitalfields."

"Ah," she said, for he'd imparted this obvious truth as if it explained everything.

"What I mean is I'm not normally well-received. Though admittedly, women don't oft refuse my offer to walk them home." He chuckled. Such an adorably boyish sound.

And she couldn't help but be ashamed of her behavior. When not clad in his blues, he was another man, not much older than she was, with feelings of his own.

She shifted her weight from one foot to the other. "I'm sorry about that too."

He turned around to place the scarf on the table by the door. His shirt stretched across his back, rippling with the movement of his body.

Her cheeks burned red hot. *For goodness sake, Poppy. He's a bloody Peeler.* The kind of man who could destroy her family if he wanted to. Not the kind of man whose arse she should be inspecting.

She felt his eyes on her before she looked up, a caress to a tired part of her that longed to be noticed. To be wanted again.

"With everything that happened with Daniel, I've grown suspicious of Peelers. You understand, don't you? Daniel almost lost his life because of them..." The words tumbled out faster than she could stop them. Anything to keep her eyes on his face and not at the tantalizing triangle of naked flesh peeking out from the opened collar of his shirt.

"Which isn't to say that you're like that." She wet her lips with her tongue.

He came back to stand across from her, taking in her crimson cheeks. Comprehension flashed in his eyes, and he too looked sheepish. "I thought you were one of the foot patrollers." He indicated his casual dress. "Would you give me a minute? I haven't a valet, but I should be able to make myself suitable."

Poppy nodded gratefully. He waved her to an open door, off the side of the entranceway. She found herself in a grand library, with windows overlooking the street. A fireplace was to the left, with two chairs and a table positioned in front.

She stood in the middle of the room, surrounded by floor-to-ceiling shelves of books, arranged by subject. Literature off to the left side, followed by poetry, plays, philosophy, and finally, a startlingly large collection devoted to policing. It was the most glorious room she'd ever seen. She longed to stay here for days, working her way through the shelves.

Knight entered, carrying a full tea tray.

"I..." She must get better at thinking about what she was going to say around him before beginning. "This room. I can't believe you've..." Poppy slowly turned in place, taking in the full width of the library. "It's incredible, do you know that? So much literature in one place."

"I'm glad you like it." His grin was contagious.

Soon, she found herself smiling too. A real, honest smile because in all of Poppy's life, she'd wanted to be in a library like this one.

She fought the urge to examine the shelf in front of her, for she'd seen a copy of Wordsworth and Coleridge's *Lyrical Ballads*. The summer of her fifteenth birthday, she'd spent many happy days sequestered in the window seat of Uncle Liam's office, reading those poems.

Instead, she followed him to the sitting area. She poured the tea into two surprisingly feminine cups, adorned with pink roses and lace. Somehow, she highly doubted he'd picked out the china. Did Knight have a lover? A wife?

He accepted the cup from her. "Ah, thank you."

She placed a lump of sugar into her tea. Then another, for from the look of his house, he could afford two lumps of sugar, and it was a delicacy she'd not pass up. "Such lovely china."

"I shall pass on the compliment to my mother," he said.

So, he was a bachelor. Relief besieged her, a strange, unsettling relief she shouldn't have felt.

He lifted the cup up, so it was at eye level, squinting as he inspected it. "You know, it's the strangest thing. I don't think I've noticed the pattern before. A cup is a cup, is it not?"

"I suppose so," she agreed.

"Yet to my mother, this cup is an example of the stellar Knight pedigree," Knight continued dryly. "It is all about appearances with my family. I have two brothers, one a clergyman and the other a banker. Both are fitting, respectable occupations for the grandsons of an earl."

"An earl?" Poppy yelped. She definitely should have worn a better dress.

"My father was the second son of a second son of an earl," he continued, sounding as thrilled as if he'd announced he was the grandson of a dung beetle. "According to my mother, that's practically royalty. I keep waiting for King William to invite me to the palace, but it hasn't happened."

So much for Edna's advice that she should set her cap at the sergeant. She felt as though she'd been stripped bare and made to stand on top of his coffee table. A crowd of jeering men would examine her wares and find her lacking.

Tainted.

Poor.

A fallen Paddy with nothing to recommend her.

A cold silence fell between them. She sipped at the tea, watching the clock on the mantel. Five more minutes before she could acceptably leave.

"I like the scarf," Knight said finally. "Silk, I see. The weaving is quite tight."

"Thank you." Weaving was the one talent she knew she had. "I made it on my aunt's handloom back home. She taught me to weave, actually."

"In Surrey," he supplied. "Your work is exquisite. Larker Factory is lucky to have a weaver of your quality."

She hadn't meant to talk about her past. But there was something about him. The quiet way in which he listened, perhaps, or the fascination that shone in his eyes as he looked at her.

Time for a new plan of action: drink one cup of tea. Then depart.

She gulped down a quarter of the cup. Not particularly well mannered, but expediency was in her best interests. The warm liquid flooded her throat with blessedly strong tea, as she drank when visiting Atlas. She had the sudden desire to seize the entire pot and run off so that Edna might experience it too.

Poppy had been spending entirely too much time around thieves.

"Are you off to the factory today?" Knight supped casually as if the tea was no great indulgence. As if he had never reused leaves until the last dregs of it came out like mud.

"Yes," she said, unsure if he was intent upon polite conversation or another round of interrogation.

"It's this case. I cannot think about anything else when I'm on a case." He leaned forward as he spoke, his usually stoic face transformed expressively. His deep baritone voice, once monotonous, now had a lilt of enjoyment to it.

She watched him closely, intrigued by the changes wrought.

"I imagine it would be hard to think of anything else when a criminal is on the loose."

"There is that to consider. But I find it fascinating we are a nation that fears its police force when the police should be beacons of safety and sanity." He peered at her expectantly, as if expecting her to voice her opinion.

"I suspect..." she began tentatively, "you presume the majority of London wishes to conduct themselves with decorum and rationality."

When he nodded, she continued, warming up to her theory. "I have been in London for three months, but in that time, I've worked beside children in the factories who are not much older than my own daughter. These conditions are not those that inspire one to be mindful, Sergeant."

"Ah, so you support the theory that poverty shall breed revolution." He propped his elbow up on his knee, resting his chin in his hand.

She'd pleased him.

"I've never thought of it in those terms." She set her cup of tea back on the table. "I confess my knowledge of theory is rather limited."

Poppy regretted this confession immediately. The first thread of panic occurring to her was that she didn't live up to his expectations—she wasn't intellectual enough—instead of worrying he'd discover her secret.

That alone should have been enough of a reason to flee. Yet his rapt gaze was still on her, and suddenly she wanted to be a part of this exchange. She could trace her usual conversations to four topics: weaving, the factory, her family, and Moira. No one had ever expected more from her.

She stood, indulging in her desire to examine the bookshelves. "How long did it take you to acquire such a collection?"

"I've been buying books since I was a boy." He came to

stand next to her, almost shoulder to shoulder, if not for the height difference between them. Plucking *Waverly* from the shelf, he ran his hands over the cover with such delicacy she knew herself to be in the company of a fellow booklover. "This one, my father sent me when I was at Eton. Back in the days when he thought I'd become a surgeon like him or a barrister. My actual profession was quite a disappointment."

She winced, knowing how it felt to disappoint family. Uncle Liam's voice echoed in her ears. "Didn't you realize the shame you'd bring upon us?"

Poppy shook her head, concentrating on the shelves again. As always, books would anchor her.

"What about this book?" She pulled down *Frankenstein*, flipping it open with relish. "I devoured this last year. The idea of a monster built from human corpses..."

"Does it remind you of the resurrection men in your brother's case?" Knight tapped at the cleft in his chin. "The cracks in the spine of that volume are from when I was helping with the trial of Finn."

"A bit, yes." She smiled ruefully. "Daniel said you were the only one who believed him. Thank you for that."

"I was just doing my job." Knight shrugged. "Plus, I admire a good bit of investigative work. O'Reilly and Miss Morgan had put together a nice case for me. That said..." He gave her a pointed look, his tone more formal. "I should hope they haven't returned to their previous illegal activities."

"Of course not," Poppy said quickly.

Too quickly.

He eyed her, the corners of his lips turning up shrewdly. She didn't know what to make of that. Would Knight turn in Kate after all? She wasn't so convinced now.

She found herself *wanting* to trust Knight, and that made him even more dangerous to her.

She ran her fingers across the spines on the shelf, soothed by the texture as much as the smell of old parchment and ink. "I cannot think of a time when I've not willed away pain with a book."

For a second, their eyes met, and Poppy saw in his gaze more understanding than she cared to admit. Kindred souls, opposite because of the paths of their lives, but joined in mutual tastes. He could spot a tight weave, and he knew the merits of Shelley, but he was a Peeler, nonetheless.

"If you like Shakespeare..." He crossed behind her, going to a shelf less orderly than the rest, with volumes stacked on top of each other. "Then this is the place for you. I've got every one of his plays, plus copies of his sonnets as well."

From the shelf, he selected *King Lear*. "This is my favorite of all his plays. I like that in the end, Lear has finally learned who he can trust. He's shed his misassumptions."

She knew who she could trust: no one. "I haven't read it."

"What is your favorite then?"

"I have always liked *Much Ado About Nothing*," she answered without hesitation. "I like Beatrice and Benedick."

"I do enjoy that one." Knight inclined toward her, his voice low and conspiratorial. "But to be honest, I've always found Claudio an absolute buffoon. Willing to shun Hero when I highly doubt that he was virtuous."

Her jaw dropped.

"Madam, my working for the police doesn't make me a complete brute," he teased.

He believed Claudio should have forgiven Hero, whether or not she'd had sex prior to marriage. But it was an entirely different matter to apply that belief to reality.

She turned, reaching for another cup of tea. Sensing what she wanted, he slid forward to pour for her—a misplaced attempt at chivalry, perhaps—and their hands brushed against each other. The slight touch was all she needed to remember pressing up against his chest. Feeling his breath against her cheek. The way he'd smelled of lemon and sage.

He hadn't moved his hand. For a second, though it seemed far longer to her, they lingered. Hands in tandem, eyes fixed on one another.

He was too near her now, yet she couldn't part from him. Idly, she wondered what it would be like for him to slide his finger beneath the neckline of her gown. To stroke her breast with the pad of his thumb.

Would he be gentle? Rough?

This was madness. She was wicked to have such thoughts.

He pulled away, pouring the tea into the cup unsteadily. A bit sloshed onto the silver tray. "Pardon me, I'm woefully clumsy. The curse of human nature—we all make mistakes."

But some mistakes were far worse than others were, and she needed to remember that.

"Sergeant Knight, it has been delightful," she told him. "Please understand how grateful I am to you for saving my brother's life. If I'd known who you were..." She pursed her lips.

If she'd known who he was, wouldn't she have turned and run the other way since he already knew too much about her family? But a hero deserved to be treated like one. "I would have told you so then. My entire family owes you a debt of gratitude."

Knight stood, bashfully surveying her. "If it all meant I'd meet you, Mrs. Corrigan, I'd do it again."

In that instant, all Poppy desired was to tell him she'd enjoyed meeting him too. That she thought him kind, inexplicably so. Her heart fluttered in a maudlin way she knew too well as the stirrings of attraction. She'd felt it before with Edward.

Trepidation clawed at her, wrapping around her heart. Women in love were flighty, irrational creatures who made the worst of mistakes. Romance was a malleable concept with no place in her life.

Moira was her focus now.

She couldn't risk Knight figuring out her whole life in London was a lie.

*   *   *

Poppy Corrigan's visit to his townhouse had left Thaddeus befuddled, an unaccustomed state for him. Outside of cases for the Met, he tended to avoid anything that might leave him emotionally confounded. People had an alarming habit of hopping from one topic to another without a single logical connector. Inevitably, the simplest of conversations turned into a two-hour affair, for which he had neither the time nor the patience. Every call at his parents' house produced the same results: he was either bored or dissected for his life choices.

Yet with Mrs. Corrigan, he hadn't wanted to steer her toward the door at the earliest opportunity. In fact, he'd delighted in showing her his Shakespeare collection. And even more curiously, she'd seemed to *enjoy* his library. No one had ever delighted in his library the way he did.

He remembered how breathless she'd been, praising his reading room. How she'd run her finger down the spine of *Frankenstein*. Before he knew it, he was imaging those delicate hands stroking him with the same reverence. Her breath uneven and heady because he'd made her experience a different form of pleasure, perhaps more exciting than even a fully stocked library.

He indulged in this vision for entirely too long. She'd thrown him off his timetable.

He looked over at his shelf of theoretical textbooks. Man is as strong as the woman he chooses, he mused, unsure where the idea had come from. In the past, he would have said man was as strong as his government, or some other acceptable bureaucratic entity.

It was inconsequential. All this talk of literature had made him maudlin.

He remained in his library for several hours after her departure, with all his notes spread about him, hoping for some sort of inspiration. Two things continued to catch his eye: the sketch of Anna Moseley and the report Joseph had brought him detailing the factory finances.

Neither made any real sense. Oh, to be sure, the sketch was well done and rather typical. This regularity disconcerted Thaddeus. What was it about Anna Moseley that had led to her murder? Why pick *this* girl?

Off the top of his head, he could think of three motives he might ascribe to the Larkers, and they all had to do with fear: fear of discovery, of losing capital, of being seen as weak. The former seemed like the most logical, knowing what he did of Boz Larker.

So, what had Anna seen or discovered that led to her death?

Mrs. Corrigan had mentioned a locked room the Larkers supposedly used to store the finished fabrics. As soon as he had a better handle on *what* this case was truly about, he'd head to the factory and demand access to that room. Until he had more information, he preferred the Larkers remain unaware of his investigation.

This made Poppy Corrigan's appearance at his townhouse more interesting. That moment when they'd both reached for the tea. He could have sworn she'd felt it too, this strange surge of longing when they touched. Had he misinterpreted it? She'd left shortly after.

He was a Met officer first and foremost, so no matter how beguiling he found it that she could converse intelligently on literature, he had a duty. He had a sneaking suspicion she knew more than she was saying. If Mrs. Corrigan had something in her past that could affect the outcome of the Moseley murder, he needed to know it.

So, he stood and went to his writing desk. He took out a paper, sharpened his quill, dipped the quill in ink, and composed a letter to Jean-Paul Beauregard. A friend from his time at Cambridge, Beauregard had moved to Surrey and set up as a solicitor.

It was not uncouth to pry into a woman's past when it was in the name of criminal inquiry. Mrs. Corrigan was hiding something. He was sure of it.

He finished the letter and folded it precisely, the edges crisp. Should Mrs. Corrigan's past bear no relation to the Moseley case, Thaddeus would burn the contents of the letter. That'd be the end of it.

But somehow, he knew he wouldn't be done with Poppy Corrigan, regardless of Beauregard's response. From the lilt of her Surrey accent to the fiery red of her hair, she riveted him. He liked how her eyes danced when she told him about *Much Ado* and the slight turn to her lips as she argued theory with him.

Soon, very soon, he'd see her again. If not at the factory, then somewhere else. He'd make the time.

Chapter Six

The next day, Thaddeus clung tightly to his truncheon as he picked between the piles of rubbish that lined Little Paternoster's Row, the back alley that connected Dorset with Brushfield Street. He hadn't the slightest inkling how Little Paternoster got its name, but it had become synonymous in these wretched days with the worst part of Spitalfields.

While Dorset Street itself was not a particularly long or wide street, it made up for this by packing at least five hundred debauched, desperate people into the small area.

This was a land of thieves—the pickpocket, the sneak, and the bullyback made their careers undeterred by the elegant criminal.

Everywhere he looked, he saw someone who had given up on life. In the doorway of number 26, a man had fallen asleep with a gin bottle, splotches of blood where the cracked glass dug into his bare hands. A slattern woman watched Thaddeus from her stoop, hands clenched around her broom, ready to use it against him. He tipped his hat to her but made no move to question her.

He'd get little information from these people.

It was not a particularly cold day, but he wore the red silk scarf Mrs. Corrigan had gifted him. Tight around his neck, the jaunty ends hanging out over his uniform, he felt somehow more courageous. The silk against his neck centered him. Though these people scowled as though he was the worst of blackguards, he knew one woman in the rookeries thought he was a gentleman.

The sounds of music and drunken revelry filtered out into the street from number 32 Dorset, the Blue Coat Boy public house. In the window, a sign advertising "rooms for let" had faded over time, as ill repaired as the rooms themselves most likely were. Thaddeus passed by the Blue Coat Boy quickly. Strickland would be patrolling the adjoining Crispin Street about this time, and he was as anxious to avoid the fool as he was a fight with one of Dorset's residents. He kept going, past three brothels, a grocer, and a chandler all crammed into one row.

Monk and Ems Moseley lived at No. 15, a crumbling dosshouse referred to as "Queen's," after the surname of the proprietor. Once, the building had been new and beautiful, built of brick, and then faced over with stucco. As with much of Spitalfields, time had taken its toll. The lodging house now served primarily as home to immigrants who called their street "Dosset" or "Dossen" and socialized with their specific ethnicity.

The presence of the Moseleys, a British family, in such a place was peculiar in itself.

Their room was located in the back half of the building. He knocked at the door, hat in his hands, contriteness splashed across his face like the rouge of one of Dorset's many prostitutes. At first, a scraping sound was the sole indication that his knock had been heard. Then, two minutes later, the door opened wide enough for half the face of a woman matching Ems Moseley's description.

Mrs. Moseley scowled. "Oy, Peeler, don't be botherin' us."

"Mrs. Moseley, I'm Sergeant Knight. I'm looking into your daughter's death." He reached forward, grabbing the door before she could slam it shut.

Distrust gleamed in her eyes. She didn't open the door to admit him. "I told ye, take yer leave. We don't admit yer kind here, do ye 'ear me?"

"Please, Mrs. Moseley," he pleaded. "I'm the one who found Anna outside the factory. When I go to sleep, I see her face. When I wake up, I hear her last breath in my ears. I can't eat without wondering if I'd been a minute earlier, she'd still be alive to take nuncheon with you."

With every sentence, Mrs. Moseley's hand tightened on the doorframe. Her knuckles were alabaster white.

"It won't take more than a quarter of an hour, I swear," he said.

"You 'ave 'alf that." One finger at a time, she released her hold on the door. The cheap wood swung open without her grip, moved by the slightest wind.

He followed her inside, shutting the door behind him. The Moseleys rented one room for the seven—now six—of them. Three straw mattresses were strewn about the right corner, threadbare blankets heaped on top. A table with a gash dug into the wood sat opposite the mats, several mismatched chairs pulled up around it. A wire rack fixed into the ceiling held the sparse wardrobes of the family. Two tots played by the fireplace, clothed in breeches two sizes too large, held up by twine.

"Go out, ye bleeders," Mrs. Moseley bid the children, her tone as sharp as the knives pinned to the thin walls.

The children took one look at her, immediately collected the bobble they'd been playing with, and scampered outside.

Mrs. Moseley caught him inspecting the place, her scowl deepening. "Wot ye lookin' at?"

"Nothing, absolutely nothing," he said quickly. "Is your husband at home?"

She let out a hollow laugh. "Does it look 'e is?"

"Ah." He remembered now why this was his least favorite part of the job.

"Anna." She barked out her daughter's name like an insult, yet he saw a stab of pain in her eyes. "Ye say ye were with 'er when she passed?"

He nodded.

"Did she..." Ems Moseley stopped, wiping her hand across her brow. "Did she say anythin'? Did she... Did she know wot 'ad 'appened?"

He seized the ends of his scarf between his thumb and forefinger, rubbing his thumb over the silk in hopes it'd make this all go faster. Scrutinized the straw mats because that was easier than meeting the gaze of a grieving woman, so hardened by this life that she couldn't express her pain in anything but acerbities. "She wouldn't tell me who had hurt her. When I inquired, she said her assailants had far more power than I could imagine."

Mrs. Moseley clutched at her apron, wringing the fabric. Already, rends had begun to appear where her fingernails had sunk in.

"I'm coming to you because I can't prove—yet—who killed her, but I think that I have an idea. Her fingers kept tracing an L. Does this mean anything to you?"

"Fuck." The color drained from Mrs. Moseley's ruddy face. "'Tis the Larkers."

She laid her head down on the table, her dirty brown locks falling about around her in a scraggly mop. He should go to her, comfort her, but all he could process was that she'd confirmed his suspicions.

He was right.

Thaddeus's heart rattled against his chest. He couldn't stand still. He wore a line into the dirt floor with his pacing, back and forth, hands in his pockets. He was so close. A few more tidbits and he'd have what he needed. If Mrs. Moseley had seen the Larkers involved in nefarious activities, he could go to Whiting.

"Are you quite certain that's who it could be?" Eagerness peppered his tone.

Mrs. Moseley's head snapped up. "As certain as I am that my girl didn't deserve none of this. I knew it. I knew that it'd be them. *I knew it.*" With each declaration, her almost-black eyes narrowed on him, and he felt the weight of her words as if she'd pelted him with her fists. "I said to Monk, I did, when she got moved upstairs. 'They're gonna kill 'er, don't ye see?' But 'e didn't care, so long as she brought in blunt."

Thaddeus stopped pacing, coming to stand directly in front of her. "Mrs. Moseley, why exactly did you suspect the Larkers? Please, the more specific you can be, the more it'll help me."

"People like them, they're vultures," Mrs. Moseley spat. "They take what they can get and what they can't, they steal. Don't matter who they 'urt, so long as they come out on top."

He remembered the bruises that had riddled the girl's body, the blood streaming down from her head. "Did Anna ever say she was being mistreated?"

"She worked at that factory since she was six," Mrs. Moseley said. "Nothing ever 'appened to her before, nothing but the normal aches and creaks from the 'ours. Two months after these Larkers come, she's home with a bruise on her temple. Won't tell me why at first, but I keep askin'. She says it 'appened at work, as punishment for bein' careless."

His stomach lurched. "And you think Boz Larker was responsible?"

"It's 'im or one of 'is men," Mrs. Moseley avowed. "I didn't wanna send 'er back, but I got four other children. 'Ow am I supposed to feed 'em all without that money? And Monk was determined. No place in this family for someone who won't work." Mrs. Moseley rubbed her palm against the back of her neck feverishly, fingertips digging into her flesh. "Anna promised she'd be more careful. She *promised*."

* * *

A day had passed since Poppy had gone to Thaddeus Knight's townhouse. One full day in which she'd worked at the factory, gone to visit Jane at the Three Boars, and returned home in time to put Moira to bed. That was all quite ordinary. So why didn't she *feel* ordinary? Everything appeared anew, from the burnished metal of her loom to the cast iron floors, scattered with fibers and dusty with footprints. Even her royal-blue dress, bought from a rag and bone shop and taken in to fit her petite frame, suddenly seemed special.

Poppy pressed the long wooden plank that served as the foot pedal. The shuttle moved, advancing the punch card forward. Another row of threads, called picks, was ready to weave. The clack as the silk moved in a predetermined rhythm was deafening, yet to Poppy, it was comforting. To her, it meant that there was order in a chaotic universe if she followed the pattern.

Jacquard had created a machine that both sped up production and allowed the weaver to be autonomous. Poppy and Poppy alone controlled the mechanism that would shift all the warp threads into the proper position for each continuing pick.

Somewhere between the sixth hour and the eighth, she'd contemplate whether all of this was worth it. If she should take Atlas's offer and run jobs with him. It'd be simple at first, serving as a distraction while he filched. Helping him categorize his various stolen goods.

But she hadn't come this far, told so many damn lies, to be a criminal.

Poppy squinted at the silk threads she'd already woven, held in place on the cloth beam. Tightly compacted, sweet roses. This might become a counterpane upon some rich aristocrat's bed. Or it'd be part of a beautiful bodice for a debutante, one who hadn't wasted her virtue on a blackguard intent on winning a bet.

The silk had infinite possibilities to become something new. She, on the other hand, was a woman who knew her place.

And it was definitely not on the arm of one charming police sergeant.

"Poppy!" Abigail's urgent voice was barely audible over the noise of the looms at work.

Poppy tilted her head to the right, where Abigail's loom was set up. They were fortunate in the Larker factory to possess twenty Jacquard looms when the majority of the new machines were located instead in the great mills in Lancashire. Hand-looms and draw looms were still operated by the Huguenot weavers, who resented the imposition of automation.

"She's coming," Abigail hissed, jerking to the right. Her blue eyes were trained on the loom, reminding Poppy of a cat watching a mouse.

Hurriedly, Poppy straightened her posture. She moved the bar at the top of the loom, the next card in the chain shifting with it, pressing the needles into the perforated holes in the card. Wherever there was a hole, the warp thread would move against the wire, or the heddle, to create the specified pattern.

But she was not swift enough in producing an appearance of diligence. Effie Larker strode across the factory floor, the clink of her duo-toned half-boots devoured by the din of overeager machinery. While most of the factory workers wore the cheapest cotton, Effie was appareled as if she expected to ride a peer's phaeton down Rotten Row that evening. She wore an expertly tailored purple gown, tucked in to display her narrow waist. Coal-black gloves reached up to her elbows, and an ebony feather bobbed with each toss of her blonde hair, whipped up in an elaborate coiffure. Her high cheekbones were splashed with rouge, and her oval, catlike eyes blackened with kohl.

The knot that formed in Poppy's stomach each time Effie appeared tightened. From her first day onward, the woman had taken a strong dislike to Poppy.

"You bunch of wastrels! All of you," Effie spat, each word clearly enunciated.

The factory workers didn't respond. Instead, they continued their tasks, not daring to be the one who attracted Effie's attention. While Boz Larker was the official boss of them, Effie's harsh tongue and baton made her feared.

It was whispered between the workers that Boz had found Effie in a Wapping brothel. She made pains to sound as high class as possible, though her natural speech patterns remained, like a Billingsgate fish market woman on laudanum.

Effie rounded the corner. "*Mrs.* Corrigan," she remonstrated, making the title sound worse than any of the vulgar names she called "her girls."

"Yes, Mrs. Larker?"

"We don't pay you to socialize," Effie snarled. One hand was planted firmly on her hip; the other clasped a long, thin switch with leather tassels.

Poppy watched the switch warily. Effie smacked the rod against her leg, wrinkling her violet dress. She tilted her chin upwards imperiously, her icy-blue eyes fastened on Poppy.

Effie's hand shot out, her fingers digging into Poppy's shoulder. Poppy winced, but experience had taught her not to move her head away.

Effie dropped her chin to whisper in Poppy's ear. "Don't think for a minute, girl, that I won't dismiss you. There's many more where you came from."

A cold chill raced down Poppy's spine, like the drips of a snowdrift, diminished by the harsh rays of the sun until nothing was left but memories.

The protest died in Poppy's throat. She couldn't move. She stayed transfixed, eyes forward, seeing not the picks and picks of woven silk stretched out across the loom.

Moira's face appeared before her, green eyes overflowing with tears, her tiny nose red and raw. She gnawed on her fist, sucking on the flesh with all her might because it was the one thing that would stop her whimpers. *Mama! Mama! Mama!*

Poppy's head swam. Her hand faltered on the loom. Her foot never hit the pedal.

She'd never be truly free.

Moira would never be safe.

Effie stood back from her, releasing her hold on Poppy's shoulder. "I knew you'd see it my way. You're a smart girl." She tapped her foot against the ground, looking at Poppy expectantly.

Woodenly, Poppy nodded. She pulled the top bar. The loom clunked back to life.

Effie rapped the switch against her right hand once, the crack echoing. Her lips pulled back in a slickly malevolent smile as she surveyed the factory floor. Satisfied that the workers had been properly motivated, she turned on her heel, entering her husband's office.

The door remained open. Out of the corner of her eye, Poppy watched Effie. She reached a hand up to pat at her pinwheel curls, her long fingernails stroking at her amethyst earrings. Boz had made her a rich woman off the backs of the workers.

When Effie turned around, leaning over the desk Boz sat behind, Abigail stood up from her loom. She loped toward Poppy, right foot dragged behind her left. "What was that about?"

"Effie believed I wasn't working fast enough," Poppy replied.

Abigail's forehead crinkled. "She's a right dragon, isn't she?"

"Don't let her hear you say that." Poppy returned to work, the process so familiar to her that she could do it in her sleep. Weaving was comfortable. An old friend that had stayed with her through it all; the silk knew her darkest sins and accepted them. It was beautiful, what she could make from this, from the basest threads into an intricate pattern.

"The Larkers don't scare me," Abigail declared, though her soft tone belied her fearless words. "Effie Larker is no better than the rest of us, you understand? We do what she says now because she has the power. But she's the same as the foreman before her, and the one that'll come after her, too, when the Larkers bore of the factory business."

Poppy sighed. "I know."

Abigail shrugged. "I've been in this factory since I could walk, Poppy, and I've seen four different owners. This is how it works. Eventually, people like the Larkers want a quicker profit. You wait and see. The Larkers might have invested in new machines, but they'll tire of us."

"I hope you're right," Poppy murmured.

If only she could last until Abigail's prediction came true. A benevolent manager could buy out the factory. One who did not delight in subjugation as Effie Larker did.

Poppy's gaze flicked to Abigail. Her friend had gone back to her loom, settling in on her high stool, her skirt ballooning around her. With her feet spread wide, Abigail wove with precision but no feeling. She'd been raised on the draw looms, and to her, that was how Spitalfields should have continued.

Abigail caught her eye, a wide smile breaking on her lips. Poppy's heart tugged. She wanted to be honest with Abigail. Wanted to have one friend outside of her brother's circle that knew her secret and accepted her.

But Abigail was precisely who she said she was. No falsities. Her mother had died when she was young, and she'd filled that surrogate role for her younger sister Bess. Their father was a drunk, gambling away what blunt he had at the hells. Abigail had confided in Poppy that she gave him only a fourth of her wages, claiming that the Larkers had cut back on pay since taking over. The rest she used to take care of herself and Bess.

That was how to survive in the rookeries: lies and subterfuges.

It was no wonder Poppy fit in here.

Chapter Seven

Five days into his allotted two weeks of investigation, Thaddeus finally had a breakthrough. As he stepped onto the corner between Wheeler and White Lion Street, he mused over the contents of Dagobert Gottlieb's letter. Assuming Gottlieb was correct—and Gottlieb was rarely incorrect—he now had enough information to warrant a visit to the Larker factory.

He'd decided to go midday when Boz Larker would least expect him. That element of surprise should work in his favor, especially when he requested access to the locked room upstairs.

Coining, Gottlieb had said. *They buy factory to hide shan. At the end, they be round the tower with it.* Thaddeus's knowledge of cant terms wasn't as all-encompassing as he would have liked, but he'd picked up enough along the way to know that Gottlieb had found out the Larkers were using their factory to pass their counterfeit currency into circulation.

It was an ingenious plan. Since Henry Fauntleroy's execution eight years ago, people had debated the righteousness of capital punishment for forgery. The Reform Act had passed a month prior, and forgery was no longer an offense worthy of death.

While Larker Factory was located on White Lion Street, the entrance to the building was on a side street. Thaddeus turned down that alley. Larker Factory loomed above the surrounding tenement houses and shops. Though it was only two stories, the ceilings were lofty to accommodate the massive looms. The original building was small and squat, but an addition gave the factory an elongated, disproportionate look. Seven windows lined the front, but the three in the side addition were boarded over, the wood rotted and swollen from London's frequent rain.

He glanced up at the top floor. One small diamond-shaped window provided sunlight for the second story, but that window faced the alley, not White Lion. Whatever the Larkers were doing, they didn't want anyone in the busy main street to see it.

He pulled open the doors to the factory. Immediately, two guards in dirt-streaked, rumpled brown uniforms surrounded him. The older of the two guards was a mass of brawn and bulk, with a wide forehead deep-set with wrinkles, gray hair combed straight back, and a gristly beard. His chin was sharp, his sea eyes sharper.

Thaddeus tipped his hat to them both, attempting to dart around them.

The bigger of the two guards planted a firm hand on Thaddeus's chest to keep him from moving forward. Thaddeus glared at the man, but still, the guard didn't remove his hand.

"Fine then," Thaddeus muttered, stepping back. The man's hand remained in the air a second later, gripping nothing.

The younger guard smirked and mouthed something that sounded vaguely like "State yer business." Thaddeus couldn't be certain, for the cacophony of the busy work floor devoured all other sounds.

"I need access to the top room," Thaddeus shouted, struggling to be heard over the din. "I'm with the Metropolitan Police."

The two guards exchanged glances. Neither one spoke. After a moment, they seemed to come to an agreement. The older guard gestured for Thaddeus to follow them toward the back office.

Workers labored at looms that spanned the full length of the room, stationed not more than a few paces apart. The looms formed three rows, with approximately ten in each row from front to back. The building had unusually high ceilings to accommodate for the sheer height of the looms, which reached far above his head. Children picked through the scraps of silk to sell in the market on Crispin Street.

He scanned the room for Mrs. Corrigan, eventually locating her toward the front. Mrs. Corrigan's loom was positioned two to the left of the blonde girl who he remembered her exiting with the other day.

If he'd thought Mrs. Corrigan beautiful the day before in the light of the sun streaming through the library windows, here, she was in her element. Perched on a tall stool, she leaned over the loom, her hands in constant motion. She'd bound her red hair in a tight top knot, and she wore no apron.

His mouth went dry as his eyes roamed down her frame. Her green dress was fitted so that she ran no risk of getting caught in the machinery, but it had the added appeal of displaying her luscious hips to full advantage. She moved with finesse and speed, each slide of the shuttle and weft an intricate dance. This was her world, the constant advancement of the punch cards, the click and clack of many looms employed in tandem.

As he walked past her station, their eyes locked. His breath caught in his throat. First, there was a flash of curiosity in her eyes, then fear. She missed a beat in the weaving.

Thaddeus couldn't tarry to watch her. The guards had already progressed three looms past him. He hurried to catch up, following the guards into the office holed in the center of the right back wall.

The older guard shut the door after them. It was then that Thaddeus started to feel apprehensive. If the men were to attack him, no one would hear his screams over the rattle of the machinery.

His grip tightened against the truncheon. He lifted his chin, eying the man behind the desk with an expression of disdain that would have made his mother proud. He had learned a few things from his mother, but the ability to deliver a proper cut direct was one of them.

Boz Larker was intimidation incarnate at approximately forty-five years of age, short yet stocky and powerfully built. His hair was ash, yet his beard and the tips of his muttonchops were tinged with silver.

"Yes, Jennings?" Larker's gruff voice reminded Thaddeus of a wire dishcloth scraping against china.

"The Peeler wanted to see you," Jennings explained.

Thaddeus noticed that Jennings didn't look Larker in the eye, but his younger companion displayed no such compunction.

"What do you think, Clowes?" Larker stroked a hand through his bushy beard, his dark eyes fastened upon Thaddeus instead of his younger guard.

Before Thaddeus had been concerned with Jennings, assuming because he was the seasoned one of the two guards, he'd hold a higher place in Larker's esteem. Yet the eagerness in Clowes's eyes disturbed him. Clowes's short nose bore a scar, from a bar fight, Thaddeus guessed. His face was heavier than

Jennings, his body thickset but squatter. With sandy-brown hair and a smirk plastered firmly in place, he radiated that egomania women usually mistook as confidence.

Yes, Thaddeus could understand why a young girl such as Miss Moseley might find Clowes appealing.

"Shall I tell the—" Larker stopped, looking Thaddeus up and down to ascertain his rank. "The sergeant to come back with his inspector?"

Clowes guffawed. "Naw, Mr. Larker, we ain't got nothin' to hide."

Larker smiled as a doting father might upon his son if said doting father was a murderer, and the son wanted to learn how to kill without discovery. With his lips pulled back, Larker's crooked teeth were exposed. Thaddeus could have sworn his front two teeth were pointed.

After this visit, he'd never read a Gothic novel before bed again.

"Well, you heard the boy," Larker said, gesturing fondly to Clowes. "Boz Larker, at your service. I assure you everything is done legitimately in our factory. What can I do for you, Sergeant..."

"Knight," Thaddeus supplied, though, in truth, he wished he could have made it through this visit without ever telling Larker who he was. "I'm here about the murder of Anna Moseley."

He let that thought hang in the air, observing the three men. Jennings's sallow complexion drained of color, while Clowes's chest puffed up. Larker, on the other hand, maintained a blank visage.

The brute didn't even flinch.

"Ah, unfortunate, that killing," Larker remarked, as though Thaddeus had informed him several yards of silk had been ruined by spilled tea. "We still haven't managed to scrub all the blood from that wall. It's a menace, really, scaring all the workers. Do you understand what scared workers mean for us, Sergeant Knight? It means that they spend less time weaving, and more time nattering."

Of all the things Thaddeus might have expected Larker to say, *that* was not included. He swallowed an exclamation of disgust, disguising it in a badly formed cough.

Larker shrugged. "Aside from her unfortunate choice of places to die, I can't see what any of this has to do with us."

"A girl is dead." Thaddeus's fingers clenched tightly around the truncheon. "You might show some compassion, Larker. She was one of your employees, for God's sake."

"God has nothing to do with this, Sergeant." From the top drawer of his desk, Larker selected a deck of cards. He began to shuffle the deck methodically, without once looking down. "If I shed a tear for every whore that died in Spitalfields, I'd never have time to run a business. Life, you see, is much like these cards. Sometimes you draw an ace, and the other times, you are beaten by your opponent."

Thaddeus stepped forward until he was in front of Larker's desk. Standing, he towered over Larker, though the older man had more girth. "Is that what happened to Miss Moseley? Was she your opponent, Larker? She got in your way, didn't she, and that's why you had to kill her?"

Larker chuckled, a low, grating laugh from deep in his throat. "So many suppositions. Do you actually think anyone will believe you?"

Ice seized Thaddeus's body. In his life, he'd met many criminals. Some had reacted with the same cavalier disregard for other humans. No matter how many times he encountered it, Thaddeus found that behavior to be disturbing.

Larker wanted him to be intimidated. To get flustered, to reveal what he'd already uncovered in his investigation.

Thaddeus met Larker's challenge with his own. "It matters not whether the people believe me. Only that the magistrate believes the evidence. I want to see the locked room upstairs, Larker. If you don't show it to me, I'll come back with four more officers, and we'll shut this whole damn factory down. How would *that* look to your scared employees?"

Larker's bottom lip twitched slightly. So slightly, it was almost imperceptible. If Thaddeus hadn't been watching for a reaction, he might never have noted it. But it was there—he'd affected Larker.

"Jennings, take Sergeant Knight upstairs. Clowes, tell Mrs. Larker I'd like some tea now." Larker waved toward the door in a motion meant to dismiss both Thaddeus and his guards.

Jennings hesitated as if he was going to protest, but he swallowed those words. He guided Thaddeus out of the office and through the factory again until they came to a staircase. Jennings ascended first, with Thaddeus following close behind. At the top of the steps, Jennings pulled out a key ring, selected a small brass key, and inserted it into the door.

"We keep the silk in here." Jennings nodded at the yards and yards of finished silk, stacked up against the wall.

The room was small, probably not much larger than Thaddeus's dressing room. It must have stretched over a fourth of the lower level. Silk covered every available surface in a whirlwind of color. Yards as vibrantly red as Mrs. Corrigan's hair atop others as brilliantly emerald as her eyes.

Thaddeus moved on from inspecting the silk to the workbench positioned in the far right corner. To the casual observer, nothing looked out of place. A hammer and awl rested on one end of the bench, next to a stack of cloth bags—purportedly for stuffing in silk that had not met the standards of the factory's clients and would later be sold in the market.

But cloth bags could also be used to sweat coins. The forger placed the coins in a bag and shook vigorously until bits of metal would flake off the money. Those bits would be collected and stored until enough metal had been scraped off to use for creating the forged coins.

The awl and hammer could be elements of coin clipping. A hole would be punched in the middle of a coin and the metal removed. Counterfeiters hammered the coin face until the hole closed again. If the hole could not be easily disguised, it could be filled with cheaper metal that replicated the effects of the original.

Rubbing his hands together, Thaddeus eyed the tools with barely suppressed delight. He simply needed to bring Whiting up to this room, show him the tools, and explain the connections he'd made. He had the Larkers—or he *would* have them. The proof was here, he knew it. He just had to have enough time to search thoroughly.

With the right push, his superiors would approve further investigation. He'd find the evidence needed, they'd arrest the Larkers within the week, and Miss Moseley's family would have the justice that the Stewarts had never received.

"Thank you, that's what I needed," he told Jennings, exiting the room and heading down the stairs.

He caught Mrs. Corrigan's eye again as he left. Inclining his head ever so slowly, he nodded. Solving the case would leave him quite free to pursue whatever this attraction was between them.

All in all, a good day's work.

* * *

By the time the bell tolled, Poppy was exhausted. Although working at the loom for eleven hours always left her fatigued, today she had other matters to be concerned with. On top of

Sergeant Knight's odd visit to the factory, she'd received a letter from Atlas earlier that morning before she'd left for work.

Poppy waved goodbye to Frank Clowes as she exited the building, following behind Abigail and Bess.

Her hand closed around Atlas's letter, secreted away in the pocket of her apron. Atlas had brought good news: Edward wouldn't return to London for the Season. While Poppy sincerely doubted that she would have run into him, the mere idea of sharing a town with him—even a town as big as London —made her skin crawl. She didn't fear that he'd exert a claim to Moira, for as far as Edward knew, Moira didn't exist. Since the day Moira was born, Atlas had employed men to keep watch on Edward.

Most of the time, Edward stayed at his family estate in Derbyshire. When he did venture to London, he spent most of his time with a fast set that gambled more in a night than Poppy made in a year. He held no occupation. As the first son of a marquess, he'd eventually inherit the title and the land that came with it.

The blackguard.

While she slaved away to simply put food on the table, Edward gallivanted from social event to social event. Yet that was the way of the world, wasn't it? The rich got richer, shoving the poor further back into the rookeries.

It was not that Poppy wanted a life like Edward's—she'd long ago disabused herself of the notion that she could change her social class, and the few fast gatherings she'd attended with Edward in the week he'd been in Surrey were too rowdy for her liking now.

Those wild days were behind her.

Instead, it was the freedom money provided that she longed for. The knowledge that she could send Moira to a good school without having to scrimp and save. Being able to spend more time with Moira, Edna, and the rest of her family. These were her dreams now, so disparate from what she'd thought she wanted two years ago.

There was little that could be done. Especially since she didn't intend to inform Edward that he had a child. Moira would grow up thinking her father had *wanted* to be with her but was taken too soon by the Lord. Moira didn't need to know the man who'd never look past her being his bastard.

"I wish you could have seen yourself," Edward had said. "Holding onto my every word, panting for me to take your virtue. You remember that when I'm gone, how easily you caved to my will."

The memory of his words twisted her stomach. Poppy could hear his voice as if it were yesterday.

Beside her on the street, Abigail and Bess recited a counting rhythm designed to teach Bess basic arithmetic. Poppy barely registered their game, her thoughts stuck on the letter.

Abigail tapped her arm. "Poppy, are you listening to me?"

"Hmm?" Poppy murmured.

Abigail rolled her eyes. "I *said* I found Lovelace to be absolutely despicable."

Poppy blinked. "I don't follow you."

"In *Clarissa*," Abigail clarified, linking her arm in Poppy's. "I was telling you how my friend brought it to our BRLLS meeting." The Baker's Row Lending Library Society was the book-exchanging club that Abigail had formed with her neighbors.

"Ah, yes," Poppy said.

"She nicked it from a secondhand shop, and would you know, it had five pages missing from it. Much better than the copy of *Evangelina* with forty gone!" Abigail paused to take a breath. "You said you read *Clarissa* before. Don't you think Lovelace is disgusting?"

Poppy grimaced. Trust Abigail to want to discuss the one

book she'd rather forget. "He's vile. But it's been a long time since I read it." Hopefully, that would dissuade Abigail.

"I find it hard to believe people so singularly evil exist," Abigail mused. "Of course, people can be malevolent. Look at the people who murdered Anna. But Lovelace's entire purpose is to possess Clarissa. Going to such extents to pursue her, abducting and raping her..."

"Awful," Poppy agreed.

Let Abigail believe that evil was limited to criminals and murderers. What had Thaddeus said? That he believed certain motivations could be ascribed to each case? If living in Spital-fields hadn't convinced Abigail that the world was full of abhor-rent people, then Poppy wasn't going to shatter her illusions.

"Poppy, look." Abigail pointed to the alleyway to the right of the road.

In the doorway of a tenement house, Thaddeus Knight waited, half-shrouded in shadows. He was already a tall man—the top hat made him appear like a giant from fairy tales. In his right hand, he held a truncheon.

"It's this case," he'd said. "I cannot think about anything else when I'm on a case."

His appearance at the factory today proved that. He was going to find out who killed Anna Moseley, even if it was the last thing he did. She'd be smart to stay clear of him. Their asso-ciation should have ended when she'd gone to thank him for saving Daniel.

All of this registered in the back of her mind, in the same way that she knew what a Bolus hook was and how to use it. Yet there was no convenient punch card to dictate her emotional response, so instead, her heart rebelled against her rational mind.

Seeing him standing in that doorway, her breath hitched. Not in fear, not in the desire to run as fast as she could from him, but instead in eager anticipation. Was he waiting for her? Had he felt that spark too when they'd locked eyes across the factory room? It shouldn't matter.

None of it should matter.

"Mrs. Corrigan." He stepped out of the doorway, into the dying natural light of this alley.

"How does he know your name?" Abigail whispered. She grabbed for Bess's hand, shoving her little sister behind her.

"He's, ah..." Poppy struggled to find the right words to label her acquaintanceship with Knight.

He's...abnormally handsome? Awkwardly endearing? Kind, sweet, and funny?

She settled on the most obvious of their connections. "He's the man who saved my brother."

"I understand," Abigail said, but her wrinkled nose indicated she didn't understand in the least.

Knight watched them both silently. His lip curled, ever so faintly, in the hint of a smile. As if he could hear her thoughts, and he'd found them particularly amusing.

Her cheeks burned. *Damn him.* She glanced up the path. Several other workers from the factory headed down the main street, and they would intersect with this gathering unless Sergeant Knight moved away from the central route. In the alley, he had at least been somewhat shaded.

"Would you excuse me?" Poppy slipped past Abigail, ignoring her gaped jaw.

Poppy stepped off the main road into the alley. "Get back," she hissed at Knight, giving him a little shove under the cover of the doorway. "I can't be seen with you."

Her fellow workers passed by a second later. The oldest of the group, a portly man known for his love of mead ale and baked apples, turned his head in their direction. He started to go off toward their alley, but then Abigail darted up to him, tugging Bess along with her.

Poppy breathed a sigh of relief as the group headed down the street, out of earshot.

"Good evening to you too," Knight said, with that slow, shy smile that shouldn't have sent a hot swell through her body but did. "How is Moira?"

Whenever people asked about Moira, Poppy always wondered what they really knew about her daughter. Yet with Knight, the inquiry sounded almost...innocent. Like he genuinely cared.

"Moira is fine," she said. "What are you doing here?"

He blinked, apparently taken aback by her brusque tone. "I wanted to see you."

Poppy narrowed her eyes. "Why?"

She was too smart for this.

Men had one reason for wanting to spend time with her. Knight couldn't be any different from the rest.

He delved into the pockets of his blue jacket, pulling out a brown paper parcel. Unwrapping it, he handed it to her.

She didn't know what impressed her more: the gift itself or his delight in giving it. Such rare, altruistic glee. Poppy had seen a similar innocent joy on Moira's face when she presented Poppy with one of her toys so that "Mama play" could occur.

Running her fingers over the binding, Poppy held the book in her outstretched palms. *King Lear,* and from the looks of it, an antique edition. She flipped the book open, running her finger down the old page. The paper was thin and opaque, reminding her of a spider's web.

"It's beautiful," she whispered. She was hesitant to raise her voice higher, for if she did, she might splinter this light, returning to the squalor and despair of a world that had torn her apart.

"It is yours." Knight grinned. "You said you hadn't read it, and I remembered I had this edition. I got it when I was at Cambridge. A book dealer had a brilliant stall in the market. I used to go every Wednesday after class."

She closed the book gently. *Confound it.* The book was gorgeous, the caramel leather front supple. The lettering was lovingly embossed onto the cover, along with a picture of Lear, wearing an ornate crown. It was the most exquisite book she'd ever seen.

And she couldn't accept it.

"No, I couldn't possibly." She shook her head, but she made no move to hand the book back.

Knight's nose wrinkled, his eyes clouding with uneasiness. "Mrs. Corrigan, I saw the book on my shelf and thought you'd like to read it. When you're done, you could read to your daughter. I have heard that babies like the sound of Shakespeare."

When she arched a brow at him, he shrugged sheepishly. "Well, at least *I* did when I was young."

She smiled in spite of herself. "I can see you, tucked in a window seat with a huge volume spread across your lap."

"An accurate picture," he admitted. "I have three other copies of *Lear* at home. I can surely part with this one. I mean nothing more from it."

Gifts came with expectations, she reminded herself. Edward had given her a necklace that night, and the morning after he'd ripped her heart open and fed it to the fire. She'd finally pawned that necklace, but it had taken her two shots of gin to part with it.

She wouldn't be beholden to another man.

Not again.

Poppy handed the book to him, already missing the weight of it in her palm. He took it from her, vacillating a moment too long so that their hands would brush again. Glove against glove, less intimate than when their hands had touched over the teakettle, but it sent a quiver down her spine.

Touching him felt like coming home.

"It was sweet of you to think of me," she said. "But I'm afraid I can't accept it."

Knight redid the paper wrapping with a careful reverence that made her wonder if he could indeed be trusted with delicate matters like the state of a fallen woman's broken heart.

His grin had faded, replaced with sheepishness. "I'm sorry if you thought I was trying to impose—"

"No, no, of course not." She didn't know why she was justifying his actions when, by all intents, it had been an improper gesture.

A thoughtful, lovely improper gesture.

He shifted his weight from one foot to the other, remaining in the doorway of that tenement house. Red spread across his cheeks, and she couldn't bring herself to add onto his crestfallen state.

"Sergeant Knight, you must understand, it's not that I don't appreciate your kindness." She resisted the urge to lay a hand on his arm. Her body had a way of talking for her that she simply couldn't countenance here. "But I don't think it'd be proper for me to be...on friendly terms with you. After all, you're investigating my employers. And in these parts, being seen with the police leads to trouble. I can't have people thinking I've nosed."

Knight frowned. "There are few things I hate about working for the Met, but that's one of them. Can't talk to a pretty woman without her getting accused of turning state's evidence."

He didn't meet her eyes when he said, "pretty woman," and the crimson upon his cheeks deepened. She loved his bashfulness, for it was the opposite of how Edward had pursued her. Free of fripperies and overly ornate praise, it felt heartfelt.

"Perils of the job, I suppose." She smiled when she knew she shouldn't. For once, she wanted to be genuine.

He laughed. "Bloody rotten."

"Good luck with your investigation, Sergeant Knight," she said, wishing she could convey all her real well wishes into that one statement.

She'd say that his compassion had touched a part of her she'd much rather keep locked up tight, hidden from sight, for it was too easily shattered. She'd say that if the circumstances were different—if she'd met him three years ago, if he wasn't a Peeler, if she didn't have Moira to take care of—she might have allowed herself to fancy him. Might have been willing to take the chance that he wouldn't end up someday bleeding to death in these very streets, felled by the very people he'd been trying to protect.

But she could only live one life and one life alone, so there was no time for regrets. Poppy Corrigan, she must be.

Chapter Eight

The station house on Wood Street was, for the most part, relatively silent today. There seemed to be a lull in arrests. Fewer thieves caught, fewer ruffians found disturbing the general peace. Thaddeus supposed he ought to be pleased about this unexplainable change, but overall, it left him without much to do on his patrol.

But as soon as he made his case to Whiting, he'd have plenty to do. Boz Larker would be brought before the magistrate. Once the magistrate heard the testimony, he'd decide whether they had substantial grounds to arrest Larker. Thaddeus had no doubt he could prove that Larker had murdered Anna Moseley. Bringing Larker in would justify him spending more time at the factory, sorting through the records. Surely, there'd be something to tie Larker irrevocably to Miss Moseley's death.

The counterfeiting charge might be harder to show definitively, but he was hopeful about that too. Thaddeus had a niggling suspicion that Larker's wife, Effie, was somehow involved—he didn't know *how* yet. He'd observed her interactions with the workers. Something felt off. He couldn't put his finger on it, but he knew enough to trust his instincts. He would have to search the factory further and find the counterfeit coins.

"Where's Whiting?" Thaddeus asked, sitting down at his desk. "I need to talk to him, but he's not in his office."

Strickland looked up from the pile of papers he'd been sorting. His desk was, unfortunately, three down from Thaddeus's station.

Thaddeus grimaced. He recognized the reports on Strickland's desk—those were the information sheets he'd given Whiting earlier that week on the Larkers' known associates. He'd tabbed each sheet with a different color so that Whiting could flip through the pages quickly.

Once again, Whiting had passed off a job meant for an inspector to someone else.

And if that person had been Strickland, he'd bet his last guinea that Strickland had moved up in consideration for Doughty's vacated inspector post. So much for Whiting's promises that Thaddeus was the likely candidate.

"Thorough report here." Strickland gestured to the pages with one brow arched sardonically. "But all the research in the world isn't going to make you look less like you're reaching for things that don't exist. So, the girl worked at the factory. It's Spitalfields—everybody either weaves at home or works at a factory where they weave."

"I've got new information," Thaddeus protested. "That's what I need to talk to Whiting about, but he's not in his office."

Shuffling through the reports, Strickland didn't look up. "He went to the interrogation room."

Thaddeus groaned, pushing his chair back and standing. "Why didn't you say so in the first place?"

Strickland smirked. "I thought I'd give you a few more minutes of thinking you could solve this case before I told you that Whiting's already got a confession."

"Puh—pardon?" Thaddeus sputtered.

"Go see for yourself." Strickland shrugged.

"I will," Thaddeus replied, turning on his heel and heading down the hall.

The station's so-called "interrogation room" was a tiny room, designed to make the inhabitant feel as though the walls were closing in upon him or her. According to Whiting, the less likely escape became to a criminal, the more willing they were to give a full confession. The whole idea seemed disdainful to Thaddeus, who far preferred coaxing information through civil conversation.

A glass panel covered one wall so that the other officers could witness what went on. When he'd first joined the Met, Thaddeus had observed from outside for hours at a time, trying to memorize the various reactions suspects had to the questions asked. From his study, he'd learned that body language rarely changed between people.

Thaddeus stood at this panel now, watching as Whiting sat across the plywood table from a small, dumpy man. He could not have been much taller than the dwarves Thaddeus had once seen in an East End sideshow.

The man was handcuffed to the metal bar drilled into the middle of the table. Thaddeus wasn't sure the handcuffs were even necessary. The suspect's expression was so devoid of emotion Thaddeus wondered if he comprehended anything Whiting said.

Whiting looked up, catching sight of Thaddeus in the window. He came to join Thaddeus outside of the room, leaving the suspect cuffed to the table.

Whiting closed the door behind him. "I was looking for you earlier, Sergeant."

"There was traffic on Pelham Street," Thaddeus replied. "A coster had set up his cart outside of Coverley Fields and the infirmary. Despite my telling him that it was illegal to sell in the street there, he insisted he was given permission—"

Whiting held up his hand. "That's enough. We're wasting time here, boy. I wanted you to meet the man you've been searching for: Raymond McPhee. A tip came in last night, and I followed it to McPhee."

Thaddeus glanced toward the room again. McPhee had rolled his eyes so far upward that the whites showed, and he stared at the ceiling with rapt interest. He kept repeating the same phrase, but Thaddeus was not close enough to hear it.

McPhee's left hand twitched every now and then. How had he managed to stab Miss Moseley with that unsteady grip? She'd been stabbed more than once. While her wounds indicated that the initial impact had been the worst, the knife had been dragged down her back and then twisted in place for a deeper, wider cut.

With McPhee's shaky hands, the likelihood that he could keep such a strong grip on the knife was greatly reduced. Add on to that a struggling Miss Moseley, and it became near to impossible.

"What evidence do you have that he committed this crime?" Thaddeus asked, unable to keep the doubt from his voice.

Whiting bristled. "He gave a full confession."

"But the chance of his stabbing Miss Moseley in her shoulder is very unlikely—"

"If you don't believe me, question him yourself." Whiting walked toward the room, holding the door open.

Thaddeus tailed behind him. Whiting was *not* going to be happy with him.

Yet he had to make Whiting see McPhee was the wrong man. He'd promised Miss Moseley justice.

"Mr. McPhee." Thaddeus took a seat across from the man.

Whiting lingered at the door. He kept glancing at the hall,

probably planning to make a quick escape to the magistrate before Thaddeus could prove once again that he was more competent than his supervisor was.

For a second, McPhee appeared surprised that Thaddeus had replaced Whiting.

Thaddeus waited for McPhee's eyes to focus on him. "Mr. McPhee, where were you on the night of Thursday, April 5th?"

"At the factory," McPhee answered without hesitation. "The Larker factory."

"Why were you there?"

"To kill the girl." Again, McPhee didn't stop to consider. That alone would have been odd. In most interrogations, suspects usually took at least a minute to formulate a story that would hopefully ensure them less time in the gaol.

"Why did you kill her?"

This direct question caught McPhee off guard. He opened and shut his mouth. Diverting his gaze to the ceiling as if it contained all the answers he needed, he considered. His hand began to shake once more.

"Girl was pretty," he settled on. "I wanted 'er."

Thaddeus arched his brows at McPhee, letting every ounce of disbelief flood into his voice. "So, you stabbed her?"

McPhee tugged on the handcuffs, his eyes widening. Alarm seized him, and he continued to pull at the cuffs, metal clacking against metal.

"I said I stabbed 'er, and I did," McPhee insisted, becoming increasingly irate with each passing second. "Why don't you believe me? I stabbed 'er. I took a knife and I stabbed 'er with it."

"Where did you stab her, exactly?" Thaddeus inquired. It took all the effort he had to make his voice flat, devoid of any emotion.

McPhee looked up at the ceiling again, and finding it provided no answers, he looked instead at Whiting. "'E's got my statement," McPhee said. "I told 'im everything. Why you make me repeat it?"

Whiting reached over his shoulder and brought his hand up behind him, squirming to reach the elusive part of his back that itched. He rolled his shoulders and angled his body so that he could use the molding to scratch.

Then, as if he could feel their eyes upon him, he started. "What?"

"I asked Mr. McPhee a simple question," Thaddeus said. "Where did you stab her? If you were truly there, you should have no problem recalling."

"In the back," McPhee spat, jerking at the cuffs. "Now let me go, pig. I said all I'm gonna."

"I should think that's enough," Whiting agreed, stepping forward.

"I'm not done questioning him," Thaddeus protested. "Inspector, I'm not convinced he was even present the night Miss Moseley died."

"I've heard enough," Whiting insisted. "Mr. McPhee has stated multiple times that he stabbed the girl, and that's good enough for me."

He took out a key from his pocket, unlocking McPhee's hand-cuffs from the metal bar. The cuffs remained on, however, and Whiting took hold of McPhee's arm to help him up from the chair.

Thaddeus exited the room behind them. Standing, McPhee was about the height of a ten-year-old boy. Miss Moseley had been frail, yes, but she was certainly taller than McPhee. Presuming she'd been attacked leaving the factory, McPhee had to stab her in the back, underneath her shoulder blade. To inflict such a wound, he would have had to take a running leap—there-fore alerting Miss Moseley to his presence.

If Raymond McPhee had managed to kill Anna Moseley

without any assistance, then Thaddeus would turn in his truncheon and top hat.

And there wasn't a single *l* in McPhee's name.

Whiting handed McPhee off to a waiting sergeant, telling him to proceed with processing McPhee. Nodding at Thaddeus, Whiting began to head down the hall, back toward his office. Thaddeus hustled after him, overtaking him in several strides. Positioning himself in front of Whiting, he spread his arms out, blocking the inspector from going farther.

"Knight." Whiting turned his name into a growl, reminding Thaddeus vaguely of a baited bear.

Were he a sensible man, Thaddeus would have stepped back and let Whiting go about his way. He shouldn't argue with Whiting, whether or not he believed Whiting was wrong to accept McPhee's confession without additional investigation. In displeasing Whiting, he risked whatever chance he had still had at filling Inspector Doughty's vacated role.

But he remembered standing in that alley at seventeen, seeing Miss Stewart's mangled corpse, slick with gore. Flies had descended upon her exposed organs in a raging black mass. Thaddeus's stomach churned. He was shoving Miss Moseley into that tumbledown hackney once more, hollering at the cab driver.

Wasn't doing what was right more important than petty bureaucracy?

And so, Thaddeus didn't lower his arms. "Sir, it doesn't make sense. How could McPhee stab Anna Moseley so many times? He's not exactly the epitome of male strength. And his name—Miss Moseley was clearly sketching an *L* on her dress. Even her mother believes it's the Larkers."

"Let me make this very clear for you, Knight," Whiting ground out through clenched teeth. "I don't care who you think murdered that girl. Raymond McPhee has confessed, and that's all I need."

Thaddeus clenched his jaw, stifling a nasty retort. "Despite there being strong evidence that he is *not* the one who killed her?"

"It is one case out of a hundred," Whiting replied. "One case that you've already spent copious time on when I need you to be devoted to your route."

"You said you'd give me two weeks to solve this," Thaddeus reminded him. "It hasn't been two weeks. I've found equipment in the Larker factory that indicates they could be counterfeiters. If I can prove that McPhee has been paid to confess—"

Whiting shook his head. "No. I will not entertain you any longer on this. This isn't a grand conspiracy, Knight. It's a simple murder for which we've found the person who did it. You should be congratulating yourself."

"But—" His arms fell ever so marginally.

Whiting darted around him. "But nothing. You will not investigate this further."

"I could look into it on my own time," Thaddeus suggested. "Fully tending to my route."

"Absolutely not," Whiting snapped. "If I hear that you've been in the Larker factory, I won't put your name in for the inspector job. You need to focus on what's to come, Knight, the bigger cases. How will you have sergeants assigned to you that need your tutelage if you're chasing after wild horses?"

Thaddeus dropped back, leaning against the wall. For a moment, he stared at Whiting, open-mouthed. He couldn't risk investigating. In that initial meeting with Whiting, the inspector had threatened to dismiss him if he disobeyed. If he lost his job, he wouldn't be able to help anyone else.

With McPhee taking the blame, Miss Moseley's real killers would go free.

There had to be a way.

"I understand," he said, for Whiting was still staring at him. "I won't go inside the factory again."

Whiting nodded briskly, pleased with Thaddeus's response. "I'll expect to see a full report on your route after you return tomorrow." When Thaddeus agreed, Whiting set off toward his office.

Thaddeus remained in that hall for a long time afterwards. If he could somehow find someone to be his eyes and ears inside the factory...

Of course. Poppy Corrigan.

The idea hit him in a flash of scarlet. Her red hair bound from working at the factory. Her soft, cadent voice with the lilting Surrey accent. And lastly, most importantly to this case, the sadness in her voice when she spoke about Miss Moseley. He could offer her a way to avenge her friend's death.

Nothing that would put her in danger, of course. Basic reports on what went on in the factory. Where the Larkers went, who entered the locked room, and so forth.

He'd have to get evidence that Whiting couldn't ignore. Technically, he'd be holding to his promise, as long as *he* wasn't the one doing the investigating.

Another visit to Larker Factory was in store. Another night waiting in the shadows for her to finish work. That prospect excited him, and not just because Poppy Corrigan presented a solution to his problem. Discourse with Mrs. Corrigan was fascinating. She had unique views on literature, and he loved to watch her mind work. The way his body heated from the inside out at the touch of her hand.

Mrs. Corrigan had his interest.

He'd have to find another book to bring her.

* * *

Another girl had received Anna's upstairs position. Abigail applied for it, but Effie claimed Abigail didn't move quickly enough for the unloading. This, Abigail suspected, was complete bunkum. The position upstairs entailed more sorting, which Abigail could do sitting, than actual lifting.

Effie had never liked Abigail. With her bright blue eyes and blonde ringlets, Abigail was undeniably a beauty. Perchance Effie saw a much younger version of herself in Abigail—in looks alone, for the two were drastically different in personality. Where Effie was coldness and malice, Abigail was joviality and light.

Poppy couldn't help but be pleased Abigail hadn't been picked. Yes, the job upstairs came with higher pay, but there was a ghastliness attached to it after Anna's death. If Knight's suspicions were correct, who was to say that Abigail wouldn't meet the same fate? Poppy had already lost one friend. At least on the ground floor, she could watch out for Abigail.

The bell had rung, and another day was ending. Another day largely like the rest, drowned in the cacophony of thirty looms working in different rhythms, the clatter of feet against iron floors, the rush for lunch with Moira. The factory granted half an hour for lunch, so usually she ate whatever she could while walking back from her house so that she could spend a few more minutes with her daughter.

Abigail and Bess left ahead of her. Poppy did a few more checks on her loom. As the last members of the factory straggled out, she took a final gander around the almost unoccupied floor. The silence encircled her, a ghost that whispered of times past. Poppy remembered Anna coming to her loom at the end of the day before Clowes had joined the factory. After Clowes came on staff, Anna had found every excuse to see him.

Just as Poppy had manufactured reasons to go to the inn where Edward stayed.

What a cruel twist of fate. Every young girl who loved unrequited seemed to end up dead, with their blood spilled on a brick wall, or their spirit smashed to shards. Poppy had learned there were many types of death: the final, inevitable passing; the loss of one's innocence; the severing of one's soul from the body until there was nothing left but a vapid void where a vivacious person had once been.

If Poppy closed her eyes, she could hear Anna's laugh again. Like the twinkling of bells, harmonious and happy. Yet no amount of willful recollection could bring Anna back to life.

With a sigh, Poppy left the factory. She carried the lantern in one hand and a penknife in the other. One could never be too careful, though she hoped she'd never have to use the knife, since she wasn't entirely sure how to inflict the proper wound. She suspected she should simply thrust forward with the blade out, but there might be a science to stabbing that she didn't know.

There were so many things that Poppy didn't know.

She stepped onto Wheeler Street, narrowly avoiding a vendor as he barreled down the path with his cart. Though her natural inclination was to dismiss the mishap as carelessness, she raised her hand in a vulgar gesture and spat out a few cant curses, because that was expected of her. The street vendor shouted back, nodded at her, and went to find another person to run down.

She had begun to think that in Spitalfields, words no longer held power. People uttered "you bleedin' bunter" with little provocation, though bunter had originally denoted a diseased whore begging on the streets. Words should hurt less when they became commonplace.

If this were true, "fallen" would hurt her less. She wouldn't wince whenever anyone referred to a "bachelor's son," or said that a woman had "broken a leg" and birthed a bastard.

No, there was no escaping one's past, no matter how widely used the language became.

Poppy held the lantern up higher as she crossed onto Lamb Street, making sure to shine the light in all of the alleyways. There, cloaked by the awning on one of the tenement houses, she thought she saw a shadow. Was it Knight, coming to meet her again?

She walked nearer, but upon closer observation, the shadow was that of another man, stretched out in the doorway underneath, shivering despite the warmth of this April night.

Disappointment surged through her. She'd told Knight not to wait for her again. Cerebrally, she recognized this, with the same part of her brain that kept a running list of finishing schools for Moira. That part of her was relieved to be done with him. He presented too many obstacles.

That was the part of her she ought to listen to, not this soul-stirring longing that whispered how he'd make her feel alive.

She kept on going, meeting no further obstacles. A few people she recognized from the factory, or from Kate's circle of acquaints. For the most part, the people of Spitalfields remained unknown to her, interchangeable in their sameness. A community of weavers smacked down by their government. None of them sparked her interest, for they were all as caught in their own lives as she was in hers. No one but Knight, with his damnably inappropriate gifts and his sweet smiles.

When she came onto Church Street, she had given up any hope of seeing Knight again. "More's the better," she muttered, as she passed by Christ Church. "He'll bring trouble, no matter how you play it."

"Who will?"

She started, tripping over a rock in the path. The lantern shook in her hand as she pitched forward. A second later, a strong hand was upon her shoulder, steadying her. She knew without looking up who it was. His legs encased in blue trousers, wide shoulders filling out his uniform coat—there was only one man who made her stomach flip at the sight of him.

Knight removed his hand from her shoulder. She wished he'd stayed close to her, wished it so much that it reverberated throughout her, a dangerous, delicious sensation. Standing here, her eyes downcast, gave her far too much time to investigate that undeniably male part of his anatomy, to puzzle about what it would be like to have him inside of her until all the cracks and fissures in her façade were filled.

She looked up. Her eyes focused not on his smiling face but on the red flower in his hands.

"A poppy for Poppy." He held out the flower to her, quite pleased with his cleverness.

She didn't take the flower. "I see. Why are you here?"

His brows furrowed. Then a thought appeared to take hold of him, and he held the flower back against his chest, frowning. "This is wildly inappropriate, isn't it? Worse than the book. Oh hell—oh, I shouldn't say that in front of you—I saw the poppy, and I thought of you and..."

She couldn't let him labor further. Setting her lantern down on the ground, she then pocketed her knife. Reaching out, she pried his fingers off the stem and took it. The thin green stem fit seamlessly in her hands. He'd chosen well: the poppy was in full bloom, the outside layer a vibrant red. The inside folds rose a bit off the other petals, the black center in stark contrast.

"I love it," she said, for against this startlingly vivid flower, she could not lie. "Even if I wasn't named after it, I'd love it."

Knight's posture loosened. He leaned against a nearby tenement. "I like the black inside that you can only see if the flower decides to open up to you. You must be patient, wait for it to be in full bloom. If you do, the reward will be great."

She dared not meet his eyes. Instead, she stared at the

poppy in her hand. There'd be no great reward for him, nothing but pain and disenchantment.

"I believe humans are much like poppies," Knight continued. "The poppy has many secrets."

"I don't have secrets," she said without conviction.

Knight eyed her skeptically. "Mrs. Corrigan, you are positively rife with secrets. Your parents named you well. You talk so little about your past; one might think you sprang from your father's head like Athena from Zeus."

She stiffened, her hands clenching around the flower. "Why should I live in the past? I am a creature of the present."

He laughed. "I am not complaining, Madame Surrey. I am well suited to the mystery, remember? Each fact you reveal is a piece to your puzzle. Eventually, I shall arrange them all and see the complete picture of Poppy Corrigan."

"Poppaea," she corrected, the name springing from her lips before she could stop it. Somehow, she craved for him to know this truth about her. It was small and harmless, but a truth, nonetheless. "Poppy is short for Poppaea, after my grandmother. My father used to take me to see her as a baby. I don't remember much, except that she had a library almost as big as yours. She was never without a book."

"Explains your love of literature." Knight reached into his coat pocket and produced a small doll, which he passed to her. Constructed from a clothespin, swatches of fabric formed the doll's dress and a cloak. Painted on the head of the pin was a merry face, framed by crimson hair.

Just like Moira's.

"I saw it in the window of a shop on my way here," he said. "It made me think of your daughter."

Poppy held the doll and the flower together in one hand. It was all so bloody, bloody thoughtful. No one, outside of her family, had been so conscientious. But this Peeler had managed to strike away at the walls she built around her heart. This bloody, bloody Peeler.

"Thank you." She didn't bother to say she couldn't accept the doll because they both knew she would. While his earlier gift of *King Lear* had appealed to her intellect, the flower and the doll appealed to her heart.

And against her better judgment, she listened to her heart tonight.

Chapter Nine

"I'm happy you're happy," Knight said. "May I walk with you toward your home? We shall keep in the shadows, and I'll disappear if you see anyone familiar."

She accepted his offered arm. They walked in silence, the flower a blaze of red in the coming darkness. Opium could be made from the poppy to dull her pain. Under that cloud, she'd forget her past sins and begin anew. The temptation was always there. This move to London had been a sort of starting over, yet she couldn't remove herself completely from the life she'd lived.

Not without giving up Moira. She'd rather remember every unfortunate choice if it meant she kept Moira in her life. But with memories came consequences. Swiftly, she peeked over at Knight, observing his calm, collected stride.

He moved with purpose and speed, a man at ease in the elements. Confident in his skills. He was a brilliant investigator, and he knew it.

Soon, Knight would discover her secrets. When he did, he'd find her inadequate. How could he not? Edward had been right. She was an easy fuck. She knew no other way to be. If she let herself get close to Knight, she'd cave to wanton desires as she had before, and Knight would leave.

And even if he *did* by some miracle accept her, if he stayed with her past their coupling, what would be the point? There'd be no future for them. He was a sergeant devoted to the most hated organization in all of Spitalfields. She didn't need a gypsy fortune teller to tell her Knight would meet a bloody end, possibly in an alley such as this one.

She'd stopped paying attention to where they were going. The streets all began to look the same. Twirling the flower in her hand, Poppy let out a slow breath. With her thumb, she caressed the outer petals of the poppy. Soft, pliable. She could slice through those petals with ease, as Edward had sliced through her old self.

"I confess, I had a reason beyond the flower and the doll for finding you," Knight said, as they crossed the narrow alleyway called Keate Court. From the alleyway, they ended up on Thrawl Street.

This wasn't the route she usually took to get home. Poppy kept a firm grip on the lantern, despite the fact that Knight had his truncheon. The sun had set.

She never cut through Thrawl Street by herself. Years ago, there'd been plans to rebuild this section and restore it to the old glory. Whatever work had been done on Thrawl Street was barely visible. Crumbling brick-fronted tenements comingled with timber-built public houses, and fancy women lined the corners to drag cubs back to the brothels.

Knight stopped in front of a shack, shorter than the two tall tenements it bordered. Set back from the street, the shack had a pointed roof thatched in approximately seven places. It appeared to be one room originally. A rectangular section with a barred square window protruded out farther than the rest of the building, an afterthought in an already clumsy construction.

"Why are you stopping?" she squeaked. Knight's presence lent her a little comfort, but he wouldn't be much of a match against a gang of thieves armed with knives and pistols. Any thought she'd had of ducking away from him before they got close to her house had vanished when they'd entered this street.

"There's something I need to ask you," Knight said.

Poppy looked from the strange cottage to him and back again. "Do we have to talk here?"

He took her arm and steered her toward the streetlight, set up directly in front of the hovel. This struck her as odd. She'd never seen any other lamps in this portion of Spitalfields, so close to Whitechapel that she could almost throw a rock over the borders.

She placed the poppy and the doll in her pocket, her hand closing around her knife just in case. "What is it?"

He shifted his weight from one foot to the other. "I need your help with this case."

Poppy frowned, sighing. "I already told you I couldn't help."

"I know," he replied. "But circumstances have changed, and I think I've found a way for you to be helpful—for you to honor Anna's memory—without the Larkers knowing. It could mean the difference between catching the right killer or not. You'd tell me if you notice anything strange."

He took a step toward that dubious house and then turned around to wait for her to follow him. "If you give me ten minutes to explain and you still don't think you can aid me, then I swear I'll never ask you again."

He looked so hopeful that the immediate refusal died on her tongue. Running a hand through his hair, his eyes never left her face. The calm that always possessed him had faded, replaced with this antsy uncertainty. He jiggled the truncheon against his right leg, waiting on her response.

He wasn't sure if she'd say yes, and somehow that satisfied

her. The great Thaddeus Knight, spectator of human nature, couldn't predict her next move. She wanted to surprise him so that she could see his reaction.

Ten minutes. She could do ten minutes without it being a problem, couldn't she? Ten minutes in which they'd simply talk. She was in control of her urges enough to get through that short of a conversation.

"Ten minutes," she said. "But not more."

"Excellent." Knight opened the paper-thin door to the cottage without any hesitation, gesturing for Poppy to enter. "Well, come along. I assure you, it's quite safe."

Poppy surveyed the shack uncertainly, half-suspecting that it would fall down the moment they entered, leaving them surrounded by an odd assortment of mud, grass, and rubbish passed off as "antique."

"Unless you're afraid," Knight teased, his wide smile doing troublesome things to her insides, a flip and then a flop combined with a surge of heat.

Narrowing her eyes, she pushed past him into the shop. Blackness met her; blackness chopped in a few places by shards of amber light. Knight came in, closing the door behind him. He stood too close to her, the narrow room allowing him no room to scoot back. Her back burnt as if lit by a lucifer, for the heat that emanated off his body was all-encompassing.

His breath tickled her neck. She wished she'd worn a bonnet instead of her rice straw hat, anything to keep her exposed skin safe from his effect.

Her eyes adjusted to the dimness as she stepped forward, chancing that she'd run into something in the dull light. She made out rectangular shapes everywhere: boxes on top of boxes, boxes suspended from the ceiling, boxes inside other boxes.

"I do no wrong," came the raspy voice from the back of the

room, English spoken through a thick German accent. "Turn around. Leave now. There's nothing for you here."

Poppy looked in the direction where the voice seemed to be coming from, ears pricked. She couldn't discern any movement. That area of the shop was dark.

"You've always been a devilish rogue, Gottlieb. Why should I believe you've ceased?" Knight smirked, as if he was privy to a secret Gottlieb had shared with him.

The rough voice was no longer cantankerous. "Ah, the Moabites man has come!"

"The one and only," Knight said. "Well, to be technically correct, one of fifteen others in the H-Division, but the only one you need to be concerned with, you vile dust-mongrel."

Poppy turned to him at his harsh words, in abject opposition to the teasing tone in which they were uttered.

From the corner of the room, a withered ancient man appeared, a lantern in his hand. He hobbled over to a table, setting the lantern down on top of it. Tawny beams bounced about the room, reflected from the crossed iron grating of the lantern.

"'Tis better to be a dust-mongrel than a rotten Herr Sergeant." Gottlieb's chapped lips split in a wide smile, leading Poppy to believe that he and Knight regularly engaged in this insult game.

Dagobert Gottlieb was an odd-looking man, to say the least. Gottlieb's skin seemed to stretch over his face, pockets of flesh with no muscles beneath. While the top of his head was bald, scraggly gray locks extended from his crown down to his shoulders. Matted hair sprouted from his chin in a beard that made up for lacking volume by having a significant length.

Forgetting the close confines, Poppy took a step back and collided into Knight.

"Oof," Knight gasped.

"Sorry," she murmured, righting herself.

Gottlieb was a person like any other, she scolded herself. How many thieves had she met in the past few months? Each had their own story. Half of Chapman Street were missing teeth, or even fingers, from bar brawls and jobs gone wrong.

"What's a matter, girl?" Gottlieb's bushy brows crumpled, reminding her of two lumps of silk tangled up in the loom.

"Nothing." The simple word stuck in her throat.

Sensing her discomfort, Knight stepped out from behind her and took a seat at Gottlieb's table. "Mrs. Corrigan, meet Dagobert Gottlieb, once Wurzburg's finest receiver."

"Poppy Corrigan." She dropped a badly executed curtsy.

Gottlieb nodded at her. He took a seat next to Knight.

"Mrs. Corrigan recently relocated to London," Knight said. "Gottlieb here has been in town since the '19, is that right?"

"Aye. Vile hep-heps. Take my house but can't catch me." Gottlieb's top lip pulled back in a sneer, his rheumatic eyes glistening. "Don't understand that I, I will outlast them."

Poppy sat down. A sad smile tinged at her lips, for if there was anything she understood, it was derision for being different. "I'm sorry you had to go through that. People... astound me. They're capable of wonderful generosity, but then they act with the utmost cruelty. I cannot fathom it."

"I appreciate." Gottlieb nodded decisively in agreement before turning his attention to Knight. "You don't visit me so late, Sergeant. What are you thinking, bringing the lady?"

Poppy frowned. She didn't like being referred to as "the lady" any longer.

"Ah, that is not a cut." Gottlieb held his palm up and made a sweeping motion to the left as if he could erase his words from the air. "I mean, you are quality, and I'm not used to that. The sergeant comes when he is confused, you see."

Poppy relaxed back in the chair. "I see." She wondered how "quality" Gottlieb would consider her if he knew her mistakes.

"There's a problem I have to discuss with Mrs. Corrigan," Knight explained. "For the Met. I need your famous discretion, Gottlieb."

The man nodded again, pushing his chair back from the table. Slowly, he rose, weary bones clicking into place with much effort. Poppy had expected him to protest at the eviction from his own home, but Gottlieb seemed unconcerned as he bid adieu.

"What time you need, you take," he told Knight.

"Thank you," Knight said.

Gottlieb stuck out his hand, brushing Poppy's shoulder, so quick she barely registered the touch. "You take care of her," he ordered Knight, his tone giving no room for discussion.

Gottlieb left in a flurry of rags. Nothing on his outfit matched: he wore a green coat thrown over the top of a dingy white shirt and a mustard vest. Fingerless gloves covered his dirty, cracked hands. He grabbed the cane resting against the chair and hobbled out the door.

Poppy watched him go, not sure what to think of him.

Knight took the seat Gottlieb had vacated, next to her. He cleared his throat, the sound echoing in the stuffy little room. "Gottlieb is a character, but he is a good man."

"He's Jewish." Surprise tinted her voice, making her feel somehow less whole because she'd expected less from Knight.

"Yes," Knight said uneasily. "Is that a problem?"

Poppy shook her head. "No. No, absolutely not. It's more that every Met officer I've ever heard of has been staunchly Anglican. To the point that all other religions are unacceptable."

"Well, I'm afraid I don't fit that description." His voice was unusually bland, and she knew she'd offended him.

"Sergeant, please," she pleaded. "You must understand me.

Growing up Irish Catholic in this country steels you toward prejudice. We weren't even able to sit in Parliament until a few years ago. You hope that people will change, but eventually, you become hardened to the attacks."

His expression softened. "I've got twenty books on religious theories from all over the world in my library, and I can't begin to tell you which one is the correct one. They're all devilishly similar in a way."

She smiled. "I thought I was the only one who thought that."

"I have to believe that everyone is worth saving, Mrs. Corrigan, or I'd go mad in this job," he said. "I can't, I won't, give credence to the theory that says we cannot be more than what we've been in the past."

She broke eye contact between them because she couldn't stop herself from wanting to rest her head on his shoulder. To lean into him, letting him shoulder her weight and her worries. At that moment, she'd feel like the odds weren't stacked against her.

But that was a dangerous thought. Whatever serenity she gained would be temporary at best. Better to hold him at a distance, so that she'd never know the pain of truly loving him and losing him. It was easier that way. Hiding behind walls had become second nature.

"I must take a more fatalistic view." She must, for if she didn't remember who she was, she'd be doomed to make the same mistakes again.

"What about presenting a better world to Moira?" He sounded so innocent, baffled by her preconceptions.

The words hurt, regardless of his intent. She drew back, fixing him with a hard gaze. "What I want—what I'll do—for my child isn't your concern, Sergeant."

Knight's eyes were on her. She knew it without looking up,

for she felt it in the tingle down her spine, in the way her nipples hardened underneath her corset.

"I'm sorry," he said softly. "It was not my intention to hurt you. Or to say that you weren't a good mother to your daughter."

"It is of no matter," she said, hating the way her voice came out strained. Were her cheeks flushed? She'd made a mistake coming to this place with him.

"Mrs. Corrigan," Knight began, and that faux appellation suddenly held more raw appeal than her own surname. It held promise, unbroken at the moment.

Avoiding his gaze should have made this less painful, but there was that damned flower in her pocket. The red petals called to her, whispering the calm of the man across from her.

"You said before you wanted me to report back to you what goes on at the factory. Is that all, Sergeant?" She used his title purposefully, reminding herself of all those many reasons why she couldn't form an association with him.

He nodded. "You've been at the factory for three months, isn't that correct?"

She swallowed, her throat suddenly dry. Tight. "You checked into me."

What else had he discovered? Panic seized her. She sucked in one breath, then another, struggling to stay calm. Yet her heart banged against her chest, the beat filling her ears. She gripped the edge of the tabletop, nails digging in, steadying herself.

Don't run. Don't run. You'll look guilty.

"I am an investigator," Knight intoned. "I look into people's histories. People lie, madam, as much as I wish they didn't."

She was the worst of liars. If he'd discovered her secret, wouldn't he be angry with her? He'd be openly confronting her. Perhaps then, he didn't know.

"I didn't devote much time to the research if that's what

concerns you," he said. "We needn't discuss it. I was looking for any connections to the case, that's all."

"I see." She breathed regularly again. Settling back into the chair, she schooled her features into civil disinterest. She swallowed down the last bit of dread. "I simply don't like to talk about my past."

"As a poppy doesn't like to reveal its secrets." He smiled.

She couldn't help but smile at that.

"I think anything you see that isn't normal would be helpful," Knight said.

She remembered Anna as she'd been two weeks before, arm-in-arm with Abigail as they exited the factory after another long day. Poppy's chest clenched every time she saw the girl who had taken Anna's place upstairs. Would that girl meet the same fate?

And if Poppy could help save her fellow workers without endangering her own family, shouldn't she do what she could?

Poppy folded her hands in her lap, an act that appeared submissive but really hid the fact that her thumb stroked against the soft petal of the flower in her pocket. "Why do you need my help?"

"My superior claims he's solved the case."

For a man who had helped to bring a murderer to justice, he didn't sound happy. He ought to be overjoyed. At least Anna's family would have some peace, knowing her killer had been caught.

"I don't understand," she said. "If the murderer has been caught, why are you still investigating? It's not the Larkers."

"That's the thing," Knight replied. "I don't think Whiting has the right man. Before Miss Moseley died, she kept tracing an *L* with her fingers. Whiting's suspect doesn't have an *l* in his name, and I can't find any prior relationship between Miss Moseley and him. There's no motivation for the crime."

"People do horrible things with little justification." She

knew this firsthand—Edward had seduced her simply to win a bet, not caring what happened to her afterwards.

"Perhaps," Knight hedged, unconvinced. "I spoke to Mrs. Moseley. She said Anna had been worried these last two weeks, as if she'd seen something she shouldn't have."

"It's Spitalfields," she reminded him. "She could have witnessed any number of crimes, none of which had anything to do with the factory. Anna was probably killed outside of the factory because it was convenient. They knew she'd be there."

Knight pursed his lips, considering her suggestion for a moment before discounting it. "When I found her, it was several hours after closing."

"You can't expect me to agree based solely on your intuition." Her protest was half-hearted. She couldn't explain it, but she *did* trust his gut. She'd seen the way his mind worked. He was balanced, forthright. She imagined him sitting in his library, weighing each alternative.

"There was another murder."

She sat up straighter. "At the factory?"

He ran his thumb across his folded hands. He didn't look her in the eye. "No. It has no bearing on this case, except that I found them both. The first murder happened seven years ago, after I graduated from Eton. She was already dead by the time I found her in an alley in Whitechapel. I was too late."

"I'm sorry, Sergeant Knight. That's horrible." She shouldn't want to bring his hands to her lips, planting a kiss where he rubbed so diligently. But she did.

He swallowed, still not meeting her gaze. "I vowed then I was going to seek justice for people like Miss Stewart. I didn't realize at the time it'd be so damn hard."

Acrimony stained his tone. It was the first time she'd heard him sound unsure of himself. She thought of him as a young boy, coming across the dead girl after a night of carousing with his mates. Had he been a rough lad? Maybe the shock of finding Miss Stewart had made him into the steadfast sergeant he was today.

He brought his index finger up, tapping at the cleft in his chin. That cleft made his face appear slightly off-kilter, the left side a smidgen higher than the right. Her heart skipped a beat at that cleft because it made him achingly real.

An imperfect creature like her.

He leaned forward, closing the distance between them until he was a hairsbreadth away from her. His eyes locked on hers, nose to nose. "I wouldn't ask for your help if I didn't need it, Mrs. Corrigan. I've got no other alternatives."

She couldn't tear her gaze away. She was captured by him, stupidly transfixed. She didn't dare take a breath, for fear that if she did, he'd scoot that last bit toward her and kiss her.

A little voice inside her kept saying, "It wouldn't be so bad." God help her, it'd probably be fantastic. He was an educated man, who probably knew all sorts of ways to make her insides tumble. They must write about things like that in books, didn't they? Maybe he had a whole shelf of dirty pamphlets in that library, and he'd practice all of the techniques on her...

His voice was so low, almost a rumble. "But I don't want you to do anything that's going to put your safety in jeopardy. If it seems like people are noticing, I want you to stop what you're doing. I will not—I cannot—have another woman's death on my head. Especially not yours."

She was important to him.

She hadn't been important to someone outside of her family in a long time.

Not trusting herself to speak, she nodded.

"And I know you've got a daughter who's depending on you." His brown eyes turned warmer, not full of pity, as she'd seen from most people when they found out she was a "widow."

This was instead something powerful. "I won't let her grow up without a parent. You must see that. If you do this for me, I'll protect you."

She was nodding again. She wanted to do what he said. To buy into his promises of safety, security, and someone to give a damn if she died.

She thought of Kate and Daniel, of Atlas and Jane and everyone they associated with. Knight would be privy to parts of her life if they worked together—continued interaction with him put the people she loved in danger. But if she could keep them safe while making sure that the Larkers got what they deserved...

If she knew anything about Knight, it was that he'd be true to his word. If he made her a promise, he'd keep it.

"I'll do it," she said. "On one condition."

* * *

"One condition?" Thaddeus held the door to Gottlieb's house open for Poppy. Nothing was ever as simple as he wanted it to be. He'd read thousands upon thousands of books, but he couldn't condense relationships. There was always some unpredictable element.

And he'd never met anyone like Poppy Corrigan.

Outside, she took off her hat to refasten it upon her head. Her simple chignon had not fared well after a day of hard labor in the factory. The poppy blossom peeked out of her apron pocket. In his library, she'd become less reserved, but here on the street, her appearance matched that buoyancy. He liked her better this way. Wanted to write some bloody awful sonnets to her beauty because at that moment, she was wild and free.

She turned back to him. "I want the people I care for to be safe. You said you'd turn in my sister if you found her fencing again. Then you said you'd have to arrest Atlas if you found him stealing."

"That's my job, Mrs. Corrigan," he said mildly, knowing that his words weren't what she wanted to hear.

She didn't flinch. "And it's also your job to find out who really killed Anna Moseley."

He nodded.

"So, if you want my help, you'll leave my friends and family alone." Poppy drew herself up to her full height, her green eyes dark. "If you hear anything about them, you'll turn a blind eye. You won't pursue them. You won't look into their crimes. You won't take any interest in them."

Thaddeus considered this. Atlas Greer had avoided police capture for years. The Gentleman Thief didn't have a history of being violent; rather, he had made a name for himself through his ability to carry out a caper without injury to those around him. Kate O'Reilly had been a fence, but she'd dealt mostly in low-end items. He had more information on Gottlieb than he did Kate, and he'd let Gottlieb go free. Daniel had never been a criminal to begin with—he'd simply been a scapegoat for Jasper Finn.

And he had to admit, Poppy's shrewdness impressed him. She bargained well, hitting his weaknesses yet not asking for something so outlandish he couldn't fulfill it. Her logic was clever.

"Atlas, Kate, and Daniel." He ticked off each name on his fingers. "Is that all?"

"Jane Putnam."

"I don't recognize the name."

"She works as a barmaid at the Three Boars in Ratcliffe. She's honest..."

Thaddeus suspected Poppy had been about to explain further but feared how he'd react. He knew how the system worked. The repeal of the Bloody Code had reduced the number of crimes that sent a man to death, leaving the prisons overcrowded. Could he in good conscience commit one of Mrs. Corrigan's loved ones to death, or perhaps worse—the wretched halls of Newgate? No, he didn't think he could.

Thaddeus let his eyes rove down her body. That fierce face made for light but hardened by whatever had happened in her past. Her threadbare dress, hugging breasts full enough to make any man's cock harden. Drawing in a long breath, he shoved his hands into the pockets in his coat to keep from reaching from her. From telling her that he'd protect her and her family.

"I accept your request," he said. "With the condition that if they're involved in violent altercations, I will proceed as the law sees fit. There's a difference between petty theft and brutal acts, Mrs. Corrigan."

Her chin rose in challenge. "I don't befriend brutal people, Sergeant."

"Then we have a deal." He stuck out his hand to her.

She accepted his hand, shaking it firmly. "Partners."

Reluctantly, he released her hand. "Partners."

And if luck stuck with him, he'd make sure they were partners in far more than fact-finding work.

Chapter Ten

When Poppy showed up on his doorstep the next evening after her work at the factory, Thaddeus was surprised. Though they'd agreed on the meeting before parting at Gottlieb's, he'd almost expected her to stand him up. For her, their alliance had been an uneasy one, and self-preservation usually topped all other notions in Spitalfields.

Closing the door behind her, he showed her into the library. In a few minutes, the housekeeper would appear with a moderate dinner of boiled chicken, buttered shrimp, roasted potatoes, and partridge soup. Nothing too fancy—intrinsically, he sensed that would put Poppy on edge.

How could he prove to her that they had more in common than she thought? He watched as Poppy's eyes widened eagerly again as she stepped into the room, immediately heading toward the section of modern novels.

They might be from different backgrounds, but this they could share.

"I'm more prepared today." He gestured to the fire he'd built. The usually cold library was toasty from the flames.

She granted him a small smile. "Aye, and your appearance is much more in line with what society dictates."

He'd managed to bathe and shave before her arrival. His neckcloth was neatly tied, and his coat was fresh from the laundress.

"What society dictates, yes, but what does Mrs. Corrigan dictate? Do you prefer me disheveled?" He wasn't sure where the flirtatious words came from so easily when he'd never been particularly skilled with coquetry. "What I mean is—"

He stopped. Her face had pinked from her cheeks to her ears. He ought to feel ashamed about embarrassing her, yet one look into her eyes, and he was certain he'd not mortified her sensibilities. Her pupils had darkened, and her breaths came heavily.

All of his books on physiology confirmed it: she was aroused.

He gulped. He was so unprepared. But by God, he wanted to be good at this. For her.

"I've been thinking about how you can accept the copy of *King Lear*," he blurted.

Her lips turned down in a pout of irritation. "I already told you it's not proper."

He could think of about seventy things she could do with him that weren't proper but would feel oh-so-good. Some of them he'd attempted before, but most were known to him through books with detailed diagrams of the different contortions a human being could undergo.

Damnation, he wasn't even sure he knew *how* to assume those positions.

He swallowed again. If he didn't look at her, if he didn't see how her bodice dropped down enthrallingly as she stooped to check out a book on the lower shelf, didn't think about how her breasts would be perfectly fitted to cup in his hand, her pert nipples ripe for his mouth...

Shaking his head to clear out those thoughts, he plucked another play down from above her head. *Macbeth*. That was safer than say, *Measure for Measure*.

"Consider the book a loan." He sounded strained like he was breathing through the scarf she'd gifted him.

She didn't meet his gaze, but her voice was huskier than he remembered it. "I haven't time to read quickly."

"A long-term loan." He shrugged. "I've practically memorized all the plays. I don't need to have a copy in front of me to enjoy them now."

"Really?" She grabbed the copy of *Macbeth* from his hands, flipping it open to a random page. "Act III, Scene III, first lines."

He closed his eyes, envisioning the page before him. "Let us seek out some desolate shade, and there/Weep our sad bosoms empty," he recited. "Spoken by Malcolm in front of the King's palace."

Bosoms. He realized it after he said it by the way her face had pinked until her cheeks began to resemble her red hair.

"Yes, well," she sputtered. "Very impressive, that. Hopefully, you have a similar recall when it comes to Anna Moseley's case."

"Ah, yes," he stammered.

The appearance of his housekeeper with the sideboard saved him from more single-syllable unintelligence. Mrs. Clery wheeled the cart into a vacant space to the right of the fireplace, poured two cups of tea from the silver teapot, and set them on the coffee table with a small pitcher of cream and a bowl of sugar cubes. All this she did without a word, as Mrs. Clery rarely spoke unless a direct question had been asked. It was one of the reasons why Thaddeus liked her so much.

Poppy blinked at Mrs. Clery's retreating back. When Mrs.

Clery had shut the door behind her, Poppy set down *Macbeth* and moved over toward the tea. She reached for the pitcher, splashing cream into her cup. "Are you aware your housekeeper bears a distinct resemblance to a ghost?"

He shrugged. "The notion has occurred to me before, yes."

"As long as she doesn't start haunting you as Banquo did Macbeth," Poppy jested.

"Well, I have not murdered any kings, so I do think I'll be safe from harm's way." He moved over to the sideboard, loading his plate.

Poppy sat in the chair by the fire, hands folded in her lap, eyes fastened on the food but not making a move toward it.

"Please, don't make me eat alone, Mrs. Corrigan." He signaled toward the loaded food cart. "I wasn't able to eat at the station, and so I asked Mrs. Clery to hold dinner in case you were hungry too. Help yourself to whatever strikes your fancy. Mrs. Clery is an excellent baker."

"Is this soda bread?" She pointed to the smaller plate to the right of the boiled chicken.

He nodded. "Mrs. Clery was born in Dublin. Was that where your relatives are from?"

"No. County Cork." She didn't offer anything more, her lips pursed.

Whatever secret she was hiding, she was no nearer to confiding in him than she'd been a few days prior. He thought of the letter to Beauregard with a tinge of guilt.

"I make excellent soda bread," she said, as she settled back in the chair. On her plate was a leg of chicken, two buttered shrimps, and the roasted potatoes. She'd skipped the partridge soup.

"I'm sure it's delicious. I'll have to try it sometime," he replied.

He did a quick calculation of what he knew weavers made

and the rent of a cottage like hers with the added cost of supporting a child. As she dug into the food on her plate with relish, he doubted she'd eaten since breakfast.

Or that she could afford a proper meal.

But he didn't draw attention to that. Pity was something a prideful woman like Poppy Corrigan wouldn't tolerate. He liked that about her.

Instead, they ate in silence, each focused on their meal. When he'd polished off a second serving of soup, he set his plate down next to the overstuffed folder on the coffee table.

Poppy finished her food. The color in her fair cheeks had returned, and he made a silent promise to concoct more reasons to invite her to dine with him. She might not let him protect her, but damn it, he could at least make sure she and her daughter were well fed. He'd have to find out which cottage was hers on Finch Street and bring her a basket of bread one morning.

"Well?" She nodded toward the file.

"This is everything I know about the Larkers." He handed her the file, careful not to drop any of the smaller scraps of parchment sticking out from the edges. Quickly, he summarized what he knew about the case.

"I had hoped that for once, the Larkers wouldn't turn out to be as bad as I'd thought." Poppy sighed. "I ought to know by now wishes and hopes are for the weak."

He hated how downtrodden she sounded. For him, work was an option, pursued by choice. He loved his work at the Met. He had enough money set upon him by his parents to take a less active vocation.

For Poppy Corrigan, working was a matter of life or death.

"When you're at work, how many men does Larker usually have on the floor overseeing the operations?" Knight asked.

She paused to count. "Two, I'd say, with his wife reprimanding those who don't work fast enough. Ian Jennings and Frank Clowes."

Thaddeus went to his desk, dipping his quill in ink and scrawling out the information on foolscap. "I met them both when I went to the factory. What's your general opinion of Clowes?"

"He's not a bad man, if that's what you mean," Poppy replied. "He's young, probably about nineteen or so. Anna had a fancy for him, but he was too old for her. I don't think he encouraged her—he seemed to treat her more like a sister."

"Do you think Anna would have acted on her feelings?" Thaddeus stopped writing, turning his full attention to Poppy. "Fourteen is on the cusp of womanhood, some might say. Anna might have entertained the thought that when she was older, Clowes would marry her."

Something flashed across Poppy's face that he couldn't quite define. Pain? An old wound? Had some sort of scandal caused her to marry Robert Corrigan?

"I'm not condemning her," he said swiftly. "Far from it. But I've seen in this profession what a foul man can do to a young woman with hopes, and it is motivation enough for murder."

She shuddered. "You think Clowes had something to do with Anna's murder because she pushed him toward marriage?"

He shrugged. "I'm considering all the options. But what particularly concerns me is that locked room. When I went upstairs, I saw bags, an awl, and a hammer. All instruments that can be used in coin clipping."

Blinking, Poppy stopped mid-turning of a page. "Counterfeiting?"

"Aye," Thaddeus said. "The more I think about it, the more it makes sense. Have you noticed any surges in production orders to justify all those looms the Larkers produced?"

She thought for a second. "Not really. I wasn't around prior to the takeover, but Abigail once said she didn't know why they'd upgraded when there already wasn't enough work to go around. It *is* strange."

Thaddeus explained his suspicions about the Larkers using the factory as a cover for their counterfeiting. He'd expected to have to elaborate on how he'd arrived at this conclusion, but to his surprise, she followed his reasoning. She even made a few surmises of her own. He'd worked with seasoned patrollers that had fewer deductive skills.

It was not often Thaddeus was impressed, but damn, he loved watching her work through a puzzle. The funny quirk of her brow as she contemplated, that dash of freckles across her wrinkled nose, the delight in her voice when she reached a conclusion.

She continued to flip through the file, grimacing at the sketch he'd had drawn of Anna's corpse.

"Ah," he said. "My apologies. I should have removed that."

"No," Poppy murmured. "Maybe I needed to see it. When I don't think of what happened to her, it's too easy to pretend she never existed."

He thought of Ems Moseley and her one-room ragged cottage. Of Miss Stewart's family, to this day wondering who had killed her.

Poppy sighed. "Death takes an uneasy toll, and we are left alone with memories."

"I'm sorry." He let out a long breath, collecting his thoughts. "You haven't spoken much about your late husband, but I can imagine in times of loss, the motions become the same. Grief has its stages, smaller in relation to how well one knew the victim."

For a second—so brief he wasn't certain he'd truly seen it—shock flared upon her face.

"Yes, yes, of course," she murmured.

"You weren't thinking of your husband, were you?" He

ought not to broach this delicate subject, but she was holding back information. How was he supposed to help if he didn't have all the details?

She shifted on the sofa so that her entire body faced him. "I don't see that it is any of your concern, Sergeant."

"It shouldn't be," he admitted. "But it is, nonetheless. I care about you."

Her expression tempered, her voice almost a whisper. "As I care about you."

"Then believe me when I inquire about your welfare, Poppy." So quickly her Christian name popped from his lips, for she'd stopped being Mrs. Corrigan to him with that first brush of their fingers in this library.

"It isn't that I don't believe you." She rubbed her thumb against the back of her bare finger, where once a wedding ring had laid.

"What is it?"

"Robert..." Again went her thumb, to and fro. "Do not think less of me when I say that I didn't mourn for love lost when Robert passed. He was a good man, yes, but he was more like a friend to me than anything else. We were very young."

He nodded. She'd been seventeen; he knew that much.

"The marriage made sense at the time," she said. "I miss Robert, but I choose to live in the present. To take care of my daughter."

"Did Robert get to meet her?"

"No." She exhibited the proper amount of chagrin at this. "I think that has made it easier. It has been Moira and me for her entire life."

Poppy's past reminded him of her Jacquard loom: each tick of the punch card was another fact, doled out sparsely to keep him interested. Was everything between them a fabrication of his mind?

If she couldn't trust him, what hope did they have?

"Thaddeus." She said his name tentatively as if trying it out first to see how it tasted upon her tongue. "I do want to help you find Anna's killer. For her family, and for you. But my past is my past, and I prefer it to stay that way. It's not a reflection upon you. Since we met, you've been nothing but wonderful to me."

His profession had made him distrust everyone around him; he saw lies in denials and omissions. Some people were simply more private than others. He should accept this. When he received Beauregard's letter, he would disregard it.

"I'm pleased you have revised your opinion of me from 'bit of a bounder' to 'wonderful.'" He chuckled.

She colored. "I'm terribly sorry about that."

"Nothing to apologize for." He waved away her concern. "You were so devilishly intriguing with your in-and-out accent. I'm a gull for a mystery, as you well know."

"I hadn't noticed." She laughed.

Her laughter made him bold. He reached out, tentatively placing his hand over the top of Poppy's. Her smaller fingers dovetailed against his palm, and she did not pull back. Heat against heat, he no longer felt so alone.

Thaddeus ought to be a gentleman and walk Poppy home. He was sure if he suggested this, Poppy would tell him exactly where to place his well-meaning concern. The thought of her roaming the rookeries alone worried him, as it had done that first night he'd met her, but he pushed it aside.

Poppy could take care of herself. She'd made that quite clear.

And so, he leaned against his door, and he prayed that she wouldn't immediately want to run home. He wasn't ready for their time together to be over. She was tonic to his soul, soothing away all his doubts.

They stood on his stoop. A full moon shone high in the sky, a glistening, perfect orb that cast the sweetest of shadows across Poppy's face. Abstractly, he marveled at the way the moon was the same shade as Poppy's dress, a sea-blue concoction with lace sleeves. Delicate as she was.

He decided that this dress was his favorite of hers for the way the waist cinched underneath her breasts. More lace trimmed her shoulders, calling out for him to touch her, to slide that fabric down and press his lips to the creamy skin of her neck and shoulders.

In the shadows of his stoop, with the moon silhouetted behind her red hair, Poppy Corrigan was a fiery angel. He'd never seen anything more striking.

They exchanged small talk about the weather. It was abnormally warm for April. A balmy breeze swayed the ribbons tied underneath her chin, holding her hat upon her head. He could attribute the rise in his body temperature to the heat—not the way she looked underneath the light of the moon.

She checked the pinning of her hat to make sure it was secure. Her fingers were callused. Another thing his family would disapprove of, for she was a working woman and her body bore the signs of it. Yet to him, calluses meant she cared enough about something to try for it.

"I think I understand now why you do what you do. There's something invigorating about going through that file." She bit her lip, unsure if her reaction had been appropriate. "Obviously, I wish it hadn't happened, and that Anna was with us. But..."

"It's the puzzle," he finished for her.

She nodded. "Precisely. Going over the different possibilities with you and weighing the options. I enjoyed tonight." Her smile sent his heart racing.

He loved that smile. Hell, he *knew* that smile. The allure of "investigation fever," as he liked to term it, had struck her too. Cheeks pinked with the notion she'd save the world somehow, she was stunning. He ached to tell her so—but he was a coward, a blind coward.

"Poppy," he breathed more than spoke.

She inclined her head toward him, imploring him to continue speaking. Had he lost his mind? Was he fit for the madhouse to think there could be something more with her?

He was a man on the precipice, readying himself to jump off a cliff, and that jump would change his life forever.

"Thaddeus." His name sounded like silk upon her lips, smooth and luxurious. A name for a man who could conquer nations, change the power structure of the world, and help others to find purpose in life.

And he believed he could do all those things with her help.

"Thank you. For meeting with me, for agreeing to help in the case."

"I want to find who killed Anna," she said. "I want to make sure they don't hurt anyone else. I have friends at the factory that I don't want to see hurt."

"We'll get the Larkers," he vowed.

Quiet descended upon them. They were peaceable in their shared determination. The warm air wrapped around them, an embrace almost as comforting as her arms around him would have been.

"It is so wonderful out," Poppy murmured. "I should go home, but Moira is spending the night with Kate and Daniel."

"How is Moira?" Though he had only met the babe once, he couldn't help but adore Moira because of the way Poppy's eyes sparkled when she talked about her daughter.

Poppy's grin lit up her face. It was a smile without pretensions, made more special because of its rarity. For once, she didn't appear to be holding something back from him.

"Moira is doing well," Poppy said. "She has learned a new word, doll, because of the clothespin doll you gave her. She quite loves it."

"I am glad to hear she likes it." He stuffed his hands in his pockets, for at least then he could tamp down on his desire to reach out for her. He'd go slowly with her, remain patient.

"Nights like these should be appreciated, not spent inside the cottage," Poppy mused. "I so seldom have a chance to enjoy the little things, like good weather or a book."

"It is a night for lovers," he blurted.

She opened her eyes, tilting her head so that she looked up at him. "Pardon?"

"What I mean is," he started, issuing a silent prayer that he'd figure out what he meant as he was speaking since he surely didn't know now. "It is the kind of night poets write sonnets about, besotted by the fanciful quality of a London without fog or rain."

She smiled again, and he let out a quick breath of relief that he hadn't botched this entirely.

"'Shall I compare thee to a summer's day?'" she quoted glibly, grasping at a handful of muslin on her skirt and giving a little twirl. "'Thou art more lovely and more temperate.'"

This side of her enchanted him. Serene and uninhibited, reciting Shakespeare from memory because such eloquence deserved to be given wings by her honey voice.

"'Rough winds do shake the darling buds of May.'" He took a step toward her, and another, until he stood next to her. So near that he might brush his fingertips against that enticing lace if he could be so bold.

She didn't retreat. Watching him intently, she gave another

swish of her skirt, daring him to come closer but not brave enough to issue a real invitation.

"'And summer's lease hath all too short a date,'" he whispered, sliding his hand around the left side of her waist. Not putting enough pressure to pull her toward him, but a gentle suggestion that she might rest her hand against his chest and lean into him. "'Sometime too hot the eye of heaven shines and often is his gold complexion dimm'd. And every fair from fair sometimes declines.'"

Poppy released her hold on her skirt. The fabric settled back into place as if nothing had passed between them. But he felt the change in the stiffening of her body against him, this emergence of sadness.

"That's what I don't like about Sonnet Eighteen," she replied. "Everything must end. There's no way around it. The happiest moments in our lives are cut woefully short, and we can never get back to them. Look at Anna or that woman you found before."

"Ah, but as the bard says, 'Thy eternal summer shall not fade,'" Thaddeus replied, his fingers light against the curve of her waist. Unsure if she'd tell him to desist, but wanting to be close to her, to quell the sorrow in her green eyes.

"Is that not true with a loved one?" he asked. "Shakespeare speaks of more than physical beauty. You may grow old, you may change, but your intrinsic personality shall remain constant. I find a woman with intelligence far more enticing than a comely chit with air for her head."

She laughed hollowly. "You say that now, Sergeant, but I think if you were presented with a diamond of the first water, you'd seize upon her far quicker than the shy bluestocking."

"I'd never tire of you." His voice came out as a rasp, for she'd shifted, so she was now flush against him.

Her hand came to rest high on his chest. Thumb on his collarbone, her lower arm across his heart.

Could Poppy hear how hard his heart thudded? He was a boy back at Eton, taking his first tumble with the barmaid at the Bitter Pill.

Her waist fit against him, positioning her against his arousal, yet she didn't move from him. Didn't shy away like a young maiden. She'd been married before, he reminded himself.

His fingers traced the line of her spine, rubbed against the lace before he held his hand flat against her back to support her. "Don't you see, there's but one woman I want? *You.*"

She shook her head. "You couldn't want me. You *shouldn't* want me. I'm not a summer night, and I'm not a happy moment that won't fade away."

He inclined his face so that their noses were almost touching. "Do you ever think that sometimes things work because they're not supposed to? That as much as we struggle to contain life to the proper strictures, it cannot be restrained?"

"Those strictures are in place for a reason," she whispered, her words tingling upon his skin. "When you go against society, you pay the price."

"Is that what happened to you?" He didn't understand the haunting darkness to her eyes, the way she shrank inside herself.

She turned her head away from him. "I married a soldier. He died. The rest is irrelevant."

Thaddeus doubted that was the end of the story. Maybe it wasn't even *the* story. But as much as he wanted to know the truth, something stopped him from solving the puzzle. For the first time, it wasn't the thrill of discovery that interested him, but that she be the one to tell him.

He shifted, bringing his hand up to her chin to turn her face back to him. "It doesn't matter. What you did in the past. Who you were then."

"I'd like that to be true." She sighed. "If only for a night, at least."

"So, let it be." He pulled her that last bit of distance to him. Ducked his head down so that they were eye level, and as her breath sucked inward in anticipation, he laid his lips upon hers. Soft at first, tentative. But he couldn't leave her, and what had been originally intended as the slightest brush of lip against lip became a consuming kiss. An embrace, as he sank his mouth on top of hers, covering those lush lips with his own.

She moved against him, returning his kiss with an equally consuming affection. Press to press, flaming his body. The moan that tore from her lips hardened his cock almost as quickly as her kisses had. He longed for that sound. He wanted to store it in the back of his mind to replay repeatedly so he could know for sure that he, a restrained, bookish man, had made Poppy Corrigan moan so loudly people turned in the street to stare at them.

"Poppy," he breathed, her name the most flawless word he could imagine. He seized her mouth again, brought his lips upon hers with the air of a conqueror. She was a case he'd solve, and yet that somehow made her more appealing.

He glided his hand down her back, squeezing her perfectly rounded bottom in his hand. And as she leaned into him, he kissed her with every ounce of passion he possessed, desperately clutching at a reality that included Poppy.

Until she pulled back, freeing herself from his embrace. He'd forgotten he meant to be a gentleman. Damnation, he'd forgotten his own name. Her lips were reddened and plump from his kisses. She drew back from him.

"That was amazing," he said.

"Aye." Stunned, she laid her ring finger on her lips, as if trying to ascertain through touch how this had all happened.

He started to reach for her, anxious to have her in his arms

147

again. She jumped back, shaking her head quickly. "That can never happen again, do you understand? This...this *thing*, I cannot do. I have responsibilities. Duties. People who depend on me." Another step away from him, out into the street. Her eyes were wide, her nostrils flared.

He'd spooked her. Damn it to hell.

"Poppy," he implored. "Poppy, please, I don't want to take you away from your family. I'd like to court you."

"*Court* me?" she repeated with disdain.

"Yes?" He was no longer confident.

Worry lines etched deep in her forehead. "Thaddeus, darling, you can't possibly mean that."

"But I do," he protested.

"No, you don't." Her lips were set in a straight line, allowing no deviations. No changes. She turned on her heel, taking that final step into the street. "If I see anything unusual, I'll send a message to you."

And with that promise, she was gone like the balmy wind.

Chapter Eleven

Guilt.

It was a strange emotion, a double-bladed sword that sliced through one's throat with alacrity. How could she justify her lapse in judgment? Agreeing to help Knight trap the Larkers had been sound reasoning, but letting him kiss her... That had been madness.

An all-consuming madness that had swept her away yesterday. She'd been willing to be condemned to Bedlam as long as it meant being with Thaddeus.

Thaddeus. She couldn't go back to thinking of him as Knight. That was too formal.

She breakfasted on dry bread and cold mutton. Chewing mulishly, Poppy reached for another hunk of the crusty bread, breaking off a piece. Through the windows, the sun streamed into the cottage on Finch Street. Edna was outside, ostensibly sweeping the porch but really flirting with Jimmy in 2B, who had taken a liking to her. Even stalwart Edna was not immune to this season of love.

Damn the weather! It was to blame for all of this.

Shall I compare thee to a summer's day?

She'd slept fitfully. Not more than two hours at a time. The slightest noise roused her, for she wavered in that half-awake state where everything carries a blurred, dismal edge. Without Moira in the crib in the corner, her room had felt emptier.

Poppy rolled her shoulders, trying to work out the kink in her muscles from sleeping so awkwardly. When she'd finally dozed off, her wicked mind had to set to work replaying the kiss. Her palms had been pressed against Thaddeus Knight's chest again, investigating the way his muscles rippled underneath her fingers, for his body was toned from patrolling the streets. In his arms, she'd felt at home, secure.

He'd nipped her bottom lip, drawing it in between his teeth. He'd kissed her as if he was the key to her lock. She gave in, gave in willingly because he'd find out all of her secrets eventually.

The dream scene had changed, and he was stretched out across her bed. He lay before her, erect and ready. She wanted to have him buried so deep inside her he'd erase the memory of Edward completely.

She'd gone to him, slipping her dress off, but Thaddeus had faded beneath her.

Like Edward, he'd left.

Now, she stood up from the table. A cold hand might as well have been wrapped around her gut. She couldn't shake the dream. Any damn part of it.

This couldn't continue. She had become a logical woman, and logical women most certainly didn't go around kissing Peelers. Police officers were the very devil.

A knock sounded through the cottage. Thank God, Daniel had come to drop off Moira, and some semblance of normalcy would return to her life. It was Sunday, and that meant she was free of the factory today. She hurried to the door, flinging it open.

Atlas Greer stood in the threshold with Moira nestled in his arms. Accompanying Atlas was one of his couriers, who carried a bag of groceries.

"'Ello, luv." Atlas leaned forward to kiss her cheek. "Danny asked me to come by. He had to go down to the docks early this morning. Bugger responsibilities, I told him, but he didn't agree with me, of course."

Poppy took the bag of groceries from Atlas's man, thanking him for his assistance. Atlas dismissed the courier and followed her inside the cottage. He closed the door behind him.

As Poppy brought the groceries over to the counter, Atlas set Moira down on the blanket by the door. Moira tottered eagerly toward the stack of blocks in the corner.

Poppy gave the bag a skeptical glance. "Dare I see what's inside?" Though carrots and potatoes protruded from the top, with Atlas, the King's crown jewels could be lining the sack bottom.

"Bit of vegetables and beef this time." Atlas tapped his nose contemplatively, watching Moira. "Growing like fresh mud on a lark, isn't she? Be a brilliant diver soon if you'd let me take her on a job..."

"Absolutely not. Moira won't be involved in anything illegal." Poppy held up the carrot she'd been unloading from the bag and aimed it at him as though it were a pistol. "And I'd shoot you if you tried. You know I would."

Atlas grinned cheekily. "Didn't know you could shoot, actually. Your new sister been teaching you?"

Poppy nodded. "Though to tell you the truth, I haven't progressed to the actual *shooting* yet. We've covered loading the pistol and storing the powder when not in use."

"Fancy that." Atlas whistled. "But don't get your bonnet strings tangled. I'd never use Moira on a job without your permission."

Atlas stood by as she placed the food in the cupboards. He

appeared at ease, slouching against her countertop. Poppy knew that if she moved to the left suddenly, he'd follow her movement as if he'd expected it all along.

The Gentleman Thief saw everything.

Sometimes she wondered if Atlas knew everything too.

"Thank you for the groceries. I shan't ask who you stole them from." Poppy patted his hand, observing Moira out of the corner of her eye. The babe had fixed upon Atlas with wide-eyed wonderment.

"Oy now, I haven't nicked food in years," Atlas reproached her. "Crime pays me better than that. I'm not going to steal from people who'd go hungry from the loss. The market stall's where I get my meals, as you do."

"Thank the heavens." She pressed a hand to her forehead in mock relief.

"Sassy lass." Atlas pulled the last item from the sack: a sheep made of rags and stuffed with sawdust. He went over to Moira's blanket, stooping to present her with the toy. "Did you think I forgot you, Miss Moira? You should know your Uncle Atlas will always bring you something."

Moira seized upon the sheep, wrapping her small hand around its middle. "Tan too!" she exclaimed, her smile threatening to envelop her apple blossom cheeks.

"She means 'thank you,'" Poppy explained. "She hasn't quite managed to grasp the k yet."

"'Tis a hard sound to make." Atlas knelt down on the blanket beside Moira, crossing his legs in front of him. "But I've no doubt our little miss here shall get it far earlier than the rest of the tots, aye, Moira?"

"Tan too!" Moira repeated, waving the sheep at him.

Atlas ruffled Moira's red hair. Poppy leaned back against the counter, watching them both.

"Saw Jane last night," Atlas said. "Cyrus has been by the

Boars again, of course. Bloody bounder doesn't get Jane doesn't want a thing to do with him. I swear the mills bashed out his brains."

Cyrus Mason had helped Kate and Daniel in their investigation into the dockworker's murder, so Poppy tolerated him, but she certainly didn't trust him. The pugilist was loud, bad, and dangerous to know. His brother, Joaquin, was the head of the rival Kings gang. The truce between the three ruling gangs of the London underworld allowed Cyrus to pass freely through the Three Boars' doors, but it didn't mean he was well liked.

With one hand clasped around the sheep, Moira reached for Atlas's shoe. She tugged it once, twice, a petulant pout darkening her pretty face when the shoe wouldn't come off in her hand. Sensing an impending temper tantrum, Poppy started to go toward them, but Atlas held her off.

"Come now, Miss Moira," he said in a singsong voice. From the sleeve of his coat, he pulled a richly colored silk handkerchief. "Do you know what this is? Would you like it? I'll give it to you if you're silent while your mum and I have a chat."

Moira snatched the cloth from him, wrapping it around her fist. She dropped it down on the top of the block stack and then picked it up, absorbed in her new game.

Atlas rose from his spot on the blanket and crossed to the chair by the fire. "I've been meaning to ask you," he began, attempting a casual tone and failing miserably. "Did anything ever come of your visit to the pig that saved Danny?"

Poppy sat down across from him on the settee, her throat suddenly dry. One look at Atlas's face told her he already knew the answer to his question but wanted to hear it in her own words.

"I went and apologized to him." She kept her tone guarded, trying to feel out how much he already knew.

"Having a sense of decency is all well and good, but you

might consider what it means to be under their eyes again," Atlas cautioned. "Do you think I like that truncheon-swinging grunter knowing what I look like? Of course not. I worked damn hard for this anonymity."

"He's not a grunter," she objected, too slowly realizing she'd given Atlas precisely what he was looking for.

Atlas smacked his palm to his forehead. "My God, Pop. Nip it in the bud. He's a bloody trap. You know what they're capable of. This sergeant might have helped saved Daniel, but he's still going to bleed blue."

Poppy stiffened, drawing herself up to her full, inconsequential height. "You needn't lecture me."

"I can't help it, lass," he sighed. "You want to rush headfirst into the fire. I already had to fish one of you O'Reillys out. Must you make me do it again?"

"I'm not Daniel," she pointed out.

Atlas stood, walking to where Moira sat on the blanket. "I know you're not, but I worry. Moira's a good girl, you know?"

Poppy's heart squeezed. "The best."

For a moment, they both observed Moira playing in silence. Fervor took hold of Poppy's heart whenever she was with her daughter. Love, serenity, protectiveness, sometimes even annoyance when Moira became fussy—all were amplified.

Before the Larker case, Poppy had felt relatively safe in this little corner of Spitalfields. She could handle everyday vices. Her associations with Atlas and Jane had kept her protected. Now, with Anna's blood smeared against the wall of the factory, she didn't feel so secure anymore.

"Did Jane say anything about the Larkers?" she asked.

Atlas nodded. "Chapman's looking into them, but I wouldn't hold your breath. Zacharias Baines would rather cut out his own liver than reveal his sources for counterfeiting. His reticence does indicate something, though, I think."

"So, you think Thaddeus was right. They're counterfeiters." She didn't bother to feign surprise. Somehow, she had a feeling Thaddeus was rarely incorrect about anything.

Atlas eyed her skeptically. "So, the Peeler is *Thaddeus* now."

"Oh, don't you start that again," she chided him, rolling her eyes.

"Like it or not, I'm going to watch out for you." Atlas shrugged, undeterred by her scolding. "I'll keep digging into your Larkers too."

"Thank you," Poppy said.

From his pocket, he pulled out a gold coin and placed it on the table by the door. "Take this."

"I couldn't possibly," Poppy said. "The groceries and the toy are enough, Atlas. I couldn't accept anything more."

"It's one coin of many, Poppy," Atlas said. "Look, I never had a family growing up. You and Danny and that mad wife of his, you're the closest thing I got to one."

In the past few months, she'd grown to think of Atlas as a brother too.

"I ran into your companion before she scurried off to tea with your neighbor. She said you've been working too much lately. Let me do this for Moira. Put it in her education fund."

"I couldn't..." She looked at the coin too wistfully, for it'd be a great addition to the fund.

"Take the damn blunt," Atlas ordered, his face scrunching up in tyrannical direction.

She understood again why legions of thieves were willing to commit any number of crimes upon his word. He wasn't a man to anger.

Pocketing the coin, Poppy nodded. "Thank you."

"And Poppy?" Atlas turned, halfway out the door. "Be careful, lass. No good can come from our kind mixing with the Peelers."

No good, indeed.

* * *

Sunday was Thaddeus's least favorite day of the week. Marred not by brutal murders, but instead by the constant disapproval of his family, Sunday breakfast consisted largely of the desire to fling himself headfirst into a hole. Being the victim of a gunshot wound or a minor explosion would have been preferable, for they would at least have provided a case to solve—and an excuse to get the hell out of his family's townhouse.

The Knights were nothing if not consistent. Every Sunday after the family returned from church, Thaddeus took his designated seat toward the end of the long, rectangular table, with Joseph's wife, Catherine, on one side and an empty chair on the other. It was a barely veiled reminder by his father of Thaddeus's place in the importance of things, for even those who were not blood relatives of the Knights had more power in the family.

Catherine, Alfred Knight liked to say, at least knew her duty.

Picking at her food delicately, Catherine finally settled on a bite of egg. Her plate was loaded high, though she'd consume a quarter of it and declare that she was too full to eat more. She wasted enough food to feed a family of four on Drury Lane.

"We missed you at church today," Catherine said, with all the sincerity of a thrice-caught purse-cutter intent on escaping a transportation sentence.

"We miss you at church *every* Sunday," his mother corrected.

"I do not believe God is concerned with the manner in which I pay my respects, Mother. He cares solely that I pay them," Thaddeus replied.

"Nathan has been working on the loveliest set of sermons." Martha Knight somehow managed to load this statement with equal amounts of pride in her middle son and disparagement at her youngest.

"Of course, he has," Thaddeus mumbled under his breath. "That is what a rector does."

He stood at the end of the serpentine front mahogany sideboard, cramming sardines with mustard sauce onto his plate that alone would have been considered an ample dinner to a denizen of the rookeries. The sideboard stretched half the width of the dining room, loaded with oatmeal and sweet cream, fried kippers, cold eel pie, beef tongue served with horseradish sauce, and four different types of rolls. He made his way next to the plum pudding, one ear tuned to the drone of his mother.

Martha was born, raised, and would probably die in London, refusing to relinquish her iron grip on the upper-middle-class community. Seated on the right side of her husband, dressed in a violet day gown trimmed in fine white lace, she appeared as ready to receive the King as she was to superintend an onslaught at Tortuga.

"Thaddeus, do you have any news?" Martha asked.

"Thaddy refused my offer of a job," Joseph put in, from his place on the other side of their father.

"And it was such a nice offer," Catherine bemoaned, her thin lips pulled into a sneer. Where her husband was brawny, Catherine was brittle and twiggy. "Joseph worked so hard on getting it for him."

Thaddeus was thankful that with his back turned to his mother, she couldn't see him mouthing a number of choice obscenities he'd learned from the East Smithfield market.

"You did *what?*" Alfred roared.

Thaddeus winced. After twenty-four years of being spoken to in that tone, he should have been used to it, but he wasn't.

"Joseph wanted me to coddle customers of the bank. That's not at all anything I'm trained for, or interested in, for that matter." Thaddeus wished his voice didn't sound so petulant. He was a grown man, damn it, he didn't have to explain himself.

He busied himself with scooping out orange marmalade, depositing it on his sweet roll. One scoop followed by another until there was so much marmalade, he'd get a toothache. But if it kept his back to his family...

"Do sit down," Martha commanded. "The servants will get you the rest of your food. I don't know why you *insist* on serving yourself. It's horrible manners. You'd think I raised you in one of those wretched tenement houses. Coddlesworth?" She turned a pointed glare toward the footman, lingering on the edge of the room and listening with far too much interest in the family squabble.

Thaddeus mouthed a "No, no," at Coddlesworth, whose upper lip turned in the barest hint of a smile. At fifty-two years of age, Coddlesworth had been with the family longer than Thaddeus had been alive.

Coddlesworth was also the only member of the household with a lick of sense.

"Sit," Martha repeated through gritted teeth.

Thaddeus sat.

"Very good," Martha praised, as though he were the family spaniel.

Proceeding to shove half the slice of plum cake into his mouth, Thaddeus earned himself a moment of silence. Speaking with a mouthful of food was high on his mother's list of hated affronts. However, this didn't protect him from his father's diatribe.

Alfred waved his fork in Thaddeus's direction, grilled trout dressed in white butter sauce dancing wildly between the prongs with each word. "Thaddeus, you will take this job, and you will do it well. Enough gadding about with a billystick, thinking you're saving the world. You're not."

Thaddeus met his father's gaze. "You know nothing of what I do."

Damn the tremble in his words. Damn the fact that he still cared what this damn family thought of him. Damn it all.

"You trundle up and down the street in that ill-fitting blue uniform," Martha complained. "Where everyone can *see* you. Your grandfather was the second son of an earl, Thaddeus. You have a *bloodline*. Yet does that ever affect how you act? No. You'd think you came from swine. I cannot possibly understand it. A good education at Eton, and you squander it."

Joseph grinned. "Never fear, Mother, no one you know would ever take the route Thaddy patrols."

"That doesn't make it better," Martha huffed, but she appeared slightly mollified.

Alfred patted his wife's hand. "When he takes the job with Joseph, none of that will matter."

It was with great force of will that Thaddeus didn't scoot his chair back and rush the door. "I'm not taking that job."

"It would please your father and me," Martha reminded him.

"You know how I live to do that," Thaddeus muttered.

His mother ignored him. "At the bank, you could meet a suitable wife, like Joseph did with Catherine."

Catherine preened.

Thaddeus didn't want a *suitable* wife. He wanted to pursue what was going on with Poppy. He wanted to pull her into his arms and kiss her with all the fire that had consumed them the night before.

He'd have to prove to her they were worth fighting for. It felt real to him. More real than anything he'd ever experienced before.

No woman had challenged him the way she did.

But she was Irish, and she worked in a factory. So, he didn't bring her name up to his family, for if they said she wasn't worthy of him, he'd not just spring up from the table, he'd hurl the chair toward the bloated sideboard.

Perhaps not. That would be a rash move, and he was a man who prided himself on his cool reasoning. But this woman made him want to be daring, emotional.

The conversation had gone on without him, as it always did. They'd progressed from the idea of him meeting a woman at the bank to a running evaluation of every debutante in their social circle.

"My friend Justine is still on the shelf," Catherine suggested.

He remembered Justine Balfour, though he couldn't ascertain why she submitted to Catherine's company. Justine was reasonably intelligent. He imagined Justine, with her demure manners and her fresh-faced looks, sitting up for him all night while he was off patrolling. Within a year, she'd hate him for putting her through that stress.

"No," he interrupted.

"No, what?" Martha asked. "No, you shall not have Justine, or no, you shall not have Hestia?"

He blinked. "Who the devil is Hestia?"

"Your language, Thaddeus." Martha glared. "She's quite lovely. The daughter of Lord Hammond."

"No to both of those possibilities, no to allowing you to select a wife for me, no to that job, no to letting you run my life, Mother, no to—"

"That is quite enough." Alfred's growl cut him short. "If you cannot be civil, son, then you may have Coddlesworth see you out."

Thaddeus pushed his chair out from the table, giving a

mournful look to the salmon he had not finished. He snatched up two of the remaining slices of plum cake on his plate, stuffed them in his pockets, and nodded to Coddlesworth. "I know the way out, Father, you needn't make Coddlesworth treat me as though I were a guest and not a member of this bloody family."

"This family," Martha sniffed, "will happily receive you when you can conduct yourself properly."

As Thaddeus strode out of the townhouse, munching on the cake, he knew it'd be a cold day in hell when he acted *properly*.

Chapter Twelve

The first visitor to her cottage that morning had been a pleasant surprise, but the second knock Poppy couldn't properly classify. As she ran to the window, Poppy's stomach twisted with the inexplicable knowledge that somehow, in some way, her life wouldn't be the same once she opened the door. She went to the window, pulling back the curtain to peep outside.

Thaddeus Knight stood outside her door, his fist raised to knock again.

Her breath hitched high in her throat. Devil take the way his shoulders filled out that double-breasted coat. That thewy expanse of chest she'd run her hands down the night before. Blast it all.

A third knock sounded. Louder this time, as if he'd caught the slight movement of the curtain and knew she was home. She held her breath, hand poised on the knob.

The best way to meet any obstacle was head-on.

At that moment, Moira let out a loud cry. "Mama!" She pattered closer to the door.

"Traitor." Poppy shot her daughter a beleaguered look. "Lord help me when you learn more words."

Moira smiled.

Poppy opened the door, standing back so that Thaddeus could enter and then closing the door behind him. He remained in the entranceway with his hat held in his hands.

Every retort she'd been about to fire off about how he shouldn't have come here died when she saw the expression on his face. The smallest of smiles turned up his lips—those blasted beautiful lips that tasted of whisky and lemon—and his dark-brown eyes held cautious optimism.

Like he'd expected her to reject him. He'd risked coming anyhow as if she was so important to him that she was worth it. No one, not even Edward, had looked at her like that before.

And so, she did what every Irishwoman raised in England would have done: she asked him if he wanted some tea.

Relief lit up his face instantly. That slight smile became a full grin, so wide it seemed to stretch from one ear to the other. "I'd like that."

Before Atlas had left, he'd fetched wood for the fire from the coster's cart a street down. He'd stacked the wood against the right corner of the fireplace. Poppy gestured toward it. "If you'd start the fire, I'll ready the kettle. There's a box of lucifers on the mantel."

Briefly, he glanced at the portrait above the fireplace of "Robert Corrigan." Almost as if he was appraising that portrait, evaluating his past competition—when Robert had never existed to begin with.

She sneaked a glance at him as she collected the tin of tea leaves Atlas had brought from the market. His shirt had come untucked from his breeches, edging up his back, revealing the waistline of his breeches. That tantalizing strip of flesh above his buttocks, tempting her with the rounded curves of his bottom.

She remembered the feel of his lips on hers, the smell of his body.

He wasn't for her.

But God, how she wanted him to be.

On the counter, she kept a bucket of water retrieved from the pump at the end of Finch Street. Dipping a cup into the bucket, she poured the water into the kettle. With one hand around the tin of leaves and the other wrapped around the handle of the kettle, Poppy approached the fireplace. He'd worked up the roaring flames and put the grate in front so that Moira would be safe.

That thoughtfulness struck her, more than it should.

She set the kettle in the rack and turned back to face Thaddeus, expecting him to have returned to his earlier place by the door. But he'd taken a seat in the chair next to Moira's blanket. He leaned forward in the seat, his elbows resting on his knees as he watched Moira play with her toy. She'd placed the clothespin doll from him on top of the sheep and was waving both about.

"Quite a fancy sheep." His voice reached Poppy's ears, pitched higher than he usually spoke. The tone she'd always expected her husband to use someday with their children, but one she'd certainly never expected from a Met officer.

"Eep," Moira agreed solemnly, holding the sheep out for Thaddeus. She kept the clothespin doll, reluctant to be parted from it more than a moment.

Thaddeus had already managed to work his way into Moira's life, even if the babe wasn't aware of it. Poppy swallowed down the panic rising within her.

This... This couldn't last. But damned if she didn't want to enjoy it while she could.

He took the sheep from Moira with all the gravity of a man receiving a commendation from the king, holding it in his outstretched palm. "This is a special sheep, you know. Why, last week, I received notice that this particular sheep—" He tapped the sheep on the head with his pinkie finger. "This sheep saved a whole hack of people from a very, very evil highway robber. A most odious wolf."

Poppy stood by the fire, waiting for the water to boil. She wouldn't be convinced this domestic tableau could ever be real.

"One must be careful of wolves." She mimicked Thaddeus's singsong voice for the benefit of Moira when her heart tore another centimeter with every word. "They want to eat the sheep."

"Your mother has heard all of this sheep's exploits," Thaddeus responded. "Outside of the carriage recovery, Mr. Sheep performed a dashing recovery of a lady's cut purse."

Moira nodded, her wide eyes focused entirely on Thaddeus. She'd stopped prattling, soothed by his voice.

Poppy watched them both silently, tears brimming at the edges of her eyes. Was she wrong in keeping the truth from him? Had she misjudged? Moira needed someone constant, someone who could be there when she needed him.

Thaddeus couldn't make that promise. He was a Peeler above all else, and Peelers had short life expectancies in the rookeries, especially when they were as determined to sniff out crime as he was. Inevitably, he'd anger the wrong person and pay with his life. Then what would she tell Moira? It was bad enough to lose one "father."

Swiftly, she rubbed the back of her hand across her eyes. There was no room in her life for Thaddeus, no matter how tempting he was.

She lifted the kettle from the fire, setting it down on the mantel so that she could place the tea leaves into the strainer.

"How did the lady's purse get cut, you ask?" Thaddeus asked. His head was down, focused entirely on the child in front of him. "You see, a thief—often a little child, such as yourself, but a bit older—will slide up behind a lady, and when her attention is on something else, he shall cut the strings of her pocketbook with a sharp tool. He must run off with the purse, as fast his legs can carry him, for he faces criminal charges if he is caught."

Poppy plucked the sheep from Thaddeus's hands, presenting it to Moira. "But people like Mr. Sheep are quite good at their jobs, my girl, and they keep the streets safe."

Rising from the chair, Thaddeus ran his hands down his breeches to smooth out the wrinkles. "I'm surprised to hear you think that now." His tone was gentle, almost tentative as if he expected her to counter him with a diatribe on the evils of Peelers again.

"It is a sheep," she stated. "Sheep don't really patrol the streets, Thaddeus."

But you do, and someday you'll pay the price for it.

He chuckled. "Nor are there wolves that waylay carriages demanding jewels. But some stories have a deeper meaning, don't you think?"

She shrugged as if it wasn't the fate of her own child she worried over, but that of all the random children in London. She was charitable, magnanimous even, caring for those little figments. "Children need stories to believe. That is the most important thing—that they're able to remain innocent throughout their childhood."

If it was the last thing Poppy did, she'd make sure Moira got to keep that innocence as long as possible.

"If I could find some way to help them all, I would," he said earnestly.

She looked up, meeting his intense gaze, and her heart tugged. She felt it deep in her stomach, this ache that wouldn't leave, sapping her of strength.

While she worried about the fate of her own family, he was

concerned with the masses. He carried their problems as though they were his own, and damn it, he'd make things better for them. How could she come between that? Distract him from his fight? These people needed a savior, far more than she needed a lover, a husband.

He didn't belong to her alone, and he never would.

"You will. You are good at your job." So good that he continued to pursue the Larkers, whether or not he had the support of his inspector. So good that she couldn't dismiss the danger that surrounded him as another fable, no matter how much she longed to.

A lopsided smile creased his lips. "You think I'm going to change the world, don't you?"

She rolled her eyes. "I hardly think that. But you do yourself credit by trying."

"Why, I do declare, Poppy Corrigan, I think you've reached a philosophical breakthrough," he joked.

"None of that," she said, echoing her earlier words to Moira. A part of her wanted to return to how she'd originally thought of him: rude, nosy, and false. It had been easier to dismiss him before she'd realized the goodness inside him: every attempt to reach out to people like her, lost in these rookeries, was out of selfless desires.

That made him far more inaccessible to her. He needed to be strong for the people, not a real, breakable man.

"I'm sorry for stopping by unannounced," he said. "But after breakfast with my family, I needed to see someone with sanity."

"Ah," she nodded, as though every day she was considered "sane."

"No matter how often I tell my mother I am fully self-sufficient and able to choose my own mate, my mother has made it her life vow to find me a wife." Thaddeus frowned, until he looked at Moira, padding toward them. "Why, Miss Moira, I do predict you shall be speaking in sentences before June. When you do that, I shall bring you a sweet to celebrate."

June. That was three months from now.

She gulped down all the words she yearned to shout out: that she longed for him to still be here then, that she wanted him, and she hoped it might last a while, even if she knew that was lunacy. Instead, she picked the most concrete of his statements to focus on.

"These women who your mother picks for you, are they all in your social class?" she asked, knowing full well the answer.

Thaddeus tilted his head to the side, considering. "I suppose so, yes."

"I see." She saw far too much: she'd been right when she'd figured his family would never accept her. What was the point in continuing this, in being close to him?

He looked away from Moira, directing his attention to her. "Why do you ask?"

"You are aware that I am *not* your social equal?" What should have been a simple fact became questionable with him, for he had that strange way of viewing people that skewed far more toward equality than the second son of a second son of a bloody earl should have had.

He blinked, surprise flitting across his face before he settled back into a more bland expression. He'd not expected her to be so bold.

"It occurred to me, yes," he said, after a moment's consideration. "But what does it matter, Poppy? I've no use for milksop debutantes. When I tell them what I do, their faces either fall—I'm not respectable enough—or they turn this wretched shade of puce like I've informed them I have seventeen mistresses, and I keep them all shackled together in a tiny harem built out of twigs."

She burst out laughing, for the image struck her as

outlandish, yet undeniably him. "You have such lovely turns of phrase."

He tugged at his neckcloth. "You understand my meaning. I need a strong woman, one who is bold and intelligent."

I need someone who isn't you, she heard, for she couldn't come to grips with his profession. Couldn't shake the image of him dead in a back alley from her mind. Couldn't stop wondering if she was putting her family in danger.

"Thaddeus," she began, intending to tell him this connection between them simply wouldn't do. "I'm afraid—"

No. She paused. That wasn't the right wording at all. What could she possibly say to make him understand? She set Moira back down on the blanket and went to tend to the tea, for at least that gave her time to think.

The tea had steeped. Poppy poured the piping hot liquid into the two mugs, grimacing at the chipped rim of one cup where Moira had knocked it off the table. She kept that cup for herself, pushing the newer one toward Thaddeus.

"The Gentleman Thief was here, wasn't he?" Thaddeus cast a thoughtful glance toward the firewood, the loaf of bread on the counter, and the tin of tea on the mantel. Good tea marked with the maker's name. Better tea than she'd be able to afford on factory wages.

She folded her arms over her chest, careful to keep her expression as blank as his. "When you said you wouldn't investigate my friends, I didn't realize that meant I had to tell you their whereabouts."

"I'm not asking so I can arrest him," Thaddeus clarified. "I made a promise to you, and I keep my promises. Call it more of a professional curiosity. I met him, if you recall, when I helped Daniel."

He frowned, stuffing his hands into the pockets of his waistcoat. "I wish you'd trust that I could help you, Poppy. I don't know what happened to you before to make you think all men are scoundrels, but I assure you, I have your interests in mind."

How could he know my interests when he doesn't really know me? The real me.

She pursed her lips. To him, trust was a natural reaction, bred out of the closeness he thought they shared. He expected it, and in return, he'd give it to her. When he eventually found out she'd lied to him about Robert—dammit, *if* he found out—that'd make her betrayal ten times worse.

"I do believe you'll hold to your promise, but I make it a point not to trust anyone," she said, trying to sound worldly. "You've been down Brick Lane. You know what this place is like. You get off your guard, and suddenly you're dead outside a factory, like Anna."

Thaddeus scrutinized the loaf of bread, the carrots, and the peas she had placed by the kitchen table. When he turned back to her, his lips smashed together tightly. His arms were locked in at his sides, his posture suddenly far more formal than it had been.

"I'm happy Greer is taking care of you," he said, a strained note in his voice she couldn't quite identify. "I, ah, didn't realize exactly how *close* you two were."

As she went toward her daughter, she regarded him out of the corner of her eye warily. "He's my brother's dearest friend. Why does it matter?"

Kneeling next to Moira, Poppy gathered the girl into her arms, kissing the top of her head. The babe struggled against her hold, frantically reaching for the doll. Poppy plucked the doll from the blanket with her free hand, giving it to Moira. Pleased, Moira leaned her head against her mother's shoulder, now content to observe Thaddeus from this new vantage point.

Thaddeus looked up from his study of the groceries, his eyes fastening on Moira. "It is quite natural to want companionship." His voice sounded gargled. "I should have accounted for this."

"What are you nattering on about?" She scowled. "You keep asking me all these questions, and I don't like it. I told you before, my past is my past. I don't want to talk about it."

He blinked. "I'm talking about your relationship with Atlas Greer, of course. I shouldn't have kissed you last night. I should've known you were involved with him when you bargained for his safety."

If she told Thaddeus that Atlas courted her, Thaddeus would insist they kept their partnership strictly professional. That'd be the end to these troublesome—but so wonderful—kisses.

Yet she couldn't bring herself to lie to him again. Not about this.

She shifted Moira in her arms so that she could look him dead in the eye. "The *relationship* I have with Atlas is fraternal, I assure you."

Thaddeus exhaled loudly, his cheeks pinking. "I'm relieved. And, ah, embarrassed."

"I'm perfectly capable of fighting my own battles." Her tone was flat, her words holding enough punch on their own. "If I had been courting Atlas, don't you think I would have told you? I wouldn't have let you kiss me. Not that I should have kissed you, and actually, I'm glad you are here so we can discuss that—"

Growing irritated by her mother's curt tone, Moira latched onto a loose curl, twisting the red hair between her fingers and giving a pull. "Ow!" Poppy exclaimed, prying her hair from Moira's hands and tucking the lock back behind her ear.

A smile tickled the corners of Thaddeus's lips. The ninny was trying not to laugh.

She narrowed her eyes. "Also, I don't need anyone to 'take

care' of me, do you understand? I thought I'd made that plenty clear. I'll help you with your investigation, but this, I can't do."

He opened his mouth to speak. She braced herself for another eloquently worded plea, for everything he said seemed to be eloquent, the product of many years spent reading dusty textbooks. She should be intimidated by that, for her knowledge was far more practical than academic.

Should be—but instead, she wanted to lean into him, to catch every word that fell from his lips as though it was gospel.

He was a good man, and he couldn't possibly survive in her world.

Moira snatched at her hair again, her face scrunching up in annoyance when Poppy ducked away in time. Letting out a fierce cry, she balled her fists up. Her lower lip stuck out sullenly.

Out of the corner of her eye, Poppy saw Thaddeus wince at the shrill shriek, but he was otherwise unruffled. "Time for a rest?" he inquired.

"I should think so," Poppy agreed. "I'll go put her down for a nap."

She crossed the short distance of the main room to her bedroom. Thaddeus waited by the fire, his gaze following her. As she opened the door, her stomach tensed with something akin to disappointment. No, that couldn't be it; she couldn't have wanted him to follow her in. What did she think? That he would toss her to the bed and ravish her with her child's crib in the corner of the room? She was a mother now.

Wantonness should be far behind her.

Poppy set Moira down in the crib, tucking the blanket in around her. She ran a hand through the babe's short, fuzzy red locks, so soft against her fingertips. "My sweet little one," she murmured. "You know that I love you, don't you? That I would do anything to protect you?"

Moira shifted in the crib, her eyes half-closed. She yawned, balling her fingers up in the blanket.

"That's why this can't be," Poppy continued. "I made you a promise that you'd know stability. That you wouldn't be in danger."

"Mama," Moira protested, reaching out for Poppy.

"I'm here." Poppy kissed the tips of her forefinger and index finger, pressing them to Moira's brow. "I'll always be here."

Moira continued to watch her. Poppy stood there for a moment longer. Protected by the sides of the wooden crib, Moira was safe.

Someday she'd grow up, and she'd start to ask questions about her father.

Poppy swallowed down her dread. She'd cross that bridge when she had to, and not before. There were enough problems to sort out currently... Starting with the devilishly handsome Metropolitan Police sergeant lingering outside the door to the room.

Shutting the door behind her, Poppy came out into the living room. Moira fussed at her absence, but in a few moments, she'd fall asleep. She always did.

Poppy rubbed her hands against her arms, up and down, trying to bide the chill that had settled low into her spine. Someday, this would all be for naught, and she'd be standing in the middle of a room like this one wondering where she'd gone so wrong.

It was unavoidable, as unavoidable as this confrontation with Thaddeus had become. From that first moment in the alley to her visit at his townhouse and then that damnably perfect kiss. They'd been set in motion by forces outside of her control, but the outcome—breaking away from him—was the only thing she could imagine.

"She's asleep." Poppy kept her voice down to not wake Moira.

Thaddeus nodded.

"Maybe you should go," Poppy suggested, with no real feeling. She didn't want him to leave. Didn't want to give up on him. For the first time in two years, she felt appreciated.

"I haven't had my tea yet," Thaddeus said with a frown.

She sucked in a breath, her resistance fading further. Why did her head always feel so muddled around him? She couldn't launch a concrete attack when he was this near to her.

"Take your tea," she sighed.

His brows furrowed with concern. "Poppy, if you truly want me to go, I'll go. I don't need tea. I don't want to be an imposition."

"You're not imposing." For once, she told the truth. Having him around was a highlight in her day, no matter how little any of it made sense.

"Then why do you want me to leave?"

No matter how hard Poppy tried to push Thaddeus away, he stayed. A little tendril of doubt formed inside her—would he stay even if he knew her secret? "I have always found Claudio an absolute buffoon," he'd said.

So, there was a chance he'd stay through that too. He'd marry her and raise Moira as his own because he'd feel that was his obligation. And he'd give up his job; sell off that part of him. Each day would dawn, and he'd lose a little bit more of himself in their union. Until eventually, he'd hate her and everything about their love.

She wasn't sure what a worse fate was: his death or him detesting his own life. Either way, she had nothing more than destruction to offer him.

Sucking in a deep breath, Poppy glanced at the clock above the mantel. "It's not that I want you to leave, but my companion will be back soon. She went to collect the washing from the rest of the neighborhood."

He rose, going to the kitchen to add sugar into his tea from the canister on the counter. He dropped in four lumps. Confound him. He didn't know how scarce sugar was, how expensive it'd be to replace, because he'd never had to fight for food in his life.

She didn't follow him into the kitchen. Rather, she hung back by the fireplace, foolhardily believing that if she put some distance between them, she'd feel at rights again. Sipping at her unsweetened tea, the warmth flooded her throat. Strong, bitter, resilient, a tea that would give her strength. A tea that would keep her steady in resolve.

"You're concerned about how it'd look for me to be here with you alone." Thaddeus mulled over the idea, tapping his chin with his forefinger. "You know, that's the first time anyone's said that to me since I joined the Met. When I'm interviewing people, in my blues, no one considers me a man, really. I'm an instrument of the law."

Poppy bit her bottom lip to stem the tide of words threatening to burst forth and proclaim that she couldn't see him as anything *but* a man. An attractive, virile man who in one week had sunk so deep into her soul she didn't know how to extricate him. *You haunt my dreams,* she wanted to whisper. *You're everything that I've ever wanted, but nothing I should have.*

So, she didn't look at him, staring instead inside the mug of tea, as though the murky brown liquid was truly fascinating, more than him baring his heart to her.

It was no use. She saw him there, too, his chin with the endearing cleft, his solid arms, those hard calves encased in breeches that made her want to reach behind him and cup his arse.

"I don't imagine that's true. Surely they can look past the

uniform." Her voice gave her away, lower, huskier. The voice of a woman aroused and too sinful to be shamed by it.

He came closer to her, not stopping until he was leaning over her shoulder. "No one has but you." His voice was low, stripped raw, doing things to her core that were certainly heathen.

This was madness.

"I—" She started, hoping that the proper words would come to her, and finding none.

His hands fell to her waist, spinning her around to face him. In a second, his lips were on hers in a kiss that challenged all her preconceptions. A kiss that claimed her entirely as his, no matter how she might protest. She'd been his from that first damn meeting in the alley.

Always his.

His lips on hers, shattering her, for he was everywhere at once. Her hands tangled in his hair, tugging his head closer to her to deepen their kiss. His hand slipped down to her chest, palming the underside of her breast. She squirmed against him, scooting so close to him she'd have been joined to him if she were any nearer. The muslin of her gown, so worn she usually had to wear a pelisse over it for warmth, was now too heavy. Too constraining. She wanted to be free.

His hand slid down to her breasts, cupping one in his palm. Arching her back, she let out a little murmur of approval. She thought not of propriety, but of the sheer bliss of him touching her. Of him.

With a growl, Thaddeus brought his mouth down to that stretch of bare skin before her bodice began. When she'd originally bought this dress in the rag and bone shop, she'd thought it too scandalous—but the price was good, and she needed another dress. Now she praised the dressmaker to the high heavens, for his lips covered her skin, leaving heat wherever he'd kissed. An all-consuming heat, a heat that'd take away her pain, leaving only this memory.

He'd managed to scoot her bodice down a bit more. The fabric gave easily, allowing him access, for even her dress wanted him. His thumb and forefinger worked at her neckline, edging it down until the top of her breast showed. He ran his thumb against her chemise, stroking just roughly enough on her already sensitive skin. And she longed for more, wanted him to undress her in the middle of her damned cottage when Edna could walk in at any moment.

Growing frustrated with her bodice, he moved back upwards again. He laid scorching kisses to her neck, sucking on that delicate space under her ears. She moaned, moaned because everything felt so perfect. So perfect, so wonderful. How could she be so wicked? Oh, she didn't care.

Thaddeus traveled up still, brought his lips back to hers. And she was an equal fire to his inferno, kissing him back with all the passion she possessed. Biting at her lip, he took it between his teeth. He nipped, grazing clumsily.

The sudden stab of pain lasted a second, but it was long enough to pull her forth from this euphoria.

"Sorry." He was quick to apologize, embarrassed by his slip. "It sounded like such a good idea in this pamphlet I read..."

Nothing about kissing him was a good idea.

Yet she couldn't help but giggle at the absurdity of him sitting at home in his great library, surrounded by classics, combing over the pages of a tattered pornographic pamphlet.

"Really," she drawled, the laughter bubbling up in her throat.

He caught her eye, his abashment fading as her chuckles grew more effusive. She loved this side of him, for it made him less intimidating. The sergeant she knew, intent on solving a crime, had a mind so clever it made her chary. But the boy in front of her, shoulders shaking with laughter because he wasn't as practiced a seduction artist as he'd wanted to be, was endearing.

And even more dangerous, because that twenty-four-year-old lanky lad she could fall deeply in love with.

Perhaps she'd already fallen for him.

She raised a hand to her lip, touched where a drop of blood had formed.

That was enough to remind her that this was all madness. She readjusted her bodice, tugging it higher. His kisses had left marks upon her skin; she was forever branded.

"Thaddeus, no, I can't," she murmured, wishing it could be anything different. That she could give herself to him. That she'd met him in other circumstances when their whole relationship wouldn't be based on lies.

He carded a hand through his hair, his eyes wide at her refusal. "I'm sorry, Poppy. I didn't mean to startle you. It's just after we kissed, I thought..."

"You didn't startle me." She shook her head, cutting him off. "It's not that I don't *want* to, but it's too soon. All of this. I promised myself after Robert that I'd move slowly."

"Of course." He smacked his forehead with his hand. "Can you believe I forgot about your husband? I'm the worst of rogues, Poppy. Please forgive me—of course, I understand that you'd want to move at a certain pace. You've got Moira to consider as well."

She'd chosen the right lie. "Thank you for understanding."

"Thank you for trusting me enough to tell me how you really feel." He smiled, a radiant smile that sliced through her reserves. His smile could set the whole world on fire, and here she was, playing him for a fool.

"Of course." She echoed him, for she had nothing left that was original. Nothing that was truly hers.

Each lie dug her in deeper, made it harder to catch her breath. A silver blade to her heart, stabbed in repeatedly, until the last shards of her identity were bloodied with falsehoods.

"I promise I'll take it slow." He spoke with the raw earnestness of a man experiencing the blooms of first love.

His eyes lit up with the hope that they were building something together. A hope she'd have to crush brutally.

Someday.

Not today.

Today, she couldn't bear to break him down. She smiled, and she said she'd meet him the next day, and she prayed to God for a rain that would wipe away her sins and the danger surrounding him.

Chapter Thirteen

Four days later, fatigue laced through Poppy's bones, so constant that she'd almost forgotten what it was like to be wide-awake. She leaned against the back bar of the loom, her feet bruised from hours of constantly tapping on the wooden plank to move the shuttle. Her left arm ached from pulling the lever that would determine when the thread passed from one side of the loom to the other.

Practice and rhythm.

Aunt Molly had drilled this into her when she'd learned to use the old handloom on the farm. While the automated loom sped up the production of woven silk, it still required her focus.

One and two, one and two, until her mind bled with the repetition. Poppy tugged on the lever of the loom again, but she imagined the lever was not a wire attached to a wooden baton, but instead, Thaddeus's hand clasped around her own, strengthening her through the rough patches. He'd been the highlight of her past few days, coming by every night after she got home from work. He'd brought supper for her, Edna, and Moira. Edna left after dinner to visit with the neighbors, but Thaddeus stayed. He'd curl up on the blanket, his long limbs folded underneath him, reminding her of a gangly colt.

Moira had taken to him. "Tad," she called him, the name usually followed by her reaching out for his coat. Last night, Thaddeus had delivered a rousing reenactment of Little Red Riding Hood using Poppy's cloak and the stuffed sheep. Moira had laughed and laughed until she eventually dozed off, burrowed against Thaddeus's hip.

It had been a perfect night.

So perfect that Poppy couldn't help but wonder when it was all going to disappear. She didn't deserve Thaddeus. He was sweet and caring. In the end, she'd only break his heart.

But selfishly, Poppy clung to these rare moments of bliss.

Those memories were all she'd have when it ended.

It was half past eight when the bell finally rang. In a giant wave, the weavers descended upon the front door, jostling for purchase. Poppy waited by her loom, not willing to risk being stepped on in the fray. Positioned on either side of the exit, Clowes and Jennings pulled open the heavy wooden doors.

Abigail and Bess stood by her side as the workers filtered out into the street.

Protocol dictated that both guards would remain outside by the doors until every weaver had left the building. She evaluated Clowes, lips pursed.

"He's not a bad man," she'd said to Thaddeus.

Tonight, as Clowes propped open his side of the door and went toward Jennings, she started to reconsider that statement. Had Clowes been complicit in Anna's murder? She didn't want to think that the stocky youth could have been capable of such evil—but then, she'd been wrong before, taken in by a pair of arresting eyes and a sweet voice.

Poppy pulled Abigail and Bess back, sheltering them behind her loom.

Clowes leaned forward, muttering something to Jennings. The older guard faced their little party, and his eyebrows immediately shot up in response to Clowes's statement. Clowes continued to speak, causing Jennings to frown. But Jennings moved back from the door.

Clowes strode toward them, giving no indication that he saw them hunched back against Poppy's loom. The loom itself almost reached the ceiling, with the reams of punch cards looped together and held on another landing attached to the top of the loom.

Poppy knelt, and Abigail and Bess followed her motion. Abigail's hand slid over Bess's mouth so she wouldn't question them. Abigail tilted her head to the side in inquiry, but Poppy simply held up her finger to her lips.

Something wasn't right.

Her ears hummed, the sound of the looms still echoing despite the veritable silence over the room. Her muscles burned, taut and ready for something she couldn't quite describe. All she knew was that Clowes hadn't followed the routine. She peeked out from behind the loom. Clowes passed by the office, motioning to someone inside. A few seconds later, Boz came out of the office. He took up the lead, Clowes following behind him as a puppy does his master.

They were heading toward the back room.

"What's going on?" Abigail murmured, concern shadowing her usually vibrant blue eyes.

"I don't know," Poppy whispered back.

"I want to go home," Bess whined.

"We will, sweetie," Abigail murmured. "Can you be quiet for a minute longer?"

Bess pouted, flopping down on the floor. From the pocket of her apron, Abigail pulled out a long string of yarn. She tied the ends together, slipping it over her hand. She moved her right middle finger to the left, picking up the left palm string, and vice versa. With the design fully formed, Abigail held out her hands to Bess.

Abigail turned her head to Poppy. "It's getting late. We shouldn't be here after the factory's closed."

"A minute more." Poppy laid her hand on Abigail's shoulder in a grip meant to both comfort and hold her in place.

The office door opened once more, and out came Effie Larker. Imperiously, she scanned the well-lit floor, and Poppy's breath died in her throat.

As Effie turned their way, Jennings closed the doors to the factory and went toward her.

"You're late," Effie huffed. "Do you think we pay you for dawdling? Where's Clowes?"

Jennings stiffened, his weathered face coloring. "Clowes's already inside with Boz."

"Very good." Effie sniffed. "That one, he's clever. Enterprising."

"What about the Moseley girl? That wasn't clever." Jennings's eyes darted from one side of the factory to the other. He fisted his hands, arms hanging down at his sides.

Poppy could almost feel the anxiety flowing off of him as he followed Effie toward the back room.

Effie spun around, her royal-blue skirt fluffing out around her as she moved. "The girl," she said through gritted teeth. "The girl is dead. Boz saw to that."

Abigail gasped.

Effie stepped back from Jennings. "What was that?"

Poppy shook her head frantically, praying Effie would forget the noise.

"I didn't—didn't hear nothing," Jennings stammered.

Effie's eyes narrowed. "These old buildings. Disgusting. I long for the time when we're free of these ridiculous covers."

"Won't be long now, ma'am," Jennings consoled her.

Effie drew herself up to her full height. "No, I suppose not. With men like Clowes, we'll be fine. He takes care of problems."

"Yes, ma'am," Jennings agreed.

Boz emerged from the back room, scratching at his thick beard. "Are you coming, wench?"

Effie's spine stiffened, her posture rigid at Boz's voice. "It'd serve you right to wait, you old rotter," she yelled back, yet she started after him.

"Should've left you in that damn brothel," Boz retorted. "Miserable shrew."

"I'm only miserable because you make me so." Effie's voice drifted back toward them as she went into the back room.

Jennings was hot on her heels. He did one last sweep of the room before closing the door behind him.

"Confound it," Abigail murmured under her breath. "Boz killed Anna, didn't he?"

Boz saw to that. A shudder shook Poppy's body, tore at the very depths of her. Everything Thaddeus had suspected was correct.

She had to find Thaddeus to tell him what she'd heard.

Bess scrambled up from behind the loom. "Someone killed Anna?"

"No, of course not," Poppy whispered.

"But I heard them talk," Bess protested. "I *heard* them, Abbie."

Abigail shifted on the floor, reaching out to bring Bess back down to a sitting position with her. "Do you remember how I told you there are certain things you mustn't ask about?"

Bess gave her an arch look. "I remember everything."

"This is one of those things," Abigail said quietly. "I need to talk with Poppy, understand?" Bess opened her mouth to object, and Abigail held up a hand. "Someday, when you're older, you can tell me there are things I can't hear either."

"But I'm hungry," Bess objected.

Poppy hunted in her pockets, finally finding the penny pie she'd meant to bring home to Edna. The coster's cart had been outside the factory as she entered after lunch. "You may have this if you sit here by the loom while your sister and I talk. Can you do that?"

Bess nodded, a frown etched into her wan cheeks.

Poppy dropped her voice low so that Bess couldn't hear her. "I'm helping to investigate Anna's murder. The Peelers suspect that Boz Larker was involved."

Abigail exhaled, the breath shaking her thin frame. "God's balls, Poppy, do you know what you're doing? This place, if you're not careful, it'll eat you alive."

"If Anna died because of the Larkers, we owe it to her family to make sure they pay," Poppy said. "Would you stand watch for me? I want to get into Larker's office. If you hear or see anything, whisper."

Abigail opened her mouth to protest, and then shut it. "For Anna. But only this once, do you hear me?"

Before Abigail could change her mind, Poppy scooted out from the loom. She edged toward the office and the possibility of this all ending. Once she found enough information to prove the Larkers were guilty, Thaddeus could take the case to his supervisors.

And after that, she'd never see him again.

* * *

Boz Larker's office appeared significantly less intimidating without him present. One floor-to-ceiling cabinet was pushed up against the far wall, while a beat-up desk with deep scratches in the wood was positioned in the middle of the room. Pulled up to the desk were two rickety chairs lined in brash mustard yellow.

Poppy had sat in those chairs when she'd first applied for work. Three days fresh from Surrey, she'd been delighted to find a factory that was outfitted with the newer Jacquard looms, considered somewhat of a fable in the shops in Dorking. London would be different. Everything would line up so that in two years, she'd have enough money for Moira's future schooling.

She should have known better.

Stepping over the threshold, Poppy carefully closed the door to the office behind her so that the noise wouldn't travel. There were no windows in Larker's office; she was safe, as long as no one came by and wondered why the door was shut. The lack of windows also meant she was separated from the twilight that lit the factory's main floor. A lantern burned on the wall behind Larker's desk. The light flickered, stuttering as the wick smoked.

The light wouldn't last more than a few minutes.

In the dark, she fumbled in her apron pocket for her tinder box and pulled it out. Three matches remained. Striking a lucifer, she held the match out. Her nose wrinkled at the near-suffocating stench of sulfur. Stomach churning, she sucked in a breath, a hard-won inhale that was as shaky as her hands. Boz had killed Anna. If Poppy was found, he wouldn't hesitate to dispose of her in the same way.

What would Thaddeus do?

He'd check the cabinet first.

Poppy nodded. She could do that—the cabinet had four drawers of equal depth and width. She held the lucifer up, grasping the bottom between her thumb and forefinger. The first drawer contained invoices for new silk, while the second

186

housed the purchase orders for the woven fabric. She opened the second drawer. The files weren't labeled; rather, the papers were haphazardly thrown into the drawers. She rifled through the papers with the hand not holding the match, checking for anything that looked like an overall report of the year's accounts.

"Got it!" she whispered, tugging on a page in the third stack from the bottom. The paper didn't budge. She readjusted her hold on it and gave another tug. The foolscap slid out, leaving the stack more lopsided but otherwise intact. She tugged out a listing of payroll and a report on suppliers from the stack beneath.

"Are you almost done?" Abigail's hiss made Poppy start.

The flames lapped at the tip of Poppy's fingers. She blew on the match frantically, her fingers singed.

"Shit," Poppy hissed. She'd almost dropped the match on the pile of papers. Setting the paper on top of the cabinet, she looked toward the door. "Is anyone coming? I need a few more minutes."

"No one yet, but do hurry."

Poppy didn't need to see Abigail to know she was wringing her hands as she crouched behind the nearest loom.

One more match.

The third drawer was marked "Weaver Records." Careful to keep the match away from the drawer, Poppy tugged it open with one hand. This drawer was the antithesis of the others: tidily marked folders slotted into the drawer, some stuffed thick and others with a lone sheet of parchment. Poppy squinted, holding the match closer.

There was a file for every employee that had passed through the Larker factory. Including her.

Bloody, bloody hell.

She flipped through the c's until she got to Corrigan. "Poppy Corrigan," the top sheet read. "Irish immigrant from

Surrey. War widow with a daughter. Past weaving history." Poppy's breaths became more regular. Nothing of concern so far.

Her heart slammed against her chest at the next sheet. "Robert Corrigan—no record of him in Dorking? Real? Daughter possibly a by-blow." And in big letters, underlined, "leverage."

She couldn't breathe. Black spots appeared before her eyes. *No, no, no!* She'd been so sure they suspected nothing.

Snatching up the paper, she deposited it on top of the other reports. The second match was about to burn out. Grabbing the stack of reports and the sheet about Robert, she blew out the lucifer and made her way in the almost darkness to the door. "Is it clear?"

"Come quickly," Abigail bid her.

She looked back at the lantern, the last sputters of light frantic.

Now or never.

Poppy gave the door a pull and slipped out onto the main floor. The sun had dipped down, leaving the factory cloaked in the gray of a new night. She nodded at Abigail, and they made their way toward the door, ducking behind the nearest loom when the door to the back opened.

The Larkers and the guards came out of Boz's office. Effie stood at the entrance to the door, and in the dim light, Poppy couldn't clearly make out her expression. But her body remained alert, spine stiff and chin high. Effie advanced toward the middle of the floor, surveying her domain.

"You're mad, bitch," Boz barked. "Ain't no one here."

"I thought I smelled something," Effie said. "Something like sulfur."

"The lantern burnin' out," Boz replied. "Think I left it lit."

"Shall we?" Clowes came forward, holding his arm out for

Effie to take. The sight of him, his boyish face splashed with pride at escorting her, made Poppy's stomach wrench. The blackguard.

Everything was silent, still for what seemed like hours as Effie remained fixed to that point in the center of the room.

Finally, Effie sighed and accepted Clowes's arm. Poppy let out the breath she'd been holding as the group went into Boz's office and shut the door.

"Run," Poppy cautioned Abigail and Bess.

She didn't need to tell them twice. They took off at a gallop. Abigail's flight was hampered by her knock knees, her pace an awkward drag-run-drag. In a minute, they were at the door.

Abigail was the last to leave.

Her breath coming out in ragged pants, Abigail leaned back against the doors, hand slapped to her stomach.

"Never, never again, do you hear me?" Abigail gasped. "This is insanity, Poppy. I'm not helping you anymore."

Papers clutched in her hands, her hat hanging on by the string around her throat, her fingers burnt and her dress reeking of rotten eggs, Poppy was certain she was far beyond anyone's help.

Chapter Fourteen

The sun had long ago set by the time Poppy made it to Thaddeus's townhouse. Night cloaked the debris-strewn streets, blackness twisting in between the alleys as if her soul had projected outward. She walked the now-familiar path to his residence without a lantern, the risk of being seen by the Larkers more terrifying than being set upon in the dark.

They'd been watching her.

That thought came to her with every step, battering her carefully constructed walls. None of this was supposed to happen. She'd researched for a week to make sure that the time-line of her faux marriage and her husband's subsequent death lined up perfectly with battles the Navy had fought in the Portuguese war for independence.

On the surface, it should have been enough—and no one should have wanted to look closer, no one but Thaddeus and his damnably inquisitive mind. All this time she had spent trying to keep him from finding out her secret, when she should have been worried about the Larkers knowing.

Everything she had worked for was crumbling down around her, and she couldn't stop it.

Poppy turned onto Thaddeus's street, the reports from Boz's office clenched tight in her fist. All except for that one page of her employee file folded and tucked securely into her apron.

Leverage.

She ran up to his townhouse. Again and again, her fist pounded his door, but there was no answer.

"Thaddeus, please!" She grew more desperate with every hit to the door. "Please, please, please answer the door."

Where could he be at this hour? Unbidden, the image of him at a tavern with another woman rose in her mind. The knot in her gut pulled tighter until she could barely breathe. She leaned her forehead against the cool wood, giving one last smack to the door.

"You belong with us," the nuns had said when they visited Uncle Liam's farm. "You've been a sinful harlot, but God will forgive you if you let us help you."

She'd failed.

The door opened. She fell forward, almost colliding with a sturdy chest clad in a white linen shirt. Thaddeus steadied her, his hands on her shoulders to keep her from sliding downward.

"Poppy."

She fought the urge to collapse in his arms, for his baritone voice expressed in that one word everything she was feeling. Worry, surprise, shock...and that stupidly eager part of her that had insisted on fleeing to him, certain he could fix all her problems, even if she couldn't tell him what was truly going on.

He ushered her inside, shutting the door behind them. "I didn't expect you."

She thrust the papers at him.

He glanced down at them, nibbling at his bottom lip as he

puzzled out the meaning. "So, I was right about the financials," he muttered, more to himself than her.

"They did it." The words spilled out of her lips. "Boz Larker killed Anna."

Thaddeus's hand lingered too long on her shoulder as he showed her into the library, warming her frigid flesh.

"You're certain?" His voice held a note of eagerness he couldn't hide. For him, this was merely another case. Solving it meant another tick on his record. An award at work.

If she hadn't already felt the splintering of her heart, that alone would have done it.

For, in the end, she was purely part of another case.

"What did you find?" Thaddeus prompted.

She ran her hands up and down her arms, hugging herself. Anything to get her blood flowing. "I heard Effie Larker say to one of the guards, Jennings, that Boz 'took care' of Anna."

He stepped closer to her until they stood within a hairs-breadth of each other. The makings of a triumphant smile tugged at his lips, those same lips that had pressed against hers so fervently. A conspiratorial expression, like they shared a secret and that drew them closer.

But Poppy knew that all secrets came with a price.

"He confessed to it?"

"Yes."

"A confession to Whiting would have been preferable, of course," Thaddeus said. "A real confession not bought and paid for like Raymond McPhee's. But we'll make do."

"That guard I told you about, Clowes? The one Anna liked? He was in it on, I'm almost positive." Poppy remembered Clowes's slick grin and had to hold her hand to her mouth for a second to keep from vomiting. "And the sick thing about it? Effie praised him for his initiative. He helped kill Anna, so he'd look good in front of his bosses. That's all she was to him, an *opportunity*."

"Poppy," Thaddeus broached. The tone one used to stall a cannon about to fire.

"Don't you dare," she hissed. "Don't you dare tell me to be calm."

The sympathy that shined in his eyes was almost unbearable. "It's hard, Poppy."

She rocked back on her feet, with her hands clasped so tight around her arms that her fingerprints would be there the next day. Even the books around them couldn't soothe her. "This isn't right, Thaddeus. There's nothing about this that's right. This was a girl I knew, a girl I was friends with. A fourteen-year-old girl who was cheerful and believed she could be something beyond this place!"

He stepped forward. "I know, Poppy, I know." He brought his arms up around her shoulders, and suddenly she was flush against him. Wrapped up in him, his heartbeat in her ears.

In his arms, she'd allow herself to believe that there could be peace. That it didn't matter if the department he worked for was the enemy of her friends, that his family would never approve of her, that someday he'd be shot down and left to bleed out in the streets because he had the audacity to try and help people.

None of that mattered.

She leaned into him more. Smashed her cheek up against his shirt, the buttons of his waistcoat jamming into the bodice of her dress. She tasted saltwater on her face, and she realized she was crying. The tears streamed down her face, wetting his clothing, but he didn't flinch. Didn't break contact between them because, somehow, he knew that this was the most important thing to her.

He was the real reason she was still standing.

"The first one is always the worst," he murmured.

She knew he meant the first murder. But she couldn't help but think that phrase applied to so many other things: the first love, the first broken heart, the first loss of dreams, the first realization that she'd never be whole again.

"What will you do now, Thaddeus?"

"I'll go to my superiors with the information. But most importantly, I'll keep you and Moira safe," he vowed.

That he thought of Moira in a time like this meant the world to her. He understood that to be with her meant taking Moira into his life too.

With one strong, large hand, he stroked her hair. "I wish I could say that it gets easier with time." His fingers continued to comb through her hair, massaging her scalp. "But that'd be a lie, Poppy, and I promise I won't lie to you."

And with those words, he tore away that facade of comfort.

I've lied to you. I lie to you every day.

He laid a kiss against the top of her head. His lips were so gentle, when before he'd been rougher, sensing that she'd wanted it hard and passionate. In the frenzy of the prior kiss, she'd not had time to think. With this tender whisper of his lips, she thought too much.

She could tell Thaddeus the truth now. Trust that he wouldn't tell anyone, that he'd put Moira first. She wanted to believe that she was right about him. But it wasn't just her life at stake. She'd been wrong about Edward. Her judgment wasn't reliable. She couldn't risk Moira's chances because she felt something for Thaddeus.

Poppy went stiff against him, rotten wood to his soft, pliable silk. He clung to her, his hands on her forearms, and she stood there dumbly. Aware of his touch but unable to respond.

She pulled back from his arms. The loss of his warmth beat through her, her body going cold again.

Running her hand underneath her eyes to wipe away the

tears, she pulled in a slow, agonizing breath. Immediately, he reached into his pocket for a wipe, handing it to her. Gratefully, she took it, dabbing at her eyes.

He took her arm, leading her to the settee in the middle of the room. Waiting until she'd taken a seat, he plopped down next to her, his lanky legs sprawled out in front of him. Her feet dangled off the high settee. With the wipe wadded up in her hands and the damning foolscap in her apron pocket, she didn't know how to proceed.

"I'm sure I must look a fright," she said.

He gave her an encouraging smile. "Nonsense. You're beautiful, as always."

She didn't *feel* beautiful. She felt wrecked. "You're sweet to say so, but I think that classifies as one of the lies you said you'd never tell me."

His smile widened. "People have imperfections. It's what makes us who we are. I believe we're better off for those rough pieces that don't seem to go together, for wouldn't life be truly dull if we were all exactly alike? There'd be no pleasure in solving the mystery."

"And there's nothing else you like better than putting together the pieces of a puzzle." Weariness tinged her voice.

He began to say something but stopped mid-opening of his mouth. For a second, he appeared lost in thought. "Last week, if you'd told me that, I would have agreed. Now, I find myself wanting something else from this case."

His gaze burned. Her skin heated with it as if he'd left an imprint on her heart. He couldn't mean her—he couldn't. And more so, she shouldn't *want* him to mean her.

"But enough about me." He rubbed at his neck, his smile fading.

"I like to speak about you." She found herself falling back

onto honesty because he seemed embarrassed that he'd bared his deepest desires to her, and she'd said nothing in return.

"I'm alive," he stated frankly. "Anna Moseley is not, and that is a grave injustice." From the table in front of them, he grabbed the reports she had pulled from Boz Larker's office. "Tell me about these."

"I'm not quite sure," she confessed. "There was a meeting after factory hours. Between Boz, Effie, and the two guards—maybe more people, but that's all I saw and all that came back out onto the floor after they'd finished conversing. My friend, Abigail, stood watch as I searched Larker's office."

"What the devil?" The hardness to Thaddeus's voice snapped her eyes back up at him.

She retreated back against the settee, frowning at him. "You wanted me to get information."

His voice softened, but worry still creased his forehead. "I told you to *observe*, Poppy. Not to endanger yourself. If they'd found you, you could have been badly hurt. No information is worth your life."

She slipped her hand in her apron pocket, fingers closing around her employment record. Oh God, she'd risked death, put Abigail and Bess in jeopardy, all to get some damn papers.

It wasn't worth it.

Thaddeus's keen glance was on her, watching her hand. "Are you quite sure no one saw you?"

She slid her fingers out from her apron pocket, smoothing her skirt. "We didn't leave until the Larkers had gone back into their office. I really don't think they saw us."

"That's good then," Thaddeus agreed. "But I don't want you to put yourself in danger again. You can continue to keep watch, but please don't take such an active role."

She bristled. He didn't have to scold her. "You needn't tell me again."

Abashed, he hazarded a smile at her. "I don't mean to lecture you. It's hard once you get into the crux of a mystery. With the flush of possible discovery coursing through you, everything else disappears. I understand why you did it. I just get concerned." He reached for her hand, squeezing it.

She didn't pull back. Rather, she returned his gentle pressure, smiling at him. "I appreciate your concern."

And she did, more than she should. When she was with him, she felt protected, as though he was watching over her.

She released his hand. Pretended that she hadn't been affected by the touch. Her judgment had become hazy around him, and she couldn't have that.

Thaddeus looked over the reports once more. "I'll need time to look over these papers in detail, of course, but I'm hopeful this will be enough to present to Whiting."

Lifting her chin, she held his gaze steadily. She ought to go back to their original arrangement before that kiss had sent everything into a tailspin. "In return, you'll protect my friends. I've delivered you evidence."

The right corner of his bottom lip twitched. He didn't say anything for a minute, but the force of his gaze upon her grew hotter as the time ticked by. "I had hoped you'd continue to work with me until the Larkers are caught. That this wouldn't be the end for us."

She swallowed. The offer was tempting. What harm could there be, other than her own heart getting smashed? The damage had already been done. She already cared for him.

Poppy pushed herself up from the settee. "Thank you for listening."

He stood, following her to the door. "I'll keep you apprised of what my inspector says."

"Please do." She was pleased with how formal she managed to sound.

But as he opened the door and she stepped outside onto his stoop, that pride dropped away, leaving the reality in its wake.

The Larkers knew everything, and she had no idea where to go from here.

* * *

Whiting was out of the office. He had left the night before in a huff, and no one had seen him since then. Nor was anyone entirely certain what had caused his bout of temper. A foot patroller remembered he'd slammed the door to his office as he left; another said he'd heard raised voices coming from inside the office, but he hadn't seen anyone enter. Whomever Whiting had met with, it hadn't been for a case that was common knowledge around the section house.

For the last twenty minutes, Thaddeus had held the reports from Poppy tight in his fist, thumb creasing the right corner. His gaze went from the clock to Whiting's empty office to the reports and back again. He'd finished his patrol route an hour ago. So much for rushing to confront Whiting with the evidence. At this rate, he'd be waiting here all night for the inspector.

He frowned, setting the reports back down on his desk. The clock in the hall tolled seven. Reaching for his cup of tea, he took a sip and grimaced. He'd forever be subjected to tepid tea.

But the tea was the least of his concerns. There'd been something strange about Poppy last night; a deep sadness in her eyes that he didn't think could be attributed to Anna's death.

He had to help Poppy realize that she was worthy of love.
His love.

Before he'd arrived at his desk, he'd retrieved his letters from the mailroom. In addition to work missives, family sent letters to the station house, knowing he spent more time there than at his own townhome. He grabbed a letter opener and slid the blade underneath the wax seals of each one. He read the first three. A letter from his cousin in Manchester, another missive containing new information on the Larkers, and a note from his mother reminding him not to miss Sunday breakfast. He frowned at the last, even as he opened the next letter.

Out of the corner of his eye, he watched several other sergeants discuss their routes. He flipped open the next letter, his mind still tracking the sergeants' conversation. Folded in four sections, tidy, uniform scrawl filled the parchment.

He'd read the first paragraphs before he realized what he was reading.

Knight,

I must apologize for the delay in answering your inquiry, but you will forgive me when you learn of the difficulties I've encountered. I reached out first to the solicitor's office, where I was rudely informed that he'd never heard of anyone by the name of Corrigan.

Next, I made my way into downtown. Again no one recalled Robert Corrigan, nor could anyone remember a soldier passing around the time indicated by you. Finally, after checking all the other shops on the street, I went into a shop called Madame Genet's—figuring that my little girls might like some new ribbon.

Knowing that you had charged me to be painstaking in my appeals, I asked the mantua-maker if she knew of Robert Corrigan. She didn't. Growing exasperated, I remarked that Poppy Corrigan must have existed in this city, for you were certain that her family, the O'Reillys, had lived there.

Oh, God, he shouldn't keep reading. But curiosity gnawed at him. He held the parchment in one hand, thumb clenched around the paper. He'd already broken Poppy's trust in reading this damned letter.

Perhaps with more information, he'd be able to help her.

With the urge to understand her better running through him, he continued to read.

The modiste's face went white.

When it was clear I had no intention of leaving, Madame Genet directed me to the office in the back. She'd never heard of a Poppy Corrigan, but she certainly knew Poppy O'Reilly.

According to Genet, Miss Poppy had been her assistant for six months when it became clear she was with child. Miss Poppy was unmarried, so you can imagine the scandal.

Thaddeus's hand shook as he read. She'd been unmarried when Moira was born? Who was the child's father then? And who in the bloody blue world was Robert Corrigan? There was a portrait above Poppy's fireplace of a man he'd assumed to be her husband.

How could she have lied about this? To him when he'd promised her honesty. And if she'd lied about this, had anything she said to him been the truth? Did she care for him at all?

Genet initially wanted to keep Miss Poppy on, for she was a talented seamstress, and Genet needed the assistance. But it became impossible to hide the girl's state, and the town rebelled. After that, Genet was forced to dismiss Miss Poppy, and she didn't know for certain what happened to the girl after her daughter was born.

God's balls, had Poppy believed he'd condemn her like her town had? If she'd expected such vileness from him, did she know him at all? He barely breathed, imaging everything that was unique about Poppy being beaten out of her until she'd become nothing more than a cast-off shell. He now under-stood why she'd looked so surprised when he'd mentioned his dislike for Claudio in *Much Ado About Nothing*. No one had treated her with kindness or forgiven her for her past mistakes.

He wanted to *fix* her problem, to make it nonexistent so that she could be happy. He'd never met a problem he couldn't solve, and this shouldn't be any different.

Yet he couldn't erase the pain of Poppy's past, any more than he could change that she'd lied to him.

When he'd kissed her, he'd felt her desire echoing through him, and he had believed it was real. He'd believed she knew him better than anyone else had.

Squeezing the bridge of his nose with the tips of his fingers, he breathed out, in, out in a slow, meticulous rhythm. He didn't know why the hell he felt like letting loose his frustration, his bitterness, when he'd seen far worse than this. A woman had died in his arms, and he'd soldiered on, but this—the proof of Poppy's lies—undid him.

Damn it all, he should have been able to piece this together sooner, for it had been right in front of him the entire time. How she'd clammed up every time he asked her about Robert—it was not the hurt of a widow, but instead the struggle for the right lie by a woman who didn't trust a soul.

He had suspected all along that there was something she was hiding, but he hadn't wanted to see *this* veracity. Foolishly, he'd allowed himself to be lulled into a false sense of security. He'd thought he understood enough that he'd put together the puzzle of what her life had been before. A marriage not made in love, but in convenience. She'd felt shame because she didn't mourn Robert as society said she should.

If he hadn't been so besotted with her, he'd have been able to treat her like what she was: a witness. Someone he should have interrogated and filed away. Instead, he'd let this consume him. The Larkers were free. He'd sent in a woman to investigate who, no matter how innocent she may or may not be now, had a child to raise.

All because he'd wanted to be near her.

He ached to tip over his pot of ink onto the letter and watch the words fade away into black oblivion. In the end, he'd still be alone in this buzzing section house, enclosed by acquaintances who thought they knew his mind but didn't understand his passions.

So, he fell back on the only thing that had kept him sane throughout a childhood of being less rugged, less polished, less willing to go along with what was expected of him, less able to take without giving back to the world around him.

He continued to read.

For your sake, my friend, I hope this isn't the woman you seek. You have always been too kind. There are some creatures in this world we cannot save.

Send my regards to Nathan and tell Joseph he still owes me forty pounds from our last faro match.

Yours as brothers in Eton,

J.P. Beauregard

Gently, Thaddeus set the parchment on his desk. Never had he longed to be ignorant, but now he found himself cursing his desire for knowledge.

Thoughts rushed through his mind at an alarming speed, half-formed and incoherent. This was not how things were supposed to work. He saw a problem, he weighted the possible solutions, and he came to the correct conclusions. He had lived his life to this principle: that everything could be worked out if all of the facts were obtained and ordered in the proper manner. Everything had a manner and a motivation. His fellow officers had always found him strange; he could look at a man's affidavit and determine what were the truths and the lies. But he *understood* these people, their rights and their wrongs.

He did not understand Poppy Corrigan.

No, Corrigan was a made-up name, one he would never use again. Poppy O'Reilly, the fallen woman. Therein laid the problem: he did not consider Poppy fallen, other than the fact that he had fallen in love with her. But he had trusted her, given her his heart freely.

She had lied to him. He could have excused her withholding information in the interest of maintaining her privacy. But in this, she had created an entirely fictional life—and she hadn't trusted him enough to clue him in on it. How could they continue when she didn't trust him? He'd lived his life believing that truth would always triumph. This belief had guided him through his studies at Eton and set him on a course to join the Met. He'd attacked every case with tenacity because he was certain truth was the light that shined through the blackest of times.

Could he still love her without her trust? He didn't care that she'd been ruined. Hell, he hated what the bastard had done to her, and he wanted to erase every memory of him from Poppy's mind.

Moira needed a proper father. Thaddeus had started to believe he could be that man. In order for him to continue on with Poppy, he had to find a way to accept her deceit. To no longer feel betrayed.

He pushed the letter to the farthest corner of his desk. Like every other puzzle, he'd make sense of this. He'd try and put his own feelings aside and do what was right for Poppy and Moira.

Thaddeus gulped down the panic that threatened to close his throat. He could design plan upon perspicacious plan, but the human heart was a fickle thing he couldn't logic into submission.

God's balls, he was so out of his element.

Chapter Fifteen

Two days later, Poppy took one last walk around her loom as the bell tolled to signal the end of the shift. Thaddeus hadn't come by the past few nights. She tried to ignore the knot in her stomach that tightened as the day wore on. His absence might not mean anything; he could be busy with work. Edna had told Poppy not to ascribe motives to Thaddeus's actions before she got all the facts. In this instance, Poppy wanted to believe that Edna's eternal optimism was correct.

After all, Poppy had given him the files to deliver to his supervisor. If everything went according to plan, the Larkers would be arrested for Anna's murder. Justice would be served.

And whatever she'd begun with Thaddeus would evaporate like the foggy London mist. Rightfully so, or at least, that's what she told herself—the ache in her heart at saying goodbye to him said something completely different.

She wouldn't think of that now.

Starting at the cloth side, she ran her finger gently along the woven silk coming forth from the reed to make sure that there were no torn picks. Effie had been in a temper all day; the last thing Poppy needed was for her to find a break in the fabric. Breathing a sigh of relief when all the threads were whole, she crossed around the back of the loom.

Usually, Abigail waited for Poppy at the close of the day, her elbow resting on the frame of her own loom. Abigail hadn't walked home with Poppy on Monday—she'd been working on the handlooms across the room and needed to finish before she could leave. And on Tuesday, Bess had claimed Abigail was home sick, but she'd stumbled over the response. Almost as if she'd been about to say something else but changed her mind.

What reason would Bess have to lie?

Yet Poppy couldn't shake the feeling that there was something more to Abigail's disappearance. She undid the tight strings of her apron, folding up the garment in her hand. Edna had told her to go enjoy herself tonight. Poppy intended to take her up on that. She'd see if Abigail wanted to go to the Ten Bells to listen to the band.

As the last ring of the bell died out, Abigail didn't appear. Suddenly, Poppy's worries seemed valid. Her friend missing one day was odd but explainable—*two* days was inconceivable. The Vautilles barely managed to pay their rent as it was. They desperately needed Abigail's pay. Without that money, Bess wouldn't be fed or clothed.

Poppy didn't need Thaddeus to solve this mystery: something was definitely wrong with Abigail. If the sinking feeling in Poppy's gut was any indication, it had nothing to do with Abigail being sick and everything to do with when they had sneaked out of the factory.

Poppy jogged to the door, catching Bess as she was leaving. "Where's your sister?"

The eight-year-old started at the sound of Poppy's voice. She didn't look up, scuffing her feet in the dirt. "Abbie's sick again."

"Then you can walk home with me," Poppy suggested. Bess started to refuse, but when Poppy suggested Bess could play with Moira, Bess skipped along eagerly.

Poppy waited until they were down the street and past the corner before she spoke again. "Has something happened to Abigail?"

Bess nibbled on her lower lip, again not looking her in the eye.

"Bess, you can tell me," Poppy pleaded. "I care about Abigail as if she was my sister too."

Bess scrunched up her fist, her gaze focused on a dirty puddle nearby. A crumbled broadsheet lay in the muck, the water smearing most of the words, except for one caption: *Woman Found Dead.*

"It started the other day when you made us stay," Bess began, fixing Poppy with the accusatory glance mastered early by children who grew up far too quickly in these rookeries. "I didn't want to stay, but Abbie said it was a good idea. Everything seemed fine the next day until she stayed late. The next morning, I woke up and she was bloody. She won't say what happened. Just tells me to go to work."

They'd found Abigail. They'd made her bleed. How had they known about her? And why hadn't they come for Poppy?

It was all Poppy's fault.

* * *

Thaddeus hadn't seen Poppy since he'd received the letter. Beauregard's missive sat on his desk. He didn't know what he thought he'd find on this fifty-second examination. More truths, more lies. When had the line between the two become so blurred?

Maybe it had started the day he'd befriended Gottlieb. That

had been his first off-the-books act, turning a fence into an asset instead of sending him off to Newgate like protocol dictated. The Met wasn't Bow Street. They weren't supposed to associate with criminals.

But he'd seen something in Gottlieb like he'd seen something in Poppy. He'd deemed them both worthy of saving.

He'd never stopped to ask if either *wanted* to be saved by him. Wasn't it their choice to make, whether or not they wanted his help? He'd thought he had all the answers—knew exactly how best to live life—but he was quickly realizing he knew very little.

Sucking in a deep breath, Thaddeus laid his head on the desk. If he remained calm, he'd become the master of his emotions. He stayed this way for five minutes, maybe twenty. He didn't know.

"Rough night, Thaddy? Don't tell me. You were out late with that redhead."

Thaddeus pulled his head up so fast from the table that his vision faded, replaced by intermittent black spots. Were his sins so offensive that God had decided to punish him by making him deal with Strickland on this of all days? He resisted the urge to slam his head onto the desk—but barely.

Strickland leaned against the wall, snickering. "'Course, if I had a dimber lass like that, I'd be sleeping at my desk too."

"What? How do you—" Thaddeus forced himself to slow down. He blinked. Once more didn't make the situation any clearer, and so he did it again. After the fourth blink, he was no closer to an answer, and Strickland had started to guffaw.

"I saw you kissing a woman outside your townhouse," Strickland supplied, through bursts of laughter. "Damnation, Thaddy, you should see your face! Redder than a whore's backside after the switch."

Christ. Thaddeus ran a hand across his bristly chin, drawing his fingers together, so his middle finger and thumb touched. If Strickland had seen him, he'd probably told the rest of their station house. So much for discretion. Strickland had a mouth the size of Hyde Park.

"You bloody, bloody imbecile," Thaddeus accused, bolting up from his chair so fast it overturned.

Strickland looked from the chair to him and back again. Slowly, he righted the chair, his eyes wide. "Balls, Thaddy, all I did was go through your files."

"You went through my files?" Thaddeus's voice was low but laced with such malice that Strickland backed up from him.

Snatching up Beauregard's letter from his desk and the reports on the Larkers, he darted past Strickland. Down the hallway, toward Whiting's office. Strickland followed him, jogging to keep up with his breakneck pace.

"What are you doing?" Strickland grabbed for his arm, spinning him around to face him. "You're going to tell Whiting I went through your files, aren't you? You little blabber. I was trying to help you."

He shouldn't respond. He should keep focused on the task at hand, yet the words were out before he could stop them. Strickland knew the precise ways to get at him. "How is invading my privacy *helping* me?"

"In the two years I've known you, you've never taken a fancy to a woman." Strickland somehow managed to appear both cocksure and slightly uncertain about Thaddeus's sanity at the same time.

"There have been other women," Thaddeus objected.

One other woman. A barmaid, after he'd given in to Joseph's demands that they go to a gaming hell together. Thaddeus had slipped out of her tenement as soon as she'd fallen asleep because he didn't know what in God's name he was going to say to her the next day.

"Whatever you have to tell yourself to sleep at night." Strickland shrugged. "When I saw you with that woman, I thought, there's no way in hell Thaddy gets a woman like that. So, I was curious. And when I found out who she was, I became worried for you."

Thaddeus arched a brow. "You, worried for me?"

"A man confessed. You're already back to your normal route." Strickland stopped in the hall. "As damn delighted as I am that you're not harboring secret fantasies about me—don't shake your head, everybody wondered about you—this isn't smart. She's a witness, or at least she would have been if Whiting hadn't shut down the case too soon."

Those last words dented somewhere in Thaddeus's consciousness. When Strickland had spoken before of Anna Moseley's murder, it had been with the surety of a man who believed absolutely in the capabilities of his supervisor.

He focused his full attention on Strickland now. "You think I'm right."

"Ah, I wouldn't go that far." Strickland turned his head from side to side, checking to see who else was in earshot. Two other sergeants were embroiled in a heated discussion of the best Covent Garden lady they'd both sampled, while a foot patroller was logging what he'd observed on his route.

Strickland lowered his voice, leaning toward Thaddeus. "It's this thing with Whiting. Everyone said he stormed out of here yesterday, but nobody's willing to fess that they know why."

"But you do." Thaddeus took a wild stab in the dark, hoping that Strickland would confirm his suspicions.

Strickland tucked his thumb in neckcloth, giving a tug. "There's this woman who was here last night. Blonde and built like an hourglass with tits the size of globes. And she was displaying them, too, in a dress that probably cost more than what we make in a year. The kind of body you want to bend over a desk and rut her from behind, to see that tight arse on display."

Thaddeus grimaced, but Strickland ignored him.

"When I saw her face as she left his office, I started to recall her," Strickland said. "If there's one thing I can do, it's remember women. Got to know which one I've tupped, lest they all get in a rage because I've forgotten them. So, when I say I've seen that woman before in your files, you can trust me on it."

Quickly, Thaddeus reviewed in his mind the portraits he'd collected in the file. Blonde, aristocratic, scandalous... *Effie Larker*.

Whiting had met with Effie Larker, and now Whiting was conveniently missing.

At every turn in this case, Whiting had gone against Thaddeus. When he'd went to the factory and confirmed his theories, Whiting had conveniently found McPhee. When he'd said the Larkers were counterfeiting, Whiting had told him not to investigate further.

Of course. This went far beyond Whiting's hubris and determination to be right.

He reviled the idea of Whiting being in league with the Larkers, the naïve part of him still believing in what the Peelers stood for and what they could accomplish. The black and white morality he'd held upon joining, that criminals deserved punishment and the law was always right. The law was for the people; the people, therefore, had a voice.

One glance up Dorset Street, and he knew without a doubt that those people were mute. Bereft. And he doubted the Met would ever become the honorable entity Robert Peel had wanted.

"Whiting's been working with Effie Larker." The words

were bitter on his tongue, sick and twisted. "Then why the hell did he let me investigate in the first place?"

Strickland tugged at his neckcloth again, his customary smirk gone from his handsome face. "Doesn't make any sense."

"The day I came in to talk with Whiting after my shift, he'd been out of the office all day, correct?"

Strickland nodded.

"How many times have you known Whiting to actually go patrol on a case himself?" Thaddeus couldn't think of a single time. That should have struck him as strange in the first place. "At the time, I thought Whiting went out looking for McPhee because he wanted to show me up."

Crossing his arms over his chest, Strickland frowned. "But now you think there's more to it?"

"What if the Larkers met with Whiting? I'd visited the factory. They could see I was getting close." Thaddeus considered this for a moment, ignoring the disbelief on Strickland's face. This idea had merit—he felt it in his bones. His focus had sharpened. The parts of this case were falling into place.

"The most likely options are that Boz Larker either offered to pay Whiting something for his silence or cut him in on the take of the counterfeiting. You know Whiting will do almost anything for a profit."

Strickland's eyes narrowed. "That's a leap, Thaddy, and a leap you'd better be damned sure of before you make it. There could be severe consequences."

Shit. He'd been so angry he hadn't thought about that. If Strickland knew he'd been involved with Poppy, was it really a stretch that Whiting would find out too? And then he'd tell the Larkers.

The Larkers would find her, they'd go after her, they'd kill her, they'd kill her daughter...

He couldn't let that happen.

Thaddeus spun on his heel, heading toward the front lobby. He had to find Poppy, lies be damned. They could sort that out later when he knew she was safe. Her truths didn't matter if she wasn't alive to tell them to him. Nothing was more important than protecting her.

Strickland stopped him again, his grip heavy on Thaddeus's arms. "Whiting's not going to be docked for his involvement with the Larkers. If you try and take him on, it'll be your word against his, and no one will be stupid enough to take your side."

Especially not me, Strickland might as well have said. Strickland had seen Effie Larker meet with Whiting, but he wasn't about to put his name on the line for justice.

"It's the right thing to do," Thaddeus said. "This place, what we do, it's in the name of something bigger than us. How can I have faith in this system when our own ranks don't follow the rules?"

"You think too much." Strickland shook his head. "Sometimes it's nothing more than a job."

Anna Moseley meant nothing to Strickland, nothing more than a sheet of paper to be filed away with the rest of the closed cases.

But Thaddeus had known Miss Moseley, felt her last breaths. He'd held the woman he knew as Poppy Corrigan—whoever she really was—against him, and he'd memorized the curves of her body.

Poppy was beautiful, and she was vibrant, and above all else, she didn't deserve to be a pawn in the Larkers' game.

Thaddeus pulled his arm away from Strickland. "I've got to get to Poppy."

"She's one woman. One woman in a sea of thousands." Strickland held up a single finger as if that gesture alone would convince Thaddeus that Poppy was inconsequential. "You're going to burn for this, and you're racing headlong into the fire.

All for what, some strumpet's cunny? Is one woman worth risking your career? Everything you've worked for? Because when this is through, you won't work for the Met. Bow Street sure as hell won't touch you."

Thaddeus glanced down at Beauregard's letter. The tiny, quill-scrawled words hadn't disappeared. The story, Poppy's lies, all remained. Maybe he'd been wrong about her. Maybe he'd been wrong about everything between them, but he heard her laughter in his ears when he went to sleep. He'd never felt so at home, so *right,* with anyone else before.

He knew, as Strickland peered at him in utter shock, that he'd accept the hurt offered by this love if it meant he could be with her. "She's worth it."

* * *

The smell hit Poppy first. Rancid and ruddy, as if someone had left a box of old rusted metal lock picks in the sun-drenched window of the Vautille's one-room flat. She couldn't breathe clearly, for every time she tried to suck down clean air, the musty stench met her.

Poppy had smelled something like this once before when a weaver's apron had caught in the machinery. Pulled forward by the loom, the woman's foot hooked on the pedal, causing it to move continuously. Her hair had snagged on the beaters.

It all happened so fast. When they were finally able to pull the woman free, her face had been permanently disfigured, her ribs smashed.

But no prior experience could prepare Poppy for seeing Abigail like this. Upon entering, Bess had fled to the bedroom she shared with Abigail, unable to stomach the sight of her sister.

Poppy was alone with Abigail.

Alone with this horror.

The curtains in the flat had been drawn back to let in the last bit of evening sunlight. Lord, how Poppy wished they were closed!

Abigail sat by the fire with a blanket draped over her legs. Soiled bandages covered her right hand, stained thick with brownish red. A purple bruise disfigured her left temple, darkest where her puffy eyelid met muscle. The flesh was tumid underneath her eyelid, a bulbous flab where once creamily pale skin had been. A similar bloated circle had formed around her eye, swelling it shut. Dried blood dotted the edge of her bottom lip where it'd been split. Only her nose was unaffected, a perky contrast to the rest of the damage.

"Oh, God, Abbie," Poppy gasped, forcing herself forward. "What happened?"

Please let it be an accident. Please, please tell me I didn't cause this.

"I can't tell you," Abigail croaked, her voice raspy.

Poppy wobbled, her legs threatening to buckle underneath her. She dropped to her knees in front of Abigail, wanting to reach for the girl's unbandaged hand to comfort her, but fearing she'd somehow injure her further. Instead, she crossed her arms over her chest. "The Larkers did this to you, didn't they?"

The slight inclination of Abigail's head told her everything she needed to know. She'd failed Abigail. Failed her like she'd failed her Uncle Liam by bringing the vitriol of the town down upon him; failed her like she'd failed Daniel, unable to keep him sober; failed her like she'd failed Moira, not giving her a proper family.

"I can help you," she murmured, even though she knew the words were false. She hadn't been able to save Abigail from this beating. She'd thrown the girl in danger, all because she'd thought she could play amateur inspector. "Please, Abigail, I know a man who can help you."

Thaddeus would know what to do. Poppy clung to that.

Every day with Abigail had been a positive spot upon Poppy's bitter existence. She'd thought Abigail possessed an indefatigable spirit because no matter how long they worked, how hard, Abigail had always been joyful.

But the Abigail in front of her was a far cry from the bold girl who had declared that the Larkers didn't scare her.

"I don't want your help." Ire combined with the hollowness of Abigail's tone, scraping her words against Poppy's exposed hands. "You're the reason this happened to me."

"No, no, I never meant for this to happen," Poppy stammered, unable to look away from the bruise on Abigail's face. Red dots littered the skin around her eye, becoming sick purplish-blue masses where the attacker had struck Abigail harder.

"They grabbed me after work on Monday." Tears cascaded down from her good eye, covering her cheeks and mixing with the dirt and gore. "They said they'd seen me depart. Because I was the last to leave."

It could have been me.

If she'd been the one to exit the building last, if she'd left just a second later, she'd be the one battered and bloodied. Poppy fisted her hand, her nails digging into her palm. She couldn't think clearly. Couldn't form a plan when she urgently needed one.

"Why, Poppy?" Abigail cried. "Why'd you have to go into Larker's office? What was so important you risked my safety and my sister's?"

"Anna." Poppy wasn't sure if that was a lie too; initially, she'd wanted to avenge Anna's death. It had become more about protecting her family and friends from future Peeler investigation, and then after that, it had been...something else entirely. She saw Thaddeus's face before her eyes, earnest and ready to love her.

"Anna is *dead*," Abigail cried. "Dead, Poppy, she's dead. She's not coming back."

Each word was a stab to Poppy's heart. "Boz Larker killed her. I wanted to make him pay. That paperwork I got from his office, Thaddeus—Sergeant Knight—will make sure it goes to the right people."

"You love him." Abigail made this a cut-and-dry statement, no question in her words.

Her surety forced Poppy forward, edging closer in a half-crawl, half-slog. This wasn't the time to talk of her feelings for Thaddeus. Whatever she harbored for him, whatever she wanted between them was immaterial. Abigail had paid the price.

"It won't matter," Abigail said. "The Larkers have paid off the Peelers. Effie told me so."

"Not Thaddeus," Poppy insisted.

She reached for Abigail's uninjured hand, intending to help her up from the chair. "We've got to get you to a doctor. Your bruises, your cuts, they need medical attention."

Abigail winced, scooting back on the chair. "I won't go with you. You weren't born here. You don't know what the doctors are like. Quacks, all of them, hawking their elixirs that aren't more than water mixed with a spot of dirt. No, I'm going to stay here, where they can't hurt me."

Poppy shook her head. "It's not safe here. The Larkers know where you live. It's on their employment records."

"They won't hurt me if I'm not with you," Abigail said, her voice deathly calm. "I've already told them everything I knew. They're not going to come after me again, as long as I stay away from you."

A shiver ran up Poppy's spine, stopping at the back of her neck, a sudden unearthly rash of coldness. "What did you tell them, Abigail?"

When her friend didn't speak, Poppy leaned forward until she was almost at eye level with the sitting Abigail. The thick fetor of dried blood clogged her nostrils until she coughed. Poppy spoke again, her voice a whip. "Did you tell them about my involvement?"

"I told the Larkers you were looking into them."

As Poppy's face fell and tears sprang at her eyes, Abigail crumpled before Poppy, her shoulders no longer so taut.

Blood, dirt, and silk fibers streaked Abigail's matted blonde curls. "I didn't want to, Poppy, please believe me."

"I know, I know," Poppy repeated, resting her hand on Abigail's knee. She intended the touch as comfort—to show that she believed Abigail—but the girl flinched.

"Where else did they hurt you?" Poppy asked, forcing formality into her tone, for if she focused on the problem at hand, she'd be able to get Abigail help. "Tell me about your injuries."

Abigail hesitated, watching her out of the corner of her one good eye. When Poppy didn't flinch and instead repeated her question, Abigail began to unwrap her bandaged hand. In stages, Abigail revealed the gruesome effect. The skin where Abigail's wrist met her hand was coated in crusted crimson, yet that was the least of the damage.

Poppy closed her eyes, hoping to God above that when she reopened them, Abigail's right hand wouldn't be crushed. That the fingers would normally extend, instead of twisting at abnormal, repellent angles.

"What—what did they do to you?" The words tasted like copper on Poppy's tongue, tasted like Abigail's blood.

Poppy reopened her eyes. She couldn't look at Abigail's

face, for if she did, she'd see indescribable pain. Hatred, maybe. Blame.

But Poppy's eyes needed somewhere to rest, and rest they did on Abigail's smashed hand. Her knuckles were red and raw; the skin was torn off completely. Almost as though a flap had been made in her flesh. The surrounding skin was higher where it still existed, a blistering contrast between the bubbling of gore over Abigail's exposed knucklebone.

"Boz held me down," Abigail whispered. "After they'd beaten my face, and I wouldn't tell them why I'd been so late in the factory. They grabbed me, and Effie jammed my hand into the frame, near where the control device is."

Poppy nodded slowly. Abigail seemed to expect an answer, and she couldn't think to form one with bile building up in the back of her throat. She swallowed, trying to keep control over her stomach.

"They turned the square bar forward." Abigail's voice was tinny, like she was somehow far away, not in this room right next to Poppy with the smell of her rotten flesh clouding everything. "You know what happens next."

The bar held hundreds of tiny holes, all fitted to line up perfectly with the needles that controlled the warp threads. The needles were sharp, accounting for the tiny pinpricks all over Abigail's hand. In theory, the needles were held in place by spiral springs, and whenever pressure was put on a certain point of those needles, they should have retracted. But Abigail's hand smashed into the frame had made the needles surge forward in line with the punch card. And on and on the process must have gone, until the skin on Abigail's hand had been wrenched clear off.

Clamping a hand over her mouth, Poppy steeled against the urge to wretch. No one, especially not sweet Abigail, should have had to endure that torture.

"I tried, Poppy, I tried," Abigail breathed. "The pain...the pain was so bad I couldn't bear it anymore."

"It's fine," Poppy told her.

Nothing was fine. Nothing would ever be fine again. Abigail didn't need to hear that, didn't need to know Poppy had given up hope. That deep in her heart, Poppy knew that this was it—this was the end. Abigail's hand wouldn't heal completely. One look and Poppy had ascertained she'd never be able to weave again. What would Abigail do for blunt now? How would she support herself and Bess?

A woman in the rookeries had very few options. A woman with knock-knees and a bum hand had one alternative: prostitution. Charming, innocent Abigail would be forced into the brothels. She'd become used up and tainted like Poppy already was.

Except Abigail didn't deserve her fate.

"We've got to get you help," Poppy said again, mustering what little bit of sternness she still had. "Your hand is going to get infected sitting here."

"I won't go," Abigail repeated.

"I'll make sure you're taken to a proper hospital," Poppy assured her. One that isn't a prison disguised as a medical facility.

Abigail shifted in the chair, starting to rewrap her hand. "If I go, who's to stop them from going after Bess?"

"I will. I know I haven't given you a lot of reason to trust me, Abbie, but I'll kill them if they hurt Bess. I'll kill them, do you hear?" Every ounce of determination Poppy had she poured into that vow until her voice was rife with it, this maddening need to seek vengeance on the blackguards who had hurt those she loved. "I know people. I know people who'll protect Bess, protect you. And I'm not going to stop until you're safe."

There must have been something in her eyes. Or maybe it

was the way she knelt before Abigail, her spine straight, her mouth smashed into the thinnest of lines. Whatever it was, Abigail stiffened, stopped winding the bandage around her hands. Her blue eyes met Poppy's green in silent agreement.

As soon as she left here, she'd send a message to Atlas through one of his couriers. Moira and Edna would need protection. She'd go to Thaddeus to get help for Abigail, but Atlas would be better for keeping her family safe. If Abigail's claim that the silence of the police had been bought, then Poppy couldn't take that chance.

But Thaddeus was sound. His father had been a surgeon—surely, he must know of a hospital that could help Abigail. If she asked him to, he wouldn't tell anyone where Abigail was.

She trusted him. She had to.

Poppy rose to her feet, clutching onto the arm of Abigail's chair to steady herself. "I'll be back with someone who can help you."

Chapter Sixteen

Thaddeus found Poppy sitting on the stoop outside his townhouse that evening. A lump formed in his throat at the sight of her, her red hair unbound, her blue dress streaked with a dark crimson that bore an unsettling resemblance to blood.

But she was here. She was in one piece.

Thaddeus stood back, his gaze sweeping down her body. Yes, that strange stain upon her gown was most definitely dried blood.

He squinted. She appeared unharmed. No bruises or obvious wounds. Just the smattering of blood, and the wildness of her hair to indicate something had happened.

"Poppy? Is everything all right?" He half-expected her not to answer, to fade away into the constant London fog.

"I'm fine," she assured him. "But I need you to come with me."

"Come with you where?" He wasn't going to follow her, not until he had an explanation.

Confusion scrawled over her face. "To Abigail's."

"Your friend's?" He blinked, jolted by the *non sequitur*. "Has something happened to her?"

She grabbed for his hand, towing him forward. "The Larkers beat up Abigail. She needs help."

They ran down the street. As they moved, Poppy informed him of Abigail's injuries. A crushed hand was concerning. He doubted it would fully recover. Still, if Miss Vautille wasn't bleeding out, recovery was possible. "We'll take her to the London Hospital. My father was a surgeon there for years. I know the staff."

Poppy breathed a sigh of relief.

"Where is her flat located?" He focused on that concrete fact because he understood facts. Street addresses, family histories, all those little entries in his color-coded case file were familiar and calming. He knew how to process that.

"Baker's Row, north of Whitechapel Road. It meets with Church Street."

He nodded. "Ah, yes, I do know the place." Church Street housed both the Ten Bells public house and Hawksmoor's Christchurch. The small graveyard next to the church was "Itchy Park," a known haunt for vagrants, prostitutes, and thieves.

Abigail would be safe at the London Hospital. But after? How could he arrest the Larkers if Whiting was working with them? It'd be his word against Whiting's unless he could get Abigail to speak out against her attackers. And even then, he wasn't sure that'd be enough to go against a respected inspector like Whiting.

Poppy stopped in front of one of the tenement houses on Baker's Row. The street was narrow, debris cluttering the drains, spilling out into the cobbled stone courtyard. The remains of a brick wall, once marking a garden for residents, stood two layers deep. The cobblestones had dissolved halfway through the courtyard, and he almost tripped on one of the sharp stones. Two children played in the courtyard, one with a ball in his hand and the other with a slat of wood. Neither had shoes.

The brick-faced tenement house spanned three floors, with what appeared to be four separate flats. Each flat had an individual entrance, with a stone-sided staircase that reached up to Thaddeus's hip. Three stone steps led up to doors of rotten wood. Blue paint flecked off of Abigail's door.

"Abigail? It's me, Poppy." Poppy knocked upon the door, and a second later it opened partially. A little girl—he guessed anywhere from six to ten years of age; children were hard to estimate in the rookeries—peeked out of the tiny gap. With ginger locks and round cheeks, the girl reminded him of what Moira would look like when she was older.

The girl caught sight of his black top hat and his blue uniform, and she slammed the door shut. Thaddeus heard her shouting to her sister indistinctly, though he thought he recognized the word "Peeler" being spat out with childish insolence.

Poppy rapped on the door again. "Bess, Abigail knows about him. Come on, let me in." She hit the door with her palm.

The door slid open a minute later, all the way this time. Thaddeus followed Poppy inside, the smell of soiled cloth and dried gore smacking him hard as he entered.

The Larkers had caused this.

And he hadn't stopped them in time.

When he had last seen Poppy's friend, he'd noticed two things about her beyond her usual physical appearance. The first, she had a beautiful smile. Though it did not affect him as Poppy's did, there was something kind about her smile, complemented by her angelic looks.

Second, she cared deeply for Poppy. He had seen it in the tenderness of her expressions, the quality of her voice.

He'd bend over backwards to help a girl who cared as much for Poppy as he did.

The Miss Vautille that sat across from him in the wooden rocker didn't resemble the carefree girl he'd observed. She leaned all her weight on her left elbow, where the armrest to her rocker remained. The right armrest must have rotted away long ago.

Thaddeus thanked God for the lessening light of evening, which cast the little flat in a gray glow. To see Abigail's scarred features in the harsh light of day would have been too much for him, for the bruises upon her cheeks and around her eyes were so similar to Anna Moseley's that he could have traced them from memory alone. If he'd had any doubt that the Larkers had been responsible for both attacks, he was now positive.

And that certainty filled him with a rage he didn't quite know how to process. He'd arrested murderers before, booked countless thieves, ruffians, and false mendicants. But none of them had produced victims that died in his arms. He glanced down at his uniform with its glossily polished buttons, a vulgar disparity from the carnage-stained bandages enveloping Abigail's right hand.

He wished for his truncheon, for the weight of the baton would be comforting. He'd feel like he could do something to protect this girl.

Taking one step, then another, he came to a stop smack in front of Abigail. His fists clasped at his sides, so tightly that he suspected his knuckles must be white by now.

He worked to compose himself, focusing his energy on what needed to be done. Get the girl to the hospital first. From there, he'd figure out what to do about Whiting. About Poppy. About his life in general if he was going to attempt herculean mental acrobatics already.

He tipped his hat to her and sketched a quick bow. "Miss Vautille."

She did not acknowledge his existence, continuing to look forward, as if she could stare through him. "Bess," Abigail called, her voice barely carrying through the flat.

The girl appeared a moment later. She eyed Thaddeus with obvious suspicion, her gaze finally coming to focus on his top hat. The Met wore top hats specifically to set them apart from the helmet-wearing military—a distinction that had not done much to quell distrust.

"I want you to go next door with Mrs. Henderson," Abigail told Bess. "She said she'd be home today to take care of you. I want you to stay there until I return."

"Mrs. Henderson has stale bread and kippers to eat," Bess whined. "Why can't I stay here until Papa comes home?"

"Because Papa may not be home until late, as you well know." Abigail matched her sister's stubborn glare. Blue eyes met blue eyes almost exactly alike.

Bess scowled, but Abigail didn't flinch.

"Don't go to the factory anymore," Abigail said.

"No more work?" Bess appeared giddy, then thoughtful. "Because you were hurt?"

"I don't have the time to explain. I don't want you to go back there ever again. Do you understand?"

"I won't." Bess gave a swift nod and headed out the door.

"Miss Vautille, I'm going to take you to the London Hospital," Thaddeus said, coming to stand at her side. He inventoried her injuries, determining the best method of removing her from the tenement house. "Will you allow me to lift you? I fear that if we have you walk to the carriage, the stairs at the entrance to your flat may cause you discomfort."

Her uninjured eye appraised him keenly. "You may lift me." She sat stiffly in the chair, waiting for him to move.

"Shall I leave a note for your father?" Poppy inquired, already searching the room for foolscap and a quill. "I won't say where you've gone in case the Larkers return, just that you're safe."

"Not that he'll care, as long as the tables are going his way," Abigail muttered underneath her breath. Louder, she said, "I suppose so. He's been in Whitechapel the last few days."

"If you can, when I lift you, please place your injured arm around my shoulder," he said.

With one hand placed behind her back, and the other underneath her knees, he brought her carefully up into his arms. Feet spread wide, he braced her weight. She wrapped her arm around his shoulder, her grip light against his coat, almost as if she feared that by touching him with all her remaining strength, her fingers would be stained blue.

Poppy trailed behind him, closing and locking the door to the flat. He took the stairs with extra caution, grimacing as Abigail moaned each time he had to step down. Once they had reached the courtyard, he paused.

There was so much he wanted to say to Poppy and no time for anything but the plainest of instructions. "Poppy, as soon as you return home, I want you to pack a bag with whatever you need for a trip away. You, Moira, and your companion will stay with me for the next few days while I figure this out."

She crossed her arms over her chest, not looking at him directly. Instead, she addressed Abigail. "I've already sent a message to Atlas. My family will be safer with him."

Her response caught him so off guard he almost stumbled. Readjusting his grip on Abigail, he took a step closer to Poppy. She watched him with a cagey mulishness, and he would've regarded this fight as futile, were it not for everything he now knew about her. Damn it! And damn her, for not believing in him enough to protect her.

"Just once—just once—it'd be nice if you trusted me enough to take care of you." He loathed how his voice sounded, pleading for something he knew damn well he'd never have. And it made him desperate in his neediness when he'd never needed anyone else his whole life. "There are things I need to discuss with you, things I can't go into here. Your friend needs a bloody doctor, and I *need* you to not disappear on me."

"Bloody hell, Poppy, do as the rat Peeler says," Abigail groaned.

"I'll meet you at the Three Boars tonight. With fifty Chapmen Street members around, no one will dare to attack me." Poppy's voice softened, the belligerence gone.

This was how she should always sound—as if he could lean into that voice and know that everything would be right in the world.

He nodded. He'd meet her at the public house. Whatever he thought about her relations with a gang of thieving brutes, they were loyal to their own. Now wasn't the time to argue, any more than it was the time to discuss her past.

"Don't come in your uniform," she cautioned.

"I wouldn't dare," he called back as he set off toward the closest hack station.

When he took Abigail to the London Hospital, there'd be no turning back. He'd be hiding not only Poppy's whereabouts but also an assault from his supervisor. As if that wasn't bad enough, he'd be actively pursuing leads that would condemn Whiting for being in partnership with the Larkers.

"My family will be safer with Atlas," he heard Poppy say again in his mind, and he couldn't help but wonder if she was right. When their two different worlds had collided, it had resulted in pain and treachery.

Each step took him away from where Poppy stood on Abigail's doorstep, away from the life he'd thought they'd have together.

* * *

The Three Boars sat in prime territory on Chapman Street, nestled in between a chandler's shop and a pawnbroker. It was widely known throughout the rookeries as the headquarters of the aptly named Chapman Street gang, led by the great thief Zacharias Baines. Born and bred Londoners knew, as they knew that the Serpentine in Hyde Park was toff land and Jacob's Island offered cut-rate trollops, not to darken the doors of the Three Boars unless they had some association with Chapman. Though Zacharias was no longer the pugilist he had once been, his cavalier son, Jason, solved problems with his fists.

Poppy perched on top of a barstool, her muddy half-boots resting on the bottom rung of the stool. She wore no bonnet; there seemed no point in propriety. No point in anything that resembled civility, for civility had not saved Anna. Civility had not taught her to avoid Edward, and civility had not kept Abigail safe.

She was the worst sort of false. Sipping at the tankard of bragget that Jane set before her, Poppy didn't look up from her examination of the mottled bar top. The mead and ale sweetened with honey went down easy, and before she knew it, she had half of the tankard finished.

This place, and all it stood for, had felt secure to her. It was a bastion of reverse privilege—those who had no proper position in a *bon ton* society allied here; shared their wealth and devoted themselves to a better good for their brethren. The church of Chapman had two creeds: loyalty to the members and the willingness to take what was not theirs to begin with. Love thy brother or meet thy death at the hands of twenty belligerent thieves. It had seemed simple enough.

In the past few months she'd lived in London, she'd become familiar with what the Baines family did to people who disagreed with them. She'd heard all the stories, seen the scars on the members of Chapman who had voiced their disapproval. She'd smelled the sweet scent of opium in the streets, and she'd watched as children swiped wipes.

And she had thought nothing of it.

Because Chapman had accepted her. They seemed to have Moira's best interests in mind, often presenting the little girl with presents when Poppy brought her by the Three Boars for Sunday nuncheon.

This acceptance was another lie, wrapped up in ruddy nankeen instead of the fancy brocade of societal power. Their makeshift family didn't matter when people like Abigail got hurt to preserve the ideals of criminal enterprise. The Baines were no better than the Larkers.

"You couldn't have stopped it, Poppy." Jane's voice was quiet, meant to console. "The boys said the wife is a clever bitch. Whatever she wants, she gets."

Resting her elbows on the table, Poppy propped her head in her hands. She let out a low groan. "Even the bloody thieves hate Effie Larker, and I decided to become her next target."

"She keeps a clean ship. Doesn't like to leave loose ends. But we'll keep you safe, you know that." Jane slid a plate of mutton drenched in thick rust-colored gravy—the color of Abigail's dried blood, clinging to her skinned hand.

Poppy picked up her fork, but she didn't cut up the meat. Didn't do anything but stare down at the plate, remembering the bubbling of Abigail's exposed veins and the gnarled bone. Imagining the tear as her hand caught against the shuttle, and layers of skin wrenched from her hand. Would it sound like the rip of paper, or the cutting of fabric? She suspected neither, for they didn't properly encompass the loss of one's ability to work, to survive.

"I *should* have known," Poppy murmured.

Furthermore, she shouldn't have done so many things. Never agreed to assist Thaddeus. Never kissed him. Never involved Abigail in this, nor put Bess at risk. Never, ever should have allowed her own interests to come before Moira's. She'd been caught up in the excitement of investigating.

"And I should have stopped Penn from dubbing. He'd still be here if I'd thought to warn him about that house. If I'd *known* that the bloody Peelers were watching." Jane reached forward, taking Poppy's free hand in her own.

Jane's touch should have been comforting. But hollowness consumed Poppy. She was unharmed, physically fit, while Abigail lay slack in the London Hospital. Poppy pulled her hand from Jane's, wrapping it up in the fabric of her apron. Her apron, slick with Abigail's blood too. The crime was inescapable.

It was all her fault.

The realization crushed her. She'd recover for a moment, start to think of something else—of Thaddeus, of how Edna had looked when Poppy left her in Atlas's loft, of Moira and if she'd settle in without fuss. Then out of the corner of her eye, she'd see the dirt on her knuckles or catch a whiff of the bile from Abigail's flat in the breeze. In an instant, she'd be back in that room again. Suffocating slowly from the guilt of it all.

And the knowledge that, in all likelihood, once she left this bar and the protection of Chapman, she'd be next.

Poppy longed to turn her mind off, to return to a time when life had been simple. To that precious day when Moira had been born, when in the light of the sun, everything had seemed possible because she had this beautiful baby girl.

Jane slid over another bragget to replace the one Poppy had already downed. "There comes a point in time that you realize the world is full of skinflints. When you've been cheated, ripped up, and abused, you spring back. You hit harder because that's the way to survive."

"How am I supposed to do that?" Poppy met Jane's glance, seeing nothing but strength shining in the woman's brown eyes. Always strong, always pushing forward, always certain she'd accomplish what she set her mind to.

God, how Poppy wanted to be like that. How she'd give her very last penny to be certain she'd done *something* right. She longed to be back with Thaddeus, to hear him tell her that he understood. That he could forgive her for anything.

For one night, at least, she wanted to know what it was like to be loved by him. What it would feel like to make love with a man who didn't want to use her up until she was so tainted by the fill of his cock, she could never be anything but ruined. Would he make her feel whole again? Would he absolve her of some of this guilt?

"Well, you don't tarry with the pigs, that's for certain." Jane wrinkled her nose as if mentioning Peelers besieged her with a horrid odor. "I don't care what he offered you. He's going to hurt you."

Poppy's voice barely rose above a whisper. "I made him promise he wouldn't investigate my family and friends. I thought I was doing the right thing."

And I did it for me. Because I wanted to be around him.

Jane's eyes narrowed. "Blast it all, Poppy, we don't need protecting."

"*You* said he was going to ruin us. *You* believed that a Met officer around meant doom." Her voice came out too tight, accusations lacing through when she knew damn well Jane had been concerned for her safety.

Poppy swigged down a fourth of the bragget in one gulp, coughing as the liquid flooded her throat. Jane's eyes had grown cold, her lips set in a thin line. Poppy knew her expression, knew it because she'd seen it every time a patron got out of line with Jane.

That was what Poppy was, another unruly member of Chapman, so far gone into the black world that she was irredeemable.

Thaddeus couldn't save her. He shouldn't want to.

In one hand, Jane held a towel for cleaning the counters. She stood up straight like the front post on a loom, a diminutive queen over this bustling land of vice. A dark curl had slipped from her chignon, framing the hard lines of her long, angular face. Her wide forehead was creased with wrinkles—Poppy realized she'd never seen Jane without those wrinkles, those marks of a life given up to never knowing if she'd see her brother free again.

"I'm sorry," Poppy murmured. "I'm sorry I said those things. I'm sorry..." She paused. How could she possibly apologize for all of this, when she couldn't even remember all the ways in which she'd erred?

Jane held a hand up, biding another patron to wait their turn. "I know, Poppy. But you're treading dangerous waters with this man, and you can't blame me for being concerned."

"I don't blame you," Poppy said.

Jane wasn't at fault here; it was *her* fault, hers and hers alone.

"I saw Kate and Daniel at a table near the stage. Why didn't you sit with them?" Jane's lips pursed in her most common expression: skepticism.

"They came with me here, but I...I wanted to be alone. Daniel keeps telling me it's not my fault." Poppy ran her thumb along the handle of the tankard, the pottery cracked. Cracked like she felt, better suited for a life in a Magdalene asylum, where all her decisions would be made for her. "I'll go back tonight with them to Atlas's loft."

She was half thankful for Thaddeus, even as she dreaded seeing him. He'd tell her they were done. He was brilliant and honorable. It wouldn't do for him to become involved with someone as impulsive as she, who failed so spectacularly at investigation her friend had been bashed beyond repair.

Jane opened her mouth to say something, but the other barkeep slid in behind the counter, bumping her as he did so. "Oy, Charlie, watch your arse," she snapped, slapping him with the towel.

"Careful, Janey," Charlie said, with a pointed glance toward the back of the room. "Jason's been takin' notice of you chattin'. He's likely to come over soon."

"Of all the nights." Jane groaned, following Charlie's outstretched finger to a table in the corner. "I'll come by later, Poppy, you hear?"

Poppy nodded. No sense in Jane being punished. She sipped at the bragget, letting the smoothness trickle down her throat. With each sip, she felt looser, less tied to a reality that was determined to break her in two. The public house became noisier with each passing moment, as night descended, and the men filtered in from their days of pilfering in the East End. Soon, the street musicians would congregate around the circular plank set up in the back of the Boars, used for a stage for impromptu shows. It was all so bloody familiar that the lump in Poppy's throat tightened.

She shouldn't be here, not now, when everything had changed. No longer could she remain blissfully ignorant of the dastardly people around her.

Not when she'd become one of those blackguards.

Good intentions mattered little when the result was pain and blood.

So, Poppy finished off the bragget and signaled to Charlie for another. When she'd boarded the mail coach that would take her from Surrey to London, she'd been waiting to begin a new life.

Now, she waited for Thaddeus to appear, and the ending of the perfect illusion she'd been foolish enough to believe possible.

Chapter Seventeen

He felt naked without his blues or his top hat. Somehow less of a man, undeserving of any sort of respect, for as Thaddeus Knight, he was simply the second son of a second son or some other bloody useless lineage. Without the outward trappings of the Met, he was a toff, born with money and dying with money. None of that mattered, not when he'd finished setting up a girl in the London Hospital under an assumed name. When he'd had to bribe guards to stay beside her door, so she'd be safe from any more reprisals.

Damnation. He had to add bribery to the list of moral ambiguities he'd now crossed. That list got longer and longer as time went on with these O'Reillys, starting with that first moment when he'd agreed to help Kate Morgan save her betrothed.

Pushing open the door to the Three Boars, he winced as the noise amplified around him, rising and swelling until his thoughts became a mottled blur. He'd known from standing on the street that it would be loud inside. The building was not particularly sturdy, with its green flaking paint and one cracked window. Yet he hadn't estimated it would be *so* cacophonous. Nor that men would turn in their chairs with the sole purpose of scowling at him—as if they knew, even without his uniform, that he was a Peeler. The Met had become part of him. If pricked, would he bleed blue now? The last four years had been about the job.

Until he'd met the beguiling redhead lolling back on the barstool. Her dilapidated boot hooked in the bottom rung of a stool that shook beneath her as she swayed to the peppy tune the band played. His gaze darted to the back of the room, left corner, where a quartet of swarthy gentlemen had collected, playing instruments that appeared a step above rubbish in the alleyways. Christ, his bloody head pounded. He yearned to be at home in front of his fire, reading a treatise on Dupin's maps.

Daniel and Kate sat toward the back, keeping a careful watch on Poppy at the bar. Jane Putnam waited tables across the room, and every once in a while, her head would turn toward the bar to observe Poppy. For a second, he was almost envious of the way Poppy's family was so close-knit, immediately rallying around her when trouble hit. He didn't dare tell Joseph what had happened, nor their mother and father. He couldn't tell anyone.

He had simply Poppy, and she couldn't be truthful with him.

She waited for him. He'd have to face her eventually—if not tonight, then when? When would they discuss the chasm widening between them? He forced himself forward. One step led to another, his boots stomping on the dirt floor, the sound devoured by the bang of a drum and the shrill of an oboe.

She hadn't trusted him, she hadn't trusted him, she hadn't trusted him.

He didn't want her lies to matter—they were pointless, emotional hurts that should be immaterial when held above these other perilous circumstances. He wanted to focus on the present, on the investigation, on finding *something* positive out of this swelling storm of excrement that had become his life.

As he watched, debating if he truly should approach, Poppy's posture went slack. Her blue dress drooped off one shoulder. Another man approached with a lecherous grin plastered over his blistering lips. "'Ey there, poppet," he said.

Before Poppy could reply, Thaddeus was next to her, his hand on her back. Too close to her rear for true propriety, but that was the language these men spoke, and damn it, he'd speak it too.

"That *poppet* is already spoken for," Thaddeus growled, his lips pulled back to show the man his teeth. He'd read about how animals staked their claim; he assumed that knowledge applied here too. "Shall we take a table closer to the band? I know you enjoy their music so, love."

Love. He did love her, in spite of it all. He couldn't refute that.

Poppy nodded. The band had stopped playing, setting up for the next song. She leaned into his touch, letting out a murmur of approval when his hand squeezed the tender flesh of the

curve between her buttocks and her back. His cock twitched to life at the sound, becoming ready for her. For something he knew damn well he shouldn't take, not tonight. Not after the horrors she'd witnessed, and certainly not after the tankards she'd probably had.

Her moan was audible enough that the brute glowered, muttered something underneath his breath, and pushed his way into the crowd. Thaddeus had won that victory, but now he'd signed himself up for another failure. There could be no acting on these hedonistic impulses. He imagined the glide of his bare hand against fine muslin until he dared to lift up the hem of her dress and touch the silken skin of her calves. The thought almost undid him here in this blasted bar because he was the worst of rogues. He wanted it rough enough to replace the pain of this day with something raw and unstoppable.

He wanted it with Poppy, wrong or not. If he couldn't have her in an honorable capacity, free of lies and secrets, then he'd take her as he could get her. Anguish set in his bones, sank him down as his hand remained on her back, fingers kneading into her flesh.

He wanted to bury himself so deep within her slick heat that he'd forget everything between them was falsified. He *needed* to forget.

Maybe he'd lost every ounce of sensibility and dignity when he'd left that girl in the hospital.

The barkeep's voice brought him back, tenor pitch and strangely frantic, as though the young man had consumed a great amount of sugar before his shift. "What'll you 'ave?"

"Gin, and a lot of it," he answered without hesitation. To his fatigued mind, it made sense to start with gin, the very spirit that had brought about his meeting with Daniel O'Reilly in the St. Sepulchre cemetery.

But when Poppy's mouth turned down in a grimace at his order, he quickly held up his hand to stop the barkeep from moving forward. No sense in disturbing her when she already appeared as though she'd seen seven ghosts, and they all spelled out her doom. "Actually, make that beer. You might as well bring me a pitcher."

"Jason'll demand you pay up front." The barkeep narrowed his eyes. His fingers drummed on the countertop to the music, and his head shook along with the rhythm.

"Very well." Thaddeus shrugged, pulling out a shilling from his pocket.

The barkeep tapped the shilling against the counter and then ran his fingers around the edges and the engraving. Satisfied the coin was not counterfeit, he proceeded to pour a pitcher of the most noxious-colored ale Thaddeus had ever encountered.

Thaddeus had half a mind to ask if they had something less...piss-colored on stock, but he stopped himself. The color was apt. He thought of Joseph's bottle of two-crown whisky, sitting on his desk at home.

Tonight, he didn't belong to that world. No, tonight Thaddeus was a man of the rookeries. Tonight, he had no principles to fall back upon.

With the pitcher in one hand and a glass hanging from his fingertips, Thaddeus helped Poppy down from the stool. Though her gaze was slightly less focused when she turned to him, her movements were swift, direct. He estimated she'd had about two mugs of whatever it was she was drinking, and she was a quarter of the way through another.

He gulped. Her height and her weight didn't bode well for extended alcohol consumption without setbacks. Probably, he ought to snatch up that last tankard from her and send her on her way to Atlas's safe house. Atlas, bloody Atlas, who she trusted to protect her better than he could.

He ought to do a thousand things but hold her close to him as they walked, the heat of her body sending flashes through him. She leaned hard into him, looking up at him with eyes he'd dismissed as alcohol-laden but somehow now looked...passionate? Yes, he was certain of it. Her nails dug into his arm, and her hip bumped his thigh muscle as they wove their way around the tables toward the back.

"Thaddeus," she breathed, her voice like hot heaven to his ears.

The answering thrum of his cock had him gulping for air. Not now, not here, not after everything had happened. No matter how much it seemed like it would abate the pain they both felt.

They found a table in a small room behind the stage area. The walls were thin, yet they served as enough boundary that the sound didn't carry as badly here. The ache of his head had lessened slightly. He splashed some ale from the pitcher into the glass and took a sip. The ale tasted watered down, stale, yet it was refreshing. After three gulps, he'd become used to the taste. After half the glass, he started to think he could get used to shit ale since it made his head feel so delightfully empty.

Poppy crossed her hands on top of the tabletop, eying her tankard but not drinking from it. Thaddeus should say something, he knew, but he couldn't think of a single thing to say except "Why didn't you trust me?" or "I want to pound into you in this derelict public house even though I know I should respect you enough to take you home." She'd righted the shoulder of her dress, a loss of tantalizing flesh he sincerely regretted.

Oh, Christ, he was a blackguard, for as she settled back in her chair, she'd begun to look as though she might sob at any moment. This was too much for her to bear. She wasn't hardened to this life of murder and mayhem. Hell, *he* wasn't as hardened as he'd thought he was.

Quickly, he swung his chair around to her side of the table. Scooting closer to her, he swung his arm around her and there they sat for a moment, him drinking the ale with one hand and his other hand wrapped around her arm.

She laid her head on his shoulder, finding the soft space where his chest connected with his arm. Each breath she took was deeper than the next.

Maybe he couldn't fix this part of her.

Finally, she spoke. "It's all my fault."

He'd never heard her so wooden, so haunted. He set the ale

down—he'd finished the first glass—and squeezed her arm. "'There is no witness so dreadful, no accuser so terrible, as the conscience that dwells in the heart of every man.'"

She turned her head slightly, peering up at him. "I don't recall Shakespeare ever saying that."

"He didn't." Thaddeus wished he had thought of something particularly apt so that he could bring a smile to her lips. He had nothing but old quotations by men that no one remembered to soothe her. "Polybius. He wrote a dreadfully dull treatise on the Roman empire."

"I'm afraid I haven't read it." She nestled back against him, breathing in the scent of his clothes as if everything about him comforted her.

That was something. He wanted to hold onto that thought, to pretend that it mattered above all else. Thaddeus could catch the Larkers, reveal Whiting's involvement, and save Abigail Vautille all in one fell stroke—he could do anything if Poppy believed in him.

He laid a kiss on top of her head. At the same time, his grip tightened around her shoulder, the perfect pairing of gentleness, and his possessive need to tell all the world that she was his. "All of this, it's not your fault, do you understand me? This isn't your doing. The Larkers are bad people, Poppy, the worst of the worst. *They* hurt your friend. Not you."

Poppy squirmed from his hold. Her sad, sad eyes rested on his face, and his heart lurched in response. "She wouldn't have been in the factory after hours if it wasn't for me. And Bess was with her! I thought I was so clever, getting that information for you. Thought I'd solved the entire case."

"You helped me, momentously." A lie, for he hadn't given the reports to Whiting, and he didn't have a damn clue how to proceed. But if she could lie, so could he.

"This isn't the life I want." She waved her hand in the air as if to indicate this entire bar had offended her in some way. "All of this, as you call it, all of this is rotten. It hurts people, Thaddeus. It would have hurt me if I wasn't already so far gone."

"No, no." He tugged her back to him, needing the feel of her upon him for anything to make sense. "You're *not* gone, love. You're beautiful. You're bold and smart, and you take my bloody breath away."

She sniffled, eying him with obvious skepticism. "I think you are saying that because you don't want to see me cry again. Men are wretched with crying women." Looking back toward where they'd come, a little smile toyed with her lips for a second before it disappeared. "My brother once told Kate she could buy a fifth gun so she'd stop frowning at him."

He didn't find it particularly comforting to know that Kate Morgan O'Reilly owned five guns, yet he wasn't surprised either. "I can solemnly promise you I shall never tell you that you may buy a fifth gun. There, does that help me sound stalwart, love?"

"You keep calling me that."

At his quick intake of air, the sudden franticness he knew must be splashed across his face because she'd cornered him, she shook her head quickly. "Never mind, Thaddeus. It is of no matter. No matter at all."

He ought to tell her he loved her. That she'd burned through every one of his last reserves. He wanted to make a home with Poppy, take care of her daughter as his own. He felt things he'd never thought possible around her. Hell, he was a bloody schoolboy, randy for her even in these horrid circumstances.

But there was something in the way she dismissed that conversation so quickly. In the way that her eyelids were now partially shuttered. She didn't want to have this conversation with him, not now, and maybe not ever. It'd offer clarification on what they were to each other.

No, she liked everything messy between them, when all he wanted to do was label and tie it all up in neat little packages.

Fine, he could give her messy for tonight. He wouldn't tell her what he knew. But eventually, when the smoke cleared, they'd have to have this conversation. He'd understand her better.

She sagged against him, using his body to hold herself up. Life had crushed her spirit, and he ached to put back the fire of the woman who had told him to go to the devil that first day.

"I keep thinking I never should have stayed in London." Weariness sunk down into her tone.

"Was it better in Surrey?"

She winced, and he knew he'd committed the gravest sin in inquiring about her past. Would she tell him what had happened?

"No, it was worse. Much worse. But I should have left Moira with Daniel and Kate, let them raise her." Realizing she'd said too much, she bit her bottom lip to stall the agony that spread across her pretty features to no avail.

"I see," he said because maybe he did. Maybe he understood what had motivated her. "Moira belongs with you. She is *your* daughter. You're a good mother, Poppy, a better mother than most."

Poppy swiped a hand across her eyes, and he snatched up that hand, pressing it to his lips.

"The greatest gift you can give Moira is to allow her to have dreams. I don't know what it's like to be a parent, Poppy, but I can see the way you interact with her. She's a clever kid, and I'd love her for how damned special she is, even if she wasn't yours."

She relaxed against him as if she had started to believe his words.

It was enough to urge him on, and he spilled out his admiration for her like a youth writing his first sonnet. "I love the way you love people, Poppy. The way you defend those who have your heart. "

I wish you could love me the same.

"When I got into this, it wasn't just to protect my friends," she confessed. "Or because I thought Anna should have justice. I...I wanted to see you again."

The world stopped around him. He saw Poppy, the vulnerability in her jade eyes, her bottom lip trembling with the weight of what she'd admitted. Tendrils of her red hair had fallen from her bun, caressing her pale cheeks. She cared for him, felt for him, hell, maybe she'd even love him someday.

He no longer heard the band play. He forgot they were tucked in the back corner of the notorious Three Boars public house, with practically every member of Chapman gang present. His heart beating so loud it slammed in his ears, he breached the distance between them, and he kissed her.

Chapter Eighteen

Thaddeus kissed Poppy like his entire universe was aflame, and she was the only one who could put it out. He broke away to kiss the salted tears that had fallen onto her cheeks, to remove the memories of pain and shame.

There'd be no shame in what they were doing. All along, she'd been meant for him.

Lips met lips hurriedly, in an almost stumbling attempt to breathe in the exact same air and know the exact same truth. He tasted mead and honey. His tongue thrust in deep, sinking into her mouth, into what it meant to be with Poppy. The lies and the secrets would remain, but she couldn't falsify this. In his arms, the rapid press of her lips against his as she gave as much as he took, she was real.

For what seemed like an eternity they kissed, two adrift sailors desperately in need of a dock for their wandering boats. His hands tightened around her waist, pulling her from her own chair into his lap. Not once did he break apart from her, for his hands had minds of their own and found her body without him ever needing to verify the location. The weight of her against his erection tore a growl from deep within his throat. Following his need, she ground against that hardness, moving her taut bottom against him in such a blatantly delicious way he almost couldn't believe that she was in his arms. She was his. His! His lips smashed against hers; his mouth was insistent. He needed everyone to know that.

This woman, Poppy "Corrigan" O'Reilly, was his.

No matter where she'd come from, where she'd been before, she was *his*.

He couldn't remember how to breathe without her lips on his. Her hands wove in his hair, pulling him closer to her, deepening the angle of their kiss. Each move of her rear made him harder until the cut of his trousers against him became uncomfortable. Until at the table next to him, a mug was shattered. Until the men at that table stood up and bellowed that he ought to take his whore elsewhere if he knew what was good for him.

Automatically, Thaddeus snapped back something fierce, but he ceased touching Poppy.

Then it hit him, that he'd let things go too far. They were in the middle of a crowded bar. She deserved honor. She deserved so much more than a quick tup in this dirty locale.

He expected she'd tear back from him, that she'd be hurt by the man's words. Wouldn't it remind her of the place in society she occupied? That she *thought* she occupied, he corrected himself, because he'd be damned if he put her in that caste. He didn't believe in castes, in—

Poppy was off of him, standing up from their blessed table. Her hand was in his. She pulled him up from his chair, too, and off they went, running down the hallway, toward some place he didn't know. He should question her, but those questions died in his throat. Whatever this was, he'd let it run its course. He had to.

She stopped in front of a door. Stopped to push him up against that door, her body coming flush against him. He'd never be the same after this night. He knew it now, knew it with the unshakable truth of a man bent on destroying all the walls he'd built up over the years.

For she'd reached up, wrapped her fingers against his neck, and brought his head down. Her lips found his and he gave up thinking they needed somewhere better than this. It was fitting, that he'd take her in this place, this home of thieves when her family was a room away.

He was fumbling with the doorknob as she kissed him, her lithe frame melded onto his. Whatever this room was, it was unlocked. He had the door open in a jiff. She backed him into the room. Boxes, crates, and kegs of ale surrounded them. The shelves were stuffed high with provisions. A storeroom of sorts, he supposed, and there were probably enough stolen goods in here to warrant several arrests. But he couldn't think of that, he couldn't be an officer for the Met now, not when this woman was tight against him, and she'd claimed his lips again. He had enough mind to close the door behind them and flip the lock when she looked at him, her eyes glazed with wantonness.

And she spoke, the sweetest of all voices. "Shall I compare thee to a summer's day?"

* * *

Poppy had stopped thinking. Thinking led to sadness. Sadness led to this overwhelming sense of guilt within her, the knowledge that she'd failed so completely. She didn't want to be that woman anymore, split apart by the injuries she'd caused.

It was much simpler, much more fulfilling, to be the woman Thaddeus seemed to see. A good mother, a brave friend, a saucy minx. Whoever he saw, it wasn't her. But for tonight she could *be* that woman.

She'd made a life now out of pretending, and damn it all, she could pretend to be someone special.

This was a mistake, of course. Another to add to her long list, but this would be one she enjoyed fully. She'd hear about it from Daniel, from Jane, from every damn member of Chapman who'd seen her paw at Thaddeus. It was a licentious, reckless display. One that condemned her again.

Yet she couldn't bring herself to care.

Standing here in this overflowing stock room, his strong, muscular body wrapped around her much smaller frame, she knew without ever saying another word that he understood her. She'd spoken that line of Shakespeare, and he knew what she needed.

He'd make her pain go away.

His hands shook as he slid her dress down from her shoulders, almost reverently, so slow was his movement. She couldn't have this—couldn't have a slow tempo because she'd remember what she was doing, and the sensible part of her would stop him. She didn't want to be sensible any longer. She wanted to be his, belonging to Thaddeus Knight of the Metropolitan Police and all he stood for. This badge of honor, goodness, and everything in between. She could believe in him when she believed in nothing else.

"Faster," she bid him on a whisper. She'd never been so forward with Edward. But here, she felt comfortable, able to express her own desires. And she longed to have it hard, to have it rough until she burst at the seams.

For a second, his eyes searched her face, as if giving her a chance to take it back. One last moment to say she'd lost her mind. But she wouldn't give in, wouldn't give up this one night with him. For whatever it meant, and whatever perdition it sent her to, she'd have him.

"I want you." She suited her words with a firm kiss, taking

his lower lip within her teeth and sucking upon it. His kiss tasted of ale. "I want this. Thaddeus, I *need* this."

"God, Poppy," he groaned. "I've wanted you since the moment I first saw you, do you know that?" His hands had ceased shaking. With steady decision, he now tore the dress down from her shoulders, past her chest, until it pooled against her thighs. He undid the fasteners to her petticoat with its heavy twine cord, scooting it downward. He lifted her up from the ground, ridding her of both petticoat and dress until she stood before him in her short-sleeved shift and stays.

He took a moment to look at her. Rather than wanting him to speed up again, she relished in the desire pooling in his eyes.

She stepped forward, tearing at his neckcloth, at the buttons of his shirt. She'd see him bared before her before she stopped. His shirt came loose, untucked from his breeches, and the athletic lines of his chest were visible. Sinewy and hard against her fingers. She couldn't stop herself from exploring, rolling his nipple between her forefingers until he groaned.

Seizing her hands, he backed her up to the boxes stacked against the wall. The stack gave some support to her back, allowed her to drag him closer, his heavier weight towering over her, yet not intimidating her. He wouldn't hurt her; he could never hurt her. Her hands tangled again in his dark mass of curls, while his lips ran hot kisses down her throat. Each touch left a brand against her skin, a mark that she'd be his, his forever.

"Poppy." He said her name like a prayer.

It had never been like this before, in her limited experience. She'd never felt worshiped. With Edward, it'd been quick and painful, no care given to her pleasure.

Yet Thaddeus's thumb stroked against her right breast, palming the tender flesh until she whimpered from the satisfaction of it all.

That wasn't enough for him.

He pinched her nipple within his thumb and forefinger. The pleasure mixed with pain brought a moan from her, and that he rewarded with another tweak, another circular massage across her breast.

"I didn't think that'd work." He grinned.

She blinked at him, too hazed to entirely understand what he was talking about.

"The book—" he started, but she kissed him, unwilling to be apart long enough for him to launch into what would undoubtedly be a long explanation of yet another tome he'd read. He shoved against her, grinding his erection into her, the hardness of him drawing out her breath. He was full, and he was ready, and she wanted every damn bit of him.

"Thaddeus." She arched her body, but she couldn't hit the right point, he was too much taller than her. "Lift me up, would you?"

He assessed the pile of boxes with doubt, instead lifting her and swinging around to the door. There, he had enough leverage. He raised her up from the ground. Experimentally, she gave a wiggle of her bottom. She gave one rub, then another, biting her lip to keep from moaning out in pure delight.

He watched her, ecstasy crossing his face with each movement of her body. "Moan for me, Poppy. Don't hold back. Don't ever hold back with me."

He bucked against her body with such force she hit the door fully. Unfettered now, she let forth a passionate cry she barely recognized as her own voice. He'd managed to pound against the exact spot—the right spot—the very best spot. Oh, if he could keep hitting there, she'd come undone.

She'd go flying.

But he stopped, setting her down on the ground long enough to undo her stays and rip her chemise above her head.

"God, Poppy, you're beautiful." His voice was so raw, so drenched in heat and need that it sent shivers up her spine.

She should feel exposed, should want to cover up. That's how it had been with Edward. Edward had changed once he saw her naked. He never met her eyes again.

But Thaddeus's gaze swept all over her, returning back to her face before flowing down again. From the tips of her toes to the secret place between her thighs and up her stomach to her breasts. They were small breasts, she knew, but the way he looked at her, she felt like she'd won some sort of grand lottery in proportions.

"Your breasts," he declared, as his hand swept up underneath her breast and took the entirety of it into his palm. "Your breasts are so bloody perfect. I'd write sonnets to them if I was the rhyming sort."

"You'll have to show me how you like them then." She was outrageously bold, forgetting how to be prim and proper. She wanted to embrace this new side of her.

The same sinful nature that had branded her would become her salvation.

And Thaddeus liked this about her, rewarding her sauciness with a flick to her nipple. He dipped his head lower so that he could envelop her breast with his mouth, taking her pert nipple in between his lips as if she was the most succulent of berries. He nibbled, and he nipped, licked and tormented until the ache within her thighs grew almost unbearable.

She needed something, needed more of him. Before even knew what she was doing, she was pushing him downward, where she desired him most. He dropped to his knees. Her legs spread without her proper command until suddenly she was unveiled before him, her thatch of unruly curls leading the way to her pink bud.

He groaned his approval, his lips sliding down her stomach,

planting kisses as he traveled. "Do you know what you do to me? You're in my dreams, all of the time." His voice came out almost strangled.

She leaned down, undoing the clasp of his pants. He sucked in a breath, and she grinned back at him. Sliding his breeches down around him, she watched for his reaction, biting her bottom lip. Then, there went his drawers, ridding him of the linen that hid his arousal. Erect and ready for her, the girth of him astonished her. She was not naive enough to wonder how his cock would fit, of course, but that his need was so potent...she was impressed with herself and in control at the same time.

She'd done this, brought this on. He wanted her that badly.

He stepped out of the cloth and came back to kneel before her. "Are you comfortable with me trying something?"

She nodded, though she couldn't possibly imagine what he had in mind. The act of sex was relatively simple. It did not leave room for experimentation.

But his hands were on her legs, spreading her wider. As she watched, he lowered his head to her cunny, and his tongue flicked against her core. She bucked up against him, a shudder rippling through her, of surprise, of want, of something she couldn't quite place. Encouraged by her response, he licked again, gliding his tongue across her folds.

He grew braver with each of her responses, taking her bud between his teeth and nibbling gently. She shook against him. He'd backed her up against the door, and she balanced precariously on his shoulders.

There weren't words for this, whatever he was doing between her thighs. All she knew was that something seized upon her, some certain force that said the pain would be gone and, in its place, there would only be Thaddeus. She didn't think about anything else but him, the strength of his fingers as he slid one long index finger inside her core, testing her out.

"You taste bloody wonderful." He'd released her thighs, his hands coming up behind her butt to lift her back up. "And you're so wet. Deliciously wet. I...I need you, Poppy. I need to be inside you if that's acceptable."

She looked at him as if he'd lost his mind, for of course, it was bloody acceptable. He didn't move, and so she nodded. "You don't need to be so gentle."

And in that declaration from her, everything changed. He plucked her up from the ground, and she wrapped her legs around the back of him, locking him closer to her. One hand fell against the doorknob to hold her steady, the other clutching the back of his neck. Within an instant, he was pushing into her, his hard cock thrusting into her tight cavern.

He paused for a second, checking her expression, and when she breathed out her pleasure, he sank in deeper. In and out he went. She used her legs to guide him, pressing against his back, allowing no separation between them.

Hot, hot sensations filled her, washed over her until there was nothing but this desperate rhythm of thrust and glide. His hands dug into her hips, steadying her against him. She had most of her weight balanced on the door. Her head came back against the wood with each of his thrusts, and somehow that ache mixed with the euphoria sent her higher because it was real and true.

This was happening. After all these moments of wanting him so badly, she had him.

His hands kneaded into her bare bottom, and the movement drove him in deeper than he'd been before, than she could ever remember being filled. Pleasure erupted within her, unstoppable and wild. If this was what it meant to be a whore, then by all that was holy, she'd be a whore every day of her damned life.

A whore for him.

"Yes," she moaned. "Yes, yes, please, yes." She couldn't think of any other words, couldn't be anything but in this moment with him.

Her cries made him move faster, his thrusts becoming more erratic. His face was a brute mask of concentration and frenzy. He drove into her without cadence, plowing her so hard she half expected to erupt from the force.

She became a creature of need and power, of lust and maybe a little bit of love. A woman who knew exactly what she wanted and how to take it. She pushed, she guided, until the sensations built up so tight within her it was too much.

Too much, for sure she'd explode, and there'd be nothing left of her when she returned. But then, he drove into her again, and it all shattered around her. Waves and waves crashing down upon her. She heard her own screams but couldn't stop the force of it—half the damn public house could probably hear them over the band, but it didn't matter because Thaddeus had filled her completely and ripped out that part of her that said she couldn't let him in.

And he came along with her, spending himself within her thighs.

Then it was over.

Chapter Nineteen

Reason and logic came rushing back to Poppy with the speed of a lightning strike. Oh God, she'd made the gravest of mistakes. She'd learned nothing from Edward, not a single confounded thing. Shoving Thaddeus from her, she slid to the ground until her bottom hit the dusty floor with a resounding smack.

Smart women didn't allow men to screw them in store-rooms. And smart women certainly didn't allow men to come inside of them, with the possibility of yet another bastard child now upon the horizon. Please, please, please, she prayed, let this pass by, for she couldn't be a mother to another child when she could barely parent Moira. Her thighs were sticky with his juices.

On the floor by her feet was an empty sack. Snatching it up, Poppy rubbed furiously at the inside of her thighs. She rubbed until her skin was raw. Until red spots splayed across her skin. But nothing changed. She was still the same.

"Oh, God, oh God, oh, God." Whispered underneath her breath, these words did nothing to soothe her. God had long ago abandoned a heathen like her. How could she have been so foolish?

"Poppy, what's wrong?" Thaddeus's eyes widened, reminding her of the alabaster plates Edna had found at the rag and bone shop the other week. He came to her, still naked.

And further proving she was nothing but a wanton whore, she wanted him again. Wanted him in her, fucking her so thoroughly she'd forget again that this was all bedlam.

"This was a mistake." She raced to her chemise. With furious fingers, she flung the chemise over her head, quickly doing up her front-tying stays. "This—this was lunacy at its best. This can never, ever, ever happen again, do you hear me? Never."

He shook his head. "No."

"No?" She stared at him as if he'd declared he was the new Gentleman Thief, for all the sense he bloody made.

"No," he repeated. "I won't allow you to think of us like that. This was beautiful."

"You're insane," she retorted. "Insane."

He rolled his shoulders in a shrug. "I prefer to think of myself as a man in love."

Her eyes snapped up, drawn back to his face. To the muscles of his chest, remembering the cords in his arms that had strained as he had tupped her. How was she ever supposed to regain sense when he looked like that?

Whatever he said, he couldn't love her. Love was a lie, as much fiction as Shakespeare's plays.

Forcing herself to look away from him, Poppy gathered up his breeches and tossed them at him. "Damn it, Thaddeus, won't you put some clothes on?"

He pulled on his breeches. She breathed a sigh of relief at that, speculating that if he was clothed, this would all be easier to discuss. But it wasn't.

She grabbed for her dress, her shoes, her petticoat, every piece of fabric that'd put distance between them. "I should go. Yes, I'll go, and then we'll never talk about this again, and it will be as if nothing ever happened..."

This was obviously a solid plan. Nothing could possibly go wrong here.

Thaddeus advanced upon her, stopping her from tugging her dress over her head. "You're not going anywhere until we get this sorted." He placed both hands on her shoulders, massaging out the kinks in her muscles.

"I love you," he repeated.

That phrase echoed in her ears, once, twice, a thousand times. She believed him. Believed him when everything in her screamed that this had been a mistake and she should run from this room. She found herself relaxing against him, daring to think that he was right.

His hands were on her face, thumb stroking across her lip. Before she'd realized she was doing so, her tongue had darted out. He tasted of salt, sweat, and stale ale, accessible and common enough that he might truly love a debased woman like *her*.

Pulling his thumb from her mouth, he stroked across her cheek, tangled his fingers in her hair. They were so close, pressed upon each other's bodies. He leaned his forehead against hers, his breath tickling her face. In his arms, she felt whole. He'd taken these disjointed parts of her and reassembled them into something better than the original.

Maybe this hadn't been a mistake.

She'd been an ingenuous girl before, but now she was a woman.

She was going to say it. She'd say those three words back to him. She did love him. It was undeniable now when the proof of that love lay between her thighs.

Until he spoke again, and her whole world shattered before her.

"I know, Poppy," he began. "I know you lied to me."

"How could you possibly—how could you possibly know that?" she stammered, pulling back from him.

"I know Robert doesn't exist," he continued, his voice flat, without the rage she'd expected. He sounded *hurt*, but not angry, and that confused the hell out of her. "So, if that's the reason you want to leave, you don't have to worry. I don't understand why you lied to me, but I'll get through it. I'm not going to abandon you. You have my heart, Poppy."

The world spun. Her grip on the dress loosened, and it fell to the floor. Exposed to him, she half expected when she looked down to see a scarlet cross burnt over her heart.

Her feet carried her forward while her mind reeled. In a fury of action, she seized his shoulders by her hands and shook him. "What have you done, Thaddeus? *Who did you tell?*"

He was stronger than her, stronger and taller. She was powerless against him, powerless because he knew everything. Oh God, she'd have to leave London. She'd have to change her name again.

Everything, everything would have to change.

"I posted a note to a friend in Surrey," he said. He explained what the letter had said, the response he'd received.

As he spoke, those words beat into her mind. She stood back from him, and she stared. She stared straight through him, saw a future she'd feared more than anything. Moira, slaved to a brothel because she had no other choice. Treated as property, forced to whore, because of Poppy's mistakes.

"It was when I didn't know you well, Poppy," Thaddeus explained. "After you'd first come to my townhouse to apologize and Whiting was pressing me to get more information. I wanted to make sure you weren't involved." He sighed, reaching for her arm to pull her closer. "I didn't mean to read the response, love. I wanted to wait until you told me. But I was going through my mail, and I wasn't paying attention. Before I knew it, I'd started reading it."

She wrenched her hands from his, retreating. The back of her knees smacked against a wooden crate. She stumbled, waving him off as he tried to help her. No, she could bloody well find her footing on her own. The box kept her from going away, but she clung to it, quite certain that her knees would give out if she didn't have something to support her.

"You looked into me because you thought to bribe me into helping you," she intoned, the hollowness in her tone shocking even her.

"No, no, it's not like that." He was quick to correct her, his head shaking so quickly she felt the rush of air the movement caused. "I'd never do that to you. I wasn't going to give anyone the information on you, not even my superior. I wanted to understand you, Poppy, to see why you were so reluctant to get involved."

"You could have attributed my reluctance to anything," she countered, as she pulled on her petticoat. The cords of twine encircled her, giving her at least that much distance from him. "I'm a widowed mother in Spitalfields, wasn't that enough? You're reaching if you think you needed more than that, and you knew damn well what my family had been involved with previously."

"I was concerned," he explained as if that fixed everything. "You were afraid, and I didn't know why."

"Because it wasn't your place to know. You didn't have a right to check into me." She fought the urge to scream, to rip at her clothes, to do anything other than stand here and have this discussion with him.

Instead, she turned her ire on him, whipping her words at

him, for language was the lone weapon she had left in her arsenal.

"You think you can patch everything up with a few choice words and a touch here and there." Her hands shook as she tried to button the back of her dress. "I told you, I told you so many times that I'm wrecked inside. But you insisted on trying to solve me."

She couldn't find the right hole to slide the button in. Her hands were too unsteady. He came up behind her, trying to turn her so that he could do up the buttons. She slapped his hands away, clutching the dress.

She was trembling now, from fear, horror, and the sheer weight of it all. She'd *trusted* him, even though there were so many reasons to stay away from him.

"You violated my trust." She hated the way her voice shook at the accusation as if the betrayal had sliced apart her heart.

"Your trust?" he repeated, shocked by the very idea. "What about *my* trust, Poppy? Anything you wanted to know about me, I told you. I never once lied to you. I told you about my mother, how I don't fit in with my family. I believed we were starting something together."

"I never wanted you to believe any of that," she snapped, finally shoving the last button into its place. "I tried to spare you. You could have gone off and been with someone else, someone who isn't fallen."

"I don't want anyone but you. I don't think you're fallen. I don't care what anyone else thinks." The flash of darkness across his face belied those words.

He stepped back from her. Smoothed his hands down his breeches. He wore no shirt still. "Poppy, can't we talk about this like rational people?"

He'd watched her frantic fight with her dress warily, as

though he expected that any moment, she'd lose her mind completely.

She flung her hands up. "So now I'm not *rational* because I didn't want you to dredge up the worst time of my life?"

Thaddeus was supposed to be different. He was gentle, and he was courageous, and he *cared*. Or so she'd let herself believe.

"You made a mistake. People make mistakes, love. None of us are perfect." He pronounced each word with the proper amount of enunciation, but no emotion.

His calm was infuriating.

"My mistake made a living person," she spat. Tears welled up in her eyes, but she wouldn't give in to them. "The most beautiful girl in all the world and she's mine. I made it possible, and I'm going to be the one who defends her. She won't pay for my sins."

Thaddeus came back to her, his hands on her shoulders. He held her tight as she cried, salt spilling down her cheeks, mixing with the dirt and grime that coated her body like a second skin.

"Sssh," he murmured, stroking her back. "I meant what I said earlier. You're a good mother, Poppy. Moira is lucky to have you. You care deeply for her, and that's all that matters."

She shrugged off his comfort. She didn't need it. *Couldn't* need it now.

"What kind of mother hates how her daughter was conceived?" Poppy shook her head. "What am I supposed to tell her when she asks about her father someday? Am I supposed to tell her I haven't seen him since that night? That's not what you say to a little girl."

"It's the truth." He dogmatically held to that point, like truth was a sword he could wield above all else.

"The truth doesn't stop my daughter from getting hurt. I'm not going to tell her what actually happened." Her voice held an edge, an underlying threat that he wasn't to reveal to Moira the truth of her parentage. "I'm going to stick to the story that her father was a soldier, that he wanted to be a part of her life, but battle took him. Robert Corrigan may be fiction, but he's a damn better father than Edward would have ever been."

"If you think that's best—" He stopped as she narrowed her eyes.

"I know it's best." Poppy didn't, but she wasn't going to tell him that.

"I don't put the blame on you," Thaddeus said as if that made a difference. "Why, if I had my way, I'd make the son of a bitch pay for Moira's upkeep. *He* made this child with you. He ought to be paying."

"You will do no such thing." Her voice, like cold steel, snapped his head up. Good, she had his attention. "Edward isn't aware I ever had a child. If you tell him, it will destroy everything I've worked to provide for Moira. And I will kill you before I let you hurt my daughter."

"I'm not going to hurt Moira." Sincerity dripped through his tone, burned in his eyes. His shoulders sagged under the impact of her words. "God's balls, woman, I love you. I want to be here for you. Won't you let me do that? I can provide for you and Moira."

He said this now. But when Thaddeus was sober, he'd regret those words. How long could he live a lie? Loving her meant keeping her secret, looking Moira in the face every day and lying to her. Thaddeus's world was one of black and white, with little room for gray areas. He'd put his own life in danger by seeking out the Larkers because he believed in justice. He believed in truth.

And that search for truth might end up in him getting killed. Now, more than ever, she knew the peril that surrounded a case. Abigail had been tortured because Poppy had thought she could help solve this mystery.

The Larkers were coming for Poppy. She'd put Moira in a treacherous situation. All to help Thaddeus find Anna's murderer.

She turned away from Thaddeus. Pulled her dress over her head and laced on her boots. She opened the door, looked back at him once. "This is how it has to be. We can't be together."

"Wait—" He called to her, but she was already out the door.

* * *

Thaddeus passed that night in a fog. He barely moved from the chair by the fire in the library, the same damn chair that Poppy had sat in when she'd visited. He imagined she was curled up in his lap, her head on his shoulder. This illusion became strongest when he drank, and so he drank more in that one night than he had in the sum of his entire life. He drank to remember her, and when that became too much, he drank to forget her.

He had not drawn the library curtains. The chiming of the grandfather clock in the hall outside of the library alerted him to the time. Six, or maybe seven in the morning. He'd lost count of the chimes.

Wearily, he pushed himself up from the chair. His gaze didn't leave the ground as he lurched to his chambers upstairs. He needed stability, a foundation to build upon.

He had neither.

For twenty-four years, Thaddeus had prayed to the patron saint of pragmatic observation. Human nature might be inexplicable upon first glance, but he who looked closely would always find an explanation to the previously unsolvable.

He couldn't comprehend Poppy O'Reilly.

His uniform was the first thing he saw when he entered his bedroom. Before he'd gone to the Three Boars, he'd hung a clean set of blues onto the door handle of his armoire. They waited for him, brass buttons shined, the pleats of his sleeves carefully pressed. Every detail was accounted for because meticulousness had made him the youngest sergeant in the entire Metropolitan Police.

He tugged the uniform down from the hanger and threw it upon the bed. The fabric would wrinkle from such disregard, but he couldn't bring himself to care. Nothing was important. Neither his stellar arrest rate nor how many books he'd read. Not even his dedication to an organization that the majority of people in the rookeries loathed.

What was the point? Whiting wouldn't pay for his sins. He'd go on corrupting the system because he had the power, and no one would stop him. So, Thaddeus would continue on, policing the same damn route, catching the same damn types of criminals because nothing changed.

Two weeks prior, he would have said unequivocally that he comprehended people. He would have cited his clever avoidance of his mother's matchmaking attempts as proof he could identify a person's motives. This intuition had prepared him, made him believe he'd know the instant he met the woman suited to his needs and interests.

He realized now he'd never considered whether or not the woman he'd selected as his future wife would want him back.

"I never wanted you to believe any of that," she'd said. As if this union between them had been nothing more than the combination of two bodies in heat. He knew better, knew that their tupping had been achingly real.

He loved her. His feelings didn't make sense. On paper, she was wrong for him, but in his heart, he knew she was right.

His hands shook as he did up the buttons to his coat. Drinking had been another bad judgment—the miles of his patrol would be hard in today's heat.

He'd made so many wrong judgments lately. Thaddeus slid

on his breeches, closing the ties that the night before Poppy had pulled apart with alacrity.

"Faster," she'd said, for she wanted him as badly as he wanted her, and reason would dictate they should have been able to act on those desires. They were both adults. They'd worked in this furious, wonderful tandem together.

It'd been better than anything he'd ever felt in his whole bloody life.

A proper man, a man of responsibility and conviction like he'd always thought he was, would never have spent himself within her. No matter how snugly her cavern gripped him or how wickedly her muscles clenched around him, doing things to him he'd not thought possible for a woman to do.

He tugged his boots onto his feet, but he didn't feel that comforting sense of purpose and righteousness. First, he'd check in at the little watch-house on Wood Street and then he'd go about his route. Whiting had taken to working night shifts, so for the next few weeks, he might avoid a confrontation.

Poppy and her daughter would disappear into the cracks of these overcrowded tenements. She did not want him. He couldn't protect her, not with Whiting around. She'd be better off with Atlas and his bloody army of thieves, for at least Whiting couldn't predict their moves. In the midst of St. Giles, distant from the Larkers, Poppy and her daughter would be safe.

And he'd live like this, without her. He'd catch the Larkers. Patrol his route. Read his books and pretend he wasn't missing this vital part of his life.

He knew no other way to survive.

Chapter Twenty

Two days had passed since she'd slipped from the Three Boars, flagging down Kate to take her to Atlas's. She couldn't bear to face Daniel. He'd want to go after Thaddeus, force him into marrying her.

And if there was one thing Poppy didn't want, it was to become an obligation.

Atlas's loft was a safe place, but it held nothing for her. She was lost without Thaddeus. She hated him for that, for ripping apart her carefully arranged life and leaving this emptiness in its place.

"Perhaps the beauty of life is that it breaks us," Atlas pondered, as he sipped from a flask of gin.

"I find no beauty in being broken," Poppy said.

Atlas shrugged. He sprawled out in a leather armchair, the lone piece of furniture in the room that didn't appear as if it'd been lifted from the pages of the fantastical novels piled up around his loft.

There was simplicity in that chair that attracted Poppy's attention. In Atlas's loft, thousands of objects crashed in together without reason. Thousands of stories that didn't give her any answers.

She was as disordered as she had been in Dorking, when the townspeople she'd grown up with had rejected her with paint-splashed signs nailed onto plank boards, driven into the freshly tilled west field of Uncle Liam's farm. *Sinner,* the signs had said, and sinner she'd remained.

Now, Poppy perched on an iron sphere, apparently made in the shape of a Roman dodecahedra, if Atlas's description was to be believed. The sphere pushed up against the diving bell that Atlas had somehow obtained years ago.

Careful not to let the spokes sticking out of the iron ball protrude into her backside, Poppy narrowed her eyes, focusing in on Atlas, shutting out the whirling kaleidoscope of objects around him. Atlas's loft provided constant stimulation. She longed for the peace of the cottage on Finch Street. Edna had taken Moira downstairs to play with the clothespin doll, citing the cramped nature of the upstairs rooms.

The sight of that damned doll slashed at Poppy's heart, but Moira refused to part with it.

Atlas yawned, stretching out as a cat would in a sunbeam. It was three in the afternoon. He had been out late the night before, off on some job or such. Poppy didn't want to know where he'd gone. With Atlas—with everyone in her life, it seemed—the less she truly knew, the better.

"You see the world through a single mindset, Pop," Atlas commented.

"Is that not all one can do?"

"There are those who claim writers put quill to paper because they want to live many lives." Atlas sat up straighter, dropping his chin into his outstretched hands and balancing his weight on his elbows.

Her nose wrinkled. "You are not a writer."

"Aye, yet I have led many lives." Atlas smiled enigmatically.

"From the orphanage to the streets to ruling the Rat's Castle. Each role made me a different person, a shade of what I once was. I have raised and crushed empires underneath my feet from this high perch."

"Are you satisfied?" She didn't know what made her ask this. Still, the need to know rose up within her, as if through Atlas's many lives, she could solve all of her own problems.

"Now, more than ever," Atlas nodded. "Because I have embraced this life. There is a release to be found in knowing exactly who you are, Poppy."

She looked away from him, her jaw clenched. Who was she? For a few days at least, she'd allowed herself to believe she was the woman Thaddeus imagined. But that had been another mirage, false as every other version of her identity.

"I haven't changed," she murmured, more to herself than to Atlas.

"*Au contraire, ma soeur*," Atlas quipped. "You aren't the timid girl who first came to London. Then, you feared simply leaving your cottage. But in time, you figured out how to navigate Spitalfields, and you carved out a little corner of your own here. You may not know all the cant, and you have that illogical attachment to a bloody *Peeler*, for Christ's sake, but you are as much one of us as if you'd been born here."

One of us. Had she truly found a home here? She'd considered this as a stop on the way to getting Moira into a proper finishing school.

She shook her head. "It counts little, for I'm in hiding again."

"Because you won't let me take care of the problem," Atlas scoffed. "One word from my men and the Larkers would be...inconsequential."

She frowned at him. "Absolutely not. Thaddeus's promise specifically didn't include murder."

Atlas rolled his eyes. "As if I need the protection of the police."

"Regardless of your hubris..." Poppy held up a hand to silence him. "Violence breeds more violence. On and on this cycle would go, never-ending, without justice."

"Justice is a bendable concept," Atlas observed.

"I am beginning to believe you may be right." Poppy sighed.

"Do you trust your Peeler?"

The question, devoid of Atlas's usual panache, caught her off guard. The answering pit in her stomach told her this had been Atlas's intention all along, to poke at her feelings with his proverbial stick and see where she stood.

"I..." she started, the lie so convenient. After all, Thaddeus had gone against her wishes. That should have been enough to strip her fragile love away. But as she raised her glance back to Atlas, his cautious but genuine expression gave her enough strength to face the actuality.

"I do trust him," she said.

"Then so do I." A grin broke out across Atlas's face, merry once again. "When I met Knight, he didn't appear a bad chap, minus the whole Met association. Were I to meet him upon a street outside of his duties, I might even like him."

A smile tugged at Poppy's lips, begging to lift the gloom that had settled over her. "High praise from you."

"And I like what he's done to you." Atlas stopped, shaking his head. "No, that is not quite right. I don't like the present danger. But you know you're welcome here, Pop, long as it takes."

"Thank you," she said. "But I don't think I understand what you mean. Thaddeus hasn't done anything to me, really."

"You've been at the mercy of your pain," Atlas remarked, in the same casual tone he'd use to explain one of his antiquities. "Edward Claremont is a dunghill flint, do you hear me? If I didn't think that acting upon the niggard would reveal you, I would've long ago. Not because of *what* he did—for I wouldn't trade my little niece for anything—but because of the *damage* that he did to you. You've been holding all this in, and it's wrecking you."

She didn't have the strength to claim Edward's leaving hadn't left a lasting stain upon her. Not when Atlas knew damn well how she'd been affected.

"Since you met the bloody Peeler, you've been...more you." Atlas stood up from the chair, coming toward her. "How I imagine you were before all this happened. Even though I deplore what Knight stands for, I can't deny the change in you. You've got a serious soul, Poppy, and a serious soul needs a love that will drown out all the noise."

Running her hands up and down her arms, Poppy hugged herself. In her mind, she was back in that stockroom at the Three Boars. There'd been pleasure, strength, and control. It had been passionate, and it had been heavy, and until the end of the month, she would not know if life had been created from their fury.

Theirs was a world of temporary. She'd found out the hard way that relationships were not permanent.

Poppy's heart pounded against her chest. Moira's and Edna's laughter echoed from the floor below, and Poppy remembered the nights spent with Thaddeus at her cottage. Those moments of brave love had been the most real she'd ever known. She'd felt like they were a family—her, Edna, Moira, and Thaddeus. Poppy wanted that again, to know undeniably that she was loved.

She wanted to know that she was home.

* * *

Whiting is on the warpath. I suggest you depart for the station as soon as you receive this.

I wish I had better news.

-MES

The summons arrived at half past six the next morning when tendrils of the sun began to poke through the cloying grasp of fog. Thaddeus recognized the letter's sender immediately. Strickland folded his letters into triangles, while the rest of England steadfastly believed a rectangle was the proper shape for an envelope. There was also the much-harassed look to the winded foot patroller who delivered the missive as if Strickland had instructed him to run as fast as he possibly could, or he'd risk reassignment to a route in the worst of the rookeries the H-Division covered.

For the first time in his tenure with the Metropolitan Police, Thaddeus would not argue with the logic of Strickland's instructions.

Pulling on the first pair of clean breeches he could find, his eye caught on a linen shirt slung across his armoire, the same shirt Poppy had unwrapped from him as if he was the greatest present she'd ever received. A spot of Abigail's blood slicked the collar. He noted it woodenly, unable to muster sentiment.

This is how it has to be.

He heard Poppy's voice over and over again as he hailed a hack to take him to Wood Street, as he sat in the carriage and finished off the rest of his flask, as he dismounted and paid the driver, and as he passed underneath the brick awning to the station house. Thaddeus entered the building. At this early hour, there were few people in the station. Most would still be in their cots at the section house in Leman Street or hitting the public houses after their night shift.

Usually, he would have enjoyed the quiet, but today with

nothing to distract him, her voice in his ears became louder, punishing in volume.

Thaddeus passed by his desk but didn't stop. His other case files would be stacked neatly, color-coded, and tabbed depending on the type of report. Almost a hundred arrests for violent theft, pickpocketing, breaking the peace, and street fighting. An occasional murder in the lot, but he'd never felt daunted before by the criminals.

In his hubris, he'd considered the Met the right arm of Lady Justice. Now he saw they were the bastard sons of a damaged system, birthed to keep the aristocrats rich and the poor downtrodden.

And Whiting was the worst damn offender of them all.

Whiting sat behind his mammoth desk in his obsequious office. Humming a cheery tune to himself, Whiting added his red seal to a report and set it down to the bottom of the pile.

Whiting didn't notice Thaddeus stood in his doorframe. Thaddeus clenched his fists at his sides and kept his posture straight.

"You wanted to see me?" Thaddeus struggled to keep his voice even, as if this was any other day at the station. As if rage didn't boil within him at the sight of Whiting's smug mien.

"Sergeant Knight." Whiting's face had transformed into a visage of abject pain as if Thaddeus's betrayal had wounded him deeply. "I hate having to do this."

Thaddeus didn't doubt that. Without him, Whiting would have to do his own work. Thaddeus would regard it as poetic justice if he still believed in the concept of justice.

"Do what, sir?"

With a sigh, Whiting began ticking off each account on his pudgy fingers. "I gave you everything, Sergeant. The hardest arrests, designed to place your name in the public eye. After the Finn case, I wrote a recommendation to Commissioner Mayne that you be placed with the Runners. I put you on the short list for the inspector job."

You did those things to keep me complacent, Thaddeus wanted to growl. All along, Whiting's duplicity had been right in front of him. But he'd been too stunned by the glory his supervisor held in front of his nose to see it.

"I've never disobeyed the Met." But Thaddeus had, damn it, when he'd started to court Poppy. It was an unwritten rule in their district to not court people from one's route.

His sins were nothing in comparison to Whiting's, yet that did not make the sting of his failure any less.

"Superintendent Bicknell received a complaint about you from Boz Larker." Whiting let the name hang in the air for a moment, watching Thaddeus's face for a reaction. "Larker claims you went to his factory and vandalized some of his equipment. His records room was also ransacked, and several key employee and financial records are missing."

The same records that Poppy had stolen that showed the Larkers were coining. Safely locked in the bottom drawer of his desk at home where the Larkers couldn't get to them.

Use your head. Don't let him back you into a corner.

Thaddeus breathed in, out, in a regulated pattern, focusing on that instead of Whiting's words. He looked straight ahead, through Whiting, because if he looked into Whiting's eyes, he'd say all the things he'd regret later.

"One of Larker's weavers was injured in the attack upon the factory. A Miss..." Whiting flipped open one of the files on his desk, scanning the page. "Ah. A Miss Vautille. Says that the equipment fell on top of her?"

Damnation. He'd never work again for the Met when this was over.

Thaddeus had expected that Whiting would claim something trivial like he'd been seen drinking in a public house during his shift. But this, there was no coming back from. Damaging equipment, injuring an employee, stealing files...he'd be lucky to get that job at Joseph's bank.

"Do you believe I did it, Inspector Whiting?" He didn't have to work to add anguish into his voice, for he remembered lifting Miss Vautille out of her chair, her mangled hand on his shoulder. The choking odor of her blood and bile. "You know me. You know I wouldn't go against policy, especially when you strictly forbade me from investigating. I've been busy with my route."

Whiting hesitated as if, for a second, he believed Thaddeus's lie. "If not you, then who? Nothing would please me more than to be able to tell Bicknell that Larker has the wrong man. But given how vehemently you kept claiming Boz Larker had committed murder, you cannot fault me for believing his claim. If you happened to know who might have committed such an egregious act..." He let that trail off, knowing he didn't need to say anything more.

Thaddeus saw it all, every insinuation, every line of Whiting's plan. Whiting would use his influence to cover up his own involvement, and after he'd use Thaddeus as a weapon. If Thaddeus gave up Poppy's name and confirmed what the Larkers already knew, he'd prove himself worthy of Whiting's trust and continue on with the Met.

In keeping his own job, he'd effectively sign Poppy's death warrant.

What have you done, Thaddeus? What have you done?

The seconds turned into minutes. Still, Thaddeus remained silent. All these years he'd prided himself on his intellect—for nothing. Strickland had been right. Thaddeus should have left this case alone. Poppy had become involved because *he'd* asked her to be.

Whiting sneered. His voice dropped low until it was but a

whisper, swallowed quickly by the cavernous office. "I've enjoyed benefiting from your work, Knight, but there's something undeniably irresistible about watching you be outwitted."

A shot of rage flashed through Thaddeus, pooling in the base of his spine. Whiting had let a woman die, and another be tortured, and here he sat, delighted with himself.

Thaddeus lunged forward, coming within a hairsbreadth of Whiting's neck. It would be so easy to wrap his hands around Whiting's throat, ending this cycle of corruption. But he'd be no better than the Larkers were.

He'd promised Elizabeth and Anna he'd get them justice.

He'd promised Poppy he'd protect her.

"I know what you did," Thaddeus hissed. "You've been helping the Larkers cover up their coining all along."

Thaddeus was that little boy again in the school courtyard, challenging a bully head-on. But this time, he didn't have Joseph by his side to protect him.

Whiting leaned back in his chair, out of Thaddeus's reach. "Bicknell has already signed off on your dismissal. I'll give you a quarter of an hour to pack up your desk, and then I'll set the patrollers upon you."

"I'm going to make you pay," Thaddeus vowed, but even he didn't put stock in the claim.

The Larkers had won. Thaddeus was no more than he'd been as a boy of seventeen, finding Elizabeth Stewart dead in the alley. His life was marked by violence from that day, bitter, gut-wrenching violence.

And so, it would go on, for he was powerless to stop it.

* * *

Martha Knight had always claimed that unfortunate events struck in threes. As a child, Thaddeus had considered this statistically improbable and had even designed an experiment to prove her wrong.

But now, Thaddeus was quite willing to admit that in this case, his mother had been right. He'd lost Poppy, he'd been dismissed from the Met, and now he had to meet with bloody Strickland.

Strickland had sent him a warning, yes. And yes, Strickland hadn't blabbed to Whiting about his involvement with Poppy. But that didn't mean Thaddeus had to like the man, damn it.

When the back door finally swung open, it was a quarter to ten. Strickland was late. Thaddeus stood, his billystick strapped at his side should he need it.

Gripped in his left hand was a fully cocked pocket pistol. The silver and wood gun was light enough to carry in a lady's reticule, yet in his hands, it felt heavy. He'd never believed in guns. Guns were too quick, allowing the shooter little time to rethink his actions before the shot fired.

"Put down your barking iron, Thaddy, lest you want your whole house to reek of smoke." Strickland emerged from the back room, his top hat held in his one hand, and a gold-tipped walking stick in the other. He swung the stick to and fro, resembling more a man at the races than one at a clandestine meeting in the dark of night.

Thaddeus regarded him with barely suppressed chagrin. This was most certainly a wretched idea, but he had no one else to turn to.

Lowering the gun, he set it down on the table by the door. From the same table, he picked up a file.

"So, you got my letter," Strickland said, his eyes narrowing as Thaddeus stepped forward, file in hand.

"As you received mine." He'd dropped the missive on Strickland's desk before leaving the station house.

When Strickland nodded, Thaddeus gestured to the

parlor on the right side of the house. Somehow, receiving Strickland in his library felt wrong. The Met had already debased the grand philosophies in his books—whatever idealism he had left, he wanted to shelter from the cruel realities of this world.

He rarely used this parlor. His mother had decorated it with the intention that it'd be his future wife's receiving room.

"Cryptic, asking me to come in the back door." Strickland stood in the doorway, inspecting the room with his customary smirk.

Refusing Thaddeus's offer of a seat on the cream settee, Strickland went to the drink cart and poured a generous serving of brandy. He took a long sip, nodding in approval.

"For a namby-pamby, you've got a good selection of spirits." Strickland held up the bottle of brandy, inquiring if Thaddeus would like a drink as well.

Thaddeus nodded.

"There's a smart lad. Good stiff drink fixes everything." Strickland brought the second glass of brandy over, eying the prissy settee with distaste. "This room looks like you raided the land of the Lilliputians and brought back their furniture."

Thaddeus blinked. "You've read Swift?"

Gingerly, Strickland took a seat on the settee. "I'm not illiterate, Knight. Just because I don't boast about my academic achievements doesn't mean I'm not erudite. I went to Oxford before joining the Met. Got a degree in mathematics, actually."

"I didn't know," Thaddeus said. Another one of his assumptions shot to hell. Was there nothing factual left in his life? He paced the room, unable to keep still.

So much of his life was now inactivity. He wanted to be the one to see the Larkers pay. The one to protect Poppy. Instead, he had to rely on Strickland's official capacity and the damn Gentleman Thief.

Shrugging, Strickland swished the brandy in his glass. "You never asked."

"Why did you join the Met? You could have been a professor or a mathematician..."

Strickland grimaced. "Professor Strickland, no thanks. You know my father expected me to join, and it was easier to go along with him. Besides, London's most adroit courtesans want Corinthians, not dusty scholars." He sipped at the brandy, smirking. "Although you seem to have done well for yourself with the redhead."

Thaddeus winced.

"Ah." Strickland raised his glass in a consolatory salute. "I didn't tell Whiting, Thaddy. Something else set him off. When I came back from my route, I could hear him raging in his office. Saying 'the bitch' would end them all. Whatever money Whiting made off this, he'd give it back if it meant he didn't have to deal with her again."

So, Thaddeus had been right about one thing, at least.

"That fits with you seeing Effie Larker earlier," Thaddeus noted. "I think she's pulling the strings. Her husband is no more than a bullyback to her. If I'm correct, which is a very large if, he's there to enforce her demands. She handles the business end of the coining."

"Counterfeiters. Fuck." Strickland groaned, leaning his head back against the settee. It creaked underneath his weight, and he quickly readjusted. "I'm bloody sorry, Thaddy."

Thaddeus went to the table and collected the file. He crossed the room to Strickland, handing him the papers. Strickland took the file, his brows arching as he flipped through the contents. With each page he turned over, the worry lines in his forehead grew deeper.

"Damnation," he whistled. "I need not ask why Whiting dismissed you. This is some fine policing, Thaddy."

"Policing I can't use." Thaddeus sighed. "I've put Poppy and her daughter in danger. Their protection is the most important thing, and I've buggered it all."

Strickland moved to hand the file back to him, but Thaddeus shook his head.

"It's yours now," Thaddeus explained. "Do with it what you will. The Met won't have me, and without them, I can't act on any of that information formally."

"What do you expect me to do with this? If I proceed, I'll end up on the street the same as you." Strickland scowled, but he didn't hand the file back. His palm pressed into the paper as if he wanted to imprint his mark upon it.

Strickland might be willing to take up Thaddeus's crusade after all.

"Whiting doesn't suspect you," Thaddeus said. "If you're as good at your job as you claim, you'll figure it out."

Every hope Thaddeus had of avenging Anna Moseley's murder was pinned on his original impressions of Strickland being wrong.

Chapter Twenty-One

Fear, Poppy had learned, was a powerful motivator. It was fear that had made her consider the Magdalene hospital in Southwark. Yet that would have been another sort of prison, for it meant a life dedicated to "reformation" in the eyes of the Church. It meant believing without a doubt that she'd sinned, and the creation of Moira had been a travesty against God.

Poppy rocked, with one hand, the crib where Moira slept. Peaceful, beautiful Moira, who cared so little about the great wide world outside of Atlas's secluded loft.

Poppy glanced over at Edna, her silver needles catching the light of the roaring fire. Knitting didn't have the comforting flow of weaving, but it still created something of beauty. It was another art of change. Of becoming something more; in that, it held another level of fear, for change brought new problems.

And it was fear that had motivated her to respond to Edward's advances originally. Fear that she'd end up alone, lost to the drink like Daniel. After Aunt Molly's death, Uncle Liam had thrown himself into the farm. He ate, slept, and dreamed of livestock and crop rotation, trying to exert his will over nature that wouldn't bend in accordance. Poppy, who had never been alone a day in her life prior to Aunt Molly's death, suddenly found herself without a confidante.

Edward had seemed so nice. So perfect, wanting to know all about her favorite books and the dresses she made for Madame Genet. When she went over those conversations now, she remembered how he'd simply stared at her in response when she mentioned the books she loved. He had never bantered with her, nor given her recommendations to expand her mind.

Only Thaddeus had done that.

She clutched at the side of the crib, nails digging into the wood. Thaddeus had claimed she was not a victim of her past. Perhaps it was not the past that held her in thrall, but fear and its many facets.

Fear not that she'd end up alone now, but that she'd end up shattered in ways she could not begin to repair.

"I fear I'm going mad," she murmured.

"It's this place." Edna placed her knitting needles on the barrel that served as a table. She darted in between the assorted clusters toward the overturned tureen that served as both Atlas's tea stand and his liquor cart. "Every time I'm about to fall asleep, I see that stuffed bear out of the corner of my eye, and I'm suddenly convinced I've ended up in the woods that bordered Liam's land."

Poppy nodded. She'd run through those woods after Edward had confessed his real motivations in seducing her. "It's been fun, poppet." Brambles had torn through her thin slippers, the thick moss coating her knees when she'd fallen over a branch.

"Have you heard from Jane?" Edna poured water Atlas had hauled from the nearby pump for them into the kettle. "As grateful as I am to the Gentleman Thief for his hospitality, I'd very much like to return home."

In her crib, Moira stirred, her green eyes opening wide. She stretched out, her fingers making grabbing motions. "Mama, up," she ordered. "Up, up, up."

Poppy scooped up Moira from the crib, holding her daughter close to her body. Moira clutched at the collar of her dress, tugging at the ivory beads Poppy had sewn into the neckline. One of the threads broke, and the bead slipped from the dress to the ground. It rolled off, lost in the sea of Atlas's treasures.

Poppy grimaced, but she didn't scold Moira. She could take a bead from the other side of the collar to even them out. When she'd been working at the factory, she wouldn't have had time to mend the dress.

Now, she had nothing but time.

And it was eating her alive.

With Moira in her arms, Poppy made her way to Edna. The older woman had put the tea on the fireplace, waiting for the water to boil.

"I'm sorry," Poppy said softly, as she bounced Moira in her arms. The babe let out a shriek of delight, but Moira's happy cries couldn't make their situation any less fraught. "I'm sorry you have to be stuck here. That I've put you in danger. That I don't make better decisions."

Edna shook her head. "Always, you apologize, whether or not it is your fault. Then always, I tell you that I trust your judgment. I'm proud of who you are today, whether or not you want me to be."

Edna planted a kiss on Moira's forehead, her expression changing from one of resigned sadness to joy. That was the effect Moira had on people: she made them feel better, no matter what their troubles might be.

"The greatest mistakes produce the best fruits," Edna said. "Isn't our little Moira the best example of that?"

Moira grinned at the cooing tone of Edna's voice. She settled back in Poppy's arms, watching Edna with wide eyes.

"You sound like Thaddeus," Poppy groaned. "He has a quote for everything. His memory, Edna, is like the lost library of Alexandria. Thousands of books, trapped in his great brain, and he can't find the right answers."

With one hand, Edna pushed her glasses higher up on the bridge of her nose, squinting at Poppy. "He does know the right answers, my dear. You simply aren't ready to see them."

Poppy frowned. "You know very well why we cannot be together. We're hiding out here *because* of him."

Edna placed the tea in the strainer and then put the strainer into the pot to brew. She turned back to Poppy, wiping her hands on her apron. "I don't think Sergeant Knight intended to place us in danger, Poppy. He did the best he could in tough circumstances."

"I know he did." Poppy couldn't hide the hint of pride in her voice. Thaddeus was, undeniably, a good man.

But he was a good man who had put her family in danger, both by looking into her past and by drawing her into his case. The latter she had gone into willingly, but the former... She'd never wanted him to know about Moira's birth.

"He knows now," Poppy said, kneeling down on the blanket with Moira. "And he thinks that because he knows the bare facts, he knows everything about what happened."

"What did you tell him?" Edna asked.

"Not a damn thing." Poppy sighed. As if sensing her mother's discontent, Moira climbed into her lap, seating herself with a loud plop. Poppy ran a hand across her head, smoothing her thin red hair.

"If I had my choice, no one would ever know. That pain from Edward... It's *my* pain. People listen to what happened, but no one really understands. Provided they have any sympathy at all, either they want to save me from my heathen past, or they want me to be a victim. I just want to be me."

"You *are* being you," Edna argued. "Dear girl, that night is as much a part of you as anything else."

Poppy shook her head. "I don't want it to be."

Edna sighed. "You see yourself one way, as a mother who must defend her child. But you are so many more things. A weaver, a sister, an Irish woman, a booklover, a seamstress, a woman with needs of her own. Every single bit of you combines to make this glorious whole. Anyone who can't see that doesn't matter."

Moira squirmed out of Poppy's lap, dangling over Poppy's legs. Poppy tapped her bottom, and Moira shrieked her glee, turning her head around to smile at her mother.

Mother, Poppy had long ago decided, was the most important role she could fill. She'd ceased being a *woman* by any other definition. Until Thaddeus, with his bloody concern. Those damnable needs he stirred up within her until too much bubbled at the surface, and she couldn't hold it in any longer.

She wanted him, his stellar moral compass, his long-winded speeches, and the way he always seemed to know what she was thinking.

"Thaddeus says that he's accepting of me being fallen, but how can he be?"

Edna passed her a cup of steaming tea. "Maybe you should ask him that."

"If I ever see him again," Poppy murmured.

If the Larkers weren't caught, she'd have to relocate permanently. Where would she go? Not back to Dorking, for she wouldn't put her uncle under that kind of scrutiny again. Nor would she go back to her family in Ireland, who viewed fallen women as debased, immoral creatures.

Edna watched Poppy for a moment, lips pursed, and spectacles perched on the tip of her squat nose. "If he is as smart as you've said, he'll find you."

"If he *does* find me, he'll want to tell Moira who her real father is. The lie will eat at him." Poppy blew on the mug, the stiff aroma of tea comforting.

"Would that be such a bad thing?" Edna asked. "By the time Moira is old enough to understand, she'll have grown up surrounded by family that loves her. Family is not only blood ties, Poppy, but a group of people who love and care for each other."

All this time, Poppy had thought she and Thaddeus were from two different worlds, and that meant they couldn't be together. Yet she couldn't think of a group of people more different in personality than her group of friends in London, yet together they worked. Pragmatic Jane, fierce Kate, tenacious Daniel, clever Atlas. What was she in the mix?

"Perhaps," she began, an unfamiliar sense of hope starting to fill her. "Perhaps when the trouble is past, I'll find Thaddeus."

"Love is a risk. If he didn't have a dangerous job, it'd be something else, Poppy. He'd have rotten friends, or he'd be Scottish." Edna's nose wrinkled at the thought. "This is a bitter world. You have to hold on to what little bit of joy you can glean from it."

* * *

To say that the Knights were overjoyed by Thaddeus's dismissal would have been an egregious understatement. Thaddeus couldn't recall a time that they'd been more ecstatic. Not when he'd graduated from Eton, not when he'd first enrolled in Cambridge, and certainly not when he'd announced he was leaving Cambridge's civil law program to join the Metropolitan Police.

Breakfast had been a series of starts and stops. Once news of his dismissal from the Met reached Martha, she'd readmitted Thaddeus to the house. In fact, Martha had even invited Miss Justine Balfour to join them, in hopes Thaddeus would consider her as a suitable catch.

Alfred interrogated him with as much determination as any experienced inspector, while Martha interrupted every few minutes to exclaim, "Finally, he'll do something respectable."

Respectable. He didn't feel respectable as he hastily shoveled in the last bit of kippers, foolhardily believing he could excuse himself from the usual gathering after the meal.

Nor did he feel respectable as his mother pulled him aside. Martha reminded him in no uncertain terms that he had to a duty to pay to Miss Balfour, and if he ever intended to remain a part of this family, he'd trot his behind into the drawing room.

Miss Balfour's expression stopped him from replying to his mother. The entire meal, Miss Balfour had poked at her food, eating in delicate, tiny bites.

When Miss Balfour's soulful brown eyes dared to rise to his face as he spoke to Martha, Thaddeus saw an unexpected flash of pain. This quiet woman with the long, oval face and the serious demeanor knew hurt. Thaddeus couldn't explain why Justine Balfour, who had both name and fortune, ached so inside, but he recognized pain when he saw it.

For he too knew what it felt like to have hopes and dreams stomped upon until there was nothing left but the crushing realization that from now on, this would be his path. He'd loved and lost. It had been four days since Poppy had fled the storeroom at the Three Boars. Not one letter had arrived from her.

Thaddeus leaned back against the settee in the right corner of the parlor, far away from the rest of the party. If no one noticed him, he might escape through the double doors behind him and make a quick getaway.

Except Martha had other ideas. She took Miss Balfour by the arm and led her over to Thaddeus. The stern look on his mother's face left Thaddeus little choice. He must exchange pleasantries with this woman or face at least two weeks' worth of scolding.

Miss Balfour smoothed out her skirt and obligingly sat down upon the settee next to him. With her hands in her lap docilely, she peered at him, her eyes wide and expectant.

"Hello," he said.

"Good morning." Her voice was so soft that it reminded him of a feather cascading to the ground, caught in a wayward breeze.

"Did you enjoy breakfast?" He couldn't have cared less if she did, but it was the civil thing to ask.

"Yes, thank you." She played with the little lace flowers sewn into her skirt, long, thin fingers moving back and forth. Fingers better suited to piano keys or harp strings, not weaver's looms.

Idly, he wondered if he'd judge women's hands by that standard from now on.

"I'm sorry about my mother," he blurted.

Miss Balfour blinked at him.

Three sentences into the conversation and he'd already forgotten what normal men said in these circumstances. Christ, it had never been like this with Poppy. Fiery, smart Poppy, who met every one of his speeches on philosophy with a clever question.

Well, he'd already embarked on this course, so he'd bumble through it, damn it. "The way my mother forced you to come talk to me. It's atrocious, I know, and you can't have enjoyed it. But when Martha Knight gets an idea into her mind, there's no stopping her. Combined with Catherine's nattering on about dresses and the like, you must find us the dullest family that ever existed."

Miss Balfour shook her head, not meeting his eyes as if she feared even this slight disagreement might provoke his ire. "Catherine is a good friend. She treats me well, and never makes me feel out of sorts." Miss Balfour looked up, catching Thaddeus watching her. "I'm content to listen, Sergeant Knight, if you want to tell me what has saddened you so."

"I fell in love." He should have couched that reveal in something less dramatic.

A blush spread over her cheeks, giving her a maidenly color to suit her maidenly dress and every other innocent, sweet thing about her.

God, he didn't want innocent. He wanted Poppy. He wanted to hear her laugh as he explained some silly thing he'd learned in another book, and to see her smile because he'd surprised her.

"Oh," Miss Balfour remarked.

Cautiously, Thaddeus met her glance. He didn't want to disappoint another woman, but his heart belonged to Poppy, and it'd be Poppy's forever, whether or not she wanted it.

But he didn't see disappointment in Miss Balfour's eyes. In place, she appeared confused.

Again went her fingers upon the little flowers on her gown. "Then why are you here, Sergeant Knight? Why aren't you serenading your ladylove? Or such mannerisms that befit a man in love." She'd whispered that last part. "I wouldn't know."

"She doesn't want me," he explained. "I put her in danger."

"You were a police officer. Such jobs have danger." Miss Balfour gave a small shrug. "I would think it takes some time for her to get used to that element of peril, yes, but if your job made you happy..."

Had he been happy? Thaddeus had always thought so. His

work for the Met had been fulfilling, allowing him to test out the theories he studied. Yet in these past two weeks with Poppy, he'd known genuine happiness. The acceptance of another mind, the rush of putting together a case with someone who understood him.

He thought of Whiting, smugly grinning in his office. Of Abigail Vautille and her crushed hand. Of the backbreaking poverty of Mrs. Moseley's life. Overlaid on those images, he saw Elizabeth Stewart again, blood crusted in her blonde locks and the sick smell of her organs poking free of her slit chest.

Death had held him in a clutch for so long he'd forgotten how to be alive.

"Sergeant Knight?" Miss Balfour ventured, a strange note in her voice he couldn't quite identify. As if the words were strangling her, and if she didn't speak, she'd suffocate entirely. "I think if you've found someone that's worth all that work, then you should go after them."

Falling silent, Miss Balfour looked over toward the card table, where Catherine had started another round with Joseph.

"Thank you, Miss Balfour," Thaddeus said.

She gave an almost imperceptible shake of her head. "It is nothing."

To him, it was everything.

It would be so easy to set upon the path his family had outlined for him. Take a modest, sweet wife like Justine Balfour, toil away at Barclay's. As he watched Miss Balfour return to the card game, he knew that he wasn't made for easy. He'd every advantage in life, but he'd squandered his chances with the one woman who made him want to be *more*.

So, he stood. He ignored his mother's pinched lips as he told her he was leaving. He had one last chance with Poppy, and he was going to take it.

* * *

Thaddeus had never been a man to fear enclosed spaces, but the rookeries had redefined his opinion of how many people could be safely packed within a yard. He walked hunched down, trying not to catch his head on the laundry that hung from the first-floor clotheslines.

Whereas the Vautilles had lived in a subdivided house bordering a courtyard, the O'Reillys had settled down in an alleyway with two bricked tenement houses that had never undergone the Georgian desire to remake everything with stucco. The houses were long and lean, given triangular roofs with chimneys each time a new section was built onto the original base.

He raised his fist to knock upon the wooden door, trepidation dripping through his bones.

The door swung open. For a moment, he stood slack-jawed, his hand still fisted.

"Sergeant Knight." Kate O'Reilly sounded far more pleased to see him than he'd expected.

Evidently, Poppy had yet to share *all* the details of their last meeting with her sister-in-law.

"Mrs. O'Reilly." He dropped his hand, wiped his clammy skin upon the leg of his tan breeches.

Damn it all, he missed his blues.

"Do come in," Kate said, standing back so he could enter.

Gulping down uneasiness, Thaddeus followed her inside. Their space was smaller than Poppy's cottage, and not as neat. Stacks and stacks of broadsheets lined the desk by the window, all advertising various news relative to the London and St. Katharine's docks. Daniel had taken a job with a shipping company.

A cursory glance around the room showed no indication

that Kate had returned to her fencing trade, but that meant little: a proper fence would hide the goods in a hole in the wall, underneath a bed, or in a cabinet used for foodstuffs.

Not that it mattered anymore, for even if he'd wanted to, he couldn't arrest her.

"Daniel," Kate called, as she dragged out a chair from the table and nodded for him to take a seat across from her. "Sergeant Knight is here. Do come out, would you?"

Poppy's brother emerged from the back room, quickly tying up his neckcloth. His eyes settled upon Thaddeus, clear and crisply green, so mimicking of Poppy's that Thaddeus felt instantly scrutinized and discovered lacking. But he'd come here to find Poppy, and he wouldn't be deterred.

Thaddeus leaned forward. "Do you know where Poppy is? Please, I need to see her." Every ounce of urgency he could muster from his fatigued soul, he put into this request. "All I know is she went to Atlas Greer's house, wherever that is."

"Yet, you're here." Kate's quieter voice held as much power as her husband's because Thaddeus knew that the four flintlocks hooked onto the wall were hers.

"If Poppy told you not to try to find her—"

Kate cut off Daniel. "Need I remind you how many times I told you to stay away?"

Daniel's body relaxed visibly, but the worry didn't leave his eyes. "It is not the same thing."

"I believe it might be precisely the same thing." Kate released Daniel's hand, gesturing to the other unoccupied chair at the table. "Sit, Daniel, lest you wear a hole in our floor with your heavy stance."

Daniel took a seat. For the second time since he'd entered their home, Thaddeus swallowed down rising dread.

"You love Poppy, don't you?" Kate smiled at Thaddeus. "I

watched your face when you came into the Boars. You were so protective of her."

Kate's eyes flashed with something he couldn't quite explain. He suspected now that she knew everything about his affair with Poppy, but somehow, she still wanted them to have happiness.

The Kate who sat before him was such a far cry from the desperate woman who had flagged him down at the Smithfield cattle market and insisted that he save her kidnapped love. If Kate and Daniel could conquer the odds, surely, there must be hope for Thaddeus and Poppy.

"I love her with every fiber of my being." Thaddeus grew more certain of this with each moment away from her. "And I'll be good to her, O'Reilly, I swear I will."

"Why did Poppy leave you?" Daniel asked.

"I—" Thaddeus began, his nose scrunching up as he struggled for proper words. "I did something wretched. I looked into her past."

A glance passed between Kate and Daniel, of swiftly biting dismay and then dawning realization. Then Daniel nodded, and Kate patted his hand.

Daniel cleared his throat, turning his chair to face Thaddeus. "Then you know why I'm protective of my sister. Why I'd do anything for her."

"I don't want to hurt her, Mr. O'Reilly," Thaddeus assured him. "My expectations at first were simply to solve the Larker case. This...this *tendre* for her, I wasn't prepared for."

"One is never quite prepared for love," Kate murmured. Another secret look passed between her and Daniel, laden with the emotions that need not be said between husband and wife.

"I want to make sure Poppy is safe," Thaddeus said. "I got her into this mess. I thought if I searched harder, if I simply knew the right facts, I could bring these blackguards before the court. That the girl who died in my arms wouldn't have died then in vain."

"It is a noble goal," Kate noted with a hint of surprise as if she'd never expected a policeman could hold lofty ambitions.

Daniel was not so easily convinced of his virtues. "I'm bloody grateful to you for saving me, and I always will be." He ran a hand through his cropped red hair, his brows furrowing. "But Knight, you involved my sister in a murder. Now she's in hiding. I wanted more for her than that, you understand? She deserved more."

"With love comes danger," Kate murmured, her brown eyes clouded, as though remembering something in her own past.

"I'm going to keep Poppy safe," Thaddeus vowed. "If she'll come with me, I want to take her to Scotland. We'll get married and find somewhere safe to settle down. Away from all this violence."

Daniel's posture loosened. "I believe you're a good man, Knight, and I've seen the way she looked at you the other night in the Boars. You make her happy. But if you hurt her..."

"I will do everything in my power to never hurt her again," Thaddeus told him earnestly.

Daniel reached for Kate's hand, a half-formed smile on his lips. "Kate gave me a second chance, and Poppy forgave me for my transgressions. I suppose I ought to give you a chance to plead your case to Poppy."

Kate grinned, squeezing Daniel's hand. "I was going to tell him where Atlas is regardless, but I'm bloody glad you came to the conclusion on your own. You can be a stubborn goat, you know."

"Not as stubborn as you." Daniel winked.

"No one is as stubborn as me," Kate agreed, turning her attention to Thaddeus. "You will see a two-story building that sits a bit back from the street. It'll appear larger from the outside as you enter. Most likely, the door shall be locked, but the lock is quite easy to pick."

"When you enter, you'll see a large room with ramshackle furniture," Daniel added. "Ignore all of that, for Atlas won't be there. Go to the wall and press the fourth brick on the seventh row from the bottom. A staircase will appear in the darkness, and you will go up the stairs and knock on the door. Whether or not Poppy chooses to receive you is up to her."

"Thank you. Thank you so much," he said, as he shook Daniel's hand and sketched a bow to Kate.

As he left their flat, he thought of the fairy tales where the hero must slay a dragon and cut through an uncharted forest to free the princess. But he'd cross any obstacle to get to Poppy and prove to her that he meant every damn word of what he'd said to her. Society might be determined to cast her as fallen, but she was far from ruined in his eyes.

She was the woman he'd win back if it took his last breath.

Chapter Twenty-Two

Curled up on the settee next to Moira, a book spread out across her crossed knees, Poppy heard the shouts. Her name repeated again and again by a voice so achingly familiar. Her hands curled tighter around the book. Her heart slammed against her chest until the sound of it beating echoed in her ears, interlaced with Thaddeus's crisp London accent.

The click-clack of Edna's knitting needles stopped. She glanced at Poppy, a smug smile sliding across her weathered face. Poppy placed the book down on the settee. Standing slowly, not trusting her knees to hold her up, Poppy stared at the door in wide-eyed surprise. She was imaging this—she had to be.

Moira grabbed the book and stuffed the corner of the hard cover into her mouth. Snatching the book away, Poppy deposited it on the tall table where Moira couldn't reach.

"Storytime will have to continue later," she told Moira, her voice sounding foreign to her own ears. Dazed. Confused.

It couldn't be. *He* couldn't be.

For if it was truly Thaddeus pounding at the door to Atlas's loft, that would mean he'd come for her. He'd somehow convinced Daniel and Kate to tell him the exact stone to push to unveil the hidden staircase that led upstairs, for even Jane didn't know the secret to entering Atlas's lair.

"I'll deal with this," Atlas declared, coming from the backroom and pushing past Poppy. Grasped in his hand was a silver dagger, too pointed for Poppy's liking.

"No, Atlas," Poppy protested. She rushed forward, the stiffness from sitting too long fleeing from her joints at this call to action. Reaching the door before Atlas, she stood on her tiptoes and peered through the hole drilled into the door.

Her heart throbbed frantically, the stab-stab-stab of her breath coming in anxious pants.

Another knock reverberated through the door. She jostled with Atlas, but he caught the knob before she could, his reflexes sharper than hers.

Thaddeus was on the top landing, his fist raised to pound on the door once more. His eyes widened as soon as he saw the knife in Atlas's hand, and he staggered backwards.

Atlas lowered the knife. "Sergeant Knight."

Thaddeus hesitated, looking from Atlas to Poppy. She elbowed Atlas out of the way, grabbing Thaddeus's hand and tugging him into the room. Atlas shut the door behind them.

The click echoed in her ears, the end of her secrets.

She dropped Thaddeus's hand, taking a step back. Surrounded by the evidence of a thousand unsolved cases, any other police officer would have surely taken this opportunity to catch the elusive Gentleman Thief.

Yet Thaddeus didn't. He was rooted in that one spot, his booted feet upon a doeskin rug. Time slowed. The silence didn't constrict around them; rather, it flowed and ebbed like the most gloriously woven silk.

Thaddeus stared openly, but not at the assorted trinkets. He looked only at her. Under the weight of his stare, everything faded away.

When she looked into his eyes, she saw love. Maybe she'd spent her life trying to find him. Simply by being himself, he'd pierced her heart. Her soul craved him, marking him as essential to survival as breathing or drinking water. As if he'd been made for her, he filled the empty, lonely parts of herself she'd long ago given up on healing.

In this stripping of every wall she'd built up around her, for the first time in two years, she finally felt like herself again.

She was free.

"You came." So many emotions were wrapped up in those two words. Surprise warred with joy and a deep-set shock until she lived and breathed this truth: he had returned.

"How could I stay away from you?" he asked as if the very idea was preposterous.

Poppy closed the distance between them. His breath hitched as she approached. He waited for her to touch him first.

She wrapped one hand around his. Then with her other hand, she glided her thumb across his bottom lip, wanting to remember the way he felt. Every caress, every kiss, had been stamped into her memory as her constant companion in this last week they'd spent apart.

His hand tightened against hers. She dropped her thumb and leaned her head against his chest, listening to the beat of his heart.

"Ahem," Atlas coughed, shattering the moment between them. "Jolly good to see you happy, Pop, but I'd rather like an explanation as to why the good sergeant is in my living room."

Poppy sprang back from Thaddeus, a blush inflaming her cheeks. "I'm sorry, Atlas. Kate and Daniel must have—"

Atlas groaned. "I figured. I'll have to speak to your brother about why we don't let policemen into my bloody lair."

"Actually, it's just Knight now. No Sergeant," Thaddeus chimed in, coming to stand behind Poppy.

"What do you mean?" Poppy asked, turning back to Thaddeus.

Thaddeus shifted his weight from one foot to the other. "Ah, you see, I've been, ah, sort of dismissed."

Atlas's eyes narrowed. "How does one get 'sort of' dismissed?"

"Oh, no, Thaddeus," she murmured. "That job was everything to you."

As if her words strengthened him, Thaddeus stood up straighter, meeting Atlas's glance. He stood a full head taller than Atlas. Even without his blues, he was an impressive man. A man of honor.

A small smile toyed at his lips, and he took her hand in his, his skin smooth, unlike her roughened hands. He'd led a more privileged existence, but now she knew that didn't mean he'd had an easier life.

"The Met *was* everything to me," he corrected. "Then I met you."

She squeezed his hand, in part to remind herself that he was there, and in part to show support. "What happened?"

"I may have told Whiting that I knew he was covering up the counterfeiting." Thaddeus shrugged, smiling sheepishly. "Basically, he wanted me to tell him you'd taken those papers from Larker's office, Poppy. There's no way under the sun I was going to do that."

"Thank you," she whispered. "For refusing to identify me, but most importantly for coming back."

"I will always come back for you," he said.

"So," Atlas ground out through clenched teeth. "Not a police officer any longer?"

"I fear not," Thaddeus replied. "If you're worried about me

arresting you or reporting you, you needn't be. My word holds the equivalence of the refuse lining the alleyway outside this place. Even if I wanted to turn you in, Greer, no one would take me seriously."

Edna came forward with Moira in her arms. "Then we should give them some privacy." Her tone left no room for disagreement.

Atlas opened and shut his mouth, frowning. "Fine. But we'll be downstairs, Poppy."

"Take as much time as you need." Edna laid a hand on Poppy's arm, her smile sunny. "And Poppy? I told you so."

* * *

They sat on the settee in the back of Atlas's parlor. Here, her knee touching Thaddeus's and her palm enveloped by his larger hand, was where she belonged.

Thaddeus had been content to follow Poppy's direction toward the settee, picking his way between Atlas's various collections with the surefootedness of a mountain goat. He took it all in stride, never questioning the suit of armor, the table littered with maps and cartography equipment, the glass-lidded box of jewels. His arched brow was the only indication he found any of this collection slightly strange.

After Thaddeus explained what had happened with Whiting, they'd fallen into silence. Poppy didn't know how many minutes passed in this way. She hated that he'd lost his job. Yet he didn't seem to want to talk more about it. She was content to be alone with him, lost in thought.

Side by side, the heat of Thaddeus's body flooding through her own, she was stronger. Her feet dangled off the cushions. She was so small compared to him, his long legs planted firmly on the ground. She wanted to be with him always, in these quiet moments that did not tinge of danger and intrigue but were simply the product of two people being in love.

But time went on in its capricious way. She was powerless to stop it. Forever, there'd be monsters that waited for her, not in the darkest alleys, but in the wild crush of happiness when she let down her guard. Life had a way of gutting her when she least expected it, and she could not help but wonder if this was to be one of those moments.

Worry clawed through bliss. She peeked over at him. His eyes were closed. He sucked in a long breath after a long breath, and his hand didn't shake against hers.

She knew this was how he appeared when he was puzzling through a case. He had heard enough of her past to assemble a neat story. All he lacked were the details. She gulped down air. Laying her head down on his shoulder, she watched as he opened his eyes. She was tired of this secret controlling her. The lies owned her until she was nothing more than fiction.

But she could be strong. She was bigger than her past. Somehow, in these last two weeks with Thaddeus, she had created a new identity.

As if he could read her thoughts, Thaddeus smiled at her. From his smile, she drew power and confidence. She could last through whatever the world threw at her.

He ran a hand through his hair, leaving his dark locks ruffled in a way that made her core seize with longing. Their fight before had been ugly and brutal. She wanted to pretend it had never happened, but she couldn't. He'd violated her trust, and she his.

Poppy turned her body so that she faced him. "I'm sorry I lied to you."

His jaw clenched. A minor movement that she would have missed had she not been studying his reaction.

"You did what you thought you must to protect your daughter," Thaddeus said. "And I shouldn't have looked into your past. It wasn't right."

She bit at her bottom lip, debating with herself. "You've been trained to question what doesn't fit. It's how you solve cases. I don't like what you did, Thaddeus, and I doubt I ever will. But if I want you to respect me for who I am, should I not do the same for you?"

"I knew it was wrong," he said, with the shame of a boy caught dipping into the liquor cabinet. "I tried to tell myself it was for the case. But it wasn't. I wanted to know more about you, and I pried into your life. I should have respected your privacy."

"And I should not have lied." Her cheeks burned. He was not the only one who had wronged here. Her failures weighed her down.

"It was not a lie born of malice. I might wish you trusted me with your secret, but I understand, Poppy."

She reached for his hand, and instantly, the quivers of her stomach ceased. Physical contact with him soothed her. "I do trust you. I think a part of me has always known that I could, but I didn't want to recognize that. It seemed safer to keep you in the dark."

"I'm aware of the basics. You don't need to tell me the rest. I love you, and nothing in your past would change that." Thaddeus spoke with such conviction that the last bit of her worries faded. They'd face the world together, and nothing would break them apart.

Nothing, not even Edward.

"I want to tell you," she said, and with that vow, she already felt lighter. "You know I was seventeen. Daniel had come back from London a changed man. He'd lost Kate, lost his job, lost everything when the Watch accused him of a murder he didn't commit. I watched my brother spiral, and there wasn't a damn thing I could do about it. He barely came home after the first month."

"I'm sorry," Thaddeus murmured. "I know the man who arrested Daniel. He's a pathetic excuse for a watchman and should never have been allowed to patrol the streets."

"You helped Daniel," she said. "You helped him when no one else would. I don't tell you this to make you feel bad, but so that you know that when I started to work as a mantua maker's assistant downtown in Dorking, I'd become used to being alone."

Thaddeus filled in the blanks. "So, when that blackguard noticed you..."

"I became besotted with him." She sucked in another deep breath. "I should have known better, of course. Edward Claremont had money and flash—what would he want with a poor Irishwoman like me? But he was so persistent. I met him in the street outside Madame Genet's. I'd dropped the packages I was carrying, and he helped me pick them up. For a week, he came by the shop as I was finishing working. He'd take me to the inn, and we'd have dinner."

Poppy expected a lump to form in her throat, as it always did when she told this story. Regret should wash over her, aching guilt that in a few minutes would leave her tattered. Yet this time, with his quiet support, she felt no shame. She couldn't change what had passed, any more than she could deny her love for Thaddeus. Some things were simply unavoidable, a forceful riot that left no room for refusal.

Thaddeus nodded, urging her on.

She lifted her chin, facing the memory head-on for the first time. "The rest proceeded as you might expect. He told me he loved me, and I believed that he'd marry me. I was foolish, and I was naïve. Neither are good excuses."

"Poppy, don't blame yourself." Thaddeus's voice sent a

shiver down her spine, for there was this edge of firmness and resolve. "*He* was wrong, not you. You love deeply and fully, and you need never fault yourself for that. It is what drew me to you. You've got a wildness to you that captivates me."

He leaned forward, capturing her mouth with his. When he pulled back, he tucked her hair behind her ear. "You bring out this side of me I never knew existed. And I wouldn't have it any other way. You make me passionate, Poppy."

The last of her defenses collapsed. She began to believe in permanence, in letting him into her life. He'd already changed her for the better. When she made a full confession, they could move forward.

"Edward Claremont was nothing like you," she continued. "While you make sure I am satisfied..." She didn't know how exactly to phrase that, so she let her gaze drift down to her hands. Her cheeks must be burning.

Lightly, Thaddeus placed his thumb underneath her chin and pulled her eyes back up to his face. "You can say it, Poppy. I will never judge you. The fact that I can make you moan my name thrills me immensely."

Her words tumbled out in a rush. "Edward didn't make me feel the things you do." She'd balanced on his shoulders as Thaddeus licked between her thighs, and at that moment, she had not cared if she was wanton.

Next to Thaddeus on this settee, she forgot to care again, for his expression spoke volumes. She didn't need words to know how Thaddeus loved her.

"After it was over, Edward got up to leave. I asked him when I'd see him again, and he laughed in my face." Grimacing, she ran a hand across her skirt. "Edward said he'd bet his friends that he could take my virtue within a week. Apparently, I won him a stallion he'd been eying."

"Son of a bitch." Thaddeus's face darkened, a hard glint to his eyes. "I'll kill him, Poppy."

"I've spent two years believing I deserved to be abandoned. That everything people said about me was true." Tears dotted the corners of her eyelids, threatening to spill. "I went to him willingly, Thaddeus. Maybe I was that much of a whore that I *wanted* to be ruined."

"No, Poppy, no." His raw voice worked its way into her mind. "Please, my beautiful girl, please don't believe that. No one deserves to be used like that. He took advantage of your innocence, and the blame is on *him*, not you."

"I know that now," she said. "And I'm ready to move past it. I want to feel whole again. I'll never be the same person I was before Edward, but I'm starting to think I like who I am now more."

"Which is very good, as I find you infinitely desirable," Thaddeus said, wrapping his arms around her. "Edward was a blighter, do you hear me? An absolute bloody blighter, who shouldn't be able to breathe, let alone insult you."

She smiled at that, for he looked so enraged at the mere thought of Edward coming near her again. It was adorable, in a sort of threatening way, and she found she quite liked this protective side of Thaddeus. He'd saved her, reminded her of who she'd always been.

Through him, she'd come to realize that she was resilient. She would not let Edward, or the people of Dorking, define her any longer.

"Now I have Moira," she said, leaning back in Thaddeus's arms. "If I am not to be defined by the actions of others, Moira shouldn't be either. I must embrace her life, all of it."

"She is the smartest of babes," Thaddeus agreed. "No one shall be able to place her in a box. I meant it when I said I'd keep your secret, Poppy. I'll *always* keep your secrets."

"I didn't want Moira to know. The people in my town made it clear how she'd be viewed as a bastard. But with you..." Poppy hazarded another glance at him, daring to hope that he meant his words, and this future for them could become a reality. "If your offer still stands, that is, to marry you?"

"Of course, it does." He tugged her closer to him, kissing her. Between breaths, he spoke against her lips. "You'd make me the happiest of men."

"Poppy Knight does have a certain rhythm to it." She giggled as he tickled her side.

"We'll go to Scotland," he said. "We can get a quick marriage there. Hide out until the Larkers disappear. I've given another officer my files. Perhaps he will make headway."

She laid her head against his shoulder. "I don't want to leave, but I'll go anywhere as long as it's with you."

He ran his hand through her hair, massaging her head. "I don't want to leave either. But until the Larkers are caught, I want to make absolutely sure you and Moira are safe."

"Perhaps Scotland will be fun," she mused. "And Daniel and Kate could come to visit."

"I hear they're doing great things with their investigative techniques," Thaddeus agreed, his fingers working through her hair. "It won't be forever, Poppy. We'll come back to London when the trouble passes. Moira will get to be raised with her family."

Poppy lifted her head up, looking him in the eyes. She saw not only him, his strong and straight jaw, the sparkle in his eyes. She saw a future with him, of nights by the fire in a little cottage. Of dinners with Moira throughout the years, until the one day when Moira brought her own children to join them.

She saw everything that he was, and she knew that, in the end, they would rise above the pain of their pasts.

"I think I'd like to tell Moira the truth," she ventured. "When she's old enough to understand."

Thaddeus nodded. "I'll support whatever you decide."

"I still don't want it to be common knowledge though. I don't believe the world will accept her." Poppy twisted her fingers into the cloth of his shirt. If she held onto him, kept him near to her, then she'd be able to face anything. She could admit she'd been wrong, that maybe there was a different way for Moira. "Maybe—maybe she should know where she comes from."

"It won't be the end, Poppy," Thaddeus told her, with an intensity that paused her fingers from winding tight into the linen of his shirt. What he said was important, always, but this speech must have special meaning. "Edward Claremont is Moira's father in name only. She will understand that, and she'll move past it. Because she will not be defined by history, any more than you should be."

"Could it really be just a part of a bigger whole?" Poppy had never dared hope that.

"I think so." He pressed a kiss to Poppy's forehead, and for a moment they stayed like that, held in each other's arms.

So much had happened in Dorking. When the town had gone against her, she'd stopped believing anyone would ever accept Moira outside of her family.

But Thaddeus had. The way he'd found out about Moira hadn't been what Poppy had wanted, but he didn't judge Moira. He didn't consider her less. And this gave Poppy hope that someday, Moira would find love of her own.

Moira could have a wonderful life without the shroud of lies around her. She'd simply *be* Moira. Her bloodline was irrelevant. Her personality, what she did with her life, all of that would matter.

"I love you, Poppaea Not-Corrigan O'Reilly." Thaddeus

placed his hand over his heart. "Do you feel that? That's my heart beating for you, and only you. Because you are bold and fierce, and even though life has tried to knock you down, you come back stronger than ever."

Happy tears dotted the corners of her eyes, splashed down her cheeks. The tension of the past two weeks ebbed from her frame. She was with him, right where she was supposed to be.

"I love you, too," Poppy whispered. Palm outstretched against the muscular planes of his chest, the pound of his heart thrummed through her fingers. "I'd apologize for not realizing it sooner, but I think I knew it all along. My heart wanted you when my mind told me this was quite irrational."

"Damn the logic," he proclaimed.

She laughed at that, his arched brow and smirk doing wonders to dissipate her fears. "What an odd statement from a master investigator."

"I'm not a sergeant anymore," he reminded her.

She sighed. "I'm so sorry about that, Thaddeus."

Pain flickered in his eyes, but he brushed away her concern, tucking a lock of hair behind her ear. He'd lost his job and with it, his sense of who he'd once been. Perhaps they'd been brought together because they both needed redefining.

"I can think of several things I'd rather think about than the Met," he murmured, the emotion burning in his chocolate eyes, leaving her little confusion about what he truly wanted.

Her hand had fallen from his chest. Sprawled across his lap, she didn't need that contact to comprehend his need. He was kind and considerate but awakened these primal desires in her. Fresh stubble littered his chin, underneath his nose. He'd been so intent on getting to her, he hadn't bothered to shave. This look suited him, left him rugged.

His dark locks stood on their ends, as if he'd run his fingers through them in the hack ride over here. She examined the planes of his broad shoulders, trailing her fingers down to his narrow waist. His eyes flashed with desire. With each touch, her body heated from the inside out, ready for the euphoria only he gave her.

"Poppy," he murmured, capturing her hands before she got to his breeches. "Are you sure? We can wait until we're married." His words came out choked; the dazed glaze to his eyes told her he was already primed.

Moira's laughter drifted upstairs, followed by Edna's chuckle. She doubted Atlas was around still; he had a habit of slipping out into the night before anyone noticed he'd left. Moira would be occupied for hours, playing with the toys Edna had stashed on the lower level.

In the heart of St. Giles, surrounded by thieves and rogues, Poppy felt safer than she'd ever been.

Chapter Twenty-Three

I f she were to be the woman society wanted, Poppy would wait. Her previous sexual experiences had been brought on by impetuousness. They'd been nights of weakness, wanting to find comfort in another's arms when the world seemed so bleak.

Society would say she'd lost the right to happiness when she'd bedded Edward. But society was incorrect—she deserved this love. When Thaddeus looked at her, she was certain she could become a person who was worthy of his affection. He reminded her to trust her own desires.

And she wanted to make love to Thaddeus. It was her decision, damn it, and she'd give herself to him because it was a natural extension of her affection. She was done being confined to rigid morals, a map for a life that wasn't hers to live.

She'd be her own guide from now on.

Fisting her hands in Thaddeus's shirt, Poppy leaned into him. "I don't want to wait. I want to be with you, always."

She pressed her lips to his, effectively ending any further questions. Locking her fingers in his hair, she angled his head so that she could take the kiss deeper. His lips hinted of whisky, of desire, and becoming unbroken.

Tentatively at first, her tongue flitted out, seeking entry between his parted lips. She'd never initiated this. Instead, she'd allowed Thaddeus to start, going off his motions. Now with him, she sought the closest forms of connection, and she did not run. This man, with his integrity and his dedication, saw a side of her buried underneath the surface.

He knew her secrets, every last shameful lie.

And he'd stayed. Stayed to run his hands down the sleeves of her jade gown, stayed to pull her closer to him until his body heat warmed her almost to the point of combustion. He broke their kiss to travel down her neck, her skin branded each place his lips hit.

She'd found respite in him before, but it had been the quiet before the storm. This time, she gave herself entirely to him.

Gently, she pushed him back from her. Her gaze roved down his frame. She'd never tire of looking at him. She liked him best when he was bare, and so she reached for his neckcloth and unwound it. Her fingers, clever and skilled from picking at her aunt's handloom, made quick work of unbuttoning his shirt. Soon, she was sliding it off him, admiring the chiseled lines of his upper arms. When she raced her fingers down his naked skin, fingertips spread out across his chest, he groaned. This led her to push harder against him, to anchor herself in his lap, dipping her mouth down so that she could kiss along his chest. Head back, he absorbed her touches in rapture.

He spun her around, burning her neck with his kisses. He undid the buttons of her dress until it pooled in her lap. He lifted her up and off of him, long enough that the dress and her petticoat fell to the floor, but not so long that she began to feel the absence of him. No, he'd never part from her. She wouldn't allow it. Corset followed and then shift, on and on until she was bared across his lap.

She rocked her hips against him. Urgency flooded her, building on the sparks that had begun with his words and rose with his caresses. His body on hers. His mouth at her center, tongue exploring her folds.

She let out a whimper, moving against him once more. Sensing her need, he gathered her up in his arms, settling her down on the settee. Undoing the clasp of his breeches, he slid the fabric off his hips, taking his smalls as well. The sight of him, powerful erection standing at attention for her, sent a bolt of longing through her body. Yet she didn't have much time to pine, for he was on the settee. He scooted farther back, trailing kisses down her body until he was positioned between her legs. Sliding a finger inside of her, he moved within her until she crooned from pleasure. Another finger joined the second within her, stretching her, readying her for him. He turned his hand so that he could flick at her bud while his finger plunged inside of her.

The sensations built high and tight within her, every nerve ending acutely aware of his presence. His scent, the salty taste to his skin as she grabbed his free hand, brought it to her mouth and nipped. It was too much. She was on edge.

Just when she thought she'd break, he settled on the settee above her, keeping his weight off of her by crooking his elbows and pressing into the cushions.

He entered her in one long stroke. One stroke to end all others, for she knew what it meant to be filled completely to the brim. Joined together, they'd faced the worst dangers, and they'd survived. She met his thrusts with her own rhythmic moving of her hips, muscles clenching around him and releasing. Reaching around him, she clasped his buttocks, urging him deeper into her. Pleasure built, and pleasure took, and pleasure seized at her cognizance until she released in a furious rush of spark and fire. He came a moment after her, groaning out her name.

They lay in each other's arms, the haze of bliss upon them. Unlike in the Three Boars, she didn't feel the cold slam of lonely pragmatism upon her, for she'd constructed a new reality with Thaddeus. One where she was loved and cherished, simply for being herself.

She'd been given a gift in Thaddeus's love.

* * *

Never had Thaddeus been a possessive man, but with Poppy, he found himself wanting to declare to the world that she was his and his alone. He'd fight her battles for her if she'd only let him. Yet her past with Moira's father was hers to own. Someday, if she wanted to face Edward Claremont, he'd stand by her side as she did so. And if she wanted to return to Dorking, he'd go with her.

He'd be content to hold her hand as she fought against the demons of her past. She might not heal tomorrow, nor even in the next year. Claremont and the rest of society had tried to shame her, but their efforts had failed.

Poppy was a woman with fire and determination, and damn it all, she was worth something. She had not deserved to be cast aside like a dirty rag. No one did.

He'd keep telling her that till she could face the world with her head held high.

She perched on the edge of the settee, her bare feet dangling over the side. Thaddeus came to stand in front of her. Clad only in his breeches, he grabbed for her hand, raising it to his lips and placing a featherlight kiss across her knuckles. He wanted to linger in this sitting room forever, pretending that their problems wouldn't exist.

There was something to be said for the protection of felonious influence. The location of Atlas's loft was widely unknown—that combined with the secret entrance assured him they were safe here. Atlas had managed to protect Poppy when the Met had failed. All those years spent arresting men he'd considered criminals...and now Thaddeus found himself deeply indebted to the greatest thief of them all.

Strange incident by strange incident, his definitions of right and wrong were collapsing. Yet instead of mourning those toppling walls, he felt unrestricted. Perhaps this was what Sophocles had meant when he'd said, "'As for me, I know nothing.'" Thaddeus couldn't return to the life he'd led previously.

Yet with Poppy so near to him, he was awake and alive like he'd never been before.

"I love you." He kissed her.

"As I love you." She smiled.

"Thank you for telling me about what happened in Surrey." He ran his thumb from her ear down to her chin, tracing the curvature of her jaw. Strong and pointed, like the woman he loved. "I know it wasn't easy."

She leaned into his touch, that small, sad smile on her lips breaking his heart. "Perhaps the truth shall set me free."

"It's a start," he agreed. "I believe pain lessens in stages. So many people bury their emotions, and they expect you to do the same. But you, Poppy, who loves so deeply and so freely—you hurt absolutely, for you feel every strike."

"I never thought of it like that," she said. "So, the pain makes the pleasure more. Without the ache, we might never know what true bliss was like."

"'*Perfer et obdura–dolor hic tibi proderit olim*,'" he quoted, clasping her hand in his. "Be patient and tough, someday this pain will be good for you."

"I know this one." She rubbed her thumb against his, her

313

pert nose wrinkling as she thought. The name came to her, her eyes lighting up. "Ovid."

"Very good," he praised. "The lady knows her Latin."

"I had run out of gothic novels to read," she confessed. "The library was right next to Madame Genet's shop, but it was a quarter of the size of yours. It was either Ovid's poetry or scientific principles."

"When we are married, it shall be your library too."

That brought a gleeful shriek from her, as she tossed her arms around his neck and kissed him. He sank into the kiss, wanting to remain in this safe place longer when he didn't have to face the reality that he was unemployed.

Bloody hell, he'd sort that all out once they were out of London. Figure out how to inform his mother and father that he'd left, and no, they certainly couldn't tell all their friends where he was. He suppressed a groan, imaging his mother's outrage. He'd probably hear her hollers all the way in bloody Scotland. If joining the Met hadn't already banned him from the family, this surely would.

Right now, he'd concentrate on the warm woman in his arms, resting her head against his shoulder. He breathed in the honey and vanilla scent of her and decided that from now on, his first job would be to remind her she was magnificent.

Poppy's hand slipped to her stomach. "There's the chance that I may be with child."

Thaddeus grinned, covering her hand with his own. He couldn't think of anything more wonderful. All this time, he'd wanted a family that loved him for him, and now he had one. "Then we shall raise both our children to know that they can be anything they damn well please."

"I never felt strong until I met you." She dropped her hand from his, leaned forward, and kissed him. A sweet kiss, a show of gratitude that left him wanting her more. "Every time I pushed you away, thinking I was protecting myself, you pulled me back into your life. You wouldn't let me stay trapped. You loved me when I couldn't love myself."

"You were a puzzle, at first," he admitted, with a sly half-smile that made her kiss him once more. When she drew back, he grabbed hold of her arm and gave a little tug, so that she was flush against his chest. "Then you came into my study, and you started to talk about Shakespeare with such fire that I thought 'This girl. She's the one I've been waiting for.'"

"So, any girl who talked about *King Lear* would have intrigued you?" Poppy teased.

"Yes, there were hordes of them lined up. You just happened to be the first through the door," he said dryly. "I can't possibly think why you'd want distance from me. Could it be because I worked the most hated job in all of Spitalfields? Or because I drew you into a case that got your friend tortured and maimed?"

His flinty questions cast a somber overtone to their reunion.

Poppy laid her head on his shoulder.

"It'll all turn out fine," he told her, but even he didn't believe his assertion.

"I'm sorry you were dismissed," Poppy said, linking her fingers with his. "It's not right. You're trying to help the people, and instead of being rewarded, you're punished."

"Thank you. I know you didn't like the Met to begin with."

"But it was important to you, and I love you," Poppy protested. "What's important to you is going to be important to me. From now on, we're a team, you hear? You and I, taking on the world."

"I like the sound of that." He laid his head on top of hers. Her devotion steadied him.

She peered up at him. "What will you do now?"

"I'm not quite sure," he confessed. "My brother has invested some of my savings in a fund that should give us a small, but secure, profit. I have enough money that I estimate we'll be fine for a year or so in Scotland, but I'll need to find a job with comparable pay to support you and Moira after that."

"You don't have to do that," she said. "I've taken care of myself so far, and I can continue to do so."

He pulled back so that he could look her in the eye. "You're going to be my wife, Poppy. While I have no doubt that you can get by on your own, I want to make sure you and Moira are safe. You shouldn't be working such long hours."

For a second, he thought she might protest. But instead, she kissed him. "I shall have to get used to being taken care of then."

"I'm sure I'll find something," he said, more to convince himself than her.

What could he do when his skill set matched police work and not much else? There wasn't a huge market for philosophers who could read four languages and dissect crimes.

Running his thumb across hers, Thaddeus remembered how smug Whiting had looked upon dismissing him. If Strickland didn't decide to take up the case, the Larkers would go free forever, and Whiting would never pay for betraying the Met.

And he and Poppy wouldn't be able to remain in London.

"We'll figure it out," Poppy agreed.

His strong Poppy, willing to fight when the odds were stacked against them.

"But we've dallied long enough." He pushed himself up from the settee, going to collect the rest of his clothes. "I'll go back to my townhouse to pick up some supplies, and then I'll come to get you. I shouldn't be long."

She shook her head. "Absolutely not. The Larkers are out there, Thaddeus. If we leave, we leave together. You'll need someone to watch your back."

"You should stay here," he told her. By the resolute set to her jaw, he suspected he'd already lost this battle.

"I'm not taking the chance that I'll lose you." She eyed him through narrow slits, her hackles raised. "I'm tired of being scared, of hiding. How can I stay here knowing you might be in danger? When we can't trust the police?"

"Stubborn chit." He sighed, but he couldn't put any effort behind his words. He loved her fire.

She hopped down from the tureen, going toward the corner where her half-boots sat on the lion skin rug. "It's settled. I'll tell Edna to keep Moira upstairs while we're out."

For a second, he watched Poppy as she moved about the room, loading her flintlock pistol. Decision, purpose, and drive, all combined in this petite woman with the Surrey voice.

Chapter Twenty-Four

When they approached Thaddeus's townhouse, it was past two in the morning. Under the cover of a cloudy, starless night and a new moon, Thaddeus handed Poppy down from the hired hack and went to pay the driver. As the carriage rolled away down the street, Thaddeus leaned in to whisper to Poppy.

Then he stopped, mid-reach, and listened. Something rustled, like the swishing of a dress, or the opening of a cloth bag. No one else appeared to be outside. Though the street-lamps provided some light, there were many dark areas where someone could hide.

Too many areas. They weren't safe out in the open.

With his hand on Poppy's back, Thaddeus guided her forward. She huddled behind him as he unlocked his front door, following him in. Blackness enveloped them. He'd drawn all the curtains before he left for Kate and Daniel's flat. As he struck the lucifer and dropped it into the lantern he kept in the front hall, it was eerily quiet.

Until Poppy's gasp ripped through the air.

His house was in shambles.

The two chairs that lined his front entrance wall were over-turned. The petite table he usually kept pushed up against the stairwell had been toppled, the third leg chopped off. Each of his painstakingly chosen portraits of ancient philosophers had been pulled down from the wall. There were great gaping holes where the paintings had once been as if someone had been searching for a wall safe.

"Christ," Thaddeus cursed.

He ushered Poppy behind him again, but he did not maintain a firm grip on her. As much as he would have liked the physical reassurance that she was safe, he needed both hands: one for the lantern, one for his truncheon, which he unsheathed from his side.

"Do you have the flintlock?" he asked Poppy, his voice low.

"Yes, but I only know how to shoot it in theory," she murmured back, hanging on to the tail of his coat.

"It'll have to do."

Thaddeus advanced down the hallway, picking his way over the remains of his once carefully ordered life. Though he shined the lantern in every corner, there was no sign of anyone else.

He knew not to become optimistic. The intruder could still be in the house. They checked his parlor, again finding nothing. This room had fared better, mostly upturned furniture and a few smashed vases.

Keeping Poppy behind him, he went to the library. God, he prayed, please let his library remain untouched.

His stomach plummeted toward his feet.

Books were ripped from the shelves, creating large gaps where once there had been meticulous organization. Ragged piles of literature covered the floor, spines cracked, pages curled back. The floor was a phantasmagoria of colors. Even the cozy corner where he'd sat with Poppy had been wrecked. The settee and armchairs had been slashed. Stuffing piled out onto the floor, white tufts mixing with equally white parchment. The remains of his favorite novels, gutted.

The library had been his refuge away from the disorder of the world, but now there was only chaos. He stood there, jaw dropped, eyes wide.

Whiting's betrayal had cost him his job, that large part of his identity. This completed the destruction of the studious man he'd been before.

He'd ruin Whiting if it was the last damn thing he did. Thaddeus imagined Whiting's face turning bright red as his hands wrapped firmly around the inspector's throat, squeezing the life out of him. Fists clenched at his sides, he stood in the middle of this devastating library and rage coursed through him. Violent, biting rage, boiling at the seams of his consciousness.

But that would solve nothing. He was a reasonable man, damn it. He'd get revenge upon Whiting, yes, but at this moment, he needed to focus.

Poppy stepped over to the sitting area and kneeled. Her face contorted wretchedly as she plucked from the rubbish his leather-bound volume of *Frankenstein*, half of the pages hanging from the spine by one lone string. There was no telling where the rest of the book had ended up.

"Oh, Thaddeus," Poppy murmured, somehow able to convey soul-shattering sadness in those two words.

He came to stand behind Poppy, drawing her body flush against his chest. He held her close to keep her safe, to quiet his mind.

"What do we do now?" Poppy whispered, huddling beside him.

Thaddeus gnawed at his bottom lip. As much as he didn't relish dragging Poppy with him, remaining on the ground floor unaccompanied was more perilous. At least together, he'd be able to protect her better.

"We check upstairs." He headed for the door, looking over his shoulder one last time. No change. He hoped the indomitable Mrs. Clery was up to the task of righting the damage.

As they slid up the stairs, those mundane thoughts sharpened his focus. He'd always been the man with the plan. Facing danger daily on patrol, he knew to ignore it all, to center his mind on the one thing that he *could* control: his own reactions.

And so, when his foot hit that final step, he saw his home with the distance needed. He'd mourn his lost things later. What mattered was Poppy's safety.

Thaddeus handed Poppy the lantern so that he could light the hall sconces. The flame flickered before gaining purchase, and soon they were bathed in a golden glow. That was comforting.

"I don't know what we'll find, so if there's danger, I want you to run."

"I'm not leaving you," she insisted, as she passed the lantern back to him. Her voice was so convincing he might have believed she wasn't scared if fear didn't backlight her eyes.

"Poppy, this isn't negotiable," he hissed.

She opened her mouth to retort, but shut it promptly, grabbing for his arm. "Do you hear that?"

A slam echoed through the hall, then another. The shutting of his trunks, if he had to guess, for the noise seemed to be coming from the bedroom. Setting his lantern down, he crept forward. He stopped at the door and put his ear to it. Poppy almost crashed into him, but she caught herself in time, hand on his back. She moved to stand next to him at the door, listening too.

"It has to be here." A woman's voice, tight with irritation.

"Effie Larker," Poppy whispered, her fingers tightening against his coat lapel.

"I ain't seen it, Missus." A man this time, vaguely familiar. "I've looked everywhere."

"Imbecile," Effie snapped, her high heels clicking on the wood floor of his room. She crossed what he estimated to be the full length of the room, probably approaching her helper. "Move over. Christ, if you want something done, you've got to do it yourself. You'd think I'd know that by now."

"We shouldn't be here." Another man's voice, nervous, higher pitched. "He was a Peeler, and he's probably got connections. I'm not getting collared for this."

Thaddeus knew this one: Jennings, Boz's older guard. He turned his head to Poppy, arching a brow. She nodded.

"No one is going to get caught if you hurry your arse up," Effie replied. "Jonah made it very clear he'd dismissed Knight. If you *listened,* you'd remember that."

"I do listen," Jennings protested, which made the other man guffaw.

"Clowes," Poppy mouthed, and then she said something Thaddeus thought may have been "I'm going to string him up by his toes for this."

Just in case, Thaddeus moved to his right a smidge to block the door from her access.

Three against two. Thaddeus didn't like those odds, but it could be worse. They ought to go now—but where the hell would they go? He couldn't turn to the Met, not with Whiting still on staff. Strickland wouldn't be home at this hour. If they went to Atlas's loft, they risked leading the intruders back to Moira.

Here, at least, they could gather information on what the trio planned. From that data, he'd form a more concrete plan.

"What's got you thinkin' it's here?" Clowes asked. "He's been gone for a few days. Might've rid himself of it if he's smart."

"Jonah said the pig kept a detailed file on the case," Effie explained. "After your fool move with the Vautille bitch, Frank, we can't take any more chances."

Beside him, Poppy stiffened. Her hands froze on the flint-lock. Thaddeus guessed she thought of her friend, laid up in the London Hospital.

"We need to leave now," Thaddeus whispered, trying to steer Poppy away. He had the information he needed.

But Poppy wouldn't move.

"You told me to get answers," Clowes protested. "How was I to know the whore'd get the Met involved?"

Effie let out a loud puff of exasperation at that.

"Besides, you liked puttin' her hand in the loom. You laughed when all the blood started gushin'," Clowes reminded her.

"What was I supposed to do?" Effie asked. "You'd already cornered her. I took advantage of the opportunity and *fixed* part of your mess."

"*I* told him not to do it," Jennings retorted.

"If you'd nabbed the little girl, Abigail would have fetched us the bloody file," Effie replied. "We could have disposed of them both afterwards. Now we've got a missing girl and a missing file!"

"You'd off the little girl?" Jennings's voice shook.

"Unequivocally. No room for sentimentality in this busi-ness," Effie replied. A smacking sound echoed through the room. The crop she usually carried, he surmised.

When she spoke again, her voice was deathly low. Thad-deus leaned farther into the door, straining to hear.

"You've got a little girl, don't you, Jennings?"

Bile rose up in Thaddeus's throat. He tugged Poppy to him, away from the door, so that she couldn't hear Effie's words.

"How'd you like it if you found your daughter slit clean

open?" Effie's voice rose in volume, cold and steely. "Because if you don't move your arse, that's what I'm going to do."

His stomach roiled. He'd known revulsion, but the Larkers were even worse than he'd imagined. God, he wanted to make them pay. But not at the risk of Poppy.

"We need to leave," he whispered, giving Poppy a push toward the stairs.

Poppy snapped to attention. Her eyes darkened, fury splashing over her pale cheeks. As if something had shattered in her, something that had been long on its way. Effie Larker had terrorized people for far too long.

His brave, possibly foolish Poppy had reached the point where enough was finally enough.

"I'll kill her. I'll kill her," Poppy murmured, rocking back against his frame.

"What was that?" Clowes asked.

Footsteps sounded through the room as all three charged toward the door.

"Run, Poppy, run," Thaddeus urged her, grabbing hold of her and giving her a push toward the stairs.

But it was too late. The door was flung open. Silhouetted against her two guards, Effie Larker was a creature of the night, bereft of the blood that should have smeared her pearly teeth. Her frigid blue eyes scrutinized Poppy and Thaddeus with imperial detachment.

Effie flicked her riding crop against her raised left hand twice. Following her signal, Frank Clowes sprang at Thaddeus, fists raised. Thaddeus deflected his blow with the truncheon, but Clowes was a strapping youth, all brawn with no brains. Swiftly, he swung at Thaddeus, and he would have connected had Effie not grabbed the back of his tunic and pulled him back.

"Patience," Effie cautioned. "Enjoy the hunt. Have I taught you nothing?"

"You're revolting," Poppy spat, peeking out from behind Thaddeus's shoulder. "You ought to be in Bedlam."

"Mrs. Corrigan." Effie's red lips curled back in a sneer. "Or should I say, *Miss* O'Reilly? How is your charming little bastard?"

"I'll rip you to shreds," Poppy vowed, starting to go toward Effie.

Thaddeus raised his arm, level at her throat. While she could have ducked underneath this, his movement served as a reminder for caution. If Poppy went rushing at Effie, he didn't know if he could protect her.

Poppy stilled.

Effie shrugged, her gaze drifting from Jennings to Clowes and back to Poppy. She arched a single brow, bemused by all she saw. "If your master will let you off the leash. But then my boys will take care of you, won't you, boys?"

Clowes nodded immediately, but Jennings held back, sneaking an almost imperceptible glance at Poppy. Thaddeus noted the reaction, adding it to his plan. There was their ticket out of this mess. Effie had threatened the man's daughter. If they could get him on their side, the odds would turn in their favor.

The longer Thaddeus kept Effie talking, the better chance she'd say something truly deplorable, perhaps enough to make Jennings cross over to them.

"Why did you do it?" Thaddeus asked.

Effie blinked. "I like money. It's simple mathematics, Sergeant." She grinned as if she'd remembered something pleasing. "I almost forgot—not quite Sergeant anymore, are you? Jonah was so sad to have to get rid of you. You made his job so easy."

"Pity for him." Thaddeus rolled his eyes. He had to get Effie back on track, so she'd tell him something new that he could use. "What did Anna Moseley ever do to you?"

Effie glanced at Clowes. "To me? Nothing. But she kept prying into Clowes's life here, and we couldn't have that."

Poppy shook against him. "So, you killed her."

"*I* did no such thing," Effie stated with a smirk. "I requested she be killed, yes. And though I would have done it myself, mind you, Boz got to her first. Quite a hassle for me, really. He's always so fired up after a slaughter, expecting things from me." She sighed, smacking the crop against her hand once more. "You must know how that is, Poppy, from one whore to another."

That was quite enough.

Thaddeus stepped forward, his truncheon brandished. This wouldn't continue. He'd end this.

In an instant, the atmosphere changed, as if a thread had been snipped in the fabric of their lives. It hit him, the raw anticipation of death. No longer were they five people engaged in an irregular cluster outside his bedroom. They were adversaries, locked in combat.

Jennings and Clowes bore down on him, while Effie Larker cornered Poppy. Blood pounding in his head, he struck out with the truncheon, connecting with Clowes's leg. "Take out the leader," Joseph had said. If Clowes was defeated, Jennings might fall back.

But the blow wasn't enough to stop Clowes. He recovered, landing a punch to Thaddeus's right arm. Jennings lingered, taking a step forward toward Thaddeus, but then stopping. He shifted his weight from foot to foot, watching the fight uneasily.

And Thaddeus could hear Poppy, somewhere down the hallway now. The grunt as something slammed into her body. Effie Larker's coolly gruesome tones. He tried to dart to the left. He had to get to Poppy.

And then Clowes's fist connected. Clowes pounded into his stomach with the strength of a man who'd grown up on these gore-stained streets. A second later, Thaddeus fell back, stumbling. Pain seared through him. Startling, awful pain, which stole the breath from his lungs and left him gasping for air.

His fall back had put just enough distance between him and Clowes that the blows no longer connected. He had the advantage of being the taller man, his arms and legs long enough to give him a better range.

He swung out blindly with his truncheon, feeling a stab of grim satisfaction when it connected with Clowes's chest. Offering Clowes no chance to recover, he drew back quickly and hit him once more. Another hit, another block, parry, parry, thrust. The moves became a dance, and he'd always found dancing to be simple. It was a matter of rhythm and numbers.

Dully, he registered the pain. Thaddeus viewed the scene as if he was out of his body, watching from a rooftop perch.

There was nothing outside of this fight. He'd break Clowes. And if Jennings came for him, he'd break Jennings too.

He'd save Poppy.

* * *

Effie towered over Poppy, sheathed in a frosty-blue dress. Despite the closeness, Poppy felt no heat emanating from her. Nothing but chilly cruelty in the cut of her sharp chin and the chisel of her cheekbones.

She was a madwoman.

Effie smiled, and it struck Poppy in the gut that she knew that smile. She'd seen it on Edward, as he'd turned around to get one last look of her, swathed in the satin sheets he'd deflowered her upon. She gripped the flintlock to her tighter, holding it in her right hand.

"Poppy," Effie intoned.

The sick taste of victory had lined Edward's voice when he'd said her name. Just like this.

Out of the corner of her eye, she tracked Thaddeus's movements. He'd the upper hand on Jennings, but Clowes had come back for more. She had to trust Thaddeus knew what he was doing.

For, in the split second she'd looked away, Effie had snaked her hand out, catching Poppy's hair. Effie tunneled her pointy nails in, digging into the tender flesh. She tugged hard.

Poppy's eyes watered. As the pain beat in her head, she clawed with her left hand at Effie's grasp. She tried to slip her fingers underneath of Effie's, to pry off a few fingers at a time. Her grip on the flintlock loosened as Effie dug in deeper.

"I'm going to enjoy killing you most of all," Effie hissed in her ear, low and lethal. "You little slut. Did you think you could hide from me? I can smell the stain on you."

Poppy kept working on Effie's fingers, applying pressure to her pinkie.

She could get a better grip if she used both of her hands, but that meant dropping the flintlock entirely. It was her only weapon. No, better to stay in this position, so that if Effie moved at all, she could wrench from her and use the pistol...

"If I had to be punished, so do you," Effie told her. "No one escapes the wrath of God, Poppaea." She rotated her wrist, bending Poppy's hair around her hand.

Poppy screamed as pain sliced through her head. Black spots dotted her vision.

But seconds later, her vision cleared. A red lock of hair hung from Effie's fingers.

She was free.

Poppy dived back, out of Effie's reach. She held the flintlock up, placing her finger on the trigger. How many times had she seen Kate take this stance? Countless. She could fake her way through this. Effie didn't need to know she'd never shot the gun before.

Effie started to go toward her but stopped when she aimed the flintlock. Coming to a dead stop, Effie watched Poppy with wide eyes, tracking her movements.

"If you take another step toward me, I'm going to shoot," Poppy cautioned.

Effie looked from Poppy to her two guards. Jennings stood off to the side while Clowes and Thaddeus continued to spar. Thaddeus was getting the better of Clowes, for while Clowes was a bigger man, Thaddeus was far spryer. A bruise already darkened Clowes's chin, while Thaddeus's shirt was ripped. But he didn't seem to be laboring hard enough that she needed to worry.

"Jennings, get her!" Effie barked.

Jennings looked at Poppy, looked at the gun, and remained where he was.

"Perhaps you shouldn't have threatened his daughter," Poppy remarked.

"You're a fucking bitch, Effie," Jennings growled. "I hope they take you down."

Still eying the flintlock in Poppy's hands, anger flashed across Effie's face. "After I slit your daughter's throat, I'll make sure you join her in hell, Jennings."

At that sick threat, Poppy's eyes narrowed. "Step back," she ordered Effie, coming nearer to the woman. "Keep backing up until you reach the banister."

At first, Effie didn't move. Poppy closed in on her. Removing her finger from the trigger, she jammed the butt of the gun into Effie's side. Effie scrambled backwards. Once Effie was far back enough, Poppy could strike her with the gun. Hopefully, the impact would knock Effie out. Then Poppy and Thaddeus could flee.

When Poppy thought she finally had the upper advantage,

something clicked in Effie. The taller woman came at Poppy in a flurry of scratches, kicks, and slaps.

Poppy concentrated on keeping hold of the gun, gripping it in two hands. She fought off Effie's attack, using the flintlock as a billystick. She kept scooting Effie back. They were at the railing.

But Poppy was not quick enough, and Effie's hand landed hard against her cheek as her foot connected with Poppy's shin.

God, the pain.

Desperate to stop the attack, Poppy slid one hand down lower on the gun, while the other gripped the middle. She thrust the gun upwards. The butt of the gun slammed into Effie's chest.

She heard the connection before the effect of it became obvious: a hard pop, that of bone-breaking from the impact. Effie was flung backwards, the force crushing her into the banister.

There was a splinter, then a crack, as the banister split under Effie's weight. Poppy barely managed to throw herself back in time.

Effie Larker plummeted toward the ground, legs flailing, mouth open in a scream. Her body jackknifed in the air. At the last second, she attempted to regain her balance, her arms pinwheeling.

There was a crack, and then a snap, as her neck broke upon impact. Her flattened corpse crumpled in an uneven heap. Red, red blood spilled from her skull, pooling in an irregular circle around her head.

Effie Larker was dead.

Chapter Twenty-Five

She'd killed Effie.

Poppy approached the gap in the railing where the balustrade had once been. She edged forward. If she took a step forward—one single step—she'd fall, joining Effie's mangled body on the ground level.

Her hand rested on the saw-toothed wood. The remaining barrier, stalwart and bold. Reminding her that in the worst of times, some did not cower. They stood up and fought.

Like the man who came to stand behind her.

Thaddeus placed his hand on her shoulder. Gently, so gently she almost didn't realize she was moving, he helped her back from the railing. He turned her so that she could no longer see downstairs, as if sensing that she needed to be removed from the scene. That if he didn't *make* her stop looking, she never would. Effie's body was burned into her brain.

Poppy could barely breathe. Any attempt at words turned into indecipherable groans. Thaddeus held her to him, stroking her back. She sobbed, long, desperate cries about this death that turned into mourning everything she'd lost in the past two years.

"It was an accident," he said.

His voice rumbling in her ears made her think for a few seconds that he was right. She hadn't intended for Effie to fall back. She couldn't have known that the banister would break.

Poppy hadn't wanted any of this.

"She's dead." Her words were muffled by Thaddeus's coat. Devoured, the way the ground had sucked in Effie.

"I know, love," he said. "No one could have accounted for that. Do you know how many times I've leaned against that banister? Hell, I might have met *my* doom."

That brought forth another round of sniffles from her. She'd almost lost him so many times in the past few weeks. From ignorance, from fear, from these vicious attacks. A life without Thaddeus, a man she hadn't even known before moving to London, now seemed unconscionable.

"Ah, shit," he muttered. "That wasn't the proper thing to say. I simply meant—"

"I know what you meant." She pulled back from him, daring to smile. To laugh, if only a brief chuckle before the moroseness stole at her mind again. Because when this was all said and done, she *hadn't* meant for Effie to die. "She would have killed you," Thaddeus said. "Poppy, you do understand that, don't you? You didn't do anything wrong."

It amazed her even then how he managed to read her thoughts. And now, in the face of this horror, he held her close.

She'd been defending her life. Defending Thaddeus, damn it. But Effie had wanted to snuff them out for the pure joy of killing, for the obstacle they posed to her plans.

Though Effie Larker might not have carried out Anna Moseley's murder, she had ordered it. Anna had not done anything to warrant her bitter end. She was disposable, and no one would miss her. No one that counted, at least.

Anna's death warrant had been sealed the day she took an interest in Frank Clowes.

Where was Clowes? Poppy had forgotten about him. She'd forgotten about everything but the mashed body downstairs.

Reluctantly, she pulled away from Thaddeus's embrace. A quick look around assured her that Jennings had fled the scene, probably as soon as Thaddeus had come to comfort her. Clowes, meanwhile, sat with his back against the wall. Taking a step closer, she saw his hands trussed up behind him with what appeared to be a…neckcloth? She glanced back at Thaddeus.

Yes. He'd definitely used his neckcloth to tie up Clowes. And he'd gagged Clowes with his handkerchief too.

This struck her as absurdly funny. So much so that she would have laughed until tears streamed down her face, had she not made the mistake of glancing down at Effie. A particularly sobering sight if there ever was one.

Poppy stepped back from Clowes, back into the sanctuary of Thaddeus's arms. Away from the man she'd once thought of as a friend.

Clowes had stood by as the Larkers murdered Anna, and he had not complained. He had tortured Abigail.

Poppy couldn't contemplate this any longer. This betrayal, on so many levels, of everything she'd thought made sense. In the beginning, she'd trusted the Larkers. Believed they'd do what was right for their employees.

She'd never imagined that devastation like this could be possible. After Edward had left, Poppy had thought she'd known the worst pain possible. Yet the torture Abigail had endured was far, far worse. Hand smashed. Livelihood gone. How would Abigail continue on after treatment at the hospital finished? Poppy barely knew how to go forward with her own life.

She was tired, so very tired.

But she was safe.

Thaddeus pulled off his coat. He took her hand, steering her down the stairs. He stuck to the outside of the steps so that he could guide her seamlessly out the door, holding his coat up so that she wouldn't glimpse the carnage. His arm remained around her, even as he opened the front door.

When they stepped out onto the street, the crisp night air slapped her face. Reminded her that outside of this violent house, London was vibrant, bursting at the seams with activity. For a second, at least, she allowed herself to hope that someday she'd move happily within that crowd, free of this perpetual gloom.

Together, they stood on the stoop. She tilted her chin up and breathed in. This area, veering toward affluence but never quite achieving it, didn't smell as her familiar rookeries did. She missed the dirt, the stale ale, the lye of soap from the washer-women. The outside of Thaddeus's townhouse smelled of fresh lilacs, of cobblestone and apple.

But it was better than the blood of inside, so she sucked in a long whiff of air. Her heart rate had slowed. Her breaths no longer came in frantic pants.

Thaddeus watched her closely, his brows furrowed. He ran his thumb underneath her chin, staring deep into her eyes as if he might be able to see into the depths of her soul if he looked long enough. Perhaps he could.

"One of us needs to alert the police." His voice held hesitancy she didn't recognize, so used to his certainty. "Are you feeling better, love?"

She nodded. Of the two tasks, she'd much prefer fetching the Met. She'd do almost anything if it meant she didn't have to go into that house again.

"The station house is on Wood Street. Go there and ask for Sergeant Strickland. Make sure *he* is the one who comes here with you." He slipped a coin in her hand. "Take the hack."

Normally, she would have protested this extravagance, but

at this point, she couldn't fathom crossing any sort of distance on foot. In the carriage, at least, she could rest. She'd keep her eyes open because in the darkness, she'd see Effie's prone body again.

She had to keep reminding herself it had been an accident.

Once, she'd been innocent. Now, she didn't know what she was. She was not the same woman she'd been before she stepped across that threshold tonight. But she had the love of a good man, a precocious daughter, and her family. While her problems wouldn't immediately disappear, it was a start.

She strode toward the hack stand. Blood moved in her veins, and her feet pounded the ground. Anna's family would get justice. No one in London would know of Moira's true parentage.

Poppy rubbed at the spot on her head where Effie's fingers had dug in. She was alive. Despite many attempts to end her, she had survived.

She'd emerge brand new from this trauma, as a phoenix did from the ashes. She'd known pain, fear, and sadness, for they'd been her constant companions since that night two years ago. And in the last few weeks, she'd come to know violence and greed, their claws sinking deep into the depths of her soul.

But now, she knew love, and she knew laughter. She'd hold onto the quiet moments with Moira and Thaddeus, and that happiness would be enough to banish the darkness.

She'd found a lantern to light her way.

A week later, Thaddeus was surprised at the knock on the front door of Poppy's cottage. He wasn't expecting anyone. Poppy was in the bedroom, placing fresh linens on the bed. Edna was visiting a neighbor—she'd been spending a lot of time with the elderly bachelor two doors down.

"Shall we see who it is?" he asked Moira, looking down at her. Bouncing on his hip, she peered up at him with wide green eyes, so like her mother's.

He stepped to the window and pulled back the shade. There was Strickland, dressed in his blues, checking his pocket watch as he waited. Thaddeus readjusted his hold on Moira, opening the door with his free hand.

Strickland entered, his smirk fading as he glanced about the room. "Bloody hell, you've gone domestic."

Thaddeus followed Strickland's gaze. The living room was in a state of absolute disarray. Moira's toys were scattered across the floor: blocks, a rag ball, the clothespin doll, and a few new stuffed animals Thaddeus had procured from various second-hand shops.

It was a bloody, bloody mess without any order.

And Thaddeus loved every single part of it.

Moira's fists grasped his coat, taking in handfuls of cloth. She let out a piercing shriek, wiggling in his arms.

Strickland covered his ears, grimacing.

Thaddeus chuckled, setting Moira down in the tent he'd created for her from two old sheets and a few sticks from the courtyard. It was Moira's new favorite place to play, now that he'd convinced Poppy to get rid of that damned blanket with the paint stain.

Strickland hurried to the other corner of the room, as far away from the babe as he could get. Only when Moira was fully occupied with her blocks did Strickland unclasp his ears. He stuffed his hands into the pockets of his coat, still eyeing Moira suspiciously.

"You, getting married," Strickland marveled with a low whistle. "Never thought I'd see that day. I was convinced your books would be your bedfellows forever."

"What do you think is in all those boxes?" Thaddeus pointed to the wall that bordered the bedroom, where the crates were stacked four wide and up to the ceiling. "There's more back at my townhouse, of course. These were what I couldn't live without."

Thaddeus had begun to move his things into Poppy's cottage, in preparation for their upcoming marriage at the end of the month. Though there'd been more space, the townhouse had become irrevocably associated with Effie Larker's death. He'd hated seeing Poppy wince when she'd brought Strickland back to the house to arrest Clowes. And if he was going to be completely truthful, he hated every night he spent in that godforsaken place away from her.

Strickland wandered over to the boxes, crouching to read the labels. "Shakespeare, Gothics, behavioral studies..." He straightened, his nose wrinkling. "What kind of man doesn't own a single adventure novel? Bloody hell, with books like these, I'm surprised you survived the Larkers."

"I'll have you know Shakespeare wrote many thrilling scenes," Thaddeus objected. "How much more exciting can you get than the execution of Julius Caesar?"

Strickland considered this for a moment. "Not exactly what I had in mind, but it'll restore some of my faith in you."

"God knows that was going to keep me awake at night." Thaddeus laughed. He walked to the table, gesturing for Strickland to take a seat across from him. The table and chairs were one of the few surfaces in the room not covered by his things. "As much as I enjoy watching you be bested by a babe, I take it this isn't a social call?"

Strickland sat down at the table. He leaned forward, elbows resting on the table. "I've caught Larker."

Poppy came forth from the bedroom, dirty sheets bundled up in her arms. "Sergeant Strickland, I thought I heard you," she said warmly, setting the sheets down on the settee. In a few seconds, she had reached their gathering at the table.

Taking the seat next to Thaddeus, Poppy reached for his hand, her fingers tightening around his.

Strickland stood and doffed his top hat, sketching such an elaborate bow, one would have thought he was meeting Queen Adelaide. "Ah, the famous redhead. We meet again."

"Enough of that," Poppy replied. "I am no grand lady, thankfully. We're a simpler sort here."

"Very well," Strickland agreed. "I was telling Thaddy that we found Larker. Caught him today in a brothel in Seven Dials. After a bit of, shall we say, persuasive questioning, the abbess said he'd been there since he found out about his wife's death."

Poppy swallowed. Thaddeus squeezed her hand. In the past week, she'd woken up three times with nightmares. But as each day passed, she'd become stronger, more like herself again.

"The magistrate has already signed off on his arrest," Strickland continued. "The trial date has been expedited due to Whiting's involvement. The superintendents are hoping that if we can get this done and over with quickly, the newspapers will forget that the Met ever had a corrupt inspector."

"Good luck with that," Thaddeus replied. "The people already have no love for Peelers. This is another spark to an already burning fire."

"From your mouth to God's ears." Strickland sighed. "But that's another matter I wanted to discuss with you. Don't suppose you'd come back to your old job?"

Thaddeus blinked. He hadn't expected an offer from Strickland.

Strickland squirmed in his chair, no longer looking so comfortable. "The thing is, I've been promoted to inspector. After Whiting's guilt was discovered, they needed someone to take his place immediately. Well, you were already dismissed, and I was the next in line."

"I see," Thaddeus said, sensing that Strickland wanted some sort of reply.

"But there's still Doughty's job to think of in the future. It won't be long until he retires." Strickland looked from him to Poppy and back again. "It'd be a better salary, Thaddy. You could move somewhere nice." He wet his lips with his tongue. "Er, not that this place isn't nice..."

Poppy smiled at that, unabashed by his reaction. "No offense taken, Inspector. The rookeries are not for everyone."

The acceptance that had been on the tip of Thaddeus's tongue tasted false. When he'd taken up with the Met three years prior, it had been because he'd wanted to change the world. He'd thought then that the best way to do it was with the police. In the past few weeks, he'd watched as power was wielded to extend corruption and punish the innocent.

As an inspector, he'd have some chance to right those wrongs. But he'd be investigating the same people that Poppy associated with daily. Her family would be at risk from him. How could he expect to be accepted as a part of Poppy's life—in Moira's life—if he put them all in danger?

And as a member of the Met, he'd be forced to go after the cases the department wanted him to, not the cases that he wanted to solve. He couldn't choose to help more Anna Moseleys. Was that what he wanted from his life? To be bound by someone else's dictates?

"No," he said, as much in answer to his own questions as Strickland's proposal. "I'm sorry, but I don't think I can come back to the Met. Thank you for the offer, but it's complicated."

Strickland's jaw had dropped slightly. "All you ever wanted, Thaddy, was to be an inspector."

Thaddeus exchanged a glance with Poppy, her eyes offering him silent support. "I want different things now."

"Women," Strickland retorted, with a shake of his head. "Never met a lad who didn't end up turned around by a dimber chit." He stood, going to the door.

Thaddeus shook his hand. "If you end up with cases you're stuck on, give me a call. I'll help you out. But that's all."

Strickland nodded. "Goodbye, soon-to-be Mrs. Knight," he called.

As the door shut behind Strickland, Poppy came to stand next to Thaddeus. Wrapping her arms around his waist, she laid her head on his back. "I'm proud of you. And I've been thinking."

He tilted his head to look down at her. "About what?"

She smiled coyly. "How you might continue to investigate."

"If I work for the Met, then I'm more than likely going to end up on a case that involves someone you know."

"That's just it," she said. "Why do you have to work for the Met to investigate? Why can't you hire yourself out privately? I have heard that aristocrats hire the Runners. Why couldn't they hire you instead?"

He considered this for a moment. "And that would leave me room to take cases not for profit from people in the rookeries."

"Precisely," she agreed. "You'd set your own hours, which would be quite a bonus if we want to add another addition to our family..."

He spun her around so she faced him. "Are you saying what I think you are saying?"

Her smile fell slightly. "No. I'm not with child, at this moment, at least."

Bringing her closer to him, he planted a kiss on her forehead. "Disappointing, yes, but perhaps it was not the right time."

Grabbing his hand, she brought him over to Moira's tent. She reached down, lifting Moira up.

"But the right time will come." Poppy caught Moira's hand in her own, waving the babe's chubby arm at Thaddeus. "And it'll be wonderful, Thaddeus. Because we'll have each other, always."

As he stood there, next to the two people who had come to mean more to him than anyone else in the world, it hit him that he'd finally found the family he'd been looking for all his life. Here, in this cottage, with his books scattered about in complete disarray and crates crammed into every available space, he'd found home.

A home he never wanted to leave, for it was no longer just a sanctuary away from the deafening outside, but a hearth. Here, he could be imperfect. They'd have battles, and they'd have the blissful mornings of apologies and devotion. This was not a love of the poets, but a love that would transcend and become stronger from those struggles.

He'd learned that home was wherever Poppy was.

"Tell me, Poppy," he said, sliding behind her to rub her shoulders. "Shall I compare thee to a summer's day?"

Epilogue

They married in the small chapel on Red Lion Street. Despite the protests of Thaddeus's parents, who claimed every Knight for the past two hundred years had been married in the same Anglican church in London proper, the ceremony was everything Poppy had ever wanted in a wedding.

Poppy no longer feared the future but looked forward to it with wide eyes and open arms. She'd pledged her troth to the one man she was certain understood her.

Together, they'd be unstoppable. Thaddeus's investigative business had started a few days prior, and he already had several cases. At night, she wove on the small handloom Thaddeus had purchased for her, this time for the sheer joy of creating something beautiful from nothing. Though the factory had passed into new ownership, Thaddeus had insisted it was more important that she get to spend as much time with Moira as possible.

As they walked out of the church hand in hand, the guests flooded the street behind them, thieves and Peelers. For one day, the two sides of the law declared a truce to celebrate the nuptials of their past sergeant and the scarlet woman who no longer had so many secrets to hide.

And it was glorious, every last minute of it, but nothing was as beautiful as coming home to their cottage on Finch Street as husband and wife.

In the story of her life, Poppy had opened a new chapter, better than anything she'd ever expected.

* * *

Did you miss Daniel and Kate's story? Read *A Dangerous Invitation*.
And check out Michael Strickland and Abigail Vautille's story in *Beauty and the Rake!*

Author's Note

The 1830s are a fascinating decade for English history for many, many reasons. The country hadn't shifted fully toward the morals of the later Victorian era, but the people started to separate from the Regency mindset as well. Particularly of note is the view of bastard children in England. What Poppy experienced is similar to many different accounts of women who had children out of wedlock, though, of course, I have dramatized it and changed it to fit the confines of my story. To be a ruined woman in England was a dismaying place in society to inhabit.

While I can't find record of a particular Magdalen asylum in Surrey, these institutions existed in both Ireland and England at this time. They began originally as homes for prostitutes, but eventually expanded toward all fallen women and women who'd hit upon hard times. The asylums provided food and shelter, yes, but the women were often made to labor without little—or any—payment. The Magdalen laundries existed well into the twentieth century.

Further evidence of change in society can be attributed to the Industrial Revolution. This brought a migration to the cities and new advances in machinery. I touch on a few inventions in this book, but there's so much more to this period that I couldn't fit within the framework of *Secrets in Scarlet*.

Poppy and Thaddeus live in Spitalfields, London. This little pocket of the East End was at this period in time considered a rookery, for great economic downturn had passed through the area. Once, Spitalfields was a teeming community of Huguenot weavers, who had emigrated from the great weaving cities in France of Lyons and Tours. Those weavers benefited from London's desire for lustrings, velvets, brocades, satins, padua-soys, mantuas, and of course, silk. A series of acts throughout the seventeenth to nineteenth centuries made it harder to import fabrics from France, and so the weavers became more in demand.

The repeal of the Spitalfields Weaving Acts in the 1820s struck the small weaving community hard. Coming upon the advent of the Industrial Revolution, the weavers no longer had the financial control they'd maintained over England's silk industry for centuries. The call for mechanization took hold, and these handloom weavers who had grown up perfecting this one tedious, delicate way of weaving were left unable to match the easier, less taxing efforts of the mechanized looms. The need for so many weavers was gone. Families were left without incomes, forced to find new jobs in an already highly overpopulated city. Some families, like the Vautilles, went to work in the factories, while others turned to different trades.

Previously, weaving had been a family vocation with each member of the family involved. The children served as a draw boys for the handlooms, while the adults worked the shuttles, etc. One type of mechanized loom that I mention throughout *Secrets in Scarlet*, the Jacquard loom, required no draw boy. Though it's often referred to as a "Jacquard loom," it's actually an attachment that can be used with many mechanical looms. It could be operated by one person, and because of its punch card system, suddenly it was possible to work complex patterns into the silk without having to reset the loom each time. The Jacquard loom, invented by Joseph-Marie Jacquard, is one of the most fascinating pieces of machinery out there, and the basic structure of it is still in use in today's fabric industry. In fact, the Jacquard loom has been cited as having a great impact on the development of computers.

While the structure of a factory like the Larker one could have existed in London, most textile manufacturing moved out to Manchester and Lancashire. There, large cotton and weaving factories were run, utilizing steam power. In *Secrets in Scarlet,* because the Larker factory is set in Spitalfields, steam power isn't used.

And one last note: until the creation of Scotland Yard later in the nineteenth century, London had no real detective force. The Metropolitan Police, created in 1828, were put into place to prevent crime. The belief behind their establishment was that increased patrolling of the streets, organization between districts, etc. would effectively eradicate crime before it could ever happen. They may not have been entirely successful in accomplishing these goals, but the crime rate did decrease after the founding of the Met.

Acknowledgments

Writing a second book is an odd experience, one I approached half in excitement and half in gut-wrenching fear that I only had *one* story to tell ever.

Yet, somehow, I found people who believed in my writing enough to keep hounding me until the book was done. Thank you, thank you, to every single person who contacted me at some point and said they wanted to read Thaddeus and Poppy's story. You're what kept me going (because let's face it, narcissistic I am).

First and foremost, thank you, Gentle Reader, for picking up this book. I know I'm one voice in a sea of many choices you have, and the fact that you chose to spend a little time in my world is incredible.

I am indebted to my critique partners, who took time out of their busy lives to rip apart my book in proper "leave no stones unturned" fashion. Rebecca Paula, Amy Jo Cousins, Emma Locke, Kristine Wyllys, and Genevieve Turner, thank you so much.

With every Rookery Rogues book, I find myself immersed in research. Jennelle Holland and Isobel Carr, thank you for helping me nail down all the pesky details.

Thank you to my editor, Meghan Hogue, for never minding when a book explodes on me, and for always striving to make my work ten times better.

Thank you to Eileen Richards, Vanessa Kelly, Lisa Lin, Samantha Maurice, Darcy Burke, Lila DiPasqua, Ki Pha, and

Kianna Alexander for your sweet texts, tweets, and messages. You've kept me (relatively) sane.

To the friends and family who have learned to accept when I decline invitations, or when I randomly stare off into space for hours and claim I'm "plotting," thanks for understanding. Your love and support throughout the years means the world to me.

And lastly, but always foremost in my heart, thank you to my husband. For endless plot talks, helping me with odd gun facts, understanding when I get creepily excited about suspense elements, taking care of the house while I'm writing, and for loving me. You are my muse, my rock, my everything.

The Rookery Rogues

Secrets in Scarlet is the second book in The Rookery Rogues. While each book reads as a stand-alone, the series is best enjoyed in chronological order. Joined by the poorest neighborhoods in London, called rookeries, the heroes and heroines in this series defy social expectations and find love in the darkest of circumstances.

A Dangerous Invitation (Kate and Daniel)
Secrets in Scarlet (Poppy and Thaddeus)
Beauty and the Rake (Abigail and Michael)
Stealing the Rogue's Heart (Mina and Charlie)

Read on for an excerpt from *Beauty and the Rake*.

An Excerpt from
Beauty and the Rake

W hitechapel, London
      October 1832

Red was everywhere.

Abigail Vautille shouldn't have been surprised. Since that fateful day when her left hand was forcibly rammed into a working loom, the color red had haunted her. Deep red scars from the punch card of the jacquard crisscrossed her skin. Pockets of exposed flesh remained, mangled red bubbles now crusted black. The bones had been reset to give her a range of movement, but she couldn't feel the brace of a cold wind on her flesh or the touch of a man's fingers against her skin.

If only she could staunch her emotions so effectively.

But, no, she was fated to face crimson. Scarlet was even the color of her once-friend Poppy Knight's hair. Poppy's investigation into their past employer had led to Abigail's torture.

Her stomach clenched at the shellacked ruby door of Cruikshank's gaming hell. A battered wreath hung in the center, the previously garnet holly berries shriveled and dead. No one bothered to use the carmine-rusted iron doorknocker. This was no longer a place that required a doorman.

Scoundrels came and went, invited by the new proprietor, Arthur Cruikshank. He was in league with Joaquin Mason, who ruled the rookeries from the back room of his main property in Shadwell, the King of Spades. With Mason's support, Cruikshank had turned this dank hole into a profitable gambling house.

Abigail knew the men here, their tells and their compulsions. Each battled a demon that only a hand of cards seemed to sate.

But familiarity didn't breed ease. The hollers of foxed men drifted from Cruikshank's, an unsettling cacophony. The building itself provided no comfort, constructed of crumbling gray stone. Gray like her constant mood. Auburn bricks made up the top floor, added after the original foundation.

Shivering in the frigid night air, Abigail drew her black cloak tighter around her to brace against the cold wind. With a glance upstairs, she brought the gloved fingers of her good hand to her lips to kiss for luck. She'd need all the help she could get in this godforsaken place.

After entering, she refused to give her cloak to the man who waited in the foyer. Cruikshank didn't employ him. When unsuspecting people presented him with their garments, he fled to sell them in the rag and bone shops. She couldn't help but admire his ingenuity.

Since she couldn't hold down honest employment any longer, she'd do best to follow his example.

Her eyes narrowed as she surveyed the crowd mingling in the lower rooms. Conversations drifted in and out, an indistinct hum. A sweet, pungent scent caught her attention from the open door to her right. Men reclined on dilapidated chaises in sleep or stupor, while two women blew into pipes, kindling the opium in their bowls until it glowed red.

"Mystery lady!" a man called, his unfixed gaze settling on her cloak. "Come back, mystery lady. Come play with me."

A lump formed in her throat. All these people, drowning their sorrows. Little she could do for them now. The longer she stayed, the higher chance she had of being a potential target for Cruikshank's less principled patrons.

She kept going, ignoring his summons, her skirts swishing against the dusty floor. Two staircases flanked the vast entrance hall. While the left staircase ended on a landing, the right staircase would take her up to the top floor where the faro and hazard tables were. The play was deep there.

She'd find her father at the back table. Inevitably, he'd be in the third chair, his hands shaking as he grasped his cards. There'd be a wrinkle where his thumb gripped too hard.

She reached down into the pocket in her cloak. No blunt. Not that she could pay the rest of her father's debts with a few coins. Settling the vowels for his last visit to Cruikshank's had taken the last of her savings. Years of hard shifts, aching knees, and pricked fingers, gone in an instant to the tables.

Now that she couldn't work in the factory, she had no way to earn back that money.

Three prostitutes lingered at the stairs, clothed in gaudy dresses with chemises peeking out of their stomachers. They roamed the halls in between their shifts in the cellar, which Cruikshank had converted into a whorehouse. He was always looking for willing lightskirts to fill the beds.

Abigail gulped as a flamboyant redhead with a gap-toothed grin caught her eye and waggled a brow.

Soon, she'd be one of them.

She mounted the stairs carefully, her uninjured hand grasping the railing for support. The hood of her cloak remained over her head, and she pretended it gave her a modicum of security. A shroud to hide behind, when it seemed everyone in Whitechapel knew her name and face.

People moved around her, passing her on the staircase and cursing her slowness. One foot in front of the other was never easy. Even before she'd lost the use of her hand, her unsteady gait had marked her as a cripple. As a child, she'd worked as a scavenger, sliding underneath the machinery to collect the broken bits of silk for reuse. The labor had distorted her body, and years of standing on her feet for fourteen hours, six days a week, had worsened her knock-knees.

Each step higher made her joints scream for relief. Her lungs, weak from the poorly ventilated conditions in the factories, burned with the effort.

But she persevered, for life had given her no other choice. Everyone she used to consider a friend had abandoned her. The sole kindness she'd known in the last six months was the whisper of a stranger when she'd been in the hospital.

Finally, she arrived at the top floor. A throng of people waited outside the faro room. Falling in line, Abigail peeked inside. Candles shimmered throughout, casting a golden glow. At least it was warmer than outside.

She'd already pawned the last of her books to pay for coal so that her little sister, Bess, wouldn't freeze in their flat. Her heart panged at the memory. Those books had been more precious to her than any other possession, but Bess had to be her first priority.

Come tomorrow when the coal ran out again, there'd be nothing left to sell.

Nothing except for herself.

She couldn't think of that now. If she did, her knees would sway, and her steps would falter. That would make her an easy mark. Already, she felt as though her movements were evaluated for signs of weakness. A chill skittered down her back. She shoved her battered hand into the pocket of her cloak and continued, trying to ignore the disconcerting sensation of being watched.

She was strong. She could survive anything.

The group behind her advanced, shoving her forward. She stumbled but managed to right herself before colliding with the man in front of her. The herd dispersed at the door, ambling to the various gaming tables. Abigail made her way toward the far corner of the room, pausing for a moment to lean against a post and catch her breath.

She scanned the crowd for her father, expecting to find him flanked on either side by intent players. Tonight, all the chairs were empty, except for three: the banker and two punters. A crowd of people watched the game proceed. The cards had split; the dealer took half of the bets on that rank. The onlookers let out a whoop of approval.

The mechanics of the game held little interest to her, for it'd always end the same: even if her father won, they'd still owe. Their debts were so high; they'd never dig out of this hole. She recognized her father: grizzly gray hair, the stoop of his shoulders, his threadbare green coat Bess had patched the week prior.

Across from him and facing her was a man Abigail did not recognize. As he purchased another check from the dealer, she swallowed back the dread that threatened to consume her. An unknown competitor meant her father might not receive leniency. Cruikshank had already told Papa that if he didn't start paying his vowels, he'd need to find a new place to gamble, or he'd have to face Cyrus. Known as an unhinged pugilist with a taste for blood, Cyrus Mason could make the injuries she'd incurred from the loom seem like papercuts.

And so, the cycle would begin again: another gaming hell and another night like this one. It didn't matter that she'd cut her meals in half for the past few months to ensure Bess had enough to eat. Or that they were three months behind on rent, and if they didn't pay up soon, they'd all be out on the bloody street.

Nothing mattered to her father except the game.

Abigail slowly steered her way through the crowd, minding her steps until she'd made it to the back table.

"'Ey now," one man complained as she accidentally bumped him. He turned, catching her eye. Even in the cloak, he recognized her. So much for anonymity.

He motioned for a few of his friends to step to the side to make room for her. "Move, mates."

Abigail nodded her gratitude, sliding into the vacated space. Her father hadn't noticed her arrival, so focused was he on the game layout.

"Come, Papa," she quietly bid. "Settle up your accounts and hope to God that this man lets you by with incremental payments."

She hated having to say those words. She hated the humiliation of having to stand there, while all the men leered at her as if she was the choicest bit of flesh they'd get all night. But if she was going to be a harlot, she might as well start expecting this treatment.

The unknown punter across from her father coughed. A cough meant to distract, to clear the air. She looked up to see who would be so polite in this den of iniquity. She focused on his features, and her stomach did a flip. A purely physical reaction, for what woman wouldn't have felt a surge of fancy for the way his linen shirt stretched over his broad shoulders. His oval face was classically handsome, chiseled with an impossibly straight nose.

The man's blue eyes narrowed. "He owes me two hundred pounds. You can't expect me to excuse so large a debt."

Two hundred pounds.

His voice rang in her ears, like the steady drum that signals a firing squad. Two hundred pounds. Each breath was harder. Her throat closed. Two hundred pounds.

The mob erupted with cheers at the announcement, eager for a potential conflict. Their hoots barely registered, for her heart pounded so hard, she feared it might burst free of her chest. The world spun around her, and she prayed the floor would swallow her up.

Yet nothing changed.

Around her, the horde grew impatient for a response. Whatever leniency they'd shown in allowing her into their midst had disappeared. Now she was a part of the spectacle, her pain on display for their enjoyment.

"'E don't got two hundred," one man jeered. "'E won't even pay me the two crowns 'e owes me."

"And 'e owes me twenty pounds!" another fellow added.

Oh, God. Her father had killed them all with the fifty-one cards of a faro game.

They were doomed. With vowels that large, surely, her father would be sent to debtor's prison. Hell, maybe they'd all be sent to Marshalsea. The thought of her little sister living in such squalor made Abigail's heart tighten. How would Bess survive?

"I can't pay you," her father mumbled as if he was just now realizing how much he'd lost. "Ain't got that."

"Then something will have to be done," his opponent announced.

Thoughts sped through her mind. Bess couldn't go to Marshalsea. It'd ruin her in a way Abigail couldn't countenance. Sorrow had seeped deep into Abigail's life, ripping apart all her hopes and dreams, but Bess deserved better.

What could Abigail offer this man? Their coffers were as

empty as their cabinets. The little blunt Bess brought in at the new textile factory already wasn't enough for the rent.

Abigail glanced down, taking in the plump curves of her breasts, her wide hips reputed to be perfect for grasping onto as a man tupped her hard. She was all the family had.

And if it were the last damn thing she did, she'd save Bess. This man knew Mason—perhaps a deal could be brokered to keep her father away from the hells too.

Abigail pushed back the hood to her cloak, revealing her blonde curls. Before her disfigurement, the factory boys had made it quite clear she stirred their attentions. But what was the price of her soul? Was she worth such an exorbitant sum?

"We can't pay you," she said, repeating her father's words. "But if you excuse my father's debts, I'll—"

The words wouldn't form. She gulped for air. A vision of Bess huddled in the corner of a filthy cell danced before her eyes. So, this was how her degradation would begin, not in a brothel, but in a hell. How could she go through with this? She'd be signing her soul away to the devil.

She couldn't think of another choice.

She needed to entice him. He wouldn't accept a single night for two hundred pounds—even as a virgin, she was not worth it. A man as good-looking as he was wouldn't pay that much for one lay with a working-class girl.

One month with her. She dismissed that idea immediately. A month away from Bess was too much. Two weeks instead. She'd start there.

"I'll spend two weeks with you. My virtue in exchange for two hundred pounds."

Books by Erica Monroe

I Spy a Duke

The Rookery Rogues

A Dangerous Invitation

Secrets in Scarlet

Beauty and the Rake

Stealing the Rogue's Heart

Gothic Brides

The Mad Countess

The Determined Duchess

The Scandalous Widow

Sign up for Erica's newsletter at ericamonroe.com and receive a free, exclusive short story!

About the Author

USA Today Bestselling Author Erica Monroe writes dark, gritty historical romance. Her current series include Gothic Brides (Regency Gothic romances) and The Rookery Rogues (pre-Victorian gritty working-class romance). She was a finalist in the published historical category for the prestigious Daphne du Maurier Award for Excellence in Romantic Suspense, and her books have been recommended reads at Fresh Fiction, Smexy Books, SBTB, and All About Romance. When not writing, she drinks too much coffee, listens to a lot of true crime podcasts, and reads a ton of books. She lives in the suburbs of North Carolina with her husband, daughter, and many rescue pets.

Erica loves to hear from readers, so please feel free to visit her website at ericamonroe.com